Before she knew it she was in his arms. His mouth captured hers—a gentle, playful kiss at first. And then, something happened—unplanned, unrehearsed.

They became a man and a woman, caught in the primeval pulse of nature, of wind and waves, roaring and crashing against the landscape. And the kiss, so gentle at first, grew into demand, exploration, as their bodies merged, seeking knowledge of shape and form and desire.

The cold wind, blowing Alpharetta's hair in a feathery trail behind her, had no meaning, for a warmth had invaded her being . . . .

On Wings of Fire

Frances Patton Statham

FAWCETT COLUMBINE   NEW YORK

To Nancy and Mimi

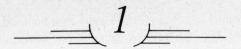

The drought of summer covered the Atlanta landscape with a thick red Georgia dust. No portion of the city was exempt from its blanket, not even the allée of dogwood trees that paralleled the drive of the Italianate villa on West Paces Ferry Road.

A forlorn Alpharetta Beaumont, standing at an upstairs window, looked down at the straight row of trees as she waited for the taxi. Like an exile leaving her beloved land behind, Alpharetta committed the sight to memory. Her eyes swept beyond the trees to the azaleas that had already formed next year's buds with their promise of delicate pinks and lavenders. But the harsh red shroud of dust covered them also.

Why couldn't it have been brilliant April instead of July—the ugliest part of the year, when the bleached blades of grass begged for rain like flowers in the desert.

A yellow taxi turned into the long drive. Alpharetta, seeing it, left the window, put on her straw sailor hat, and began to walk down the stairs with the suitcase in her hands. No one was in the house to stop her, not even Min-yo, the houseboy. She'd seen to that. Now there remained only one more thing to do before walking out the front door.

She took the two letters from her handbag and placed them on the Louis XV table in the hallway. The first was addressed to her guardians, Reed and Anna Clare St. John, and the second to Ben Mark, her fiancé. With an unsteady hand, she removed the diamond engagement ring and, as the doorbell chimed the driver's impatience, she dropped it into the envelope, which she hurriedly sealed. Without looking back, she rushed to open the door, lest she change her mind.

The long mirror in the hall recorded, for a brief moment, the slender young woman with her flaming red hair partially hidden under the straw hat and her exotic green eyes luminous with unshed tears. Then that image was gone as she opened the door.

"You called a taxi, ma'am?"

"Yes. If you'll just take my bag . . ."

She followed the driver down the steps and waited for him to open the taxi door for her. "Where to, ma'am?" he asked, while he slid under the wheel.

"Brookwood Station," she replied, the muscles in her throat constricting.

"A mighty hot day to be travelin'," the driver commented, turning his head slightly to wait for her verification before he started down the drive.

"Yes. A hot day."

"Just about the hottest day of the summer, so far," he added.

With a fleeting smile on her lips, Alpharetta responded, "Do you know what the temperature is?"

"Already a hundred 'n' one by the thermometer at the cab stand. I expect it might even get up to a hundred 'n' three by late afternoon."

Mercifully, the traffic drew the driver's attention and Alpharetta, having made the responses that courtesy demanded, settled down on the seat and rode the rest of the way in silence. She was determined not to think of the past week. She would have ample time for that later. Her main concern now was that the train not be delayed. If Ben Mark should discover the letter and follow her to the station before the train pulled out, she was lost. The excuse she had given for breaking off their engagement was a flimsy one that wouldn't bear up under a challenge, but the true reason was too painful to divulge to anyone.

Alpharetta had been gone less than twenty minutes when Min-yo, the Chinese servant, returned with the week's groceries. As he walked through the side entrance, a sense of desolation momentarily touched his bones and caused him to shiver, as if a good *shen* had been suddenly replaced by *kwei*, or ghosts in the house. But then, as he hurried on toward the kitchen and began to remove the groceries from the brown sacks, the pleasure from his successful shopping soon made him forget his initial foreboding.

Min-yo smiled as he placed the three small steaks in the refrigerator at the far end of the kitchen. It had taken his own shoe stamp and a bag of rice to convince his brother, who ran a laundry downtown, to part with the meat stamp. Because of his swap, the St. Johns could have a hung shao beef that night, instead of macaroni and cheese. As Min-yo continued to plan the evening meal, he heard the screen door to the side entrance open.

"Hello! Anybody home?"

Min-yo, recognizing Ben Mark's voice, left the kitchen. "Good afternoon, Lieutenant," Minyo said, seeing the tall man with hair as black as his own pigtail. Only Ben Mark's hair was cropped close to his head in military fashion.

"Is my fiancée home?" Ben Mark asked, seeming to get a special pleasure from the sound of the word.

"I go see. You like to wait in living room?" Min-yo asked politely.

Ben Mark strolled down the hall as Min-yo hurried up the winding stairs toward the suite of rooms that Alpharetta had occupied ever since Nurse Jenson had been dismissed. He smiled as he walked by the door of the bedroom where the young Alpharetta had spent her first night in the house. He remembered it well. Eight years ago. The shabby old valise that contained her one good dress . . . her desire not to be any trouble.

The door to the suite was wide open. Min-yo knocked on the panel and called out, "Missee, your lieutenant is downstairs." He waited a moment, and when there was no answer he called out again, "Missee."

"Min-yo." The voice from the downstairs hall was deep, masculine, urgent. The houseboy retraced his steps down the stairs.

Ben Mark St. John stood by the hall table and in his hands he held an opened letter.

"What is it, Lieutenant?" Min-yo inquired, not alarmed at first by the sight of the letter. Alpharetta often left notes propped by the gold ormulu clock on the table, especially when she was going to be late for supper.

"Alpharetta has gone." As spoken by Ben Mark, the statement seemed far more serious than the situation warranted.

"She be back," Min-yo assured him.

Ben Mark then opened his hand to reveal the ring. "No, Min-yo. Not unless I can find her in time. She's broken our engagement."

"But why, Lieutenant? I already saved eggs for wedding cake."

Ben Mark, visibly upset, asked, "When was the last time you saw her?"

"About hour ago—before I went to market."

"And my uncle? Where is he?"

"At farm. Miss Anna Clare, too."

With Min-yo trailing him, Ben Mark left the entrance hall and walked into the back hall where the telephone hung. He gave a number to the operator and, as it rang, he waited impatiently for someone to answer.

"No one seems to be there," the operator advised.

"Just let it keep ringing, operator," Ben Mark requested.

And so the ringing began again. Finally the scowl lifted from Ben Mark's face as a voice came over the wires.

"Al, here."

"Al, this is Ben Mark St. John."

"How're you, Lieutenant? I heard you were—"

"I'm trying to find Alpharetta," Ben Mark interrupted. "Has she called you about taking the Piper Cub out today?"

"No, sir. It's still sitting in the hangar. You want me to get it ready?"

Ben Mark hesitated. There was no way he could keep it secret. The news would be out soon enough. "No, Al. If she comes, find some excuse not to let her fly it. And Al, could you make sure she doesn't hitch a ride with anyone else?"

"No danger in that. The only other plane in the hangar has been taken apart. I'm working on the engine right now." After debating with himself, Al finally blurted out, "You two have a lovers' quarrel or something?"

"Something like that, Al. And I've got to keep her from leaving town until I get a chance to talk with her."

"Then, I'll walk on over to the hut and check the next

commercial flight. If I see her, I'll have her call you for sure, Lieutenant—if it's the last thing I do."

"Thanks, Al."

Ben Mark hung up the phone and turned to the Chinese houseboy who had been standing beside him and unabashedly listening to the conversation. "Come on, Min-yo. You'll have to ride with me."

"Where we go to find her?"

"To Brookwood Station on Peachtree. And if she isn't there, we'll drive to the main rail terminal."

Ben Mark put the engagement ring in his pocket, and with Min-yo hurrying to keep pace, he walked down the hall and out the side door to the Jaguar parked near the curved marble steps.

As he backed his car around and headed out, another car turned into the driveway, blocking his path. Long, flowing red hair was visible in the open convertible.

"Alpharetta!" Ben Mark's relief was evident in his voice. But even as Ben Mark stopped the car and got out, Min-yo knew it was Belline Wexford. He was too far away to see her eyes—turquoise, instead of green—the only exterior characteristic different from Alpharetta. But he had always been able to tell the two women apart, for Alpharetta radiated *husn*, an inner beauty, even from a distance.

The disappointment showed in Ben Mark's face as he realized his mistake. "What are you doing in Alpharetta's car?" he demanded.

"What's the matter, cousin? You don't seem very glad to see me."

"I was hoping you were Alpharetta, coming back home."

Belline disguised her jealous twinge at the mention of the other woman's name. "Isn't she here? I was just returning her car. I had a blowout this morning."

"No, she isn't here. She's left for good."

Belline laughed. "Why, whatever did you do to her, Ben Mark, this close to your wedding day?"

"Oh, shut up, Belline. Just get the convertible out of the way. Min-yo and I have to get to the rail station to try to stop her." Then thinking of the small amount of fuel in his own car, he suddenly asked, "How much gas did you leave in?"

"About half a tank."

"Then, move over. We'll go in the convertible, instead."

Ben Mark motioned for Min-yo to switch cars, while he slid into the driver's seat. As soon as the Chinese houseboy had climbed into the rear seat, Ben Mark, with Belline at his side, backed the second car onto West Paces Ferry Road and started toward Peachtree.

At Brookwood Station, Alpharetta sat on a hard wooden bench and waited for the train. Once before she'd tried to sever her ties with the St. John family, when Anna Clare's nurse had persuaded her that she was no longer welcome in their home. That decision had also brought her to this same passenger station on Peachtree Road. But Reed had arrived in time to stop her. Today, she didn't want to leave Atlanta any more than she'd wanted to on that day long ago. But within a matter of weeks, she had been forced into it, to spare the St. Johns embarrassment.

Perhaps when the war was over—perhaps when circumstances were different, she could tell Ben Mark she loved him, would always love him. And perhaps she would be able to come to terms with her real mother.

The word *mother* had an alien sound to Alpharetta. She felt so much closer to her distant cousin, Anna Clare, than to the strange woman who'd suddenly appeared on her doorstep, claiming kinship and demanding money. How ironic that her engagement announcement to Ben Mark St. John would be seen by the mother who had deserted her when she was a baby. She hadn't even known she was alive until that Saturday in May.

Alpharetta knew she would never forget that day, as long as she lived. It had started out so gloriously. She and Ben Mark had been flying for most of the afternoon. She remembered the color of the sky with its rolling white clouds, the sun catching the glitter of rocks jutting from the Chattahoochee River. Following the water's meandering path, they flew low, tipping the Piper's wings to acknowledge the waves and hurrahs of the people floating lazily downriver in their inner tubes, silver canoes, and brightly colored rafts. She was almost afraid that day, she was so happy—with her fiancé home on his weekend pass, with their marriage only two months away, as soon as Ben Mark graduated from flight school. Even the guilty feeling from using the rationed gasoline was forgotten when she saw the pleasure registered on Ben Mark's face.

By six o'clock that same evening, her happiness was shattered, and in its place lodged a wariness that refused to go away. And with good reason. For the confrontation with her mother settled nothing. Though she had given her most of her savings, the woman had returned the next week to demand more money. It was then Alpharetta realized what she must do, however painful. Ben Mark's pride was at stake and she could not ask him to accept such a woman as part of his family. He deserved better than that.

It was hard enough for him to accept the fact that her father and brothers had once been arrested for making moonshine. But when her father died, and Reed loaned Conyer and Duluth, her two brothers, enough money for a down payment on the cattle ranch in Nevada, Ben Mark relaxed. Of course, it had helped, too, when Reed began to treat her as a treasured daughter, instead of Anna Clare's poor, distant relative. But with her mother's appearance, all that would change.

Alpharetta stared down at her unadorned finger, with its telltale circle of white where the ring had resided until an hour before. Quickly, with a feeling of loss, she covered her left hand with her right and stared at the clock on the wall. In a few minutes, the train should be pulling out of the main terminal. When it stopped briefly to take on passengers at Brookwood Station, there would be no possibility of turning back. By morning, she would be in Washington.

"Excuse me, miss. Is this seat taken?"

Alpharetta looked up at a woman with two small children. She shook her head and moved over to make room for them on the bench.

"We're goin' to Chattanooga," the tow-headed little boy volunteered as he squeezed his small frame into the space between Alpharetta and his mother, who held a sleeping baby. "To meet my pa. He's got a new job at the shipyard in Norfolk. And we're movin' with him."

"Ennis Thompson, I've already warned you about botherin' other people. You just sit still and finish your Orange Crush."

The woman's sharp voice woke the baby in her arms. The infant began to cry and the mother, looking toward her son, commanded, "Get Sister's bottle from the duffel, Ennis."

Hurrying to obey his mother, Ennis leaned over. In the process, he spilled his beverage on the bench and it splashed onto Alpharetta's yellow dress. She stood up quickly and began to mop the stain with her handkerchief.

"Ennis Thompson," the mother began again to the accompanying shriek of the baby.

Seeing the sorrowful look on the little boy's face, Alpharetta said, "That's all right. No harm's done."

"Maybe you'd better sponge it off right away," the woman suggested, "with water."

"Yes, I'll do that," Alpharetta replied and fled toward the restroom. Once inside, she fought to maintain her control as she began to clean the dress. But she burst into tears, the damage to her yellow dress of little consequence compared to her broken heart.

Just beyond the traffic light where Ben Mark stopped, rose the Palladian-style Southern Railway Peachtree Station, known more familiarly as Brookwood, its classical motif and red brick walls in Flemish bond proclaiming the genius of its architect while denying its utilitarian function as a suburban passenger depot.

Ben Mark waited for the light to change and then drove into the parking lot. "Belline and I will check inside," he said to Min-yo as the three climbed out of the car.

"Then I look on platform," Min-yo volunteered.

Belline matched Ben Mark's stride as they walked to the double doors of the building.

Once inside, Belline saw that the hot station was crowded with women, children, and crying babies—not a pleasant place with the odor of sweating bodies, the smell of milk gone sour, and the strong scent of disinfectant drifting over the transom from the restrooms all but overpowering. She turned up her nose. Before the war, few people used the station other than those who lived on the smart north side of the city. Now, to Belline, the station was different—spoiled.

"Belline, check the restroom," Ben Mark ordered as he looked up and down each bench.

"All right," she said grudgingly. "But I can tell you now that Alpharetta wouldn't be caught dead in there."

Belline reached into her white summer purse and quickly pulled out a handkerchief before she touched the knob on the door to the public restroom. The door closed behind her, and she gingerly surveyed the empty room. Hanging on a wooden peg next to the washbasin was a straw sailor hat with yellow ribbons—exactly like the one—

Belline stopped, listened to the soft sobs coming from the enclosure. She hastily spun around and fled from the restroom.

"Well?"

She stared at Ben Mark. "I think we're wasting our time," Belline murmured.

He nodded. "She's probably at the main terminal."

"How about the bus station?"

"I hadn't even thought of looking there," Ben Mark confessed.

"If only we knew in which direction she was going . . ." Belline sympathized. On her way to the car, Belline wore a satisfied smile as she deposited her handkerchief into the trash bin attached to the lamp post.

Later, after dropping Min-yo at the bus station, Ben Mark and Belline traveled toward Spring Street and the downtown rail terminal.

Many times the size of Brookwood on Peachtree Road, the main terminal had an altogether different ambience. Unlike the smaller station, it had a sense of urgency. At Brookwood, the only military uniform was a mock sailor suit worn by a six-year-old, but here clusters of khaki and sailor-white moved back and forth. Interspersed with civilians, the servicemen walked faster, talked faster, with surreptitious glances toward the clock running out of time for them.

Ben Mark, also aware of the clock, frantically searched the sea of faces for familiar red hair and endearing green eyes. While he stood and watched the boarding of the passenger trains, a wave of young women rushed past him. They all looked alike—brown-haired, solemn young women, with no distinguishing features to tell one from the other. When the last one had disappeared, a disappointed Ben Mark turned to Belline.

"She's not here, either," he said.

Two miles north, a tear-stained Alpharetta emerged from Brookwood Station and took her place on the platform. In five minutes, the train arrived; her luggage was hoisted to the baggage compartment, and boarding a passenger car, Alpharetta Beaumont left Atlanta behind.

2

In the rapidly plunging temperatures of early evening, Lieutenant Daniel "Marsh" Wexford, stepbrother to Belline, shifted the weight of his paratrooper equipment on his back as he stood with his friends, Gig and Laroche, under the wings of one of the C-47s waiting to take off from the Tunisian airfield.

The three men had come a long way since their basic training together at Fort Benning, as members of the 82nd Airborne Division. Although Marsh was now an officer, he still felt a special kinship with Gig and Laroche, who were as different from each other as night and day, not only in looks, but in personality, too. Laroche, small, dark and taciturn, was the perfect foil for the taller, sandy-haired Gig, with his high spirits inclined to get him into trouble as soon as he opened his voluble mouth.

In silence Marsh glanced down at the slip of paper handed him—to verify the secret destination not divulged by the high command until the actual moment of lift-off.

Soldiers of the 505th Combat Team:

Tonight you embark upon a combat mission for which our people and the free people of the world have been waiting for two years.

You will spearhead the landing of an American force upon the island of Sicily. Every preparation has been made to eliminate the element of chance. You have been given the means to do the job and you are backed by the largest assemblage of airpower in the world's history.

The eyes of the world are upon you. The hopes and prayers of every American go with you . . .

> James M. Gavin

Crumpling the paper in his fist, Marsh Wexford looked up as an irreverent whistle escaped between Gig's teeth. And Laroche said in his soft Louisiana Cajun accent, "You think we've fooled the Axis, Lieutenant?"

Towering over the dark-complexioned Laroche by more than eight inches, the tall blond giant shook his head. "The Germans, maybe. But not the Italians."

"Well, they fooled *me*," Gig conceded. "I took Sardinia."

Marsh laughed. "How much did you lose on the bet?"

"The price of a camel," he readily admitted, glancing in the direction of the tents.

Like desert flowers, the tents had blossomed overnight, stripes of red and green in vertical lines hobbled to the ground by large wooden stakes. The wind now swept over the land bereft of trees, and caused the openings of the tents to flap in rhythmic sequence. Sensing the change from an earlier calm, the camels lowered themselves awkwardly to the ground.

Soon the tents would be taken down and the Berbers, with their camels, would vanish into the vast expanse beyond the Kasserine Pass, for the long awaited day had finally arrived.

As the paratroopers began loading, a uniformed corporal from the weather station ran toward the group and stopped before Colonel Gavin, who stood slightly apart from the others.

With his voice rising above the roar of the engines, the corporal shouted, "Sir, we've just received word that the wind is now up to thirty-five miles an hour. I thought you'd want to know."

The three paratroopers, overhearing the ominous message, halted in line and stared at the colonel. Most had never jumped when the wind was blowing more than fifteen miles an hour. Yet Marsh knew it was far too late for the invasion to be postponed. The entire Allied war machinery had been set in motion and there was no turning back.

The colonel, silent for a moment, thanked the corporal and gave the signal to continue loading.

Marsh, Gig, and Laroche found seats in the rear of the
transport, but their brief camaraderie and humor had suddenly changed to sober realization. By the time the moon
reached its zenith, they would thrust downward into the steel-
jawed mouth of the enemy. And to make matters worse, they
were flying to meet their fate on wings of the dreaded *sirocco*,
the hot, dust-laden wind that swept over that portion of the
Mediterranean like a devil unleashed from the dungeons of
Hell.

Seated in the rear of the C-47 with Gig and Laroche on either
side of him, Marsh could feel the buffeting of the high winds
against the plane. It would be difficult to maintain course in
such a gale and practically impossible to parachute to a designated spot. Marsh should know.

He shifted his body uneasily and thought of another day
of high winds, when he had landed five miles off course in
the swampy terrain of the Chattahoochee River bottoms near
Fort Benning. He had not only acquired blisters from his walk
back to camp that afternoon, but had also received the nickname that had stuck to him like the thick, sucking mud to his
boots.

For the past hour, the paratroopers had watched for the
red light over the door. And now Laroche, putting into words
the question on every paratrooper's mind, joked, "You think
the pilot will find the island, Lieutenant?"

"Eventually."

"Hey, maybe we're going to Sardinia. Maybe I haven't lost
my bet after all," Gig remarked over the steady loud drone
of the plane.

Just then, antiaircraft fire sounded in the distance. Navy
guns flashed red from the flotilla of ships making its way
toward the island that for centuries had been labeled the step-
ping-stone between Africa and Europe. Tonight, if everything
went according to schedule, Axis-held Sicily would be the
rock that stubbed the military toe of the great boot of Italy.

As the sky turned red, the alert light inside the C-47 also
turned red. Soon it would be time to bail out, to engage the
enemy waiting below. The men stood up and attached themselves to the line.

The green light came on; the cargo door opened and Gig

responded immediately. But then he stopped, causing Laroche directly behind him to lose his balance, as the rhythm of the jump was interrupted.

The commanding officer, seeing the balk, ordered in a harsh voice, "Jump!"

"Sir, we're still over the ocean," Gig shouted, as he gripped the umbilical cord that still attached him to the plane.

The officer swore; the cargo door closed as the copilot realized his mistake. The men sat down again while the light went out.

Ten minutes later, when the light came on again, there was no mistake. They were over the rugged terrain where the fighting had already begun.

In smooth formation the paratroopers left the plane. Gig first, Laroche next—and then Marsh Wexford, followed by the others.

Like great white blossoms unfolding in midnight-blue fields, the paratroopers of the 82nd Airborne filled the sky. To Marsh, the jump began in the same manner as all the others—the initial surprise, like touching an icy patch and having his feet slip out from under him. Then a rapid descent. But along with the sameness was a new feeling—of fear, that he would be out of the fighting before it actually started.

This was the moment he had inwardly dreaded—the suspension of time that held him pinned in the blinding glare of the kleig lights, that moment of impotence when his rifle was of no use, when he had to trust to lady luck *and* God, not to become a casualty before he ever hit ground. For this was no practice jump. There would be no truck waiting below to take him and his buddies back to camp—only the enemy waited, with live weapons in hand, to prune the fragile blossoms of silk before they had a chance to take root on the rocky hillsides.

Whipped by the wind, another parachute came perilously close to colliding with his own. A burst of shells exploded a few feet from Marsh. He plunged rapidly, past the other paratrooper whose suit was now covered in blood, his ammunition kit still attached to his left leg. The sudden descent caused Marsh to look to his own parachute. Through the fretwork of holes he could see the sliver of moon above. He pulled the rip cord of his auxiliary chute and once again Marsh was jerked upward. The sky now contained a blossom of a different color—gray silk amid the field of white.

He continued to plunge, driven by the wind, until the uneven landscape came up to meet him. Thrown at an angle, he managed to hit ground, knees bent, head and arms in fetal position, the jolt of his descent absorbed by every bone in his body, like a jump from a runaway merry-go-round with the calliope going full blast in his head.

He had no time to recover from the jolt. Marsh rolled toward the protection of rocks a few feet away. Within seconds, he had retrieved his weapon kit and divested himself of both parachutes. Marsh Wexford smiled. He had survived the first test, but the second would begin all too soon. With his carbine rifle in his hand, he started along the road toward the sound of battle.

Pierre Laroche, landing on the other side of the stone wall, was not so fortunate as Marsh. Despite protection by his strong combat boots, Laroche's right ankle had taken the brunt of the fall. "Hell," he muttered, and then caught himself. He had to be careful not to make any unnecessary noise. Quickly, he cut himself loose from the parachute's harness and reached for his rifle. But he knew that his oath and his noisy movements had already called attention to him.

Marsh, hearing the commotion on the other side of the wall, dove for cover, leaping from the road into the grapevines beyond. There he waited with his finger hugging the trigger, ready to fire.

At the witching hour, with the moon overhead, the roar of great guns in the distance, the two paratroopers began to stalk each other, not able to tell friend from foe. Finally, Marsh, taking a chance, called out, "George."

Laroche, recognizing the code, felt a great relief. "Marshall," he responded, and limped toward the road to meet Marsh Wexford.

Soon there were nine of them, all certain of merely one thing. They had not landed at Gela, their destination. With no idea how many miles away and with their only compass the sounds of the intermittent guns to the west, they trudged—one limping from a bad sprain, another with a superficial arm wound, and yet another with a phosphorus burn on his cheek.

Along a sixty-mile stretch of land, paratroopers fell from the sky, some so far off course that they landed on the opposite side of the island, in front of the British army. Even then, they were luckier than their British counterparts. One out of every three gliders carrying the British paratroopers plunged into the sea.

And so, with one hand, the wind brought tragedy, while it also gave cover to the sitting-duck convoy of ships, LSTs and LCVPs on their way to unload the Allied armies on the rocky shores of the island. Certain that no enemy would be about in such weather, the Axis felt safe enough to ground their observation planes until the gale lifted.

Yet, the island was not unprotected. Its strong defense was made up of airfields—more than thirty of them—and strong, concrete pillboxes several stories high, linked together in concert over the rugged land.

Marsh and the others with him stopped to examine their small cache of weapons—four carbines that had already jammed with sand grains; three M-1s; a bazooka; assorted grenades; knives and pistols—none alone capable of demolishing either the dreaded German Tiger tanks, with their 88 mm guns, or the stoutly built pillboxes of the Italians.

Cautious of the tall towers of death that loomed in the darkness, Marsh and his men had gone less than a mile when they attempted to pass a pillbox overseeing an intersection on the main road on which they traveled.

A rapid fire from the pillbox suddenly pinned them to the ground. They exchanged fire with the soldiers inside, but their weapons were no match for the enemy's.

Marsh, crawling past Laroche, said, "Cover me, corporal." He began to edge toward the side of the pillbox. Laroche had no time to see what Marsh planned to do. He emptied his clip, firing straight ahead to keep the Italians busy returning his fire. Marsh suddenly stood, hurled a grenade through a side slit of the pillbox, and fled. In seconds, the concrete walls exploded and crumbled to dust.

Into the night the paratroopers went, cutting lines of communication, answering small-arms fire with their own; hurrying, yet chafing at their slow progress toward the beach. Laroche said nothing, but Marsh knew the walking was painful for him.

As they stopped for a brief respite, in an olive grove by the roadside, Marsh whispered, "How's your ankle, Laroche?"

"Damned sore," he responded. Yet when the rest was over, Laroche was the first to begin walking again.

As they marched toward Gela, Marsh hoped the majority of the troopers had landed close enough to the combat zone to keep the Axis on the high ground busy while the amphibious landing of American troops, tanks, and heavy guns took place.

Marsh looked at the luminous dial on his watch. It was now 02:45, and the moon had almost disappeared. He waited for the shelling to begin in earnest, but the only sound he heard in the night was a Sicilian coming down the road on his donkey.

The nine took cover and waited. The Sicilian, with a blanket draped over his stooped shoulders, hummed a song in his ancient, cracked voice, to the steady clop of the donkey's hooves. He seemed completely oblivious to the invasion in progress.

"Do you speak Italian, Giraldo?" Marsh whispered to the paratrooper at his right.

"Just a few words."

"Then ask the old man the way to Gela. And requisition his donkey for Laroche."

Giraldo nodded and removed the knife from his boot. He waited until the donkey had almost passed, then rushed to the road. "*Scusi, signore. Dovè . . .*"

Giraldo stopped. He was staring at the barrel of an M-1 rifle pointed between his eyes. The old man sat erect, with no evidence of a curved spine. He took his time, examining the uniform of the man who had stopped him. Finally, he spoke in English. One word. "George."

With an embarrassed laugh, Giraldo responded, "Marshall."

"Glad to see you," the man on the donkey said, grinning and lowering his rifle. As Marsh and Laroche watched from the shadows, the blanket fell to the ground, revealing the uniform of the 82nd Airborne.

"Gig," Laroche called out, recognizing his friend. "Durned if it isn't Gig."

The paratroopers, who had been hidden at the side of the road, emerged, and a happy Gig Madison joined Marsh and Laroche.

3

*I*n a villa high in the hills halfway between Biscari and Gela, an SS officer, Heinrich von Freiker of the Siegfried Panzer Division, swore at the news. The enemy had landed on both sides of the island.

While his aide waited discreetly outside the door, Heinrich sat up on the side of the bed and tried to assemble his thoughts.

It was not surprising that the British had chosen to land at the ports of Siracusa and Augusta on the southeastern tip. But for an amphibious force to try to land on the rugged west coast in high seas, with no adequate port, was a foolhardy venture. Yet the Americans had done it. And his orders now were to get his Tiger tanks to the ridge overlooking Gela as quickly as possible.

That meant he would have to backtrack in the vulnerable staff car to the *Kampfgruppe* where his men were billeted, with the danger of meeting enemy paratroopers on the way.

He looked toward Paulina, with her tousled black hair spread over the white pillowcase. Suddenly he reached over and gave her a smack on her backside. "Wake up, Paulina," he said in Italian, the soft sibilant sounds marred by his gruff, guttural accent.

She stirred slightly and gave a small moan. Heinrich, impatient at her laziness, grabbed her arm and jerked her toward him.

"Enrico," she complained.

"Heinrich. My name is Heinrich," he shouted. "How many times do I have to tell you, you stupid Sicilian?"

Caution crept into her large brown eyes. "What is it, Heinrich?"

"I want you to leave. Now. I have to get dressed."

"But it must be the middle of the night." Despite her protest, she got out of bed, took her clothes, and fled.

"You may come in, Metz," Heinrich called out, and his aide walked back into the bedroom.

"What time was the landing?" Heinrich inquired.

"The paratroopers at midnight; the ground forces at three."

While Sturmbannführer von Freiker dressed in the uniform with the eagle of the Third Reich on prominent display, Metz began to pack his superior's clothes. When Heinrich had finished brushing his dark hair with the silver brush, Metz packed that, too.

A brief scowl was recorded in the ornate mirror as the thirty-two-year-old Heinrich looked at his short hair—darker than he would like it to be, a legacy from his mother, whom he had never forgiven for passing her coloring on to him, while his sister had inherited the blond Aryan look of their father.

Abruptly he turned from the mirror and walked out of the room, his mind dismissing his family, Paulina, and everything else but the impending fight with the Allies.

The villa's large front door creaked as it closed. The servant Vittoria hurriedly put the bar in place over the door and, taking the lamp with her, went back to her room off the kitchen.

Hiding in the closet under the stairs, Paulina waited until she heard the motor of the staff car. Then, in the darkness, she groped her way back up the stairs, walked into the bedroom, and crawled into bed. She wasn't about to leave the luxury of the villa in the middle of the night, especially since there was no telling how long Heinrich would be gone. A week. Maybe even longer. Pulling the soft comforter about her shoulders, Paulina di Resa went back to sleep.

As the bright Sicilian sun made its way over the hillsides to color the tips of the olive trees, Vittoria's scream from inside the villa awoke Paulina. She sat up, brushed her hair from her eyes, and ran to the window. Groups of men were walking onto the graveled entranceway, their uniforms neither Italian nor German.

Calling to the woman, Paulina raced from the window to the chest on the opposite side of the room, where Heinrich had stored his spoils of war. She pulled out the Moroccan silk caftan just as Vittoria, dressed in peasant black, came to the door of the bedroom.

"*Convicts!*" she screamed. "*Convicts*." And in her Sicilian dialect, she continued, "They will kill us all."

"Hush, Vittoria," Paulina demanded. "Help me put this on. And stop your hysterics."

"But the bar will not keep them out. They will break down the door and kill us. Herr Freiker told me so."

Warily, Paulina asked, "Did you count them? How many are there?"

"Nine," the woman replied, her hands trembling as she held up as many fingers in front of her face.

A knock sounded and Vittoria whimpered in terror as Paulina straightened the caftan on her shoulders. The knock was a good omen. She had dealt with the enemy long enough to know that if the soldiers didn't break the door down immediately, there might be some way to reason with them. But she would have to be extremely careful, since she was an interloper, too, merely the mistress of the German officer who had requisitioned the villa for his own.

She turned to the woman and said in a severe voice, "Go downstairs, Vittoria, and open the door wide."

"But—"

"If you want me to save your life," Paulina cut her off, "do as I say."

The woman obeyed. She walked down the stairs, while her hand was busy making the sign of the cross. She unbarred the heavy door and then opened it.

As if on cue, the aspiring actress Paulina di Resa summoned up an imperious voice worthy of a marchesa and inquired from above, "Who is it, Vittoria?"

"*Convicts*," Vittoria replied, for directly in front of Marsh and Gig stood Giraldo, shaven-headed like all the members of his team before initiation into battle.

Wearing the green silk caftan with her long black hair flowing behind her, Paulina stood at the top of the staircase. She waited a moment for the soldier's eyes to become adjusted to the darkened interior. Then she began to walk, floating slowly downward toward the cool black and white tiles of the square entrance hall.

The wide-open door provided a clear view, assuring the soldiers that no one was hiding inside to shoot at them and, just as important, it established a frame for Paulina's dramatic descent.

The eyes of all five paratroopers at the door were on the woman as she swept down the stairs and stopped a few feet from the opened door.

"*Scusi, signora,*" Giraldo began. "*Mia . . . mia . . .* " He stopped and turned apologetically toward Marsh. "Jeez, Lieutenant, I can't remember the words."

Paulina smiled. "It's not necessary for you to speak in Italian," she assured him. "I speak English."

At her admission, Marsh stepped forward. "I'm Lieutenant Marsh Wexford, 82nd Airborne Division, American Army. On behalf of the Allied liberating force, I request food and water for my men, immediately."

Paulina's solemn brown eyes reflected her earnestness as she looked at the tall blond man before her. "My servant and I will gladly share what food we have in the house, but it won't feed an entire army. How many are with you?"

Marsh hesitated at the question. "Just give us as much as you can spare. My men will divide it."

So the lieutenant was smart enough not to divulge the strength of his force. Paulina looked out over the vista. If there were others, beyond the nine Vittoria had counted, they were still hidden.

"Very well. The water is in the courtyard," she said, "if you wish to fill your canteens. When the food is ready, I will have Vittoria bring it out to you."

"Thank you, *signora.*"

She inclined her head and closed the door, hurriedly putting the wooden slat in place. "Quick, Vittoria, go to the kitchen and fix every scrap of food you can find. But hide the wine."

Paulina stood and watched while the five left and joined the others to begin walking toward the well in the courtyard. She knew they must have observed the villa before she awoke. Otherwise they would not have been so bold. But she had done it—kept them out of the villa itself. With a slight regret, Paulina looked at the tall blond lieutenant as he disappeared. That one, she would not have minded inviting inside. But the others—no.

Around the curve of the road, Laroche came on the donkey. The soldier clicked his teeth, urging the donkey forward.

"Come on, P-35," he said to the animal that Gig had named after the obsolete single-seater fighter plane. "It's time for your oats."

The donkey, sensing that food and water were ahead, broke into a trot for the first time since Gig had turned him over to the Cajun. At the ludicrous sight, Marsh and Gig forgot their precarious situation for a moment.

Vittoria, already preparing the food in the kitchen, prayed that it would not be long before Tonio, her son, returned with the Italian soldiers.

She filled large, wooden trestle bowls with bread, sardines, cheese, and olives, and hurried to the courtyard to set them down on the concrete bench near the well.

Like a swarm of starving ants, the soldiers stampeded toward the food, while Vittoria fled back to the kitchen. She was deathly afraid of what the soldiers might do, for they were all murderers, hardened convicts who had been pardoned by their government and released from prison to become paratroopers. At least that's what Herr Freiker had told her. If she had not believed him at first, she did now; for the shaved head of one of the soldiers proved it.

Unaware of the German propaganda designed to scare the civilians, the paratroopers ate, then drew lots for sentry duty. They had survived the night in enemy territory, but it was too dangerous traveling in broad daylight. So while half the men slept, the other half stood guard. Throughout the southwestern part of Sicily, other small groups of paratroopers did the same, little realizing the havoc they were playing with their hit-and-run warfare.

By midmorning, Vittoria could stand it no longer. The Italian soldiers had not come to rescue them. And Tonio had not returned. If something had happened to her son, it was all her fault. Stealthily, Vittoria took her black shawl from the nail driven into the kitchen door, wrapped the material around her head and shoulders, and tiptoed upstairs where Paulina sat staring out of the bedroom window.

Hearing the woman, Paulina turned. "Have they gone, Vittoria?"

"No. They're still in the barn. I came to tell you that I'm leaving—to find Tonio."

Paulina frowned. "The soldiers will not let you leave, Vittoria. You should know that."

"I'm going through the dungeon. You can come too, if you'd like."

"No. It's too frightening. There're spiders, and probably snakes, too. Besides, the opening in the hillside might be blocked."

"I have to find Tonio," the woman said, her maternal instinct overshadowing her fear.

"Then go, Vittoria. But I shall stay here."

Paulina turned her back to stare again through the window. Vittoria would never understand. The American soldiers were sure to move on, and if Heinrich did not return to throw her out, then the villa was hers. She had never lived in a real house before—only a poor tenant's hut on land owned by an absentee landlord. And a shabby one-room *penzione* in Rome, when she had struggled to become an actress. No, Vittoria would never understand her feelings, all those years that she had spent as a thin, knobby-kneed, sallow child, gazing at this very house and longing for just one glimpse inside. Paulina's hands tightened against the smooth silk caftan. It would take more than fear of a few American paratroopers to make her give up the villa.

The sixty-ton German tanks rumbled down the road, their three-foot-wide treads crushing everything in their path. Soldiers, hidden in the irrigation ditches, listened to the sound and began to dig deeper with their entrenching tools. Finding them ineffective, they removed their steel battle helmets and began to use them instead, measuring their spaces every few minutes to make sure they were deep enough so that the tanks might pass over them without crushing them.

Heinrich von Freiker rode ahead of the tank convoy in the staff car, with Metz at his side. The main army of the Americans had landed; the 45th Division was already hurtling toward Livorno. Now there was no telling how long the fight for Sicily would last. Heinrich had little faith in the Italians and even less in the Sicilians. It would be up to the Germans to keep the Allies from driving them all into the sea.

From the moment he had left the villa early that morning, Heinrich had regretted leaving his war chest. He looked toward the hills where the rocks reflected the afternoon sun. Suddenly he slammed on his brakes, throwing Metz abruptly against the windshield. Heinrich realized he was only three miles from the villa. If he hurried, he could retrieve the icon, at least, and catch up with the convoy before they engaged the enemy.

He shifted gears, backed the car off the main road, and took the small, uneven hillside road leading to the villa.

"Keep your eyes out for snipers," Heinrich ordered Metz, who was nursing the bump on his head. "I'm going back to the villa for a few minutes."

Metz obeyed, taking his pistol from its holster. He had learned long ago not to protest his superior's actions.

Marsh Wexford, coming off sentry duty, was disillusioned. The initial excitement of the jump and the tension of the past eight hours in enemy territory had worn off, leaving in its place a let-down feeling. He had been prepared for all-out war, not this hit-and-run business or holing up in a Sicilian barn until it grew dark again.

Methodically, he spread the khaki army blanket over the lumps of straw. It was finally his turn to go to sleep. He was dog tired, but he knew he should clean his rifle first. He eased his large frame to the blanket and reached for the carbine that had seen no duty since it had jammed at his first encounter with the enemy. Dismantling it, he laid the parts on the blanket, then took the oily rag from his kit and began the painstaking cleaning and polishing. To Marsh, it made no sense to spend so much money in training a paratrooper and then to arm him with a battle weapon that wouldn't work when he needed it most.

The soft, muted whistle of a familiar song broke through the quiet. Marsh grinned. He didn't have to turn around to see who it was. But he glanced up anyway, to see Gig sitting in the light from the barn opening. The paratrooper was busy, going through the same motions as Marsh—cleaning the dust and grains of sand from his rifle.

Marsh would never forget the first time he'd heard that song, "Praise the Lord and Pass the Ammunition." His step-sister, Belline, and his cousin's fiancée, Alpharetta Beaumont, had sung it for the bond drive at Fort Benning last Easter Sunday morning. They had been good sports to come down from Atlanta at the last minute when the other program had fallen through.

Poor Barney Oldfield, the public relations officer who'd once worked for *Variety*, had gone to all the trouble to get his friend, Gypsy Rose Lee, to agree to fly down from New York—and then his invitation was cancelled by the general.

It would have been a landmark sale, no doubt about it, if it had gone through as planned—having the stripper peel off the bonds attached to her body as each was sold, with the higher priced bonds in the more strategic spots. What a spoil-sport the general had been.

Marsh grimaced. Those days seemed so long ago. He finished cleaning his rifle and covered it. Then he lay down on the lumpy straw to go to sleep, to the muted tune on the other side of the barn.

Laroche stooped down from his perch on a rock overlooking the wide expanse beyond the villa, and picked up an olive twig. He took out his knife and began to whittle the green stick into the shape of an alligator, as he had done on so many lazy days by the bayou. But he glanced up regularly to make certain no one slipped by him on the road below. A cloud of dust in the distance caused him to stop whittling. He put his knife back in his boot and watched until he saw the vehicle, a German car with a swastika on its side. When he realized it was turning into the small, winding road toward the villa, Laroche threw down the carving and hurriedly limped to the barn to alert Marsh and the others. It was a pity to wake the big, blond paratrooper, for he had just settled down to sleep.

"Lieutenant," he said, standing over Marsh and shaking him awake. "There's a German patrol car coming up the road to the villa."

The news hit Marsh like a dash of cold water in the face. He grabbed his rifle, and within seconds the paratroopers were in position, concealed behind the shuttered windows of the stone barn. Marsh took the barrel of his weapon and slowly pushed the shutter just wide enough to see out.

There had been no visible activity from the house ever since the peasant woman had brought the food to the courtyard and vanished back inside. She and her mistress appeared to be the only residents of the villa. Marsh had no delusions as to where their sympathies lay. But regardless, he had been determined that no harm would come to them from his own men. And so he had given orders for the paratroopers to stay clear of the house.

Now he waited for the military car to come into view. He heard the crunch of the tires and the squeal of brakes, as the car stopped in the curved gravel entranceway of the villa. The German officer who was driving got out, leaving the other soldier in the car. On the main road in the distance below, there arose a steady chug of armored units moving in convoy.

Heinrich, unaware of the paratroopers, walked to the front door. Impatiently, he grabbed the twisted metal ring of a knocker—the Sicilian wolfhead. The clang of metal was loud. "Vittoria," Heinrich called. "Open the door."

Marsh was clearly uneasy. He had two alternatives, neither one attractive—certain betrayal to the convoy below if he fired his rifle, and certain betrayal if he allowed the German to talk with the women inside the villa.

With Heinrich's aide in his sight, Giraldo inclined his head toward Marsh questioningly. Marsh quickly made up his mind. He shook his head and a disappointed Giraldo lowered his rifle.

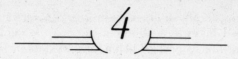

4

*P*aulina heard the sound of the German car as it came up the roadway to the villa. And when she recognized Heinrich von Freiker and his aide, Metz, she was no happier to see him than Marsh. Curiously she stood near the window overlooking the graveled entrance and waited to see what the American paratroopers would do.

Heinrich's angry voice cut through the stillness. "Vittoria!" He rapped on the door, and still Paulina waited. There were no paratroopers in sight; she heard no shots ringing out. Had they already left the barn? Or were they merely watching to see if someone let Heinrich inside?

Better to do nothing, she finally decided, and crept cautiously back into the bedroom, closed the door, and climbed into bed. If Heinrich forced his way into the house, she could pretend to be asleep. Then he couldn't fault her for not opening the heavy door for him.

In a few minutes she heard the sound of boots, the harsh click of metal against the marble tiles. So he *had* found a way inside. She closed her eyelids, letting just enough light through the shuttered lashes to see when the door opened. Deliberately she slowed her breathing.

The bedroom door burst open and Heinrich rushed to the chest in the corner. Then, as if he sensed someone else in the room with him, he froze. With a rapid turnabout, he faced the bed with his pistol drawn. Incredulously, he watched the green silk caftan come to life, as Paulina stretched, opened her eyes, and sat up.

Her brown eyes mirrored surprise. "Heinrich," she said. "What are you doing here?"

"I might ask you the same question, Paulina." Heinrich's features showed no sign of amusement.

"I never really left, Heinrich," she confessed with a little laugh. "I was too sleepy."

Eying her suspiciously, he turned again to the chest and began to search for the jeweled icon amid the silken materials. His left hand groped without success. Frantically, he laid his pistol beside the chest and began to use both hands, pulling the silken material out, little by little, blue and sapphire, tangerine and yellow, decorated with gold threads, until, in a frenzy, he turned the chest upside down, spilling the contents over the floor. A bracelet of topaz stones, an old brass lamp, gold necklaces, a marble egg, a piece of carved ivory, and loose, semiprecious stones rolled onto the floor. But the box containing the priceless icon was missing.

"What have you done with it, Paulina?"

"With what?"

"The jeweled icon."

"I don't know what you're talking about, Heinrich."

He picked up his pistol and pointed the weapon directly at her. "Give it to me, Paulina. Now. Or I swear the stolen robe you have on will be your burial gown."

In a quiet, warning voice she said, "You don't dare shoot me, Heinrich."

"And why not?"

"The sound would bring the American paratroopers from the barn."

Heinrich laughed. "Don't try to bluff me, Paulina."

Watching and listening from the barn, Marsh heard the shot the same moment as Heinrich's aide, who had waited uneasily for his superior to reappear.

As Metz leaped from the German command car with pistol in hand, Marsh said, "Okay, Giraldo."

The exchange between the paratrooper and the German was brief. Metz slumped to the ground while Marsh, Gig, and Laroche stormed the villa, with the others in a covering position.

Heinrich ran from the bedroom to look out the upstairs window. Damn! So she was right, after all. He saw his aide lying on the ground beside the car. Heinrich knew then that he could never make it in that direction without being killed, too.

The great rumble of the Tiger tanks drawing closer caused the chandelier overhead to rattle as Heinrich barricaded the bedroom door with furniture. Then he opened the French doors to the small balcony off the bedroom—and saw the sheer drop to the rocks below.

He was trapped—unless he could find the spiral staircase hidden behind the panel in the bedroom alcove. At least the Mafia knew how to construct their villas. And for once he was grateful to them.

With the loudening sound of his own tanks vibrating in the room, he searched for the concealed staircase while beyond the bedroom door, a voice called, "Signora, are you inside?"

Heinrich broke into a sweat as he saw the huge chest moving slowly from its place in front of the bedroom door. But the hidden panel turned; Heinrich quickly disappeared. In the last brief light before the panel closed, he saw the figure of a blond American paratrooper.

Marsh burst into the room with his rifle lifted to his shoulter. A pale Paulina, hugging the white embroidered pillow, stared at Marsh from the bed. With Heinrich nowhere in sight, she watched as the American searched for him. His eyes roved over the room, the empty alcove, the open balcony doors. Marsh frowned while he crept to the balcony doors, pushed one wider with his combat boot, and rushed onto the empty parapet. He examined the roof above, the rocks below. No one could have escaped in either direction. The woman must have barricaded the door herself as a protection against intruders—his own men, probably. And the shot he heard must have come from another room.

Walking back inside, he looked toward the woman. "You're all right?" he questioned.

"Just frightened," Paulina answered. She made no attempt to move from her position. Marsh felt sorry for the woman. Her face was deathly pale, waxen, and her brown eyes were great pools of fear.

Along the hall a trampling of feet sounded. A cautious Marsh lifted his weapon to his shoulder, but it was Gig joining him from the floor below.

"Did you see the German?" Marsh asked, lowering his rifle.

"No sign of him," Gig answered, "but the men are still looking."

"What about the servant? Did you find her?"

"No. Not a trace."

A frowning Marsh turned back to Paulina. "You think the German may have shot her?"

"No. Vittoria left this morning. To get help."

The confession didn't surprise Marsh, that the women had chosen to betray the paratroopers. Yet the news left him with the puzzle of the fired shot and the German unaccounted for. Suspiciously, Marsh took his rifle and lifted the coverlet of the bed, but he found nothing underneath.

Laroche hurriedly limped to the open bedroom door. "A tank's headed up the hill toward the villa," he announced.

It was too much to hope for—that the American tanks could have traveled that far from the beaches. "A kraut?" Marsh asked.

"Yes."

With his suspicion corroborated, Marsh snapped out orders. "Gig, have the men retrieve their equipment from the barn—on the double. And bring everything into the house.

"Laroche, stand guard downstairs at the main entrance."

Gig, running from the barn with the donkey, P-35, fell to the ground as an 88mm shell racked the stone structure, removing a chunk of tiled roof and taking one wall with it. Gig absorbed the ground shock through the palms of his hands, then got up and tugged at the donkey.

"Come on, P-35, before they make hamburger out of us both."

The donkey's stubborn streak had been effectively removed by the sound of guns. He willingly went with Gig toward the kitchen door.

"Hey, Madison, you can't bring that animal into the house," Giraldo shouted.

"He's part of the equipment. I got orders," Gig retaliated

and pulled the donkey inside just as another shell hit the barn, demolishing the roof.

Seeing Marsh leaving the bedroom, Paulina stopped him. "Lieutenant?"

"Yes?"

"There's an escape route from the dungeon below—to the hillside. You and your men should have no trouble finding it."

Another shell hit. The chandelier fell from the bedroom ceiling and narrowly missed the bed where Paulina lay. Bits of plaster and glass covered the rug while chalky dust permeated the air. As if the devastation to the room were a minor irritation, Paulina continued, "Go, Lieutenant. Now."

Still not trusting her and afraid that it was a trick, Marsh said, "I think you'd better come with us."

"No, Lieutenant. I won't be going anywhere."

She unclasped the pillow from her side, revealing the deep, red stain of blood that marred the green silk caftan.

"I'm done for, as you can see." She managed a tiny smile as she reached toward Marsh. "Take my hand. Please."

Reluctantly, he did so.

Her face changed. Her eyes narrowed; her voice took on a strident quality. "Promise me—you'll find Heinrich von Freiker and avenge my honor."

What could he do? The woman was dying. It mattered little if he promised to kill one more German. But to Paulina di Resa, it evidently meant everything.

"I promise."

Paulina's face relaxed. With a slow, weak gesture she pressed her other hand to her side and then, in Marsh Wexford's palm, she drew a cross in her own blood. "Go now," she ordered. "Before it's too late."

Staring down at the cross of blood rapidly dissolving into the grooved life line in his own palm, Marsh Wexford had an uncomfortable feeling that, by this act of Sicilian vengeance, he was irrevocably linked to one Heinrich von Freiker.

5

Alpharetta Beaumont sat in the meeting room of the Bluebonnet Hotel in Sweetwater, Texas, and waited for the orientation to begin.

Surrounded by other women pilots, she was silent, thinking of the busy days since she had left Atlanta. A steady hum of whispered conversations filled the air before a uniformed woman, Adrienne McBain, came into the meeting room and walked to the podium. Then the conversations ceased, as the older woman looked over the rows of young women assembled before her.

She smiled and then began to speak. "Miss Cochran has asked me to welcome you into the Women Airforce Service Pilots' program. You have reason to be proud today, for all forty of you in this room have passed the grueling physical examination to determine your fitness for the program.

"Your depth perception is outstanding; your reflexes quick; your health excellent; and your patriotism unquestionable."

A murmur rippled through the room, an almost imperceptible sigh of relief. And each young woman leaned forward to capture the words about to be spoken.

"Although you will be trained for noncombat roles, you will soon realize that, in wartime, these are just as necessary as the bombing of a German munitions factory or the shooting down of a Japanese fighter. For this reason, you will be treated as any other military air cadet, subject to the same regulations, the same rules—with the exception of two.

"Congress has not yet authorized flight pay for women, so you will receive compensation under civil service until a bill is passed to militarize the women's program. General Arnold has been assured of its passage. The other exception is that, from now on, any floor of this hotel, beyond the first, is off limits. Please remember this, for any infraction of this regulation will automatically terminate your part in the WASP program."

A hand went up in the back of the room.

"Yes?"

"My parents are on the third floor right now, Miss McBain. Does this mean I can't go up to tell them good-bye?"

The woman smiled again. "No. There are exceptions to rules. Relatives staying here are the exception." Her face grew serious again. "But I think each of you understands. The program is new. Miss Cochran had to fight opposition on two continents. We cannot afford any cloud on the program *or* the women involved. Now, are there any further questions?"

She waited a moment. No one spoke. "Then, let's get on with our assignments." She glanced at her watch. "It's now 1400 hours. The bus will leave from in front of the hotel for Avenger Field in thirty minutes. At the field, you will be divided into bays—six women to a bay. As I call your names, will you please form your groups, two by two.

"Happy Anderson?"

"Here."

"Flossie Aronson?"

"Here."

"Alpharetta Beaumont?"

"Here."

"Mary Lou Brandon?"

"Present."

Alpharetta turned around to find her partner. Mary Lou smiled at her in acknowledgment, as Miss McBain continued, "Agnes Cavanaugh? Lark Dennison?"

Thus the first bay was completed. All six stood up, took their luggage, and walked out the lobby of the hotel and toward the bus.

As she matched steps with Alpharetta across the hot concrete of the parking lot, Mary Lou Brandon inquired, "Where are you from?"

"Atlanta. And you?"

"Originally from Topeka. But I've been a test pilot for a company in California for the past three years."

The woman, tall and tanned, looked athletic, with her long legs in easy stride, her honey-colored hair pulled back in a straight style that contrasted with the curled tresses of the majority. Seeing Alpharetta push her red hair from her neck, Mary Lou confided, "You're going to have a problem."

"Why do you say that?"

"Your fair skin is going to burn in this Texas heat."

Alpharetta laughed. "Oh, that. Actually, the heat is the least of my problems. I'm much more concerned about the mechanics of an airplane engine. I've only worked on car engines with my fian—with a friend," she corrected.

"Don't worry. You'll master that in no time," the woman assured her with a self-confident air.

"I hope you're right," Alpharetta replied, less certainly.

As they approached the dusty old bus at the edge of the parking lot, Mary Lou hailed the driver. "Is this the limousine to Avenger Field?"

Sitting in the shade of the lone tree, the driver took one look at the woman and scowled. "Just put your bags in and be sure to shove 'em all the way to the rear." He made no move to help.

"There's a decided drawback, Red—coming at the beginning of the alphabet. First in, last out."

Alpharetta flinched at the nickname. In an apologetic voice she said, "My name's Alpharetta, but you can shorten it to Retta, if you like."

"Then Retta it will be," she responded, not at all embarrassed by the gentle rebuke.

Soon the bus was filled. The driver started the engine and the town of Sweetwater disappeared, to be replaced with a monotonous countryside of buffalo grass and mesquite.

Windswept particles gathered momentum, finding their way through the open windows of the bus. Alpharetta's dress was covered in a white silt that resembled finely sifted flour. She held her handkerchief over her nose and mouth to avoid breathing it into her lungs.

Mary Lou, seated beside her, choked and coughed, even

though she had also covered her face. "Close the window," she gasped. "I'd rather die of heat stroke than be asphyxiated by this Texas dirt."

Alpharetta, agreeing, pushed the window up.

Finally Avenger Field loomed in the distance and, to the sound of a Dakota making its approach for landing, the bus came to a stop.

"All right. Out you go." The driver's voice still sounded grumpy as the women filed from the bus and retrieved their luggage. An army officer sat in a jeep nearby and watched until they were all out. Then he began to walk toward them.

There was something about the officer that caused each woman to stop talking and stand at attention.

Tall, stern-looking, eyes veiled by aviator's glasses, Major Grier came to a stop directly in front of Alpharetta. He examined one row and then another of the women, and again his eyes came to rest on Alpharetta. Her position in line was not the best, sandwiched as she was between Mary Lou Brandon and Agnes Cavanaugh, both extremely tall in comparison to her own height of five feet, four inches. Somehow she felt that the waiver on her physical exam because of her weight— 110 pounds—was emblazoned across her forehead. Alpharetta, so close, could see the muscles tightening in the officer's jaw as he spoke, although she tried to stare straight ahead.

"You have already been given a welcome," he said, his voice devoid of warmth. "I see no need in repeating it. Only a warning. No allowances will be made for your being female. As long as you are in training here at Avenger Field, you will be treated like any other flying cadet. Good luck. You're going to need it."

He turned abruptly. "Lieutenant Gifford, you may take over." With those parting words, he climbed into the jeep and signaled the driver to leave.

"All right, you guys. Pick up your suitcases and follow me." The froglike voice, seemingly coming from nowhere, startled Alpharetta. Then she saw the officer standing a short distance from the hood of the bus. She picked up her suitcase and joined the line, following the lieutenant to a Nisson hut that served as a supply warehouse.

"Here, try these on for size." A pair of mechanic's coveralls was thrown in Alpharetta's direction. And the supply sergeant waited for her reaction with a grin.

She looked down at her dress and back to the supply sergeant. "I don't suppose you have a fitting room?"

He laughed. "This ain't Neiman-Marcus, Beaumont."

Self-consciously, Alpharetta tucked her dress around her and stepped into the coveralls while he watched. Her feet and hands disappeared in the excessive length of sleeves and trouser legs.

"Do you have another size?" she inquired.

"Larger or smaller?"

"Stop being so cute," Mary Lou Brandon cut in. "Give her a smaller size, and while you're at it, find me a pair that's longer in the crotch."

Curiously deflated, he complied with Mary Lou's requests.

Armed with her first uniform, bed linens, and towels, Alpharetta went back to her place in line. Within a half hour, she and the six others in her bay had been deposited into a Nisson hut that she would call home for the next several months.

In the bay, she emptied her suitcase, stashed it into the locker at the end of the bunk assigned to her, and began to put the sheets on the bed. She was careful to stretch the linen taut so that there was no sag in the middle. Once that was finished, she stripped herself of the dusty yellow dress, hung it up in her locker, took her towel and soap, and leisurely walked toward the showers. It was then that she discovered where everyone else had vanished so quickly.

"Hurry up, Aronson. You can't stay in there all day."

"Oh, this water is already ice cold," another voice complained from the adjacent shower stall.

"No wonder. You've used all the hot water washing your hair."

Impatiently, women from the two bays lined up before the shower stalls, urging the others to hurry. In her first lesson in communal living, Alpharetta took her place in line. When her turn came, she felt no need to hurry since no one else remained to take a shower after her. The water, running in riverlets across her face, washed away the heat and dust of the summer afternoon. Alpharetta reveled in the feeling, even in the inadvertent shiver as the water trickled down her body and disappeared in a small, whirling eddy at her feet.

Just as she was toweling herself dry, she heard a male voice outside. "Inspection in two minutes."

Alpharetta, with the towel wrapped around her, raced to the bay, grabbed her underwear from the locker, and began to dress. But before she could step into her mechanic's coveralls, the door had already opened and Lieutenant Gifford walked into the bay with the commanding officer.

"Attention!"

Each woman stood at attention before her bunk, her posture ramrod straight, her arms at her sides. All except Alpharetta. Like a mannequin in another pose, she held her coveralls stiffly in front of her and silently prayed for death before the two reached her bunk.

Her wish was not granted. Major Grier, taking note of her state of undress, turned to his junior officer. "Lieutenant Gifford, from now on you will give the cadets *five* minutes notice before an inspection."

"Yes, sir."

"The cadet's name?"

"Beaumont, sir."

"Two demerits for Beaumont." He walked on to the next bunk, as if Alpharetta no longer existed.

"I see I'll have to take you in hand," Mary Lou confided that evening at mess. "But I thought your college days would have prepared you for the community washroom."

"I didn't stay on campus, Mary Lou. I was a day student."

"And how did you get back and forth to school? By bus?"

"We had a chauf—" Alpharetta stopped suddenly. "By car."

"Oh, one of those—poor little rich girl driven back and forth by the old family retainer."

"No, it wasn't like that at all." Anxious to change the subject, Alpharetta said, "But I've learned my lesson—about the showers. I won't get caught last in line again. You just watch."

"That's the spirit, Red."

Training began in earnest, the women spending sixteen hours a day divided among the classroom, with problems in meteorology and navigation, and the hangars, taking apart and reassembling the airplane engines, and the cockpits of the BT-135, made Consolidated-Vultee, with their two-way radios—crafts referred to as "the Vibrators" because of the sound made by their propellers. And through it all, the women known as Cochran's Convent because of the severity of the rules that governed them, worked hard, despite the disparagement of the civilian male pilots assigned to train them.

"Flying is a man's job," Gandy Malone grumbled each day to anyone who would listen. "They got no business sending these dames down here for us to waste time on. The sooner we wash 'em out, the sooner we can get back to training the men."

Gandy began a methodical persecution of each woman assigned to him. And on the afternoon that Beaumont and Brandon reported to him, he felt particularly pleased with himself.

There was something that riled him about Brandon's confident swing as she walked across the field. She looked much more of a challenge than the small redhead beside her, and he'd always enjoyed a challenge.

As Alpharetta and Mary Lou neared the place where Gandy Malone stood beside the training plane, Mary Lou, with eyes straight ahead, spoke out of the side of her mouth. "Look at the old geezer, waiting for us. He's already planning something dirty, mark my words."

"Don't make him angry, Mary Lou. You remember what happened to Lark yesterday."

"I can take care of myself. But I worry about you. Don't let him push you around, Red."

Alpharetta sighed. How could she keep her flying instructor from taking advantage when she couldn't even defend herself from her friend?

"I wish you wouldn't call me that."

"Right-o." Glancing around quickly, a satisfied Brandon saw the stubborn resolve in Alpharetta's face. She hoped it would be enough to get her through a miserable afternoon.

"Pull up your wing, dammit," Gandy shouted through the radio to Mary Lou. "Now go through the maneuver again, Brandon. And this time, act as if you know how to fly."

Alpharetta listened to the abuse meted out by Gandy Malone, who had rushed up the steps to the tower. She not only felt sorry for her friend in the air, but fearful for herself. In a few minutes, she would be the object of his derision. And she didn't look forward to it.

"Brandon, do you read me? Brandon?" There was no reply to Gandy's voice. He could have been talking to the moon for all the attention paid to him.

Alpharetta put her hands into her coverall pockets and looked anxiously upward at the plane. With the mind of its own, the plane climbed in altitude until it was almost out of sight of the base. Then, it banked, made a 180-degree turn, and with full throttle, came soaring toward the hangar.

"You're losing altitude too fast. Pull up, Brandon. You're going to hit the hangar."

Gandy ran down the steps. He fell to the ground as the plane barely skimmed over the buildings on the base, causing the windows to rattle. The noise brought Major Grier from his headquarters, and within a few minutes his jeep drew up beside a livid Gandy Malone.

"What's going on, Malone?" he questioned.

"Radio contact broken, sir," he said disgustedly. "And she's too far away to see any ground signals. We'll just have to pray she has enough experience to get the plane to the ground by herself."

"Who is it?"

"That Brandon woman."

Alpharetta saw an amused spark light up the major's eyes. "I don't think you need to worry, Malone. She'll come down when she's good and ready."

The three watched while the plane maneuvered back and forth, going into nosedives, pulling up in a graceful chandelle, and presenting a visual display that would have made the most daring combat pilot proud. Then, as if suddenly tired, the plane leveled off, came in smoothly for the landing, and taxied up almost to Gandy's feet.

Mary Lou Brandon climbed out of the cockpit with a serious expression on her face. She pulled off her flyer's helmet and faced her instructor. "You'd better do something about the radio, Malone," she said sweetly. "I couldn't hear a word you were saying."

Too angry to acknowledge the woman, he shouted at Alpharetta. "All right, Beaumont. Get on your parachute and climb into the cockpit."

Somehow, Gandy Malone didn't seem so formidable after that. With quiet assurance, Alpharetta took over the controls, adjusted her goggles, and tested the radio. The official voice from the tower came in loud and clear. "BT in take-off position. Clear to go."

The major, standing beside Mary Lou, watched the procedure with interest. And Gandy, subdued for once and conscious of the major's scrutiny, became civil in his instructions. Even the timbre of his voice had suddenly changed.

"Take her up, Beaumont. And watch the nose."

Hoisting the old plane into position, Alpharetta took off, soaring into the air with a grace that denied the plane's limitations. Over the barren, dusty acres she flew. For the first time since she had left Atlanta, she felt the thrill of being aloft. The experience removed her from the pain of the past few weeks, for in the cloudless sky, she was another being— floating through space, riding the wings of the wind, without a care. It was a healing experience, and she was sorry when the instructor signaled for her to return to earth.

Below, the other woman pilot watched with a pride in the way Alpharetta handled the plane. With a new respect for her friend, Mary Lou Brandon realized that the small red-headed Alpharetta Beaumont could take care of herself from now on.

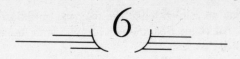

6

*U*naware of the young American woman aloft in the same plane his British cadets had once flown, Wing Commander Sir Dow Pomeroy of the Royal Air Force was at that moment making a reconnaissance flight over Mount Etna. Montgomery's troops below had reached an impasse on the eastern side of Sicily, where they were unable to breach the defense of the Germans.

The plans for the Allied invasion had been laid skillfully. They called for the establishment of beachheads on both sides of the island, with British and American armies moving rapidly from opposite directions toward the port of Messina, to keep the Germans from escaping across the strait to Italy.

But no one had allowed for national pride—in pitting Patton's brand-new U.S. 7th army against Montgomery's veteran British 8th army. It had not sat well with the Americans when the egotistical Montgomery had demanded the road assigned to Patton, relegating the U.S. 7th to guard duty of his left flank while Monty took the island. Pomeroy had an uneasy feeling that if the situation were not soon resolved to everyone's satisfaction, it would bode ill for future joint endeavors, or even the remainder of this one.

With a sense of frustration, the wing commander gave his pilot the signal to return to Tunis. And on the way, his mind turned to another worry, the letter from his fiancée, Meg. She'd written:

> I went to see your father yesterday, just as you requested. Poor dear, he's so upset about his ruined rose

garden now planted with rutabagas and Brussels sprouts.
Even plowing up the front vista almost to the door to
accommodate the corn was not nearly so devastating to
him. He even jokes about the view to Father, saying our
marriage will not unite two great houses of England,
merely two government corn crops. I do hope you will
be able to visit him soon. He maintains the proverbial
stiff upper lip so well, but I know that deep down he
misses you terribly. And so do I—miss you, darling . . .

An unidentified plane spotted off his left wing tip brought
him back to the problems of war close at hand. The pilot,
reacting immediately, veered into the cloud bank and left the
second aircraft behind.

Early the next evening, Dow Pomeroy sat opposite a frowning
U.S. Army Air Corps major and took a swallow of bourbon.
He set his glass on the umbrella table and gazed out toward
the azure sea, visible from the marbled terrace of the white
palace that served as headquarters for Allied Air Operations.

"Well, Pomeroy, how do you *expect* the Americans to feel?"
the major inquired. "Montgomery got his pick of the seaports.
Patton's army was dumped on the rocks. Now Montgomery
has decided he needs Patton's road to Messina, too."

Dow shifted uncomfortably in his chair. "He's in a poor
position, Lawton," he defended. "With no room to maneuver.
He probably isn't even aware of the inconvenience to you
Americans." Dow smiled suddenly. "Remember Monty's the
one who defeated Rommel in North Africa. Don't you think
he deserves *some* special consideration for it?"

"Patton won Mareth for him, Pomeroy. As for El Alamein,
I'll grant you that victory. Only he should have done it sooner,
seeing he had access to all communications going in and out
of Rommel's headquarters."

Pomeroy laughed. "Your nationality is showing, Lawton."

Lawton grinned. "So is yours, Pomeroy."

Seeing the aide approaching them, Dow said, "Shall we call
a truce until after dinner?"

The Americans were clearly unhappy at the turn of events.

For the British Alexander, in charge of Allied land operations in Sicily, had requested Patton's army to give up the Vizzini–Caltagirone road, twenty-five miles inland, to the British. And the U.S. 45th Division was rerouted almost all the way back to the landing beaches, to start over again, allowing the enemy time to reassemble its defenses.

Marsh Wexford and the others who escaped through the dungeon route to the hillside beyond the villa, caught up with their division. And on July 16, the town of Agrigento was captured. By the next day, the airborne troops relieved the hard-fighting 3rd Infantry Division. In six more days, the city of Palermo was occupied. After an all-night march, Marsh, Gig, Laroche, and Giraldo arrived in San Margherita, and by the 23rd, with the surrender of Trapani, the 82nd Airborne Division had completed its Sicilian campaign.

In the shadow of the old convent on Mount Erice, the paratroopers, too specialized to be used for routine ground fighting, rested and cheered as Patton and his army swept over the island and finally captured Messina—Montgomery's objective—only a few minutes before the British 8th army arrived from the other direction.

With the surrender of Messina, the battle for Sicily was over. But Heinrich von Freiker, with what was left of his panzer division, escaped through the straits to Italy, while Marsh and the other survivors of the 82nd Airborne returned to Africa to train for the next invasion.

At Avenger Field, Alpharetta graduated from the vultee trainer to more advanced aircraft, and her progress was duly noted with satisfaction by the commanding officer and grudgingly by Gandy Malone. In the classroom, she became known for her unusual ability to spot hidden targets in aerial photographs.

It was not so surprising to Alpharetta herself, trained as she had been from childhood by her father, with his hidden moonshine stills, until that way of life had been interrupted by the law and she had gone to live with her wealthy cousin, Anna Clare St. John.

The quiet, understated Alpharetta and the flamboyant Mary Lou Brandon temperamentally mirrored the two women responsible for the acceptance of women pilots for service—Nancy Love, the women's liaison for the Air Transport Command, and Jackie Cochran, director of training.

Now, halfway through the training program, Alpharetta's group had been measured for their first uniforms beyond the shapeless mechanic's coveralls they'd been issued at first. And they eagerly awaited their arrival.

The official uniforms came on a Saturday morning. The six women in Alpharetta's bay self-consciously dressed in the white shirts and general's pants, or dress pinks, with overseas caps. Armed with a pass to town, they hitched a ride into Sweetwater in time for lunch at the Bluebonnet Hotel.

So used to being together twenty-four hours a day, Flossie and Happy, Lark and Agnes, Mary Lou and Alpharetta never gave a thought to pairing off with anyone else. Bound by nothing more substantial than the alphabet, they had grown in sympathetic spirit beyond all blood ties.

As Mary Lou Brandon straightened her cap before the mirror in the ladies' room of the hotel, she glanced at Alpharetta by her side. "You know, Beaumont, I never would have chosen a Southern girl half my size for a friend back in Topeka," she admitted in a surprised voice.

Alpharetta laughed. "I don't have any friends like you back home either, Brandon."

"But Lord, how you needed me those first few days. You really were a baby. Frankly, I thought you were going to get lost in the shuffle."

Agnes Cavanaugh, coming out of a stall, took a place at a basin. "I don't know about that, Brandon. Beaumont sure did get noticed that first inspection—in her bra and step-ins. For days, the lieutenant looked at her and then back at us in those formless zoot suits. I think he was trying to decide if we all had the same kind of figure Beaumont does."

"The major wasn't averse to looking, either," Flossie piped in. "No, Brandon, there was no way they were going to lose Beaumont."

Having taken enough teasing, Alpharetta said, "I'm hungry. Let's go into the dining room."

Seated at a table between Doric columns that supported the

decorated ceiling overhead, the six chatted happily while luncheon was served by Maria, a Spanish-speaking waitress. They tried to ignore the interested glances from the U-shaped counter, yet were only partially successful. The uniforms were too new for the women not to feel self-conscious. Over the steady hum of the ceiling fans, they talked.

"We could even go to a movie tonight," Happy suggested. "We'd have plenty of time to do our shopping beforehand, and then be back at ten P.M. for Charlie to pick us up."

"I need to buy some stockings," Lark commented. "I have a run in my very last pair."

"Why don't you buy some leg makeup, instead?" Agnes inquired. "It's much cooler."

"I would if I could paint a straight seam. But I can't."

"Use your slide rule, idiot."

The waitress, amid the laughter, removed the heavy china plates that had no food left on them, and then brought the tall, frosted glasses of parfait. Just as Mary Lou lifted her long-handled spoon to taste the iced dessert, her face turned white. She laid the spoon back on the table and abruptly stood up.

"I—Excuse me. I think I see someone I know."

She brought him to the table to meet them. And the change in Mary Lou Brandon was electrifying. Gone was the brittle manner, and in its place was a softness that, despite the uniform, despite her height, highlighted a femininity that the woman had kept concealed until that moment. Only love could do this to a person. Alpharetta, aware of the transformation, felt a sudden emptiness.

"This is Kyle," Mary Lou said. "Kyle Arrington. And this is my bay—Alpharetta, Flossie, Happy, Lark, and Agnes."

"Hello, Kyle. Hi! How are ya? Howdy—hello," they chanted individually, and in one concerted breath added, "Sir!" like a chorus in a Greek drama, for he was in uniform—summer khaki—an army officer, and they were in uniform, too.

"My pleasure, ladies." His white, even teeth shone in a dazzling smile, his good looks enhanced by the dramatic tan.

"Beaumont, can I see you for a moment?" Mary Lou inquired.

"Certainly." Alpharetta rose and followed Mary Lou to the

far window where they could not be heard, while Kyle sat down at the table with the other women.

"Do you mind dreadfully if I don't go with you? Kyle's asked me to spend the rest of the day with him. But that sort of leaves you at loose ends."

Alpharetta smiled. "Go with him, Mary Lou. I'll be fine—with the others."

"You're sure?"

"Of course I'm sure." Then thinking of the return trip to the base that evening, Alpharetta said, "Will Kyle bring you back to the airfield?"

"No. I'll meet you in front of the hotel at 21:30 and ride in the jeep.

"All right. I'll see you then."

Kyle stood as the two returned to the table. Mary Lou leaned over to retrieve her shoulder bag. Digging into it, she said, "Here's the money to pay for my lunch."

Alpharetta eyed the untouched parfait. "You're not going to eat your dessert?"

"No. You may have it," she replied, aware of Alpharetta's fondness for ice cream. "I'll see you later," she said and, with a wave, left the hotel in step with Kyle Arrington.

"Where's Brandon going?" Flossie asked Alpharetta as the redhead sat down again and reached for Mary Lou's parfait glass.

Before Alpharetta had a chance to speak, Happy replied, "That's obvious, isn't it? With Kyle."

The five soon left the hotel, and in the sleepy Texas town that was now bursting at the seams in wartime, they shopped, buying the items not available at the base.

Their uniforms were heavy, and by late afternoon each was sorry she had not worn a sundress into town. Thirsty, they walked into a drugstore, wedged themselves into a wooden booth at the back, put down their packages, and waited for the boy to come and take their orders.

Removing her cap and smoothing her dark hair, Lark complained, "I hear they're designing sissy berets to go with our uniforms. Isn't that a letdown."

"The British commandos wear berets," Alpharetta defended.

"And there's nothing sissy about *them*," Agnes agreed.

"What color are they?"

"Red."

"Red? Aren't they likely to get their heads shot off—with such a bright color?"

"Maybe it has the opposite effect. My father wears a red hat when he goes hunting, so he won't be mistaken for a deer," Lark said.

Flossie glanced at Alpharetta seated across the table, with her flaming hair partially hidden under her cap.

"You ever have any trouble, Beaumont—being shot at?"

"Not yet. But Gandy might change that if I'm not careful. I'm keeping my fingers crossed that he won't assign me to tow targets for the new gunners to practice on."

"Towing gliders is almost as bad."

"What I'd really like to do is ferry planes to England," Alpharetta admitted.

"Fat chance. We'll all probably wind up doing something like delivering the general's piano or his Scottie dog."

"Waiter, could we get something to drink?" Agnes called to the boy behind the fountain.

The conversation continued in a light-hearted manner. They ordered, drank their sodas, and left to finish shopping before the stores closed.

It was almost 9:30 by the time the five came out of the picture show. Happy, with a Kleenex tissue in her hand, sniffed, "I just hate sad endings—especially when it's Alan Ladd who gets killed."

"Don't you think Brandon's friend, Kyle, looks a little like Alan Ladd?" Flossie asked.

"Maybe."

"No, I don't think so," Agnes replied. "And it's just as well—because Mary Lou is no Veronica Lake."

Alpharetta looked quickly at her watch. "I hope she's already at the hotel, waiting for us."

"She'd better be. Charlie won't wait. You remember the last time we caught a ride with him."

When they arrived, Mary Lou Brandon was not at the designated spot in front of the hotel.

"There's Kyle's white convertible—under the tree," Lark commented, for she had seen them driving down the street in it that afternoon.

"So she must be around here somewhere."

"I'll bet they're in the lobby," Alpharetta suggested. "Watch my packages while I go inside to get her."

With a mischievous smile, Flossie said, "And if you don't find her there, maybe you'd better knock on Kyle's door."

"You don't think she's—no, she couldn't be," Happy said.

"Happy's right. Anything above first floor is strictly off limits. We *all* know that," Lark agreed.

Miffed at Flossie's insinuation, Alpharetta walked inside the hotel. She hurried past the empty lobby and headed toward the dining room. All the tables were empty. As she walked through the lobby again, she shyly approached the registration desk.

"Excuse me, please," Alpharetta said, her face showing her embarrassment. "Do you have a Captain Arrington registered here?"

The clerk, suspicious at her question, replied, "Yes, we do."

"Is he—is he in his room?"

"I believe both Captain *and* Mrs. Arrington have come in," he sniffed, eying her with even more suspicion.

At that information, Alpharetta felt miserable. What could she do? How could she contact Mary Lou without breaking the rules herself?

"I'm a friend of theirs," she explained to the clerk "I . . . I wanted to tell them good-bye, but I don't suppose they have a telephone in their room?"

"No. But if you wish to leave a message for them, I'll see that they get it tomorrow morning when they check out."

"There's no way I can get in touch tonight? A bellhop or a maid, perhaps?"

"No, I'm afraid you're out of luck. This *is* Saturday night, you realize. Everyone else has gone home, and it's against the rules for me to leave the desk." He pushed a pad and pencil toward her. "But if you'd like to write a note," he repeated, "I'll see that they get it tomorrow."

Alpharetta had no recollection of the message she wrote. She folded the paper, addressed it and handed it to the clerk.

And she watched to see in which pigeon hole he put the message. Room 225.

"Come on, Beaumont. We're late." Waiting impatiently in the jeep, Charlie called to her as she walked slowly out the door of the hotel and down the steps.

"Where's Brandon? Didn't you find her?" Agnes inquired.

"No," she said. But her green eyes, widening in chagrin, were not on Agnes, but staring at the two people coming down the street. Alpharetta watched from the shadows while her commanding officer, Major Lee Grier, walked up the side steps with his wife and disappeared into the Bluebonnet Hotel.

She quickly made up her mind. Mary Lou had saved her life too many times for her to abandon her friend now, regardless of what she had done.

"You all go ahead. I'm going to ride back to the base with— with Mary Lou and Kyle."

"All right. But don't dally. Curfew's at 2200."

Agnes had no need to remind her. Shielding her eyes from the sudden gust of wind, Alpharetta felt a sense of loneliness as the jeep disappeared.

7

Alpharetta stared down at her uniform and was doubly sorry that she had worn it to town. Not only was she vulnerable to the desk clerk's reporting her to the base authorities, but if she got past him without being seen, she could still be recognized by her commanding officer, Major Grier. Regardless, she had only one course she could pursue—to contact Mary Lou and see that both of them got back to Avenger Field by curfew time. But if they were caught on the second floor, they might as well not return to base at all.

While Alpharetta stood outside the hotel and pondered her next move, the lights in Sweetwater went out, one by one. And within moments, the town that had been so lively in the afternoon, became a ghost town, with only two people visible—Alpharetta on the outside; the bald desk clerk on the inside.

But a clink of bottles behind the hedge on the right indicated that someone else was out in the night. Alpharetta started walking toward the noise.

A small boy, pulling a wagon filled with empty soft-drink bottles, came into view. Evidently, he had been raiding the hotel's garbage cans.

He was the answer to Alpharetta's prayer. Rushing toward him, she did not see the flicker of alarm crossing his face at her sudden appearance out of the darkness.

"Would you do me a favor?" she inquired immediately.

He stared at her in silence, but in dubious tones he finally asked, "What?"

"I'll give you a dollar if you go into the hotel and tell the people in Room 225 that I'm waiting for them down here."

He removed his dirty baseball cap and scratched his head. "I dunno."

"Two dollars," she bargained.

He made up his mind in a hurry. "All right. But ya got to watch my wagon and make sure nobody steals it."

"I will."

"How do I get to the room?"

She walked with him closer to the front door. "You see those steps? Past the desk clerk?"

He nodded.

"They go to the mezzanine. You can find the stairs to the second floor from there. Room 225. Don't forget."

With a fleeting look toward his bottles, the boy opened the door and, hunching his thin shoulders as if to make himself invisible, he walked across the hotel lobby.

He was almost to the steps when an irate voice challenged him. "Stop. You know better than to come off the street to play in the hotel. Out. Go on. Out."

Embarrassed, the boy looked toward the front door in the direction of Alpharetta.

"Go on home," the desk clerk ordered, "before I call the sheriff."

His finger pointed toward the door and Alpharetta, disheartened, watched the street urchin retrace his steps to the outside.

When he drew beside her, he looked up and said, "The man wouldn't let me." He reached down to pick up the tongue of his wagon.

Hearing his sigh, a disappointed Alpharetta quickly pushed a dollar bill into his hand. "At least you tried. Thank you."

She stood in the shadows while the boy proceeded down the street, to the clinking accompaniment of the empty glass bottles. Suddenly he stopped, turned around, and came back to Alpharetta.

"Why can't *you* go?" he asked.

"I'm in uniform. It's against the rules."

"Maria wears a uniform and *she* goes inside."

"Do you mean the woman who works in the dining room?"

"Yes."

"Well, that's different. She's a waitress. I'm—" Alpharetta stopped. Of course. Why hadn't she thought of it before—the print dress hanging on its wire coat hanger in the last closet of the ladies' room.

All at once, a picture of Min-yo, the houseboy at the St. Johns', flashed through her mind. For eight years he had hung his street clothes in the half bath off the utility room near the kitchen, and when his work was finished, he had always swapped his white coat and dark trousers for the clothes he traveled in.

What if the worker at the hotel was accustomed to doing the same thing as Min-yo? A hopeful Alpharetta sent the child on his way and hurried again into the hotel. The desk clerk looked up briefly, saw that it was not the urchin, and went back to his work while Alpharetta walked to the powder room.

Crossing her fingers for luck, she opened the last closet. The print dress was gone. But in its place hung a waitress' uniform—black cotton, with white frilly apron and cap. On the lapel of the dress, pinned to the puffed white hankerchief, was a nameplate that read MARIA.

"Thank you, Maria," she said under her breath and began to remove her own uniform. She pulled the black dress over her head, tightened the belt, and looped under the excess length. She placed the frilly cap on her head and then tied the small white apron around her waist. She hung her own uniform on the coat hanger.

The powder-room mirrors reflected her image in all directions at once, distorting it into tiny facets like the compound eyes of a fly, as she quickly grabbed a linen hand towel, draped it over her arm, and opened the door along the corridor from the lobby.

She knew better than to try the elevator in full view of the desk clerk. She would have to use the stairs instead. At that moment, Alpharetta felt she had wasted an enormous amount of time, yet her watch told her that only ten minutes had elapsed since the jeep had left for the base.

She waited for the desk clerk to turn his back. Then she streaked past the lobby and disappeared toward the mezzanine. From that landing with its curved iron railing, she found the steps that led upward. Alpharetta, listening, began to climb the stairs. Halfway up, the dimly lit treads took a sharp-angled turn. She adjusted her body and leaned toward the wall until the steps straightened again. And then in front of her a closed door signaled that she had reached the second floor.

Now to see whether the door were locked or not—she pushed. The door opened easily and she walked into the hall. Her eyes were cognizant of the brown-patterned wool runner along the entire length of the corridor, past the elevator shaft and the small velvet bench against the opposite wall. A steady drone of electric fans drifted over the open transoms of the individual rooms. But the only respite from the heat was a gentle breeze that swept through the open window at the end of the corridor.

211—213—215. The numbers went up as Alpharetta passed by each door. Before she reached 225, she heard a voice behind her.

"Oh, miss."

Alpharetta froze and then reluctantly turned around. Standing in the hallway, before an opened door, was the same woman Alpharetta had seen earlier with Major Grier.

"Yes, ma'am?" Alpharetta's voice croaked.

"Could you please bring some extra towels for Room 217?"

"Yes, ma'am. Right away, ma'am."

Clutching her one small hand towel, Alpharetta fled the rest of the way down the hall. As she reached the door that held the numbers she'd been searching for, she glanced over her shoulder. The woman was still standing outside in the corridor, observing her.

Alpharetta knocked on the door, tentatively at first, then more urgently when there was no response. Finally she heard some movement inside and a sleepy voice called out, "Who is it?"

Alpharetta glanced again down the hallway. "Maid," she answered, for with the major's wife in hearing distance, she couldn't reveal her identity.

She heard his grumbling as Kyle walked to the door and unlatched it. Before the door had opened all the way, Alpharetta rushed inside, to Kyle Arrington's sleepy surprise.

At first, he didn't recognize her, dressed as she was in the black and white uniform. But Mary Lou Brandon, waking up, stared incredulously.

"Beaumont! What are you doing here?"

A furious Alpharetta said, "You missed your ride back to base."

Mary Lou, rubbing her eyes, peered down at her watch. She groaned and looked from Kyle to Alpharetta. But Alpharetta had already turned her back to walk into the antiseptically white bathroom with its tiled walls, where she stripped the bath of its clean white terrycloth towels.

When she came out, Alpharetta said, "I'm taking your towels. Major Grier and his wife are down the hall in Room 217. She stopped me and asked for extras."

Mary Lou looked horrified at the news. "You mean the major's here in this hotel?"

Alpharetta nodded.

"Well, you certainly can't go back to their room. The major will recognize you for sure."

"And what else can I do? Their door's wide open and his wife will be watching for me in the hallway."

"Isn't there something you can do—to disguise yourself?"

"I *am* in disguise, in case you haven't noticed. But I'll try to hide my face as well as I can. Now, listen. When you see me close the door to their room, hurry on down the back stairs. And wait for me outside."

"You're taking an awful chance—for me," Mary Lou said in a repentant voice.

"I know."

Mary Lou, in a sundress she'd evidently purchased that afternoon, hid her uniform in the bag while Kyle walked to the mirror to comb his hair.

"Ready?" Alpharetta asked.

"Ready."

Alpharetta emerged from the room first, with the towels in her arms. In their place, she'd left Kyle the one small linen hand towel from the powder room below.

Slowly she began to walk down the hall. Her pulse quickened, her breath grew shallow as she reached Room 217. Taking a deep breath, Alpharetta knocked at the open door. "Maid," she called out.

"Come in."

Shielding her face with the towels, Alpharetta edged sideways into the room and closed the door behind her. She gave a momentary start when she saw the major sitting in a chair beside the bed. Luckily, he didn't bother to look up.

Alpharetta went straight into the bathroom, placed the towels on the racks, and listened for footsteps down the hall. To make sure Mary Lou had enough time to get down the stairs without being observed, she turned on the water in the claw-footed tub, then the lavatory, ran the water for a minute and then wiped the porcelain fixtures dry.

With a feeling of impending disaster, she wanted to run from the bath into the hallway, but she knew that would only call attention to her. So forcing herself to walk slowly, she came out of the bath. As she reached for the doorknob to open the outside door into the hall, she called over her shoulder, "Good night, ma'am."

"Oh, just a minute. Lee, honey, do you have some change?"

Behind her, Alpharetta could hear the jingle of coins as the major reached into his pocket. And from the corner of her eye she watched the major's wife approach.

The woman pressed the coins into Alpharetta's hands while she stared down at the floor. "Thank you, Maria," she said, reading the name on her lapel.

"Thank you, ma'am. And good night."

"Oh, Maria?"

"Yes, ma'am?"

"Leave the door open, will you? It's much cooler that way— for now."

Alpharetta did as she was bid and, with her knees not quite steady, she walked down the corridor.

As she pushed the door open to the stairwell, she heard the major's wife above the sound of the fans. "Well, she certainly was shy. Stared down at the floor the entire time I was talking."

Alpharetta didn't wait to hear the major's comment. She ran down the dimly lit stairs and, without thinking of the desk clerk, rushed across the lobby into the ladies' room where she changed back into her own uniform.

By the time she arrived outside, a subdued Kyle and Mary Lou were waiting for her in the white convertible. They had exactly ten minutes to reach base and check in.

On the three-mile trip back to Avenger Field, no one spoke. The wind, sweeping over the arid countryside, caught up swirls of tumbleweed that, in the glare of the headlights, resembled oversized gray animals scurrying toward shelter before the storm.

The car drove past the archway decorated with the Fifinella, the gremlinlike figure designed by Walt Disney as a mascot for the women pilots. One minute before curfew and lights out, the two women reached the Nisson hut. Without a word they undressed in the dark and climbed into their cots. But sleep eluded them for some time.

The next morning, a tired and contrite Mary Lou Brandon sat opposite Alpharetta at mess. The others around them had finished their breakfasts and the hall now contained only a few stragglers.

"I swear nothing happened," Mary Lou vowed. "We took a terrible risk, I know, going up to his room. But after dinner, we had nowhere else we could go except to sit in his car. And we were both so bushed. I haven't had a decent night's sleep since we started training. You know that. Up before the sun— calisthenics after dark. And if you hadn't come to the door last night, I wouldn't have wakened until this morning.

"But why did you have to choose the very weekend the major's wife came to visit?"

"How did *I* know she was going to check into the hotel? Charlie told me she was moving near the base."

"What? You mean she's going to be here, permanently?"

"For the next several months, anyway."

Alpharetta groaned and laid aside her cereal spoon.

"What's the matter?"

"You realize she actually *saw* me, *spoke* to me—and gave me a tip?"

"That doesn't mean she'll recognize you," Mary Lou replied. "You're not the only one in the world with red hair."

Mary Lou narrowed her eyes as she carefully scrutinized Alpharetta's appearance. "On second thought, Beaumont, have you ever considered dying your hair another color?"

Alpharetta made a face. "I'll just have to avoid the major's wife. That's the only thing I *can* do, under the circumstances."

8

Six days later, when the September sun bore down on the airfield with merciless heat and searched, like a vain narcissus, for its reflection in each piece of burnished chrome and glass, Air Cadet Alpharetta Beaumont sat in the classroom and studied the camouflaged target map before her.

"Did you find the objective, Miss Beaumont?" the civilian instructor, Avery Canfield, inquired.

"I think so."

"Then, will you inform the class?"

"It's halfway between Sections A and B—at 33 degrees north."

"Does everyone agree?" the instructor asked, looking toward the other cadets for confirmation.

A hand went up. "I think it's actually at C," a voice from the back of the room responded.

Still another commented, "I'll take Beaumont's word for it."

The instructor smiled. "You'd do well to go along with her. She's correct."

He looked at the young red-headed woman and asked in a teasing voice: "Are you sure, Miss Beaumont, that you're not color-blind, too?"

"Oh no, sir. I mean—I *am* sure."

Avery Canfield was still bitter. A first-rate pilot, he was partially color-blind, and so could not pass the Army Air Corps tests. But his very weakness had given him an unusual ability. He could spot from the air almost anything camouflaged by man—tanks, planes, vehicles painted in their khakis and greens, the colors that had no meaning or reality for him. Yet he was grounded—a civilian instructor biding his time during the war in a dust bowl in Texas.

The hands of the clock above the blackboard advanced in a sudden, awkward movement, the click causing the entire class to look upward. It was now four o'clock, or 1600.

As if the sound of the clock had returned him from a thousand miles away, Canfield walked back to his desk. "All right. Time's up. See you on Monday."

The scraping of chairs heralded the rapid departure of the cadets. All except one.

Alpharetta slowly folded her map and, in no hurry, returned it to the rack on the far side of the room. For the first time in the past six days, she felt relaxed, no longer looking for the major's wife around every corner, no longer feeling compelled to wear her leather flight helmet in the heat. She was glad that the major's wife evidently had taken no interest in the women cadets under her husband's command.

She began to walk out of the room, but before she reached the door, her instructor's voice stopped her.

"Oh, Miss Beaumont—may I see you for a moment?"

"Yes, sir?" She took a step closer and waited for Canfield to speak.

"I almost forgot. I have a message for you. The major wants to see you in his office."

"N-now?"

"Yes. You'd better hurry."

"Do—do you have any idea what he wants?"

"No, I don't. But if I were you, I wouldn't keep him waiting."

Alpharetta's spirits plummeted. She'd been recognized, she knew. Somehow the major's wife had found out and informed her husband.

"It can't be that bad, Miss Beaumont."

"What, sir?"

"You look as if you've just been sentenced to the guillotine."

Alpharetta forced herself to smile. "Maybe it's only solitary confinement."

Avery Canfield laughed, and then, pensive, he watched the young woman disappear from his classroom.

Despite Canfield's suggestion to hurry, Alpharetta walked slowly toward the commanding officer's headquarters. She held her flight helmet in one hand and stuffed her other hand in one of the many pockets of the mechanic's coveralls.

"Cadet Beaumont reporting to Major Grier," Alpharetta said to the man seated at the desk inside headquarters.

"Go on in to his office, Beaumont. He's waiting for you."

She knocked at the door and when the major answered, she opened it. "Air Cadet Beaumont reporting, sir," she repeated.

He said nothing at first. His eyes assessed her, from her red hair to her feet covered in sturdy brown oxfords. "My God, Beaumont. Those are just about the scrungiest, poorest-fitting coveralls I've ever seen."

"Yes, sir."

"Well, it isn't your fault. Don't take it personally."

"No, sir."

He didn't ask her to sit. Instead, he got up from his desk and began to pace. "I've talked with your tactical officers and your instructors. They all speak highly of you."

"Thank you, sir." If he were going to wash her out, she saw no reason for him to soften the blow with compliments.

"Tomorrow, a group of Allied dignitaries is flying in to see the women's program in action. I've chosen you, Miss Beaumont, as one of the cadets to accompany them while they're on base. You're to report to the airfield at 1200—in dress uniform. A driver will pick you up a few minutes prior to that in front of your building."

Alpharetta couldn't believe his words. She wasn't being washed out of the program, as she had feared.

"You'll eat in the mess with them—and answer any questions pertaining to the training program," he continued. "I can't tell you how important tomorrow is, Miss Beaumont. I expect your behavior to be exemplary."

"Yes, sir. And thank you, sir."

"That's all, Beaumont. You may go."

Alpharetta's elation was short-lived. On her way back to the Nisson hut, she began to worry again. Did commanding officers' wives greet visiting dignitaries, alongside their husbands?

Remembering the night at the Bluebonnet Hotel, Alpharetta realized her only hope lay in appearing very self-assured the next day, no matter what happened. And if she met the major's wife, she would have to convince her that it was mere coincidence that she resembled the maid, Maria. She already had one double in the world—Ben Mark's distant cousin, Belline Wexford. She might as well have another. Her career depended on it.

That evening, she washed her hair and saw to her uniform. Mary Lou Brandon did the same, for she had been chosen to take part in the aerial display.

The others in the bay, like Arabs in the marketplace, offered their prized possessions to both women.

"I have a new lipstick—Chen-Yu," Lark said. "You want to use it tomorrow, Beaumont?"

"It's too purple, Dennison," Flossie Aronson said, declining for Alpharetta. "She'd look like she's been in the blackberry patch."

"Thanks a lot," Lark replied sarcastically.

Alpharetta smiled. "I think I'll use my same lipstick, thank you."

"A wise decision, Beaumont," Agnes agreed.

"Hey, you want to use my pancake makeup, Brandon?" Happy offered, pulling the new jar from her locker.

"I thought you were saving it for a special occasion."

"Tomorrow *is* a special occasion."

"Well, yes," Mary Lou replied, "if you think it will hide my peeled nose." She rubbed the area where the Texas sun had taken its revenge.

"It should. Especially if you put enough on."

"But what if she flies too near the sun?" Flossie inquired. "I'd hate for her face to melt in front of the French duke or that English lord."

"You really think we're going to have royalty tomorrow?" Happy asked, impressed at Flossie's words.

"Nobility," Agnes corrected. "Not royalty. Unless the King of England comes, too."

"Beaumont, I envy you. I really do," Lark confided.

Around noon the next day, Alpharetta hurried from class, changed her coveralls for her dress uniform, and walked outside the Nisson hut to wait for the jeep that would take her to the far end of the airfield.

Her hair, burnished copper, caught the jealous rays of the sun. It was remarkable that one so fair-skinned had remained impervious to the ravages of the Texas sun. After the initial burn, her skin had taken on a golden glow that refused to deepen into the muddy, weathered tan that now afflicted Mary Lou Brandon. In the gentle glow, her eyes appeared even larger, drawing the unwary viewer into sudden hidden depths, a cool green desire surrounded by the uncompromising heat of wind and sand.

Alpharetta, oblivious to the picture she presented, had her mind on the next few hours of her life. At the sound of each jeep, she looked up, but no vehicle stopped.

Then the thunderous noise in the sky gave birth to alarm. It was a long-range bomber—not the usual one- and two-engined planes stationed at the base. And she realized it must be the plane carrying the important guests. She should have been at the runway already. What had gone wrong? Had she misunderstood the instructions?

At that moment of indecision as to what to do next, a staff car rounded the corner, slowed, and came to a stop. Alpharetta paid no attention, until the driver got out.

"Miss Beaumont?"

"Yes?"

"We'd better hurry. The dignitaries are getting here twenty minutes ahead of schedule."

She walked to the car and waited for the driver to open the door for her.

In a teasing voice, he said, "*You're* not the dignitary, Miss Beaumont. You'll ride up front with me."

"Sorry," Alpharetta responded. "I wasn't thinking." She moved to the front of the car and climbed in. From her behavior the driver decided the woman was quite used to being chauffeured in limousines. She had that air about her.

Major Grier was already standing on the field, not with his

wife, Lavinia, but with Lieutenant Gifford, two other tactical officers, and three air cadets from the various bays. A relieved Alpharetta hurriedly joined them as the plane came in for landing. The cars were lined up behind them, waiting for their important passengers.

The plane grazed the runway and bounced up and down before settling into a smoother pattern. Alpharetta winced visibly at the sloppy landing. If it had been made by any one of the four women cadets now witnessing it, Gandy Malone would have had their heads.

Nevertheless, the plane was down. It taxied toward the group; the steps were put into place and the men inside slowly began their descent from the military craft. Major Grier quickly moved toward the steps, leaving the women cadets, like ignored Chinese wives, many paces behind, until the official greeting was consummated.

From her vantage point, Alpharetta took note of each dignitary filing down the unsteady metal steps. She recognized the uniform of the Royal Air Force, the Free French, as well as the U.S. Army Air Corps. Then came an extremely familiar face. He was dressed, not in any official uniform, but civilian clothes, his rotund figure encased in a jumpsuit not unlike the mechanic's coveralls Alpharetta had worn that very morning.

Suddenly Major Grier signaled for her to step forward. "Sir Nelson, may I present your guide for the day, Air Cadet Alpharetta Beaumont. Air Marshal Sir Nelson Mitford."

"Sir."

She saluted; he acknowledged and with no further ado, Major Grier said, "You may show him to his limousine."

She led the way to the waiting car; the driver also saluted and held the door for the air marshal. And Alpharetta climbed into the front seat opposite the driver.

"Is it always this hot in Texas, Miss Beaumont?" the clipped, Oxford accent politely inquired, as they waited for the others to join the small caravan.

"Only about six months out of the year—or so I understand."

The air marshal asked no more questions. And Alpharetta, remembering her brief conversation in the taxi as she left

Atlanta, felt amusement that she was being treated in the same manner as the driver. One small mention of the weather had fulfilled the obligation of polite conversation between people of dissimilar interests or rank.

The procession arrived at the officers' club and, as soon as the car carrying Air Marshal Sir Nelson Mitford stopped, Alpharetta responded immediately. Alighting from the car, she waited to direct him.

In pairs, they all walked inside—dignitary first, followed by his aide for the day. The club, decorated in flowers, gleaming prisms of crystal goblets, and glazed white china upon white linen, held a festive air.

Just inside the private dining room stood a woman, also in white, with one small bunch of artificial violets pinned to her breast.

Major Grier stepped forward. "Gentlemen," he said, "may I present my wife, Lavinia."

At the name, Alpharetta froze.

lpharetta stared at Major Grier's wife. As she was pre-sented with the other cadets, she faltered at the un-expected smile in her direction.

Lavinia Grier bore no resemblance to the woman at the Bluebonnet Hotel.

"I'm delighted to meet you at last," Mrs. Grier said. "The major's letters have been filled with news of his women ca-dets."

"It's *our* pleasure," Alpharetta replied with genuine sincer-ity.

Like one given a reprieve, she took her assigned place at the table. She couldn't believe her good fortune. Here, she'd been avoiding the major's wife all week, had even worn the hot flight helmet to hide her red hair. And it hadn't mattered at all. Though outwardly calm, Alpharetta was betrayed by her sparkling green eyes.

Still unbelieving, she looked from the major to the slightly plump but pretty Lavinia at the end of the table. And then her own happiness at not being caught was tempered by the knowledge of the major's infidelity.

The Frenchman seated directly across from Alpharetta watched the subtle changes in the young woman's face from one moment to the next. One second, an overwhelming joy, and the next, a vague sadness—a paradox.

Trying to sort out her ambivalent feelings, Alpharetta, like the British air marshal on her left, was serious and reserved. Content to listen to the conversation around her, she never-theless responded politely to questions directed to her.

"I think you'll enjoy our aerial display this afternoon," Major Grier advised. "We have some top-flight pilots flying this afternoon."

"Good enough to fly the B-26 bombers?" General Meyer suddenly asked, leaning toward Major Grier.

"I thought they were being taken out of service," he replied.

"They've gotten bad press, Lee, because of all the crashes in North Africa. But it's my opinion that if we can show the women flying them safely, then maybe . . ."

"There's not a male pilot around who'll touch one," another replied, "even if the women *do* fly them. They've already been labeled widow-makers."

"Well, we'll see. We'll see." General Meyer continued, "I'm already impressed with your cadets, just talking with them. And I propose a toast to the continued success of the women's program."

The other male voices joined in and wineglasses were lifted in salute.

After lunch, the dignitaries toured the classrooms and questioned the cadets and the civilian instructors at length. And at 1500, they arrived at the stands set up for them to view the aerial display.

Few clouds interrupted the sky's monotonous expanse of blue. And the wind was merely a zephyr, lighting on the shoulder with the gentleness of a butterfly and then leaving without a fuss.

Gandy Malone presided over the lineup of aerial maneuvers and Alpharetta, seated in the stands between the British air marshal and the Frenchman, watched as each plane took flight. Mary Lou Brandon, the former test pilot, had been chosen for last. Gazing over the airfield, Alpharetta remembered the initial encounter of Mary Lou and Gandy, which had since grown almost to vendetta size, and she kept her fingers crossed for the smoothness of the afternoon.

"Great take-off." The people in the stands clapped, but Gandy, bracing against the exhaust of the plane, stood with his thumbs in his side pockets and his perpetual frown encased in the weathered bronze of his face. He was far too busy following the path of flight, ready to criticize the least deviation from his almost impossibly high standards, to listen to the applause behind him.

Now all five planes were aloft and the dignitaries in the stands watched them through their binoculars.

Lavinia Grier, on the other side of the white-mustached air marshal, leaned toward Alpharetta. "Just watching this makes me quite proud to be a woman," she said. From that moment on, Alpharetta felt a distinct kinship with the major's wife.

For another twenty minutes the flights continued. Then the planes came down, one by one, and the aerial display was over.

"Good show," the air marshal complimented.

"*C'est magnifique*," the Frenchman said, watching Mary Lou Brandon climb from the plane. Alpharetta was unsure as to whether the Frenchman meant the compliment for the woman herself or for her expertise in the air.

"I've made up my mind," General Meyer commented to Major Grier. "The women will be trained to fly the B-26 bombers."

In less than a half hour, Avenger Field was back to normal. The long-range bomber had departed; the air cadets were returned to their bays, and Major and Mrs. Grier left the base to celebrate the success of the day.

Mary Lou Brandon paced up and down in front of the Nisson hut for at least fifteen minutes before Alpharetta finally returned. The moment she stepped out of the limousine and waved to the departing driver, the tall, long-legged blonde rushed to meet her.

"I saw the major's wife. Did she recognize you, Beaumont? What did she say?"

Alpharetta, with a frown, hesitated as she thought of Lavinia Grier.

"For heaven's sake, don't keep me in suspense. I nearly died when I saw her walking beside the major."

"Mary Lou, it was the other way around. I didn't recognize *her*."

"What? What are you saying?"

"The woman in the Bluebonnet Hotel wasn't . . . Lavinia Grier."

In no more than a whisper, Brandon croaked, "You mean the major was with another woman last Saturday night? He wasn't with his wife?"

"Evidently not."

Mary Lou whooped with laughter. "Here we've both been in agony for the past week—afraid you'd be found out at any moment—"

Her laughter was infectious. Alpharetta joined in until a sobering thought caused her to stop. "Who do you think it could have been—at the hotel?"

"It doesn't really matter, does it, just so long as it wasn't his wife."

"I expect it matters to *Mrs.* Grier."

"Who's going to tell her? She certainly won't find out from *us*." Mary Lou, with a feeling of lightheartedness, said, "Come on, Beaumont. Let's go somewhere to celebrate."

"I'm staying on base," Alpharetta replied, "to soak my foot. The air marshal stepped on it twice."

Fourteen days before graduation, ten women out of the forty were selected for specialized bomber training. Agnes Cavanaugh and Mary Lou Brandon had been selected without restriction, with Alpharetta Beaumont also, if she could remove the waiver from her physical examination. Otherwise, she would be sent to Davis Field.

"But maybe you don't want to fly the bomber," Happy said one evening while sitting on her cot and painting her nails with a clear enamel. "I hear they're called widow-makers."

"That's the nicer name for them," Flossie spoke up with a laugh. "They're better known as Flying Prostitutes."

"Why do they call them that?" Lark inquired.

"Because of their small wings. No visible means of support."

When the laughter subsided, Alpharetta said, "Of course I want to fly them. But 120 pounds! How in the world am I going to gain ten pounds in the next two weeks?"

"Easy. We'll just stuff you with ice cream," Brandon responded. "Since you love it so much. You'll have ice cream for breakfast, for lunch, for dinner."

"And I'll give you my bread," Cavanaugh offered.

"You'll be the prize goose, Beaumont—stuffed for the fair."

The diet began with the entire bay as conspirators. Several

days later, Alpharetta shook her head at a second helping of chocolate ice cream with marshmallow topping.

"I don't want any more. Last night I even dreamed I was a banana split."

"You'll never gain the weight, Beaumont, if you don't keep on eating," Brandon advised.

"It's the calisthenics," Lark argued. "No matter how much we eat, the calories get burned up in all that exercise."

"Maybe you can claim you've hurt your knee," Happy suggested. "And get out of the exercise."

"If I did that, they might put me on the sick list. Then I wouldn't graduate with the rest of you. No, Happy. Just hand me the ice cream." Alpharetta picked up her spoon and forced herself to eat. "You realize, of course, that you're destroying my love for my favorite dessert?"

"Maybe you should switch to bagels—the ones with cream cheese," Flossie said with a sparkle in her hazel eyes.

During the two weeks, Alpharetta secretly monitored her weight, but all attempts to gain the necessary ten pounds failed. On the day before her official weigh-in, she was eight short of her goal.

The next day, as a dejected Alpharetta came off aerial duty in the late afternoon, Mary Lou Brandon was waiting for her with the message to report to the flight surgeon's office.

"It's no use. I might as well not go."

"Don't worry. You'll pass the weight test."

"How? By putting lead in my shoes?"

"Don't be a smart-mouth, Beaumont."

"Sorry."

"Just tell me—you really want to fly the B-26s?"

"You know I do."

Mary Lou Brandon smiled. "Then Mama Brandon is going to fix you up. Come inside the hangar with me."

Alpharetta walked into the empty hangar with Mary Lou. From her shoulder bag, Brandon withdrew a small, smooth rock and dropped it into one of the pockets of Alpharetta's coveralls.

"Now for one on the opposite side, so you won't list when you walk." She put one in another pocket. Six rocks in all were deposited into various pockets.

"Now let me see you walk, Beaumont."

Speechless during the entire procedure, Alpharetta began to move gingerly toward the opening of the hangar.

"You walk just like you have rocks in your pockets," Brandon accused. "Try it again, and please see if you can look a little more natural."

Up and down the hangar Alpharetta practiced, until Brandon was satisfied. "Now let's go."

They began to walk slowly across the field with Mary Lou Brandon shortening her steps to accommodate the rock-burdened Alpharetta. And with every few steps Alpharetta lamented, "I should have stayed in Atlanta. I never should have come to Texas. Just think of the disgrace when I'm shipped home . . . "

"Shut up, Beaumont. And try not to clunk as you walk."

When they reached the flight surgeon's office, Mary Lou turned to Alpharetta and said, "Go sit down and I'll check you in."

"That's not necessary. I'll do it myself."

"All right. But be careful."

Along the wall a double row of wooden chairs faced each other. In the first chair rested a cadet with her ankle strapped in Ace bandages and her crutches propped up alongside her.

Mary Lou nodded, took her place down the row, and waited. Soon she saw Alpharetta walking slowly toward them.

As Alpharetta passed by the seated cadet, the woman inquired, "Calisthenics too much for you, too?"

"Oh, no. I'm just coming to be weighed in."

Alpharetta negotiated the space warily as the cadet watched. Leaving a vacant chair between them, she sat down near Mary Lou. The dull thud of a rock hitting against the wood of the chair reverberated down the row at the same time a nurse appeared from around the corner. The cadet, reaching for her crutches, lost her grip and one slid to the floor, making even more noise than Alpharetta. Not daring to look at either cadet or the nurse, Air Cadet Beaumont suddenly found an interesting view outside the window.

"Maybelle Tyson," the nurse called. The injured cadet smiled and hobbled down the hall with the nurse.

"You don't have to say anything," Alpharetta whispered.

"At least she didn't blow the whistle on you."

"Alpharetta Bumont?" The medic mispronounced her name but she did not correct him.

"Yes?"

"Come with me. We need to put you on the scales."

In the formless mechanic's coveralls, Alpharetta stepped onto the scales. The medic adjusted the first weight—one hundred pounds. And then he began the important maneuvering of the second weight.

Standing there, Alpharetta had a terrifying thought. What if she weighed *too* much? Almost afraid to look, she saw the scales indicator drop. The medic pushed the weight back, and then she watched it balance at one hundred twenty and one-half pounds.

In a matter-of-fact voice, the medic said, "Well, Beaumont, looks like you passed."

"Is that—all?"

"Yes. I'll send an official notice to the C.O. this afternoon."

Alpharetta stepped down from the scales. "Thank you," she said and walked slowly back to where Mary Lou was waiting.

"Did you pass?"

"Yes. With a half pound over."

In a smug voice loud enough for the medic to overhear, Mary Lou commented, "I told you the ice cream would do it."

Out the door of the infirmary the two pilots went. And Alpharetta whispered, "Let's hurry someplace, Brandon, where I can get rid of these rocks. I feel like a moving Gibraltar."

"How about an ice cream sundae—to celebrate?"

"Never again."

On the afternoon of graduation, the women dressed in their slacks and white shirts, and stood at attention as the commanding officer pinned their wings on each uniform. At the head of the line stood the women from the first bay—Anderson, Aronson, Beaumont, Brandon, Cavanaugh, and Dennison. At the end of the stands stood the tactical officers and civilian instructors.

Avery Canfield had no need to hide the pride he felt at

their success. He smiled, in contrast to the frowning Gandy Malone, unable to show his feelings. For at the rear of the stands sat the new group of women who'd arrived on the cattle wagon that very afternoon. He'd have to start from scratch again.

When the ceremony was over, friends and relatives of the women who had just received their wings walked onto the field—small groups gathering together, intimate families laughing. Feeling a momentary loneliness, Alpharetta began to walk away when she heard someone calling her name.

"Alpharetta!"

The voice, familiar, loving, caused her to stop and turn around. Walking toward her were her guardians, Reed and Anna Clare St. John.

For a moment, Alpharetta stood, unable to respond. Then she found her voice. "Anna Clare. Reed. What are you doing here? In Texas?"

"The major invited us," Reed answered. "We're awfully proud of you, Alpharetta."

"Proud? For . . . for running away? Without even saying good-bye?"

"We understand, dear," Anna Clare said. With a pleased expression she said, "And I think you'll be happy to hear the news from home."

"Is . . . Ben Mark all right?" Alpharetta bit her lip as the name slipped out.

"Yes. He's fine. Rennie, his mother, had a letter from him last week."

Smoothing over the awkwardness, Reed said in a jovial voice, "Well, let's not stand in the hot sun. Let's go back to the hotel to celebrate."

He reached out and touched Alpharetta on the shoulder. His gesture, so natural, so unrehearsed, unleashed a sudden love in Alpharetta's heart.

"I'm glad you came," she admitted.

"So are we," Anna Clare agreed. "We wouldn't have missed seeing you get your wings."

"We're staying at the Bluebonnet Hotel. I suppose you're familiar with it?" Reed asked.

"Oh, yes."

"They really have very good food in the dining room," Anna Clare offered. "And such a nice waitress."

"Maria," Alpharetta supplied the name as she walked toward the parked car.

By the time they reached the hotel, the dining room was full. Even the bar stools at the U-shaped counter were taken. While the three waited for a table to be cleared, Alpharetta saw Maria in her black uniform with the frilly white apron and cap. As she rushed back and forth to the kitchen to fill orders, Alpharetta remembered that frantic Saturday evening before she'd finished her training. Yet it seemed a lifetime away.

Toward the end of the luncheon, as they waited for dessert, Reed cleared his throat. "Alpharetta, there's another reason we came out to Texas to see you—besides seeing you get your wings."

"Oh?"

"We know the real reason you left Atlanta so suddenly."

Alpharetta looked down at her skirt and smoothed a wrinkle with her hand. "Then you've met my . . . mother."

"Merely the woman who *pretended* to be your mother."

Alpharetta looked up. "What do you mean—*pretended* to be my mother?"

"Your own mother died five years ago—in Birmingham," Reed informed her. "The woman who bilked you out of your savings was just a con artist who once knew your mother."

"You mean my mother was alive? All that time? Why didn't my father ever tell me?"

"He probably thought it was best for you not to know that she'd abandoned you," Reed replied.

Alpharetta nodded. "He was a proud man, you know. I guess it was easier for him just to pretend she'd died." And with a hesitation in her voice, she inquired, "Do you know anything about her?"

"Only that she married again. But the man was an alcoholic."

"Did she . . ." Alpharetta swallowed and began again. "Did she have any other children?"

"No. You and your brothers were her only children."

"The woman who posed as my mother must have known

her well. She knew things about me. About my father . . . my brothers . . ."

"You should have come to me when she first approached you," Reed admonished.

Anna Clare, who had remained silent, suddenly spoke up. "But the woman won't ever bother you again. Reed has seen to that. And now that it's all settled you can come home with us. Ben Mark still loves you. I know. And I'll be happy when you two patch things up between you."

The smile vanished on Alpharetta's lips. "I can't go back with you. I still have a job to do."

"But surely you're not thinking of staying in the flying service," Anna Clare argued. "It's entirely too dangerous, ferrying those huge planes all across the United States. If you want me to, *I'll* write Ben Mark and explain—"

"No, Anna Clare. I can't let you do that for me."

"Alpharetta's right," Reed agreed. "She's the only one who can put things right between her and Ben Mark."

"Well, then, will you promise to write him?"

"I don't even know where he is."

"He's stationed in England," Reed informed her.

"And Belline is, too," Anna Clare added, "with the USO. She left Atlanta shortly after you did."

At that information, the light went out of Alpharetta's eyes. Then, disguising her mixed feelings, she smiled, the warmth of her smile reaching out to encompass Reed and Anna Clare and even Maria, the waitress, who at that moment, brought the bill.

Watching Reed dig into his pockets for the money, Alpharetta began to make plans. She had heard that some of the Americans were ferrying planes with the British women in Air Transport Auxiliary, on the various routes across England to a base in Scotland. As soon as her stint with the B-26s was over, she would apply for transfer, for it was impossible to explain things in a letter. Far better to see Ben Mark face to face in England. Unbelievably happy, a grateful Alpharetta quickly followed Reed and Anna Clare St. John out of the dining room in the Bluebonnet Hotel.

With Reed and Anna Clare returning to Atlanta, Alpharetta

left for Kansas to begin training with the widow-maker B-26s. And in Tunis, high-ranking air officers in Allied Command began to reassess the role of paratroopers in an invasion, as the air officers in Kansas began to reassess the role of the planes no one wanted to fly.

Wing Commander Sir Dow Pomeroy sat at the planning table as the discussion began. From their experiences in Sicily and Italy, the command realized that if men so specially trained were to be used effectively, then a method of dropping them closer to target would have to be found. Dow could not forget the disasters that had plagued both British and American paratroopers.

"Pathfinders—that's what we need. An advance group going in first, to light flares on the ground for others to follow."

"Isn't that awfully risky?" a cautious officer questioned.

Hank Lawton, becoming excited at Dow's suggestion, responded, "It's a hell of a lot safer than having an entire division dropped in the wrong area—like Sicily."

"How many are you talking about—in a pathfinder group?"

"No more than eight or ten. One officer, a sergeant, and the rest enlisted men."

"It might have possibilities," a grudging voice acceded.

"We can try it. If the concept doesn't work, we'll have to come up with something else."

"Does anyone have a better suggestion?"

No one spoke.

The action taken that day directly affected Lieutenant Marsh Wexford and seven other survivors who'd received their initial taste of war at a Sicilian villa. For as soon as Marsh volunteered to form one of the pathfinder units, Gig, Laroche, and Giraldo, and the other four immediately signed up with him. So the closely-knit team began its training for Operation Overlord, the projected invasion of the European continent.

10

As the airfield at Prestwick, Scotland, came into view, Alpharetta glanced at her watch. It was now eleven o'clock, double summer British time. She was thankful to be arriving only forty-five minutes behind schedule, for it had been a rough, turbulent trip.

The plane had been in the air for over twenty hours and she was tired. Alpharetta arched her back in the copilot's seat and reached for the radio transmitter to request clearance for landing. It gave her a special pleasure to be able to do so.

As she spoke, her voice was met with an incredulous silence from the tower. She repeated her message. "F-4236, Firebrand, requesting approach clearance. Over."

The air controller recovered quickly. "F-4236, Firebrand, you are cleared for approach to Runway 5. The winds are variable from east to west at twelve knots." Then, in a soft Bogey voice, he added, "Sweetheart, do you read me?"

The copilot grinned at Alpharetta as she made a face. But he remained silent, watching her prepare for landing. Alpharetta realized that it was a momentous occasion, for even Jackie Cochran, with all her hours in the air, had not been allowed to land a mere two years back. She'd had to give the controls over to the male copilot, even though she had flown the entire way across the ocean. But Cochran had made it possible for Alpharetta to be at the controls today. She didn't care that she wasn't listed as the official pilot. It was enough that she'd flown all the way from Air Transport Command's base in Montreal and was getting ready to land on foreign soil.

The smudge pots of the runway suddenly changed from tiny points to lantern size. Alpharetta brought the fighter down as smoothly as a goose skimming over water. With the engines still running, the plane followed the waving flags to a holding destination along the tarmac, to be sandwiched in between other fighters under the camouflage netting.

As far as she could see, planes were lined up on every available inch of space. And from that, she knew something was going to happen soon. There was an electricity in the air, for the frantic race to fill the entire British Isles with men, tanks, planes, and supplies for the European invasion had begun.

"You'll be all right, love, going into London by yourself?" Randy, the pilot, asked as they both climbed from the plane.

"Of course," she assured him. "You just go on home to your wife before the fog gets you. I can take care of myself."

Later, Alpharetta ignored the whistles and wolf calls of the men as she walked, with her luggage, toward the military bus bound for the railway station. When she had reached the station, she walked along the platform and looked for a vacant compartment, or at least one that had a space left.

She saw no vacancies—only closed doors, full compartments, and crowds of military people rushing toward the aisles of the passenger train. It was almost as if all the armies of the world were in one spot, seeking seats on the same train.

All around her were uniforms of different shapes, sizes and nationalities—British, American, colonial troops—each with distinctive headgear—glengarries, soft khaki caps with their edges bent out of shape to give a more casual appearance, boxy, staid, militarily correct hats worn by army officers, sailors' tams with their ships' names carefully removed from the bands. And caught up in the swarming mass was Alpharetta in her uniform, with silver wings across her breast to signify the air transport service.

In the momentum, Alpharetta moved up the steps and onto the train, her luggage dragged behind her. "Excuse me, please," she murmured as she edged down the aisle of car after car, while she too searched for a seat and, at the same time, tried to keep her balance against the train pulling out and gathering speed.

Afraid the entire trip to London might be spent in the aisle with her luggage, she heard a friendly voice call out, "In 'ere, ma'am. There's a tuppence of space just about your size."

Alpharetta smiled at the soldier. Relieved to have found a place, she squeezed into the small area made for her and used her luggage as a cushion for her feet.

As soon as she was seated, the same young soldier, as if eager for her denial, asked, "You meeting someone in London?"

"Yes," Alpharetta responded almost apologetically, for his eagerness turned to immediate despair at her reply. The light went out of his blue eyes, and his round, ruddy face with a slight sprinkling of freckles across his nose momentarily lost its vitality.

"That's the luck of the Irish for you, Paddy," the soldier opposite him teased.

"Would you . . . would you like your seat back?" Alpharetta inquired.

"Now what kind of Indian giver would I be, to do such a thing as that?" He grinned sheepishly. "Besides, you might change your mind in the next twelve hours when you see what charmin' fellows we can be."

"Well, I want to warn you," Alpharetta said with a yawn. "I haven't slept in twenty hours. So don't take it personally if I go to sleep in the middle of one of your jokes."

"Oh, don't apologize, ma'am," the second soldier said. "Paddy's jokes are known for putting people to sleep."

The third soldier, silent during this exchange, joined in to needle his friend. "Paddy's our secret weapon. In Sicily, we sent him over the lines to tell jokes to the Germans. That was the only way we could get past Mount Etna. Once the Germans were asleep . . ."

"Paddy got a medal for it, he did."

The corporal, taking the teasing good-naturedly, said, "Actually, it was the bazooka that did it."

Alpharetta leaned back, closed her eyes, and listened to the sounds of the train and its passengers—easy camaraderie; laughter begetting laughter; jokes shared in a frenzy that comes at wartime; bubbling gaiety to hide the horrors they had already experienced.

She thought of Marsh, training for the coming invasion. With a sudden need, she reached into her shoulder bag for his letter.

She was glad she had begun writing to him again, once she reached Kansas. They had been so close—the four of them—Marsh, Ben Mark, Belline, and herself, especially when Marsh was stationed at Fort Benning. But then the war had separated them. Now it was easier for her to see Ben Mark again, for it was Marsh who had arranged for all of them to meet at the Ritz for tea.

As she reread Marsh's latest letter for the twentieth time, Alpharetta experienced an excitement coupled with a vague uneasiness. The letter was guarded, as if he were keeping something from her that she should know. Finally, she folded his letter and dropped it into her shoulder bag.

The train quieted. The three soldiers began to play cards. Alpharetta looked out the window for a time as the express sped through the countryside. The glimpses of green were at odds with the gray buildings and steel-gray rails and orange vats rusted from the English mist. She stifled another yawn behind her hand and, lulled by the monotonous sway of the rail car, Alpharetta drifted exhaustedly into a sound sleep.

Former Wing Commander Sir Dow Pomeroy, now promoted to air vice-marshal, was not in the best of moods. The fog surrounding London had not only grounded his scheduled flight to the city, but now, permeating the entire countryside, it had brought even his car to a standstill.

Pacing up and down on the rail platform, he waited to hear if the stationmaster could stop the approaching express train from Prestwick to London. That was his only hope of arriving in time for the meeting at the Air Ministry.

It was disappointing enough to be missing the dinner party for Harry, but it was imperative for him to be in London by early morning to be briefed on his new assignment.

Group Captain Freddie Mallory, aide to Dow Pomeroy, brought his commander good news. "The message has been sent, sir. I think you'll be more comfortable, though, waiting in the car until the train arrives."

"How much longer will it be, Freddie?"

"Approximately an hour."

"This damned fog. I might have known it would spoil things."

Within the hour, the train slowed and came to an unscheduled stop. Heads lifted from makeshift pillows, and wary men listened for sounds overhead—for the Luftwaffe, for the secret weapon that was supposed to make the blitz resemble child's play, while outside, the swirl of fog closed even tighter.

"It's all right, chaps. Just a high-ranking officer getting on." The news traveled up and down the train. And the passengers went back to what they had been doing before—some sleeping, others telling jokes and dealing cards.

But the conductor, searching for a comfortable spot where he might place the air vice-marshal, stopped before the compartment shared by Paddy and his friends.

"Sorry, laddies," the conductor apologized. "But I'll have to move you to another section of the train. We have a VIP getting on, unexpected-like."

They all groaned. But one of the soldiers, Rhodes, inquired with a grin "What's the army code on that, Paddy? Do we move for a mere VIP?"

Looking out the window toward the platform and, recognizing the rank of the waiting officer, Paddy replied, "That's no ordinary VIP. It's a V*G*DIP."

"Well, why didn't the conductor say so in the first place?" The young soldier picked up his duffel bag and leaned over to awaken Alpharetta.

The conductor stopped him. "Let the lady sleep. No need for her to move, too."

And so it was that Alpharetta's newly made friends, Paddy, Rhodes, and Matthews, vanished into another car of the train while their places were taken by Sir Dow Pomeroy and his aide, Group Captain Mallory, for the remainder of the trip into London.

With nothing to disturb her, Alpharetta continued sleeping until a sudden noise outside the train erupted. With a start, she sat up. Disoriented, not knowing day from night, she struggled to get her bearings, looking around to find some point of reference, something on which to anchor her split-second flight from dream to consciousness. Slowly the outlines of the rail compartment came into focus. She had not gone to sleep at the controls of the fighter plane, after all, but had already landed and was on the train to London.

She gazed around the compartment for Paddy and his friends, but all three were gone. Seated opposite her, instead, were two British air officers, seeming very much at home and unconcerned over the noise that had awakened her.

A puzzled Alpharetta smoothed her hair and straightened her uniform. "Excuse me, please," she said, looking toward the more approachable of the two. "Could you tell me what happened to the other occupants of this compartment?"

Freddie Mallory looked slightly uncomfortable. "I have no idea. But I presume the conductor found places for them elsewhere."

His tones were clipped, precise. As soon as he had answered, he returned to reading his book.

His supercilious reply angered Alpharetta. So they had pulled rank on Paddy and the other two, ousting them from their comfortable places. Alpharetta looked from one to the other in an accusing manner. Her initial urge, to get up and leave the rail compartment, too, soon evaporated as she recalled the crowded conditions of the train. And so, ignoring the two men, Alpharetta sat quietly, her hands, small and slender, folded calmly in her lap. And she made no effort to converse.

At first, Dow Pomeroy was relieved. Despite her uniform, he knew from her brief question that she was an American. And for that reason, he'd been deliberately aloof. Every American he'd met so far had been entirely too talkative and friendly. It seemed to be a national trait. And he'd had no wish to carry on a meaningless conversation with someone he would never see again. Yet it intrigued him that the woman had not reacted according to the stereotype. Beyond that first question, she'd made no effort to speak with either him or his aide.

As the hour passed and the silence continued, Dow glanced up from his newspaper from time to time. He saw that, although her uniform was travel-worn, the woman opposite him had a patrician look about her—and the coloring he so admired in women. Hair, titian red; eyes, emerald green. There was something vaguely disturbing but familiar about her.

Dow's memory swept over the long, cold portrait corridor

of Harrington Hall, the family estate, where ancestors stared impersonally from their gilt frames—men in formal dress or uniform; women in ethereal white, each with the family coronet upon her head.

As a boy, he had spent many a long, rainy afternoon staring up at and memorizing the features of each generation. For a fleeting moment he visualized the portrait of the young women opposite him. She gazed from her frame with a serenity in keeping with the gallery. And on her head was the diamond coronet belonging to his family from the time of the Norman Conquest.

Alpharetta's green eyes intercepted his scrutiny and Dow quickly averted his gaze. What was the matter with him? He must be coming down with a fever. Else his mind would not have become so frivolous, imagining that the complete stranger, and an increasingly hostile one at that, who sat across from him even remotely resembled the family portrait of the titian-haired beauty he'd had a schoolboy crush on.

Taking refuge behind his newspaper again, Dow became aware not of the printed words, but of the speed of the train hurtling itself toward Liverpool Station.

The train slowed and stopped. Dow, making no pretense to ignore her any longer, openly watched as Alpharetta stood, adjusted her hat on her red hair, and reached for her luggage. Group Captain Mallory, redeeming himself slightly, opened the outside compartment door for her.

"Thank you," she said, her voice aloof. And then she was gone.

Waiting for the crowds to disperse before venturing onto the platform, Air Vice-Marshal Sir Dow Pomeroy sat impatiently, trying to conjure the face of his fiancée, Meg. But he was not successful. He saw only hair of burnished copper and eyes of green staring at him from a large gilt frame.

Alpharetta followed the crowd onto the street where a fine mist sprinkled the city and vied with the fog to give discomfort. Within a few seconds she was alone, lost in a darkened silence, as if somehow she had taken the wrong turn and missed the exit.

Her sense of equilibrium vanished. Even her shoes disappeared from view as she stared toward the pavement. Onward she groped, with her hand stretched in front of her, until she bumped into the side of a vehicle parked at the curbing.

"Do you wish a taxi?" a voice from the darkness uttered.

"Yes. Oh yes, please," Alpharetta answered, relieved to hear the sound of another human being.

Her luggage exchanged hands and was relegated to the front seat of the taxi while Alpharetta settled herself in the back.

"To Rainbow Corner, off Picadilly Circus, please," she announced.

All the street signs, all the highway signs had been taken down for the duration of the war. Marsh had warned her about that. Only he hadn't warned her about the thickness of the fog that wrapped itself around the city, making it twice as difficult to find one's way.

Realizing how lucky she was to have literally bumped into the taxi, Alpharetta sat upright, straining her eyes and wondering how the driver could find his way ahead, when visibility was no more than a few inches. But the driver, more used to the fog than Alpharetta, steered his taxi behind a large red double-decker bus. And in front of the bus, a man carrying a shielded lantern walked on foot to guide the bus driver.

Traveling at a snail's pace, Alpharetta, like a blind man whose other senses have become more acute, could now hear the noise in the darkened streets. Occasionally, soldiers loomed from the curbing and stepped back again, their American voices cutting through the mist briefly, like their flashlights.

At times, even the taxi driver had to pull to the curbing, get out, and trace the outline of numbers on the sides of the buildings to see how far they had traveled.

Once, when the vehicle had come to a brief stop and Alpharetta was alone in the taxi, a soldier bent his head to peer inside and exclaimed, "Hey, Mama. Buy me that." Then the light caught the glitter of the silver wings on her uniform. Quickly he straightened and disappeared.

Finally reaching Rainbow Corner, Alpharetta said, "You'll wait for me, won't you? I shan't be long. I just have to pick up my billeting."

The taxi driver replied, "Yes, miss. Take your time."

She left her luggage in the front of the taxi and walked toward the sound of voices. Luckily for Alpharetta, her billeting was assured, for with the thousands of GIs on pass, lodging was a problem. A central housing service at Rainbow Corner had been set up to help the soldiers find accomodations. Even then, on any given weekend, as many as a thousand men slept on cots in bomb shelters.

"This is the key to the flat," the woman at the desk explained to Alpharetta. "And the address. You'll be sharing the flat with five others by tomorrow. Oh, and here's the key to the park." She held a second key for Alpharetta.

"I beg your pardon?"

"The key to the park," the woman repeated. "The gate is always locked."

Dubiously, Alpharetta took the second key as well. "Thank you," she said, dropping it into her shoulder bag, too.

She walked out of the building and edged cautiously toward the waiting taxi.

By the time Alpharetta reached the flat near Berkeley Square and used the key to open the massive front door, it was close to midnight. With no idea that, at the same time, Dow Pomeroy's batman was building a fire in the black onyx fireplace three doors away, a shivering Alpharetta, wearing her long pink woolen underwear, crawled between ice-cold sheets and began to dream of her meeting with Ben Mark St. John.

11

The sun, so timid in its early-morning journey, began to fight its way through the fog of London by mid-morning. Alpharetta had gotten up late and, although not wanting anything more substantial than a cup of coffee, she had forced herself to eat breakfast. It would be at least five hours before she met the others at the Ritz for tea.

After eight months of separation from Ben Mark, Alpharetta was philosophical about waiting only hours more. Yet she had to remind herself that she not only needed to eat, but to find something to pass the time until late afternoon. Else she would be in no state to see anyone.

She put on her coat, tied a scarf around her neck and, venturing out onto the street, began to survey the surroundings she hadn't seen the night before.

Directly in front of her was a park surrounded by walls and shrubbery. She walked to the closed gate and peered inside. Benches, sheltered under the limbs of trees, were empty, and the few pigeons, strutting along the walkway, cocked their heads and listened, as if waiting for her to enter and feed them. But Alpharetta was empty-handed, and it was cold. She backed away from the gate and began to walk down the street from the flat. At the corner, she automatically looked up for a street sign, but no markings indicated where she had been or where she was going.

Farther down, in front of another square, she saw an old-fashioned hack, with a FOR HIRE sign propped up on its seat. The sight of the horse and the driver immediately dredged up memories of early days on another continent, when she was the moonshiner's daughter, living within the shadow of Stone Mountain, where figures carved in stone recalled yesterday's heroes of the South.

Like a child again, she wanted to see other monuments, other heroes, in this land where her cousin, Anna Clare, had been presented to the queen at the Court of St. James—and to ride through the familiar streets described by Anna Clare in that year of her greatest triumph.

Alpharetta signaled to the driver, and as the hack came to a stop beside her, she climbed into it. Her enthusiasm was evident in her voice.

"I want to see it all," she said, "the Thames, the Tower, Trafalgar Square, Soho, Parliament, Big Ben . . ."

When the driver gave her a dubious look, she laughed and pulled out of her shoulder bag a one-pound note. "Or at least this much of the city."

His solemn face denied his pleasure at her exuberance as he tucked the money into his leather pouch.

"This your first time in London, miss?"

"Yes."

"Not like it used to be," the driver apologized, "before the Jerries got to her. She was a grand old lady, she was. Just like the Queen Mother. Now her face is dirty, like that flower woman on the steps. But lucky at that, I guess—to be alive."

Massive stone buildings greeted Alpharetta in all directions, as well as arched gateways into the parks, wrought iron with speared spikes of gold now dulled, old brick with scaffolding indicating repairs underway, side by side with the dry rot of unpainted wood—and great empty spaces where façades had once stood—the old and the new—uneasy bedfellows in a land that had borne the brunt of nightly bombing, and somehow survived.

They drove along the Strand, with the driver pointing out Nelson's Column and the four lions at the base of the fountain in Trafalgar Square—and once again, empty spaces near the Cathedral.

Farther away, along the greens of Hyde Park, Alpharetta watched snatches of cricket and baseball games, with onlookers everywhere—some with their own chairs, others perched under the trees or sitting on stone steps. As far as she could see, there were American uniforms, with a sprinkling of other nationalities. As one group of soldiers passed by and waved, Alpharetta asked, "Is London always this crowded with Americans?"

The driver nodded. "Especially on weekends. But they'll disappear soon," he predicted, "just like the children when the blitz began—overnight, without a word."

His prediction sobered Alpharetta. She shivered from the cold and the driver, turning back to look, asked, "Would you like to stop for a hot cuppa?"

"That would be nice," she admitted. "It's frightfully cold."

The absence of children was apparent in Picadilly where a Punch and Judy show was in progress. An organ grinder's grizzled monkey passed his tin cup in the square for ha'pennies among the grownups, while the hawkers had cleverly changed their childish wares to souvenirs that no soldier on leave could resist. The campaign medals on their uniforms were at variance with their carefree behavior. With oddly youthful, amnesiac faces, the soldiers were determined to experience a lifetime in one weekend, with the past forgotten, with no certainty for tomorrow, only the promise of the immediate hour.

Climbing down from the hack, Alpharetta suddenly made up her mind. She had been spectator from the slow-moving vehicle long enough. She wanted a hot cuppa, as the driver had called it, and then to walk briskly in the streets, to become a part of the crowd. And so she said good-bye to the driver and began to walk toward Marble Arch and into Lyons Corner House.

"I say, what enormous luck to see you again."

Alpharetta looked around. At her left elbow stood a smiling Paddy, the Irish soldier from the train. And beside him were his two British companions, Rhodes and Matthews. Feeling alone in a city filled with people, Alpharetta returned his smile.

"Paddy! What happened to you on the train? When I woke up, you had turned into an air officer."

"A clear case of the frog and the prince, my dear Watson," Rhodes, the more profane of the companions, answered before Paddy had a chance to explain.

"Actually, the conductor moved us."

Remembering her feelings when she'd discovered the change, she said, "Why didn't you wake me? I would have moved, too. The rest of the trip was quite boring."

"You were sleeping like a baby, you were. And the conductor took pity on you."

Paddy, with his eyes searching for a companion, quickly said, "Are you alone?"

"For the moment."

"Then take pity on three boys far from home, ma'am . . ."

"Wait a minute," Alpharetta said, interrupting him with a laugh. "*I'm* the stranger here."

"Then all the more reason for you to have us as guides, so *you* won't get lost. Where to, ma'am?"

She wrinkled her nose. "Why do you keep calling me *ma'am*? I thought that title was reserved for the Queen."

"But *you're* the queen of our—"

She held up her hand. "Don't finish it, Rhodes. I don't think I can take it this early in the day. I'm going across the street for something hot to drink."

"Paddy, get out and stop the traffic while I spread my coat for the lady."

A military car slammed on its brakes as Alpharetta suddenly stepped from the curbing almost in its path. One of the soldiers pulled her back to safety. Then the three enlisted men saluted the high-ranking officers as the car started up again.

Inside the Packard, Dow Pomeroy scowled as he recognized the red-headed woman from the train. She had lost no time in finding her friends again.

"Watch the traffic, luv," Paddy cautioned a visibly shaken Alpharetta.

"I will," she replied, "as soon as I get used to Englishmen driving on the wrong side of the street."

Her voice contained a slight petulance to hide her embarrassment, for she had recognized the vice-marshal, as well.

They sat in the café, the four of them. It was a pleasant diversion for Alpharetta to be surrounded by the soldiers. But she didn't linger after the hot liquid had revived her and brought warmth to her hands and feet.

"You're making a terrible mistake," a disappointed Matthews admonished as Alpharetta left them.

"You'd have a lot more fun with us," Rhodes insisted.

"I know," she admitted sympathetically, and then was gone, to shop at Selfridge's before finding her way back to the flat.

By the time she reached her quarters, the flat was vastly different. Scattered clothes and suitcases provided evidence of the arrival of the five with whom she was to share the flat for the weekend. But the flat, empty of people, resembed a cocoon from which the moth had hastily flown.

Alpharetta dressed far in advance of her appointment. In the mirror she stared at the new outfit she'd bought, not at Selfridge's, but at the small export shop around the corner that catered to foreigners.

Beautifully woven green wool and silk, the ensemble had been far too expensive, even with its two skirts—one, street length; the other, long, suitable for evenings in drafty, unheated English houses. Completing the ensemble were a blouse, a coat, and a stole of Highlander tartan that could be worn around the neck or about the waist. Alpharetta carefully draped the stole over her blouse and pinned it in place with the small brooch of green glass and rhinestones, a gift from Anna Clare, who had dug it out of an old trunk at the foot of her bed.

Alpharetta reached for the matching green coat and stopped. She looked again at the image in the mirror and what she saw troubled her.

She continued to stare, adjusting the stole, trying it differently, removing the pin and then attaching it in another position closer to her neck.

But the trouble was not in the ensemble itself. It was beautiful, as it should be at the price. Her eyes left the mirror and looked toward her discarded uniform, draped over a nearby chair. Slowly, the real reason for her dissatisfaction dawned on her. For once again she had used Ben Mark's standards to judge. He didn't care to see women dressed in uniform—either British *or* American. So, she had been a spendthrift, paying much more than she could afford for a mere piece of cloth to win Ben Mark's approval.

She began to remove the expensive outfit. In viewing her uniform as Ben Mark would see it, she was denying the many hours of hard work that had won her the right to wear it and its silver wings.

Had she not already learned a bitter lesson from her fear of what Ben Mark might say about the woman who'd posed as her mother? If they were to have a future together, then there was no need to hide what she was, or had been. With her decision, Alpharetta found a quiet inner peace and serenity.

Marsh Wexford sat uneasily in the atrium of the Ritz and gazed over the palms to the door whose patched glass gave a distorted view of the street. His knees were at the same level as the table top beside him.

Tall, handsome by any nationality's standards, the paratroop officer was unaware of the murmurs of approval at the other tables filling with young women in a ritual as old as the watering hole at eventide, when societies of both jungle and civilization came together, species of like kind.

In a hotel known for its elegance, even in wartime, the casual bystander would see no outward manifestation of Marsh's uneasiness. For he was accustomed to the Paris salon of the Vicomtesse d'Arcy, the family friend with whom he had stayed twice in his life. Of course he remembered almost nothing of the first time. He had been only two years old— a small waif rescued from the battlefield of World War I. But the second time he'd been an eighteen-year-old student at the Sorbonne. For over a year, he'd remained with the vicomtesse, until his adoptive father died and he had returned to Atlanta.

No, it was not the elegance of his surroundings that made him uneasy, but the coming together of his stepsister Belline and Alpharetta Beaumont, both in love with the same man, his cousin, Ben Mark St. John. Despite the broken engagement, Marsh knew Alpharetta loved Ben Mark as much as ever.

Alpharetta's serenity lasted only until she reached the entrance to the Ritz. And then it left her entirely. What would she say to Ben Mark, after so long?

She gazed down at the uniform and for one brief moment regretted changing her mind. But no. She was proud of the uniform and what it represented. Why then, was her pulse racing so uncontrollably, echoing its dismay into her ears? She took a deep breath and slowly walked into the hotel.

Outwardly she was calm, aloof, her nervousness apparent only in the slight circular motion of her thumb against the forefinger of her right hand, as if she were manipulating the worry stone used by the ancients.

Marsh, watching the door, recognized her. He rose from the table and went to meet her. Truly glad to see him, Alpharetta smiled and held out her hands to him. As envious female eyes at a nearby table watched, Marsh took both hands, drew her to him, and kissed her.

"It's good to see you, Alpharetta."

"Am I . . . the first one here, Marsh?"

"Yes. I suppose Ben Mark and Belline will both be late, as usual. You remember how they both were."

"Yes."

Glad of a chance to talk with Marsh first, Alpharetta forgot her nervousness as they shared experiences and he questioned her about her flying. Her eyes took fire as she described the past few weeks, the challenge of the transatlantic flight. But as the time passed, Marsh realized how vulnerable she was. Every moment or so, she glanced toward the entrance and then returned her attention to him. He should have written her, to warn her. Suddenly, he leaned toward her.

"Alpharetta, don't be too disappointed, if—"

"Hello, you two," Belline said, sweeping toward the table whose pink cloth cascaded to the floor. "Sorry I'm late. We had a rehearsal for the show this afternoon."

Belline still wore an exotic makeup, and the deep pink wool dress, by no means government issue, brought out the highlights in her red hair as she cast off the more subdued brown coat she'd worn.

"Ben Mark should be here in a few minutes," she informed them. "He said he'd come straight from Grosvenor House."

"How are you, Belline?" Alpharetta asked.

"Better every day—in every way." She laughed. "At least that's what we're supposed to believe." A guilty flush began to spread over Belline's face, for she remembered the episode at Brookwood Station months before, when she had hurried Ben Mark out of the depot while Alpharetta was still in the restroom.

"How long have you been in England, Belline?" Alpharetta inquired politely.

"About four months. I was in Cairo before that."

Captain Ben Mark St. John, sauntering into the Ritz from the side entrance, saw Marsh's reflection in the mirror beyond the palms. And seated with him was Belline. He started toward them when he became aware of a third person at the same table—a woman in uniform with the same red hair as Belline, the same slender figure.

He stopped. Anger grew and became a palpable thing, a lump in his throat that refused to be dislodged. Alpharetta! Eight whole months and no letter, not a single word from his former fiancée. Yet, suddenly, here she was, in London, with no prior warning from anyone. Not Marsh. Not even Belline.

He had been set up. His eyes, cold, calculating, assessed Alpharetta from his vantage point behind the palms. He took in her uniform, the silver wings on her breast. And at that moment, he was sorry that he had ever taught her to fly.

An angry Ben Mark backed away and headed for the bar instead. He needed more time to get himself together before facing Alpharetta.

Marsh, deciding not to wait any longer before ordering, signaled the waiter who was hovering nearby.

"We'll go ahead and order now. The other member of our party seems to be delayed."

"As you wish, Lieutenant."

Despite the wartime austerity, the tea table was still creditable, the absent delicacies of earlier days made up for by ingenious substitutions and the elegance of the service—silver teapots, fine porcelain cups with gold trim, lovely old pink linen napkins to match the tablecloths.

After the second drink, Ben Mark felt fortified enough to face his former fiancée. With a slight flush to his cheeks, he started toward the other room, as Belline excused herself.

"Coming to look for me?" Ben Mark asked as he and Belline met outside the bar.

"I had an idea you might be in the bar."

"Why didn't you tell me—that Alpharetta was going to be with you?" he demanded.

"So you've seen her."

"Only through the palms."

"And you couldn't face her without getting drunk first?"

"I only had two drinks." He grabbed her wrist and whispered, "Why didn't you warn me?"

"Please, Ben Mark. Don't make a scene. Let's go back into the lounge, where we can talk."

When they were seated, Belline began, "I know how awkward it is for you to see Alpharetta and Marsh together. But you assured him that it was all over between you two. Marsh really believed what you told him. So it's not as if he's taking her away from you, Ben Mark."

"You mean they've been seeing each other?"

"Not much chance for that, until this weekend. But I know they've been writing to each other. Please, Ben Mark, don't spoil things for Marsh. He wants all of us to be friends."

A bitter twist to his mouth marred Ben Mark's dark good looks. "It's not fair. Alpharetta always brought out the best in me."

Belline laughed. "But you have me now. And I understand you much better than Alpharetta ever did. Come on, Ben Mark. Perk up. I'll help you get through this afternoon."

"You promise?"

"Yes. And you can help matters along by calling me *darling*."

Ben Mark laughed for the first time in the conversation. "The same old Belline. Still jealous of Alpharetta."

"Now, why do you say that? Alpharetta doesn't have *you* anymore."

"And you think you do?"

"For this weekend, anyway. Shall we go?"

Arm in arm they walked toward the room where Marsh and Alpharetta waited, surrounded by mirrored images of uniforms and silver teapots, incongruous symbols of war and peace.

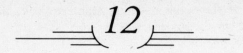

*B*en Mark!" Alpharetta's face turned pale as she said his name.

"Hello, Alpharetta. Hello, Marsh." Ben Mark quickly shifted his attention to his cousin, politely standing, and reached out to shake hands while Belline slid into her seat again.

Flanked by the two men in American uniforms—one man, blond, the other, dark, resembling the men in wartime posters in every American city—the two women sat, similar in looks, yet vastly different in personality.

"So what brings you to England, Alpharetta?" Ben Mark asked casually as he pulled out the chair opposite her.

Her voice was almost inaudible as she replied, "I ferried a fighter plane from Montreal yesterday."

Their eyes met for an instant before Belline cut in. "What will you have, Ben Mark? A cup of tea? A rhubarb pastry? Waiter, could we have another pot of hot water?"

"Nothing for me, thanks. I can only stay a few minutes." Ben Mark looked around the room, at people still wrapped in their coats as they sipped tea and engaged in conversation, their low-toned, well-bred behavior denying the discomfort of the unheated room. "God, it's cold in this place," he complained. "You'd think they'd come up with *something* to heat the building."

"Rumor has it that there's a war going on out there," Marsh chided gently.

At his dark scowl, Alpharetta quickly inquired, "Have you flown many combat missions, Ben Mark?"

"Oh, I've shot down a few Jerries, plowed up a few fields in Holland. But right now we're practicing our dive-bombing at the Wash, getting ready for something big."

"What plane are you flying these days?" Marsh asked.

"The Jug." He laughed. "At least that's what we all call it. A P-47 to you." Ben Mark glanced at his watch. "Look, this is great, seeing you again, but I've got to run." Looking at Belline, he added, "Are you coming, darling?"

A crestfallen Alpharetta sat, saying nothing as Belline smiled and answered, "Of course."

Marsh, attempting to salvage the fiasco of the meeting between Alpharetta and Ben Mark, said, "I've booked a table for dinner tonight—for four."

"Some other time, Marsh." With an immobile, impersonal face, Ben Mark mouthed, "It really was great to see you, Alpharetta. Let Belline know the next time you're coming over, and if we're still in England, maybe we can all get together."

"It . . . it was good to see you again, Ben Mark."

When Belline and Ben Mark departed, Alpharetta stared down at the cup in her hands and fought back the tears.

Marsh, furious with Ben Mark's behavior as well as his sister's, reached over and placed his larger hand on Alpharetta's to comfort her. His gesture, recorded in the mirror, was not lost on Ben Mark as he took one last glance at his former fiancée.

"You did well, cousin. I was proud of you," Belline whispered.

"One of my better performances," Ben Mark acknowledged in a bitter voice as the two left the hotel.

"I didn't know—that he and Belline . . ."Alpharetta stopped and swallowed. Her voice could not be relied upon to finish the sentence.

"Alpharetta, he's not worth it—even if he *is* my cousin."

"He didn't even notice me. I bought a beautiful dress to wear today. But that wouldn't have mattered, either. Will you . . . will you excuse me for a few minutes, Marsh?"

He stood. "Take as long as you want. I'm in no hurry."

She rushed to the powder room. And it was as if the eight

months had never passed since the time she had fled Atlanta. The same hurt was there in her throat as on that July day. But now it was a double loss, of hope regained and hope vanished.

The specter of Belline appeared in the mirror beside her. But hadn't she always been there, like a silhouette, from the time Ben Mark had first entered her life?

No one but Anna Clare suspected that she knew the truth, that she and Belline shared the same father. Alpharetta had been sworn to secrecy and even her father, Tucker Beaumont, had died without confiding to her that he had sired another daughter. Alpharetta had always wanted the sister that she had been denied in childhood. But instead, she had been handed an adversary who had just taken Ben Mark from her.

She struggled with her disappointment. And she began to find excuses for Ben Mark's behavior. She had expected too much from him. After all, *she* was the one who had broken their engagement and fled. It was too much to hope that he would welcome her at their first meeting, even if Marsh had tried to prepare the way.

Conscious of Marsh waiting for her, she blew her nose and left the powder room. As she walked back to the table, she rounded the corner just as another man in uniform approached. To avoid collision, she quickly stepped aside, but the man, waving good-bye to his friends, continued walking backward until he stepped on her foot.

"Oh, I say, I am sorry."

As Alpharetta came face to face with the white-mustached officer, she recognized Air Marshal Sir Nelson Mitford, the British officer who had accompanied General Meyer to Avenger Field to view the women pilots' program in action.

"It was my fault, Sir Nelson."

Her use of his name startled him, for his was not a household name like Monty's. "Do I know you?"

"I was Cadet Alpharetta Beaumont, your guide, sir, when you visited Avenger Field in the United States."

He peered at her as if trying to place her. Then the light came into his eyes. "Yes, of course. I remember now. You're the one with the uncanny knack for reading aerial maps. And what are you doing in England, Miss Beaumont?"

"I'm flying air transport now, sir."

"Well, I hope your foot won't give you any trouble with your flying, Miss Beaumont."

"No, I'm sure it won't."

He walked past her and Alpharetta, with a slight limp, returned to the table.

Acting as if the confrontation with Ben Mark had never taken place, she managed a smile as she said, "I just bumped into someone I know."

Marsh, prepared to be sympathetic to a devastated Alpharetta, was completely surprised at her quick recovery. "Who?" he asked.

"Air Marshal Sir Nelson Mitford. He stepped on my foot."

Marsh laughed. "I know him. He was on Tedder's staff. They called him 'Pelican' Mitford behind his back because he's so clumsy on land. He didn't hurt you, did he?"

"I'll get over it," she admitted. "But he's really done me a favor."

At Marsh's quizzical look, she added, "You know the old comic routine: To take your mind off your headache—"

"You hit your knee with a hammer," Marsh finished for her. Relieved at her ability to make a joke despite her disappointment, he said, "I still have those reservations for dinner."

"That's not necessary, Marsh. If you'd like to cancel them—"

"No."

Three hours later in the pink-marbled dining room of the Ritz, tapers protected from sudden drafts by glass bathed the tables in a warm, soft glow and danced a *pas de deux* on the high ceiling, wreathed in golden garlands.

At eye level, lovers sat, hearing the pulse of their own music beyond that of the small orchestra near the dance floor, and reaching toward Venetian wineglasses—long-stemmed, green, like tulips of wine on fragile stems.

Each night it was different, yet always the same—the touching of hands, the fleeting smile, the sadness hidden under the surface concealing earthly desires in full bloom that could suddenly be snuffed out.

Tonight was no different. The dream continued even amid the quiet acceptance of danger.

Into this atmosphere, Marsh and a regretful Alpharetta entered. Dressed in the green wool and silk, with hair like re-fined gold still molten from the furnace, Alpharetta took her appointed place opposite the blond-haired man. Regret, shared, became a powerful force. Although so different from his stepsister Belline, their façades were alike. Alpharetta could never be more than a friend to Marsh. But tonight she needed a friend most of all, for Ben Mark had deserted her, even as she had reached out to him.

Marsh held her in his arms, his mind on another woman in green, Paulina di Resa, who had died in the villa in Sicily, while Alpharetta was wrapped in her own dream. But others at the tables and on the dance floor, had no way of knowing that they dreamed different dreams, least of all a frowning Dow Pomeroy.

"Dow, you're not listening."

He turned to his fiancée, Meg. "Sorry, darling. What were you saying?"

"I said one of the children at the nursery came down with measles yesterday. I'm sure we're going to have a regular epidemic."

"Would you like to dance, Meg?"

He had not heard a word she had said. She sighed. "If that's what you want to do."

They left their table and walked to the dance floor as the small orchestra began to play "A Nightingale Sang in Berkeley Square."

In Berlin, over one hundred musicians began tuning their expensive instruments for the Berlin Philharmonic Orchestra's Saturday evening performance.

General Emil von Freiker, seated midway in the orchestra section of the hall, was particularly happy for two reasons—first, the orchestra was playing Beethoven's Ninth Symphony, and second, his son Heinrich, on medical leave, was seated beside him.

General von Freiker was tired. The lines in his face revealed his age as well as worry over the progress of the war. Himmler, the head of the SS, was becoming more cruel by day, and Hitler, the madman, unable to sleep, was becoming schiz-ophrenic as he prowled at night. Together, the two seemed intent on destroying as many lives as possible, even those of ordinary German citizens.

But tonight, Emil was at no one's call save his own. He sat patiently during the first half of the concert and waited for intermission to enjoy his glass of schnapps before the second half of the program.

After intermission the choir began to gather behind the orchestra for the great choral finale. Frau Emma von Erhard was soprano soloist. Only through General von Arnim was she able to sing at all these days, for her Austrian husband had refused to join the Nazi party and had been shot. Von Arnim, interceding directly with Himmler, had kept the woman from being arrested with her husband. It would be interesting to know what gift Himmler had received in return.

"Heinrich, do you remember the first time I brought you to hear the Beethoven Ninth?"

"*Ja, Vater*. I was six years old."

"And you embarrassed me," von Freiker said fondly, "squirming before it was half over."

"I like Wagner better than Beethoven, *Vater*."

"So does the Führer," the general commented in a dry tone. And for one brief moment, Emil von Freiker, veteran of two world wars, decided that he liked peace better than war.

In anticipation of the music to come, Emil watched the musicians tune up, with his attention finally focusing on the three cellists adding to the cacophony. Proud Germanic heads leaned forward as great, powerful arms, clothed in black, bowed their instruments. While Emil watched the wrist movements of the three, they began to resemble the German woodcut of the three bears, for the patches of hair, visible on the backs of their hands, were almost as thick as the short, curled hair on their heads.

Emil became amused. To pass the time, he began to look for a Goldilocks in the vast choir behind the orchestra. It didn't take him long. The shaft of light in the center of the choir acted as a spotlight on one young soprano. Emil smiled. There she was, the woman *mit goldenes haar*.

Emil turned to say something to his son, but Heinrich was occupied with his binoculars, intent on examining each female singer in the chorus.

Emil's attention returned to the stage. The *Koncertmeister* took his place in the first violinist's chair and the audience grew quiet again as the conductor, followed by the soloists, walked on stage. Frau Emma von Erhard bowed with the others, and when the applause had died, the conductor lifted his baton for the music to begin.

Emil leaned back and closed his eyes, but Heinrich, using his binoculars, ignored the conductor and instead watched the young blond woman hidden in the soprano section of the chorus.

Waiting all season for this one night, Emil was not disappointed. The music grew in majesty and magnificence, gaining in rhythmic momentum with each theme hurled above the tympani, like Thor throwing a thunderbolt into the midst of the orchestra and then finding rest in the melancholy voice of the violins.

When the orchestra was spent, when each theme was renewed and discarded, the human voices began—first, one; then, four; and finally the entire chorus, searching for an ode to joy, a hymn to recall the brotherhood of man and to touch the soul of Emil von Freiker, seated in the great hall.

But then a discordant note swept over the hall—the sound of air-raid sirens. A stunned audience fled comfortable seats to seek uncomfortable shelter from the bombs of the Allies.

In the rush, Emma von Erhard called to her daughter. "Gretchen! *Hier!*"

The young woman, who was the one Heinrich had been watching on stage, struggled to reach her mother. But Gretchen, with the chorus between her, was swept along with the others in their flight to the stairs and dark catacombs underneath the hall.

In the audience, Heinrich stood, watching the exodus, while Emil von Freiker raised his fist to the skies. Damn them—for spoiling his evening.

The German people, so used to reading of the Luftwaffe's nightly blitz of London, were stunned that Allied bombers had penetrated into their capital city. How had such a thing happened, when they were supposed to be winning the war?

Emil von Freiker took small comfort in the knowledge that any day now their powerful new rocket weapons would be aimed toward London with devastating results. His night was spoiled.

He refused to take shelter with Heinrich, choosing instead to walk toward the outside of the building, where antiaircraft guns were pointed toward the brightly lit sky.

Emma von Erhard did not rest until she had been reunited with her daughter. Huddled together in the shelter, they listened as the others did, for the sound of bombs.

Emma had another reason besides the bombs to be worried. Her daughter Gretchen had narrowly missed being sent to Himmler's brothel for his SS officers. Warned by von Arnim, Emma had shaped her fifteen-year-old daughter into a child. Strapping her young breasts with gauze, unpinning her hair to let it fall to her shoulders, and dressing her in a school girl's uniform with heavy black stockings, she had made her four years younger in appearance.

But now Gretchen was eighteen and the masquerade threatened to come to an end because of the maturity evident in her face—blue eyes, porcelain skin over high cheekbones, a mouth that promised a soft sensuality. Gretchen's only salvation was in being small and slender.

"Frau von Erhard?" Emma recalled the SS officer at the door of her apartment three years earlier.

"*Ja?*"

"I have come for your daughter," he said, stepping inside.

"My daughter? What do you want with my daughter, Herr Captain? What has she done?"

"I have orders to take her to Leipzig. Please see that she is ready in five minutes."

Emma gazed at the clock on the mantel. "There must be some mistake, Herr Captain. Gretchen has not yet come home from school."

The officer frowned. "School? That information was not on her dossier. Your daughter is at university?"

"Certainly not. She's far too young to be enrolled there. But you may see for yourself. Please have a seat," Emma said. "She will be home in a few minutes."

The SS officer reluctantly sat in the fine old chair with its faded velvet upholstery. If the woman were not telling the truth in the hope it would give her daughter time to escape, her efforts would be futile. The apartment house was surrounded by his men.

"Would you like a glass of wine while you wait?"

"That would be most pleasant, Frau von Erhard." He felt almost guilty taking the wine from her, for he could tell she lived a frugal life. But then his heart grew hard once again. The great Frau Emma had brought it upon herself—she and that husband of hers. If he had not been so stubborn . . . He began to drink the glass of wine without regret, for it was nothing in comparison to what he was taking from her.

He had been told that the woman was intelligent, but she hadn't blinked an eye when he mentioned Leipzig—as if she had no idea what awaited her daughter. Yet in her ignorance, she was far easier to deal with than the old grandfather an hour earlier. The bile rose in his throat as he thought about it.

"Here she is—my granddaughter." The old man, weeping, had stood aside for SS Captain Manfred Schönbrun to view the body of the young woman lying on the cot. Freshly drawn blood indicated the choice she had made. Seated in Frau Emma von Erhard's apartment, Manfred wanted no repeat performance.

"I think I hear her now," the woman commented with a smile. "You know how noisy schoolgirls are, when they've been held in restraint all day."

Walking down the cobblestoned street, Gretchen passed the *biergarten* on the corner where old men gathered each afternoon, and turned into the narrow street where she lived with her mother. The window boxes were bare of flowers.

She stopped, for the dreaded black Horch parked outside the apartment building spelled trouble. Gretchen shifted her school books in her arms and, looking at her friend, Elsa, she said, "Come on, Elsa, let's sing."

"I'm too scared."

"No, you're not. Come on." Tucking her arm into Elsa's, Gretchen began singing in her small, high soprano voice as they skipped along, laughing, singing, bumping into the streetlight and then bounding across the street. They both wore armbands with swastikas over their white blouses, and as Gretchen approached the steps where the amused SS men had watched their arrival, she batted her eyes flirtatiously and lifted her arm in salute.

"Heil Hitler!" she said to them.

And they responded, "Heil Hitler."

Gretchen and her friend burst into giggles and ran up the steps into the apartment.

"*Mutter! Mutter!* You'll never imagine . . ." Gretchen stopped, wide-eyed, in the open door.

"Gretchen," her mother scolded, "we have a guest. Please remember your manners."

"I'm sorry, *Mutter*," she said, her eyes staring contritely at her black brogan shoes. And Captain Manfred Schönbrun, gazing in dismay at the flat-chested child before him, said "This is your daughter?"

"Of course. Gretchen, you must curtsey to our distinguished guest."

Again Gretchen shifted her books, and with an awkward charm she curtseyed toward the SS officer, the slight run obvious in one of her ugly black stockings.

The SS officer stood, clicked his heels in acknowledgment. "There has been a mistake, Frau von Erhard," he said. "I bid you *guten tag*."

"*Guten tag*, Herr Captain," Emma replied, and when the door was closed, mother and daughter collapsed into each other's arms.

"Frau von Erhard?" The SS officer clicked his heels and Emma, so immersed in the past, froze.

"My name is Heinrich von Freiker, and I had the pleasure of hearing you in Vienna some time ago."

Although he spoke to the woman, his eyes were on her daughter. The old fear struck in Emma's breast. "How kind of you to remember. May I present my daughter, Gretchen?"

Heinrich again clicked his heels, just as the sirens signaled the all clear.

Gretchen acknowledged the introduction, but Heinrich's bold stare disconcerted her. And the childlike bewilderment that had served her so well in the past vanished before the frank desire written in the officer's eyes.

The crowd began to move from the catacombs. For the musicians, there was no need to reassemble on stage for the remainder of the performance. The audience was anxious to go home. Emma, also anxious, walked with Gretchen to the dressing room where her daughter removed her choral robe.

Outside the musician's entrance, Heinrich was in no hurry to leave. He wanted to see Gretchen without the black choral robe. When she appeared, dressed in a schoolgirl's outfit, he was disappointed. She had seemed much older, and yet— He narrowed his eyes and stepped back into the shadows to watch her, unobserved. Something was not quite right. For in the meager light, he saw a woman masquerading in a child's clothing.

13

In London, the soldiers disappeared overnight, just as the cabbie had predicted to Alpharetta. Ben Mark returned to his squadron and began a nightly bombardment around Pas de Calais on the French coast. Marsh also vanished, rejoining the 82nd Airborne Division in its final training before the Normandy invasion. And a sad but wiser Alpharetta continued to ferry much-needed planes to Prestwick in a stepped-up program, with no time to revisit London.

Across the channel, in the town of Ste.-Mère-Église, the old bellringer, Maurice Duvalier, rose a half hour before six A.M. on June 1, 1944, dressed, retrieved his sabots near the doorway, and began his daily journey toward the church in the square.

Maurice was the only Frenchman authorized to be about before the Angelus signaled the end of curfew, since it was he who rang the bells at the beginning and the end of each day. As he walked along the street, he made as much noise as possible to alert Hans, the German guard, for he had no wish to be shot.

Hearing the uneven sound of Maurice's limp on the cobblestones, Hans glanced at his watch and smiled. The night was almost over. The villagers would be let out of their confinement for another day of work, and he could go back to the barracks for hot sausages, *brot,* and steaming black coffee.

"*Bonjour, monsieur,*" Maurice said, as he came into the square.

Hans, leaning against a wall, nodded to the old man in his

peasant garb, patched neatly by his late wife, Lalu. *"Guten morgen,"* he replied.

It had been the same for the entire year, each speaking in his own language, with neither one giving a hint that he spoke the other's language fluently.

Hans unlocked the outside door leading to the church tower and relocked it as Maurice disappeared inside.

Removing his sabots at the second-floor level, Maurice quickly climbed the narrow wooden steps to the bell tower, his limp miraculously disappearing. He had only five minutes to listen to the wireless before ringing the Angelus.

Hidden in the niche behind the coils of rope, the short-wave radio waited with messages from England for the French Underground. It had taken Maurice a long time to smuggle the parts past Hans, and an even longer time to put the radio together, because he could never work on it more than five minutes at a time.

He carefully turned the wireless on, tuned it, and, knowing how easily sound carried from that far up, held the single earphone tightly to his right ear.

The static was disconcerting and the news from the BBC was of little interest. But just as Maurice made ready to turn the radio off and put it back in its hiding place, he heard the signal for which he had been waiting for the past six months—the first line of *"Chanson d'Automne." "Les sanglots longs des violins de l'automne . . ."* It was the first alert that the invasion forces were gathering.

Down below, an impatient Hans waited for the old man to sound the Angelus. He was getting slower and slower, and if he got any worse, Hans decided he would have to talk with the curé and get a replacement.

As if the old man understood, he began, tremulously at first, but then gathering force, to ring the bells that reverberated over the countryside. And when the job was done, Maurice knocked on the locked door and waited for Hans to let him out.

The German relocked the door behind him, and with his night duty over, Hans took the key and headed toward the barracks.

An excited Maurice, forcing himself to keep the same slow,

leisurely, limping pace, walked home. He knew that when the second line of the song was broadcast, the landing would be only forty-eight hours away. *"Blessent mon coeur d'une langueur monotone."*

At La Roche-Guyon, in the stronghold of the Counts of Rochefoucauld, Field Marshal Rommel, the former Desert Fox of North Africa, left his quarters with his aide, Lang, to inspect part of his Atlantic Wall.

For two months he had stared toward England and waited uneasily for the imminent Anglo-Allied invasion. April passed, and then May. Now it was June, and still no sign of ships in the channel.

The Wall had been a farce when he first arrived in November 1943. But he had proceeded immediately to fortify the entire section of frontier, using a half million men as laborers and all the equipment he could muster, even stripping the old Maginot Line and the Siegfried Line of their materials, and erecting concrete cones strapped with deadly mines. The cones were invisible at water's edge but capable of blowing apart the landing craft as they struggled toward the beaches.

On the beaches themselves, mines were attached to metal-tipped stakes—Rommel's asparagus—planted in rows and connected to each other with barbed wire, the disaster appointed for those soldiers lucky or unlucky enough to reach shore. And if they reached the grassy knolls beyond the stretch of beaches, Rommel had designed an even more sinister welcome—a living hell of fire and brimstone in the shape of pipes leading to kerosene tanks, automatic flame-throwers capable of incinerating everything and everyone in its path, at the press of a button.

But he had not stopped with mere coastal defenses and gun batteries in the chalky bluffs. Remembering the paratroopers and gliders of Sicily and Italy, he flooded the low-lying areas beyond the rivers and forced young girls of the surrounding villages to whittle sharp-pointed stakes that would impale the paratroopers in the open fields, if they were not drowned.

Despite all his preparations, a tired Rommel recognized a major weakness to his defenses. He desperately needed the panzer divisions under Hitler's direct authority. And so, with the meteorologists in Paris assuring him of bad weather for the next several days, Rommel left the village of La Roche-Guyon for Germany, to see the Führer.

In England, in the air planning room, Air Vice-Marshal Sir Dow Pomeroy listened for the news—that General Eisenhower, Supreme Allied Commander, had given the signal for the 5,000-ship invasion convoy to set sail. Closely coordinated with their arrival, the planes carrying the British and American paratroopers were waiting for takeoff.

Like oriental ancients viewing the heavens for favorable signs, the Allied meteorologists had examined both the projected days of low tide and the nights of moonlight in June, since the paratroopers needed a late-rising moon while the landing crafts required a pre-dawn low tide, when Rommel's beach obstacles were visible.

They settled on three days—and only three—when the signs were right—June 4, 5, and 6.

On the morning of June 2, Dow looked up as Colonel Hank Lawton of the U.S. Air Corps entered the planning room.

"Well, the great armada has started," Lawton announced. "All we can do now is wait for our turn."

Dow nodded. Operation Overlord had begun—at last.

Like the long body of a segmented Chinese dragon in a parade, the convoy started its lumbering trip across the channel, with troops, guns, tanks, and fireworks of the most grievous kind. Slowly, it wound its way through the waters, with minesweepers in formation ahead, and its long dragon tail trailing all the way from Portsmouth.

But the heavens, governing man and earth, the wind and the tide, became dark with clouds. A major storm began. High waves lashed against the ships, and the winds tugging at the barrage balloons overhead gave the dragon a drunken appearance as the ships listed. And the men on the smaller vessels leaned over the rails and lost the sumptuous meal that all men facing a sentence of death are given.

Suddenly, with the French coast only forty miles away, the invasion force received orders to return to port. And the mammoth task of turning the head of the dragon around in rough seas began, with the added danger of being spotted by the Luftwaffe.

"Hell!" Sergeant Giraldo looked toward Lieutenant Marsh Wexford, when he heard the news at the holding grounds of the 82nd Airborne. "I wonder what went wrong."

"The weather. There's a gale blowing in the channel," Marsh replied, the dejection just as obvious in his face as in the others seated around him.

"How long do you think it will last?" Laroche asked, looking up from the alligator he had been whittling from a small piece of wood.

"Can't last long," Gig volunteered. "Else the men will go stir crazy, holed up in the ships."

"The stand-down is for twenty-four hours," Marsh offered.

"How about a game of poker?" Giraldo suggested, "to pass the time?"

Laroche laid down his knife and piece of wood; Gig pulled out his deck of cards, and the four, with nothing else to do but wait, put their minds to winning at cards, if not on the battlefield. And in the hangars and the tents, other groups did the same.

Again Maurice Duvalier hurried toward the bell tower in the town of Ste.-Mère-Église. He had been baffled by the broadcast of the first line of *"Chanson d'Automne,"* on two consecutive days. But there had been no sign of the second line. He was becoming increasingly nervous. And yet he and his friends had waited four years for their liberation from the Nazis. Now that the invasion alert had been given, it was hard to wait any longer.

The guard on duty in the evening was not nearly so pleasant as Hans. Far more suspicious, too, he would stand and watch Maurice maneuver the stairs, and sometimes not bother to close the doors, as if by watching Maurice at the bells he could be assured that the old man did not use the ringing of the hours as a signal for the people in the village. To distract the guard from his usual scrutiny, Maurice had brought his small grandson, Ibert, with him to the square that night.

A man with the responsibility of the entire free world upon

his shoulders, General Eisenhower, the overlord, sat with his advisors in the library of Southwick House and summoned the head meteorologist, Group Captain J. N. Stagg. In the same manner that King Saul sought the advice of the witch of Endor before battle, so Eisenhower listened to the scientific advice of Stagg.

A slight break in the weather was all they could hope for—it would be a mere twenty-four hours before the storm began again. Eisenhower looked at Air Chief Marshal Tedder, Deputy Supreme Allied Commander; at Montgomery, in charge of land forces; at Leigh-Mallory, Allied air commander; and at the naval commander, Admiral Ramsay. They had already called off the invasion for June 5. They now had a half hour to decide if the invasion should take place on June 6. The men were divided. It was up to Eisenhower to decide.

He thought of the thousands of troops, the thousands of ships waiting. It was impossible to keep them at their holding stations much longer without the Germans finding out. Finally, he stood.

"I don't like it a bit more than you, but there it is. I am quite positive we must give the order."

With his decision, a new D-Day was confirmed. June 6, 1944.

The dragon unwound its long body from the ports and once again began its lumbering way across the channel.

The next morning, Maurice, in the bell tower, heard the second line of the poet's words: *"Blessent mon coeur d'une langueur monotone."* The invasion was in 48 hours.

Joyfully, he rang the Angelus; not in six steady peals against the wind, as he usually did, but in sets of two, with a space between. *Vic-toire! Vic-toire! Vic-toire!*

To some of the people waiting in their houses, it was the ordinary Angelus, no different from any other morning. But to a few, it was the sound of liberation and the call to arms.

As the great invasion force continued on its way, with the Americans headed toward the infamous beaches labeled Omaha and Utah, a frustrated General George S. Patton, Jr., the hero of the Sicily campaign and also its antihero, because of the soldier-slapping incident, was left behind in England. Slapping the hysterical soldier with his glove almost cost Patton his military career, since an officer was not allowed to touch an enlisted man.

He had been given no part in the planning of the Normandy invasion, no part in the initial fighting. He was used merely as a decoy for the Germans against a Calais attack farther north. And yet he was the general on intimate terms with the treacherous hedgerow country of Normandy. A military student in France in 1913, he had become familiar with the entire area from Cherbourg to Samur, not once but twice. For again, in World War I, he had trained his tank corps in that area.

It was Montgomery who had been chosen to lead the land battle, and the plans included the set piece that was a trademark of the British Field Marshal.

Kept informed, however, of the plan by Bradley, Patton was concerned, for he was well aware of its dangers. The Allies could be boxed in because of Montgomery's caution.

"Monty is supposed to take Caen on D-Day," Patton said. "Well, Brad, he won't do it. He'll take his time, and in the meanwhile, the Germans will get ready for the counterattack."

Lieutenant Marsh Wexford and the members of his pathfinders unit were only concerned with their part in the invasion. Leaving the airfield a half hour before the other paratroopers, they double-checked their equipment.

One of the most important pieces was a child's cricket, a metal snapper that could be purchased in any five-and-dime store for a few pennies. Laroche took out his and snapped it once. Gig responded with two clicks, laughed, and then put the cricket up. But Marsh was thinking of the flares and equipment he would need to light the landing field for the others to see where to jump.

No matter how often they had practiced, he knew there was a wide margin for error, especially going into territory he had never seen. They had studied the maps that were now hidden in their helmets, but he remembered the drop in Sicily and wanted no repeat. He took off his helmet to look at the map once again.

"I declare, Lieutenant, you've got to be the ugliest S.O.B. in the entire infantry," Giraldo teased, and quickly added, "sir," because of his rank.

Marsh laughed and ran his hand over his head, which had been shaved in the Mohawk manner. His once handsome face was blackened with charcoal.

"You really started something in Sicily, Giraldo," he retorted. "Now we're all just as ugly as you."

Giraldo grinned, while Laroche took up for Marsh. "The lieutenant can wash his face and grow some more hair. But there really isn't any hope for you, Sergeant."

"Just wait till we get to Paris. I'll show you what the mam'selles like," Giraldo boasted.

Gig said, "Have you forgotten so soon? Laroche won all your money at poker."

"He's too short. They'll beg to go out with me. Money or no money."

"But I speak the language, monsieur. *Vive la différence!*"

"I hope you speak it better than Giraldo spoke Italian in Sicily," Marsh countered.

"Geez! Look below. Have you ever seen so many ships in your life?"

They passed over part of the convoy, ten lanes wide, twenty miles long, and in the brightness of the moon, they recognized the magnitude of the operation—and the vast importance of the paratroopers' mission to serve as a buffer between the Germans and the beaches, to destroy the bridges and hold the ground against the Germans until the great dragon could give birth to its young and wash them ashore.

Flying low along the coast, the plane carrying Marsh and his men passed through a field of flak. A light peppering of small-arms fire was heard, like hail on a tin roof. And in the distance, flames burned—houses and buildings caught up in the crossfire of the enemy.

The alert light came on—then the green.

"Here we go," Marsh said, and the pathfinders of the 82nd Airborne jumped. The invasion of the European continent had begun.

14

*O*nce again Marsh Wexford parachuted into enemy territory. But it was different this time. The responsibility for his entire combat team rested on him.

Now the goal was not merely to stay alive, not even to engage the enemy, but to clear the designated landing area of its deadly mines and obstacles, and then to light the way for the others who would drop from the skies in less than a half hour.

Weighed down by heavy equipment, Marsh could see burning houses in the distance, and people rushing around in the town square.

The sound of bells in the church tower reached him as he approached tree-top level, for Maurice, summoned by the curé with permission from the German garrison, was signaling for help to fight the local fires. As Marsh plunged into a nearby orchard, he saw two men in peasant garb running past him. If they saw him, they gave no evidence.

Landing in a hedgerow, Giraldo was hopelessly tangled in the thick bocage that had divided the fields for centuries. And Gig Madison, crashing through the glass roof of a farmer's greenhouse, awoke the owner's dog to a vicious barking.

Two other members of the pathfinder unit, Hardie and Kaminsky, also landed in the orchard. After a quick snap of the cricket, they were answered by Marsh. The three joined together and began a frantic clearing of the designated landing area in the field nearby. Crawling inch by inch, with their bayonets prodding the ground ahead like blind men's canes, they flattened themselves to the ground as a burst of machine-gun fire ripped through the field. Suddenly a grenade silenced the machine gun positioned in a small opening cut in the hedgerow. Giraldo, with a chirp of the cricket, rushed through the slit that allowed passage from one field to the other and joined the three men.

But Gig Madison was having trouble of another kind.

"Steady, boy. I'm your friend. *Ami,* that's what I am. *Comprenez-vous?*"

Gig stood at the entrance of the greenhouse and faced the Great Dane that was almost as tall as he. Animal lover, he had no wish to shoot the animal, and, too, a shot would bring someone to check. Yet the growl was unfriendly and the dog was blocking his escape.

Staring at the dog in the moonlight, Gig slowly and deliberately reached into his pack and removed the can of Spam that would have been his breakfast. Regretfully, he opened it with the metal key, took his knife, sliced off a piece of the meat and offered it to the dog. In one gulp, the Great Dane swallowed it and looked to Gig for more. He cut another slice and began to walk from the greenhouse with the dog following. Another snap of his powerful jaws demolished the second tidbit of Spam. By the third slice, Gig had made a friend for life.

"All right, Caesar, but you got to be quiet," Gig admonished, reconciled to the dog's following him.

With a click of the cricket, Gig found the others and, working steadily, they cleared the field as the distant roar of the DC-3s signaled the first wave of the 18,000 paratroopers.

Overhead, Lieutenant Colonel Krause, carrying the American flag that he vowed would fly over Ste.-Mère-Église before morning, looked down. He too saw burning buildings in the square, but there was no sign of flares from the pathfinder unit.

"There it is, sir," the pilot called out. "The drop zone."

Now outlined in red, the field beckoned the combat team. In other areas, the paratroopers jumped in the darkness, some landing in the flooded areas where they were dragged under by the weight of their equipment and drowned. Others were carried by the wind into the very square of the town and floated down into the burning buildings, their screams and the explosions of the ammunition attached to their bodies adding to the horror of the night.

The German garrison, realizing the invasion was taking place, called for help. But their message was never received, for Maurice Duvalier and the French Underground had cut the communications wires.

By 4:30 A.M., Lieutenant Colonel Krause hoisted the American flag on the pole at the town hall. Ste.-Mère-Église was liberated. It was the first success, the small glimpse of glory before the storm that was to come.

"Has anybody seen Laroche?" Marsh questioned as he lay against the hedgerow in exhaustion, the silk of a discarded parachute offering him a slight warmth from the wind and mist.

"Not a sign," replied a saddened Gig Madison. He had looked for him everywhere; had shone his light into the trees where dead paratroopers still dangled in their harnesses. "I found Williams and Smith, though," he added. "Poor guys. They never had a chance." Gig continued to pull fragments of glass from his hands.

"You should go to the schoolhouse, Madison, and get those cuts attended to," Marsh suggested.

Gig shook his head. "I hear they've got wounded krauts in there too. I wouldn't be able to control myself."

"He's scared the medics will keep him, or send him back to England," Giraldo said. "And then he wouldn't get to go to Paris."

A sniper's fire caused them to seek other shelter. Caesar, the Great Dane, moved with them. Cautiously they crept through the orchard, but the Great Dane, leaving Gig's side, loped toward the well outlined in the moonlight, and began a low growl. From down in the depths of the well came the sound of a cricket.

"Jeez, you don't think . . " The lieutenant held up his hand for Giraldo to be silent.

Marsh took his cricket, snapped it once, and waited. From deep inside the well came the correct answer.

With Gig covering their exposed position, Marsh and Giraldo laid down their rifles and began to pull the rope up by hand. At the end of the rope was a half-drowned Laroche.

With odds of one in a million, Pierre Laroche had parachuted and landed in the well as neatly as a golf ball putted from the green.

"He's so little. You think we should throw him back in?" Giraldo teased as Laroche perched precariously on the wooden bucket.

"For God's sake, get me out of this miserable position. My butt's frozen stiff to the bucket." Laroche's teeth chattered and clicked as Marsh held the rope steady and Giraldo lifted him bodily to the ground.

For a full day and night the paratroopers fought to wrest the bridges and causeways from the Germans. But the bulk of their equipment never reached them. The gliders crashed into the swamps and onto the mined fields, and the men fought against insuperable odds. With no radios to make contact, the troopers weren't even sure that the amphibious forces had landed on the beaches.

But the Germans were well aware of the soldiers coming ashore in the landing crafts. The initial surprise of the attack was quickly negated by the force of their powerful guns. Unknown to Allied intelligence, the areas directly behind Omaha and Utah beaches, the sites chosen for the Americans to come ashore, contained an entire German army, gathering for its annual maneuvers.

One week after the Normandy invasion, Montgomery still had not taken Caen. With the field marshal stopped at Caen, the Americans slowly progressed through the treacherous hedgerow country, with their casualties mounting by the kilometer. By the end of June, 14,000 Americans had given their lives, out of a total 21,000 Allies dead. And the number of their wounded was equally as devastating.

Two other devastating events occurred during the month of June. One involved Congress, the other, the powerful secret weapon of the Germans. It was the latter that changed Alpharetta Beaumont's destiny.

With the invasion in full swing, the need for even more planes became paramount. On the morning of June 12, Alpharetta ferried a long-range bomber from Montreal to Prestwick. And once again, she continued to London. This time, the weather was clear enough for her to take a connecting flight rather than ride the train.

Through the Air Transport Auxiliary, she had received a strange summons from Air Marshal Sir Nelson Mitford. The letter contained little beyond the necessary information of time and place of the meeting.

The other letter she carried with her, from Mary Lou Brandon, was long and indignant. In part, it read:

> I am absolutely furious. I guess you've heard the news—that Congress is reneging on its promise to authorize flight pay for us. It was the powerful lobbying against the bill by the civilian male pilots that did it. (They're scared they'll have to go to war.) So I guess this sounds the death knell for the WASPs. I heard it's only a matter of months before the army closes down the whole program. And just when we've gotten our santiago blues, the first really decent uniforms we've had. You think the British could use another flyer?

Alpharetta felt a disappointment for Mary Lou and the others with whom she'd trained. They all wanted to continue flying as long as anyone would give them planes to fly. Alpharetta had just been luckier, that's all, signing on with the ATA in England.

When Alpharetta arrived in London, she checked into the Savoy Hotel. After a bath, she crawled into bed. She had only three hours to sleep before her appointment with the air marshal.

Thirty minutes before Alpharetta was to report, Sir Nelson Mitford sat in conference with Air Vice-Marshal Sir Dow Pomeroy.

"Pom, this young woman is incredible. I've never seen another like her. She's tailor-made for the special mission. And I'm assigning her to your personal staff."

"But she's an American," Dow commented, not happy at the prospect.

"I've cut all the red tape. You don't have to worry about that. The only worry you'll have is to see that the plan goes through as scheduled, before those bloody secret weapons of the Germans annihilate the entire British Isles."

Alpharetta awoke with her alarm clock ringing in her ear. She dressed and went downstairs, where the military car was already waiting to take her to Air Defense Headquarters in Stanmore, Middlesex, northwest of London.

Inside the headquarters, a huge table map of Great Britain was surrounded by members of the British WAAF (Women's Auxiliary Air Force), with red metal arrows plotting the path of intruders into its air space. From its galley vantage point overhead, the operations staff looked down into the room and watched, ready to alert the cities and send out fighters to meet the intruders the moment the coastal radar units spotted them. Observing the procedure of putting the red arrows in place, Air Marshal Sir Nelson Mitford was informed of Alpharetta's arrival. He quickly left the galley and walked into his private office.

"Miss Beaumont, it's good to see you again."

"And you, too, sir."

"Sit down. Sit down." He waved to a nearby straight chair. "We have quite a bit to talk about.

"It was opportune for me to bump into you several months ago at the Ritz," he said, and then wasted no time in coming to the point. "I've received permission to borrow you for a while from Air Transport Auxiliary, if you are willing, Miss Beaumont. Do you have any objections to working elsewhere, at least for the next several months?"

"Will I be flying, sir?" a puzzled Alpharetta inquired.

"Well, yes and no. All I can tell you at the moment is that you're to be assigned to the staff of Air Vice-Marshal Sir Dow Pomeroy in a very hush-hush project. You will be a member of a small, select group. No one will be able to get in touch with you directly—only through me. What do you say, Miss Beaumont?"

Alpharetta, staring at the white-mustached air marshal, knew he was only being polite with his inquiry. If ATC had given him the okay, the matter was out of her hands.

"When do you wish me to report, sir?"

"We'll leave the exact time up to your commanding officer,"

Mitford said. Going to the door, he called out, "Oh, Pom, would you step in here for a minute?"

An unsmiling Air Vice-Marshal Sir Dow Pomeroy halted as he recognized Alpharetta.

"You!" he said, and continued to stare in consternation at the woman who had plagued his dreams and disturbed his thoughts for weeks. Just when he had finally rid himself of thinking of her, she had suddenly appeared again.

"Have you two met?" Mitford inquired, oblivious to the undercurrent.

Dow quickly recovered. "Not officially."

"Then, may I present Miss Alpharetta Beaumont. Your commanding officer, Miss Beaumont—Air Vice-Marshal Sir Dow Pomeroy."

"Sir!" Alpharetta responded, saluting.

Wanting to find fault with something—*anything*, Dow said, "If you're going to be on my staff, Miss Beaumont, you'll have to improve your salute."

His scowl, usually so intimidating to others, had no effect on Alpharetta, veteran as she was under Gandy Malone's tutelage.

"Yes, sir," she answered, gazing at him with unwavering green eyes. "Do you prefer the British or the American salute?"

Mitford, recognizing they were getting onto treacherous ground, interceded, "Now, now. Let's not get bogged down in protocol. The main question, Pom, is when you want her to be ready to leave."

"I'll have my aide pick her up tomorrow morning. Where are you staying, Miss Beaumont?"

"At the Savoy."

"Then please be in the lobby at 0800."

She nodded and then addressed Mitford. "Is there anything else, sir?"

"No. Run along, Miss Beaumont."

She quickly moved back as the air marshal lumbered toward her. She hurried to the door with a salute and, with the guard accompanying her, she walked out of the underground caverns of Bentley Priory and climbed into the military car waiting to take her back to the Savoy.

That night, Alpharetta wrote three letters, to give her new mailing address. The first was an answer to Mary Lou Brandon, the second to Reed and Anna Clare St. John, and the last one, a joint letter to her brothers, Conyer and Duluth, both serving on the same ship somewhere in the Pacific.

In the early hours of the morning, an air-raid siren awoke Alpharetta. She got up and sleepily pulled aside the blackout curtain to peer into the dark, but she saw nothing. There were no telltale signs of enemy plane engines, no returning fire of guns. Within minutes, the all clear sounded. Alpharetta crawled back into bed. A few minutes later, the sirens warned the city again. Off and on, a baffled London awoke, listened, and then went back to sleep. The majority of its residents were unaware that the first V-1 rockets had hit a section of the city, and a new reign of terror was to begin.

15

*F*light Lieutenant Reggie Minton could hardly believe his eyes as he stood in the lobby of the Savoy—or his luck, either, when Alpharetta Beaumont walked toward him. He'd been inwardly lamenting his forced incarceration on the deserted crags of Scotland with no one more interesting than Birdie Summerlin, the staff secretary. And here Pomeroy had planned all along to take this gorgeous creature, too.

Suddenly remembering the secret arrangements, he frowned. Maybe there was something between her and his commanding officer. But no. Pomeroy wasn't like that. Besides, he had a fiancée at home. Yet some of the American generals had wives at home, too, and that hadn't seemed to make much difference.

The flight lieutenant shrugged. "Miss Beaumont?"

"Yes?"

"I'm Flight Lieutenant Minton. The car is waiting. Will you follow me?"

The chauffeur, a sergeant in the British Army, stood at the curbing. He opened both doors and took Alpharetta's luggage to place it in the trunk of the staff car. Alpharetta saw that the other figure in the back seat was Dow Pomeroy.

"Good morning, sir," she said and climbed into the front seat, leaving Flight Lieutenant Minton to ride with the air vice-marshal.

A surprised Minton looked at his commanding officer and then climbed into the back.

At first, the seating arrangement pleased Reggie, for it indicated that there was nothing between Pomeroy and the woman. But then he grew wary again. Maybe the two were just being discreet.

They left London behind and headed north. No one in the car spoke. To Alpharetta, it was ridiculous, this unnatural pall of silence. She didn't even know the driver's name, or how long it would take them to arrive at their secret destination.

Vowing that she was not going to ride the entire way in silence, or be intimidated by the man in the back seat, she turned to the driver. "My name is Beaumont," she said. "Alpharetta Beaumont. And what are *you* called?"

"Eckerd, mum," he replied.

"Well, Eckerd, how long is it going to take us to get there?"

He hesitated. Dow Pomeroy, looking up from the papers he had been examining, supplied the information.

"We will spend the night at Harrington Hall, Miss Beaumont, and arrive at headquarters sometime tomorrow."

They lapsed into silence again. And somehow to Alpharetta, it just wasn't worth the effort to continue the conversation, even to finding out what and where Harrington Hall was. From her bag, she pulled out her sketchbook and pencil and soon became absorbed in recording the scenery along the way—a flower, a tavern sign, a tree. The route alternated between expanses of open country and small villages, heralded by blank signposts that gave no clue to the traveler unfamiliar with the land.

They crept through the villages, and once they reached the open countryside, they picked up speed. To Alpharetta, the towns had an almost medieval look with their cobblestoned squares, wooden doorways, tea-shop signs, and old stone churches with tall steeples. In the country, a castle or manor house occasionally loomed in the distance, amid trees older and larger than any Alpharetta had ever seen. Images of Shakespeare, the old oaks of the Druids, and the two beautiful white swans that were the only survivors of the park in London, filtered their way from her mind to the sketchbook in her hands.

Once she turned to Eckerd to ask the name of the town they were passing through and then quietly went back to her sketching. By midmorning, they stopped for petrol and to stretch their legs. And then they drove on.

About the time that Alpharetta was becoming sorry that she had not eaten an English breakfast before checking out of the Savoy, she heard Dow Pomeroy addressing the driver.

"I think we can stop along here, Eckerd," he instructed from the back seat, and the sergeant immediately began to slow down.

Alpharetta, surprised, saw nothing more interesting than old ruins a hundred yards from the road, shaded by a large tree and a clump of purple and yellow wild flowers growing amid the stones.

"I expect everyone is hungry by now," the man added. "Eckerd, you remembered to pack the silverware?"

"Yes, sir. And the corkscrew this time, too, sir."

The flight lieutenant climbed out of the car first. "I'll go ahead and make sure the place is uninhabited."

While they waited for him to return, Dow said, "Miss Beaumont, I presume you have picnics in Georgia?" Before she could answer, he continued, "But no. You have barbecues. I remember that from reading *Gone With the Wind*."

Alpharetta smiled. "Actually, we have both."

Sergeant Eckerd removed a rattan picnic basket from the floorboard of the back seat and, with the aplomb of a waiter setting the table at Maxim's, he spread a white linen cloth on a slab of ancient stone amid the ruins that Reggie had pronounced safe. There was no need to mention the wild pig since it had fled, Reggie decided.

Without being asked, Alpharetta became Eckerd's helper, removing the china plates and cutlery from the basket. In a natural, unobtrusive manner, she became the hostess, serving the picnic fare while Eckerd attended to the wine.

Once they were all served, each searched for a place to sit in the circle of the ruins. Knowing that enlisted men did not share the same mess with officers, even in the wilds, Sergeant Eckerd found a place away from the other two men. But he was not alone for long. Alpharetta joined him. And Dow Pomeroy, with a frown, let it be known that he was not pleased at this.

Ignoring his look of disapproval, Alpharetta wiped her hands on her napkin and said, "And what area of England are you from, Eckerd?"

"Yorkshire, mum. From the city of Leeds. Are you familiar with the city?"

Alpharetta shook her head. "Only through the geography books." She closed her eyes and tried to recall schoolgirl lessons. "Wool and . . . wool and steel," she said and opened her eyes.

Sergeant Eckerd grinned. "And we have ruins, too—like this," he said. "In the middle of the city—Kirkstall Abbey."

They continued talking while they ate, the sergeant getting up several times to pour the wine and Alpharetta following with the tray of sandwiches. When they finished eating, she helped Eckerd gather the china and utensils to place in the basket. While he carried the basket to the car, Alpharetta removed the white linen cloth from the slab of stones, shook it before folding, and followed him. By the time she reached the Packard, the two officers had disappeared behind the ruins. She climbed into the front seat while Eckerd remained standing by the car door.

When Dow and Reggie returned, the older man hesitated, and then in a low tone said to Alpharetta, "We still have a long way to go, Miss Beaumont. It might be a good idea for you to make a rest stop before we proceed."

Feeling self-conscious, she took his advice and headed for the copse of bushes behind the ruins.

When she had disappeared, Dow turned to his subordinate. "I say, Minton, it might be a good idea for you to ride up front for a while."

"Yes, sir."

A shot rang out, startling the three men into action. "Hell's bells, I'll bet it's the bloody pig," Reggie Minton said. "I should have warned her."

With their weapons drawn, the three began to run toward the ruins. Reggie knew he would never forgive himself if the wild pig had attacked her.

"Miss Beaumont! Miss Beaumont!"

The men fanned out from the ruins, carefully stalking the animal and searching for some sign of the woman. Suddenly, Alpharetta stepped from the copse and paused long enough to place the small Baretta back into its holster.

"What happened? Are you all right?"

Without answering the questions, Alpharetta glared at Dow

Pomeroy and said instead, "I don't think much of your rustic rest stops, sir!" and walked past them.

"You think she got him?" Minton whispered.

"I doubt it. I expect the shot merely scared the boar away," Dow suggested.

The sergeant, ahead of the other two, called out, "Look at this, sir. Jolly good shooting, wouldn't you say? Right between the eyes."

Alpharetta walked as far as the stone slab of the ruins and, with her knees refusing to support her, sat down. When the men returned, Dow realized Alpharetta's state of shock and helped her up from her seat and back to the car.

In the space of one short morning, two men out of the three were hopelessly in love with Alpharetta Beaumont.

The journey continued and by late afternoon the car turned off the main road and approached a manor house through a smaller, tree-lined avenue winding over rolling hills and meadows where cattle grazed.

The vista, despite its formal terraces and statuary, no longer contained the gardens and wide expanses of grassy green so common to the country houses of England. Instead, the terraces were planted with grain—deep, luscious green corn that rippled in the breeze as the car came to a stop in the courtyard of washed pebbles embedded in stone.

Alpharetta looked up at the red brick, three-storied façade, the old leaded windows still intact, safe from the London blitz that had shattered even the windows of Buckingham Palace. A spume of smoke curled and wafted into the sky from one of the tall, massive old chimneys atop the gray slate roof, steep-pitched against the late afternoon sun.

Alpharetta's suspicions were confirmed by the man seated beside her.

"This is Harrington Hall, Miss Beaumont." And as an afterthought, he added, "My father is expecting us."

From his brief explanation, she knew that they were spending the night in the ancestral home of the Pomeroys.

The door to the manor house opened and a smiling young woman walked toward the car. "Dow, darling, we've been waiting all afternoon for you to arrive."

The air vice-marshal, climbing out of the back seat and

walking past Eckerd, leaned over and kissed the woman. "Meg, it's good to see you."

Sergeant Eckerd then helped Alpharetta out, and as she appeared and Meg realized someone else was with Dow, she stiffened.

"Meg, may I present Miss Alpharetta Beaumont, a member of my staff."

Without acknowledging Alpharetta, she said, "I didn't realize you had another woman on your staff, Dow. What happened to Birdie?"

"She's still my secretary," he informed her. "Miss Beaumont, this is my fiancée, Lady Margaret Cranston."

Recovering her sense of etiquette, Meg looked at Alpharetta. And although not liking what she saw, she smiled and said, "Welcome to Harrington Hall, Miss Beaumont."

"Thank you."

Arm in arm, Meg and Dow walked toward the front door, manned by a stooped old butler dressed in black, while Flight Lieutenant Reggie Minton walked beside Alpharetta.

"We have tea waiting in the family drawing room," Meg informed Dow. "Father's here, too."

"Welcome home, Master Dow," the old man said, seeing the air vice-marshal as the same small boy he had fished out of the pond thirty years earlier.

Dow smiled and nodded. "You'll see to the bags, Andrew?"

"At once, sir."

"Miss Beaumont is to be put in the green room, Andrew."

"The green room?" Meg questioned. "Wouldn't it be better if she were—"

"The green room," Dow said, emphatically. "You'll show her to the room, Meg?"

She disguised her lack of enthusiasm. "Come with me, Miss Beaumont."

"We'll expect you down shortly for tea," Dow said and watched the women disappear along the hall toward the curving stairs. "Reggie, you know your way?" he inquired, turning to the airman.

"Yes, sir."

"Then, I'll see you in the small drawing room later."

Dow left the hall and walked into the downstairs room where a white-haired old man sat beside the fire.

"Dow, my boy, we'd about given you up," the booming voice greeted him as the man slowly rose from his chair.

"Hello, Father. Don't get up."

Seated in the opposite chair and hastily putting out his pipe was the old man's companion. "Lord Cranston. Good to see you again."

"Jolly good to see you're finally here, Dow. Meg was afraid you'd gotten held up in London, with those blasted bombs coming down everywhere."

"What are you talking about, sir?"

Sir Edward, Dow's father, replied, "The rockets. It's been on the news all day—the bloody secret weapon of the Germans. You didn't see any of them?"

The news disheartened Dow. So it had started. "We left early this morning."

"And a good thing," Meg interposed, walking into the room. Then she sighed. "I guess we'll have more little urchins than ever sent up here. And the school's so crowded."

Dow, excusing himself, washed up and returned to the room a few minutes before Alpharetta and Reggie appeared together. After they were introduced to Sir Edward and Lord Cranston, the tea arrived and Meg began to pour.

This was so much more formal than the picnic at the ruins. To Alpharetta, it was as if she had suddenly stepped into one of the English novels that her teacher at Agnes Scott had enjoyed reading aloud, and holding up as the epitome of manners and civilization, with the tea ritual remaining steadfast and unshakable even in the darkest hours.

She thought of Marsh's letter from Normandy. "Can you believe it? The British officers actually took tea before leaving the gliders," he had written of the invasion forces. And yet, sitting in the warmth of the wood-paneled room, with only a dog lying by the fireplace missing from the picture, Alpharetta thought there was something endearing about it—like a salute to civilization before the horror began.

Sipping her tea and eating the cucumber sandwiches, Alpharetta was lost in her own past. A softness shaded the shimmering green of her eyes, as she remembered the tea parties with Anna Clare, the dressing up in clothes from the old trunk at the foot of her bed, those earlier times when her cousin was confused from the excessive medication administered to her by the nurse, and her only consolation was living in happier times. Alpharetta had enjoyed pretending, too, until reality shattered her dreams. But she'd learned her lesson with Ben Mark. Never again would she pretend to be anything other than what she was, never forget her humble beginnings, or attempt to deny them.

Glancing toward Alpharetta, Meg was not happy with the jealous stirrings in her mind. They were new to her, caused by the woman with red hair. She sat, saying nothing, yet Meg could tell there was an awareness in the room of her every move.

"I understand, Miss Beaumont, that you're an American?" Sir Edward asked, drawing her into the conversation that had been entirely too personal up to that moment.

"Yes, I'm from the South. Atlanta, Georgia."

"And your father? Is he in trade, Miss Beaumont?" Meg inquired.

The slightly disparaging tone made no impression on Alpharetta. She was merely passing through from one assignment to another. The people in the room had nothing to do with her.

Quietly and unflinchingly, she answered. "My father is dead. But while alive, he was in whiskey—legal and illegal."

Meg gasped at her answer. Quickly she put her napkin to her mouth.

But the old earl, seated on the adjoining chesterfield, laughed appreciatively at Alpharetta's answer. "Like your ambassador to the Court of St. James, eh? I understand he made his fortune in whiskey, too."

"But my father was never rich. And the government put a stop to his occupation."

"Ah, yes," Lord Cranston said with a sigh. "The Prohibition—an exercise in futility." Then, addressing his host, he said, "How is your home brew coming along, Edward?"

"Had to throw out the last two batches," Sir Edward complained. "Turned to vinegar. Don't know what happened." With a twinkle in his eye, he turned again to Alpharetta. "Perhaps you'd like to see my still after you finish your tea, Miss Beaumont?"

"Really, Father," Dow admonished, not liking the direction the conversation was taking. "She wouldn't be interested."

"I . . . I would very much like to see your still, Sir Edward." Alpharetta didn't look at Dow as she responded to his father.

"Good. Well, that's settled then." Glancing at his son, he chastened, "Seems to me that you'd be glad to have a chance alone with your fiancée, since you might not be seeing each other for a long time. You care to come too, Reggie?"

"No thank you, sir. I have reports to make out."

"Well then, we'll see you at dinner, if not before." Sir Edward rose. "Come along, Miss Beaumont."

As they left the room, Meg said, "Oh, Miss Beaumont, in case no one has thought to tell you, we dress for dinner."

In the evening twilight, Alpharetta moved about the room assigned to her. Her clothes had been laid out and the hot bathwater drawn by the maid as soon as she'd returned from the stone barn. Sir Edward, allotted so many gallons by the government for home consumption, had derived a great deal of pleasure from showing her the still and discussing its problems. But she was certain that the serious Dow Pomeroy would not be pleased at his father for relating stories of their ancestors, one a smuggler.

As she put on the long skirt belonging to the green silk and wool ensemble purchased in London, she remembered why she'd bought it, and a momentary sadness touched her. Yet, in the formal atmosphere of Harrington Hall, it was the only part of her wardrobe suitable for dinner.

In the bedroom, Alpharetta was surrounded by priceless possessions, comfortable family pieces that looked as if they had been there forever, the wood beautifully polished, the green silk moire on the walls and at the windows slightly faded from the sun, yet still elegant.

The bed itself was the largest piece of furniture, and as she gazed at it, she wondered at the generations who'd occupied it. The feather mattress seemed so high that she would surely need the footstool to climb up to it when she retired.

The mirror at the dressing table was ancient, too, with the patinaed gilt frame intricately carved with birds and garlands of flowers. With its mercury backing slightly spotted and worn at the edges, the glass proclaimed that it had reflected many an image over the years.

Alpharetta sat down before it and began to brush her red

hair, coiling it onto the top of her head in a more elegant style than she ordinarily wore. As she did so, her eyes played tricks on her. Alpharetta turned around quickly, but the woman she had seen in the mirror had vanished. Feeling foolish, Alpharetta finished brushing her hair, pinned the green glass ornament to her blouse, tied the scarf about her waist, and left the bedroom, even though it was much too early for dinner. But the reflection in the mirror had unnerved her, as if someone had been in the room, watching her get ready for the evening.

Dow Pomeroy, far from spending his free time in the afternoon with Meg, had been on the telephone to Middlesex, being briefed by Sir Nelson Mitford concerning the rockets, and in conference with his ADC, Freddie Mallory. Birdie, his secretary, was already at Lochendall with his batman, arranging for the arrival of their commanding officer the next day. Then Dow closeted himself with Reggie for an hour and a half in the upstairs library.

With nothing else that he could do until he arrived on the northern coast, a restless and worried Dow Pomeroy dressed for dinner and prayed to get through the evening without severely alarming his father or the others over the serious threat of the German rockets.

As Alpharetta wandered the length of the long corridor and gazed up at the family portraits, Dow Pomeroy said from behind her: "So you found the rogues' gallery."

Not taking her eyes from the paintings, Alpharetta inquired with a lilt to her voice, "Which one was the smuggler?"

"My father's been talking again, that I can see—regaling you with all the family skeletons, no doubt. He's the third one from the left."

She moved down the row, acknowledging the one Dow pointed out; stopping before another and still another until she turned abruptly to stare at Dow Pomeroy. Alpharetta's green eyes searched Dow's face, impersonally, as an artist, looking for the family resemblance. And then she turned her interest to a particular portrait. The face was nearly the same—sandy-colored hair and mustache, the brow proud and full. But the eyes were different—hooded, enigmatic, not at all like the hazel ones that stared at her with undisguised dislike at that moment.

Seeing a hurt, vulnerable look, Dow backed away, ashamed of himself. How could he explain to her, when he couldn't, even to himself, this unreasonable antipathy, even to the way she was wearing her hair?

"If you will excuse me, I left something in the room." Alpharetta fled from the gallery and returned to the green room where she remained, staring out the window, until it was time to join the others downstairs.

Reggie Minton's eyes lit up when she appeared in the drawing room later. With a drink in his hand, he came to greet her.

"I say, you look smashing in green. But then, Diana of the Hunt usually wears green, doesn't she?"

Meg, overhearing his comment, joined them. "Do you like to fox hunt, too, Miss Beaumont?"

"No. I hunt only wild boar," she said.

Appearing at her side, Dow Pomeroy laughed and added, "But she doesn't use arrows, Meg. She much prefers a Baretta."

His smile was charming, his manner completely changed, as if the previous half hour had never occurred. "What can I get you to drink, Miss Beaumont?"

"Sherry, please."

The formality of the evening became even more oppressive over dinner, with the stone fireplace and twin five-branched candelabra providing the only light in the baronial hall. The candelabra, too tall to see over, divided the six people at the long mahogany table. Sir Edward sat at one end, with Lady Margaret to his right and Reggie Minton at his left. And down at the other end sat Lord Cranston, Alpharetta on his right and Dow to his left, immediately opposite Alpharetta.

And to make matters worse, the gregarious Lord Cranston was unusually quiet. Finally, toward the end of the meal, the man spoke.

"Miss Beaumont, I hope you don't mind an old man's curiosity, but may I inquire the origin of the brooch you're wearing?"

"It was given to me by my cousin. Merely a good-luck piece, worth little."

"And your cousin's name?"

"St. John. Mrs. Reed St. John."

"Her first name," he insisted.

"Anna Clare," she responded, puzzled at his insistence.

The old man looked as if he had seen a ghost. "Her maiden name was . . . Carleton, perhaps?"

"Yes. But what—"

"And she was presented at the Court of St. James in the year—"

"*Lord Cranston.* You're the Lord Cranston she's spoken of so often."

All at once, it came back to Alpharetta—the party in Lord Cranston's garden; his marrying the heiress from Charleston, instead, because he needed to pay his estate taxes—all the stories that Anna Clare had told her, over and over.

Lord Cranston let out a triumphant laugh, and the three at the other end of the table stopped their conversation to hear what was happening.

"Edward," he roared, pushing the candelabra to the side so he could get a view of his old friend seated at the other end of the table. "You know who this young lady is? She's a cousin of Anna Clare Carleton, the woman I almost married."

He turned back to Alpharetta. And in a confidential manner, he said, "My dear, the brooch may be a good-luck piece for you—but it's quite valuable, as all good emeralds and diamonds are. I should know—since I was the one who gave it to your cousin."

"I don't know what to say, Lord Cranston."

It didn't matter that she had few words. Lord Cranston took over, asking her numerous questions that spilled over from the dinner table into the night, until Meg finally rescued Alpharetta from her father, long past bedtime.

Dow was unable to sleep. He took a flashlight and walked to the storage room beyond the portrait gallery, where two portraits, transferred from their ornate frames, were waiting to have the damaging mildew removed.

From the worktable, he picked up one fragile canvas and shone the light on it. Yes, he was not mistaken. The woman assigned to his staff had the same coloring as the woman on the canvas, but the striking resemblance lay in the same elusive, mysterious quality of remoteness, as if she could never be fully possessed—vulnerable, yet complete in herself, demanding nothing, and because of that, producing a fealty of heart, fierce in its desire to protect, to love, and yes, even to possess the very part that was guarded, withheld.

A doubly troubled Dow silently closed the door and started back to his room. Why had Alpharetta Beaumont suddenly appeared in his life, threatening his carefully laid plans, devised, not by the heart, but by expediency?

As he made his way back to his room, he silently swore at his superior, Mittie, for placing him in such an untenable position.

By the next morning, Dow was still troubled, for he realized that Alpharetta was the real enemy to his peace of mind, not only for the previous evening, but for the weeks to come.

As the staff car was brought into the courtyard, Sir Edward said, "You must come again soon, Miss Beaumont. And we'll sample our brew to see if it's any better, now that you've pointed out my error." He gave her a conspiratorial wink.

"Thank you for such a delightful time, Sir Edward. I loved being here, even if you *do* have ghosts in Harrington Hall," she teased.

Sir Edward laughed. "Well, now, I hope you didn't sight more than one."

"Are you ready, Miss Beaumont?" Dow interrupted.

"Yes, sir."

"Then I suggest you get in front with Eckerd, since Minton and I have reports to go over."

Alpharetta did as he requested and, out of the corner of her eye, she saw Dow walk back to the open door of the hall and say good-bye to Meg and her father.

Then he returned to the car and the military vehicle left the pebbled courtyard and retraced its way down the avenue past the fields of corn.

As they rode, Dow paid no attention to the reports. Finally he addressed Alpharetta casually: "You saw the ghost of Harrington Hall, Miss Beaumont? On the stairs, I presume?"

At the question, she turned to face the back seat. "No. I

thought I saw a woman staring at me in the mirror of the green room. But when I looked around, she was gone." Alpharetta laughed. "I have an overactive imagination," she confided.

With a wry twist to his mouth, he said, "I'm glad, Miss Beaumont. For what's to happen in the next few weeks, even the next few minutes, is going to tax even the wildest imagination."

"I beg your pardon?"

"Just wait. You'll find out soon enough."

Leaning toward the driver, Dow said, "Turn right, Eckerd, at the next lane."

A puzzled Alpharetta watched while Eckerd, instead of driving toward the intersection with the main road, detoured down a small, secluded lane, still on the estate. As they drove through the private gates of a small replica of the main house, Alpharetta decided that Dow must be stopping to see a relative living in the dower house.

"Reggie? Eckerd? You both know what to do?"

"Yes, sir."

"Miss Beaumont, come with me."

"I'll be happy to wait in the car."

"I think you would be happier changing your clothes in the house. Come with me," Dow repeated to a startled Alpharetta.

16

A half hour later the military vehicle had been hidden in the garage and replaced with a black Rolls-Royce. Eckerd had exchanged his army grays for a regular chauffeur's uniform, and a self-conscious Reggie, dressed in country tweeds, walked from the carriage house with a huge sheep dog named Brewster straining at the leash.

Inside the dower house, Alpharetta changed from her own uniform to the green wool and silk coat ensemble with the short skirt, as she had been instructed. And when that was done, she walked into the small anteroom where Dow was waiting for her.

"Sit down, Miss Beaumont."

She did so in a small corner chair with crewel embroidery of white, red, and green.

"I don't know any other way to begin, Miss Beaumont, except to give you the facts as quickly as possible. It's top-secret information, and what I'm going to tell you must not be repeated to anyone.

"For some time now, the War Office has known that London was due another Armageddon, courtesy of the German's new rocket missiles. For the past six months, the Allied bombers have searched for and bombed the launching sites at Pennemünde, Pas de Calais, and even the Volkswagen plant in Germany where the rockets are manufactured.

"But two days ago, Miss Beaumont, as you know, the buzz bombs started hitting London. The city has already suffered considerable damage from them, according to Sir Nelson, even in that short length of time, and will continue to do so, for we have no effective air defense, whatsoever, against them. Yet these weapons are nothing in comparison to the second missile the Germans are putting into production. There is no way the bombers can get to them, since the Germans have moved their operations into tunnels deep within the Harz Mountains."

Alpharetta sat and listened. She was conscious of the serious expression on the man's face. She didn't dare interrupt him, although she was anxious for him to get to the point—what the missiles had to do with her secret mission.

"What I'm about to tell you is known by only a few high-level people. For once, we have been lucky. Part of a fired test missile has fallen into the hands of the Swedish Government. And although the country is neutral, we have a chance to smuggle the fragments out for our scientists to examine. And that's where you come in, Miss Beaumont." He looked at her and hesitated.

"I'm to fly to Sweden to pick up the pieces," she prompted.

"Yes."

"When do I leave?"

"It's not quite so simple as that," he said. "We have our contacts working on it from both sides. But I want you to understand. It's a dangerous mission. You would be flying over enemy guns."

He acted as if he were waiting for her to back out. "I've been shot at before," she said in a calm voice.

"And you're not afraid?"

It was her turn to stare before answering. "Of course, I'm afraid. But that's never stopped me." Except once, she confided to herself under her breath.

"Well then, it's settled. When we get into the car and head for Lochendall, there will be no turning back.

"Oh, there's just one other thing, Miss Beaumont."

"Yes?"

"Sir Nelson has provided a cover for you, so no one will suspect what we're up to."

She waited for his explanation. He cleared his throat, and in an embarrassed manner, he said, "You will go to Lochendall as my wife."

"What?"

"Don't be alarmed. We'll only be pretending to be man and wife, of course."

"Won't Lady Margaret . . . mind?"

"My fiancée is not to know."

"But what about the people at Lochendall?" Alpharetta continued, dismayed at the plans. "*They'll* know I'm not Lady Margaret."

"Only my personal staff will be at Lochendall. And as for the villagers, I doubt they even know that I'm engaged to be married." He stood up, as if to put an end to her questioning. He walked to the safe behind the mantel, opened it, removed its contents, and walked back to Alpharetta.

"Hold out your hand," he commanded.

She held out her hand and watched as he placed a ring on her finger. It was too large. He removed it and replaced it with another. Satisfied at its fit, he added a second one. "Since you seem to like emeralds so much," he said. "And I suppose a proper husband would give you jewels to match your eyes, Miss Beaumont."

She stared down at the wedding rings on her left hand and, amused, she said, "I don't believe a man would call his wife *Miss Beaumont,* sir."

"You're absolutely right. I'll have to become accustomed to calling you by your given name. Alpharetta, is it?" He inclined his head in a questioning manner.

"That's correct."

With no hint of a smile, he said, "And I suppose it wouldn't sound true to form if you kept calling me *sir.*"

"I suppose not."

"Don't look so glum, Miss Beau—Alpharetta. Your assignment won't last forever. The honeymoon will be a very short one."

Far into the night the black Rolls-Royce traveled, with the sheep dog, Brewster, asleep on the floorboard between Dow and Alpharetta. In the wee hours of the night, they arrived at Lochendall.

Seeing no sign of civilization past the small village they passed through, Alpharetta knew that the place was appropriately named—the arm of the sea at the end of everything.

In the darkness, she could hear the lashing of waves against the rocks—a lonely, remote sound as she stumbled from the car toward the house that was secured by gates and a seawall to protect those within from the ravages of nature and other enemies.

Invisible to her in that starless, clouded night were the military landing strip two miles away and the hidden laboratory where rocket experts waited to examine and attempt to rebuild the German Vengeance rocket from the fragments she was to smuggle out of Sweden. And down below, also out of sight on the rocky beach, was a small cabin, manned by one lookout, with eyes searching for invaders from both air and sea.

Late the next morning, Alpharetta was introduced to another member of Dow's staff, sent ahead to open the house. She was Birdie Summerlin, Dow's staff secretary, acting out her new role of housekeeper.

Only the few liver spots on her hands announced Birdie's age. And they were of no consequence. Far more important was the warmth that charmed Alpharetta immediately and caused her to respond to the brown-haired woman with a smile.

"I hope the clothes fit," Birdie whispered to Alpharetta as she served a late breakfast to the two in the dining room.

"Yes, thank you." So it was Birdie who had selected the wardrobe and placed it in the bedroom for her arrival. Sir Nelson had evidently gambled that she would not back out, even though Dow Pomeroy had offered her the chance in the dower house.

As she ate her breakfast, the gardener from the village was busy repairing the ravages of the wind in the sea garden outside the window.

"Alpharetta?"

"Yes, Dow?"

The man smiled at the moue on Alpharetta's face as she said his name.

"At least it sounds more natural this morning than it did yesterday."

"Well, it's difficult to call my commanding officer by his first name."

Looking out the window, Dow lowered his voice. "You can still back out, Alpharetta, if you're having second thoughts this morning."

"But you told me yesterday that there was no turning back, once we reached Lochendall."

"You've had more time to think about it—to remember that your Amelia Earhart lost her life in a similar mission."

"Connie Jenkins also lost her life at Avenger Field when the prop fell off her plane, but that didn't stop the rest of us from flying."

The gardener drew closer to the window and stopped his clipping. A look of caution entered Dow's eyes. He ordered in a quiet voice, "Come and sit with me, darling."

"What?"

"Don't argue. Just do as I say," he whispered.

Reluctantly she obeyed, leaving her place at the end of the table. She perched precariously on the chair arm until Dow drew her onto his lap and then hid his face in her mass of red hair.

"Please," she said, struggling to get out of his embrace.

"Be still. He's watching us."

"Who?"

"The gardener." As if he were whispering words of love to a new wife, Dow brushed his lips against her ear and said, "We're surrounded by spies, you know."

"You think the *gardener* is a German spy?"

"He's a stranger," Dow replied against her cheek. "I don't remember him from the village—and I've come here all my life."

"He doesn't look—"

"Careful, Alpharetta."

She turned her head away from the window, for the man was peering at her. "He may just be curious," she suggested.

"Perhaps."

His mouth was dangerously close to hers and Alpharetta was aware of a new electricity in the air.

The sound of clipping started again.

"Dow?"

"Yes?"

"Is he gone from the window?"

He looked. The gardener had moved to the hedge at the far wall.

"Yes."

"Then I'll go back to my place and finish my tea, if you'll release me."

He acted as if nothing had happened between them. He picked up his teacup as she walked to the other end of the table. And in a pleased, rather dispassionate voice, he said, "You behaved quite well, Alpharetta—just the way a shy young wife would probably act on her honeymoon."

"I don't think so."

"Oh? Why do you say that?"

She gazed at him with her innocent yet seductive green eyes. "Because if I were *really* married to a man, we would both be having breakfast in bed right now, *not* engaging in polite conversation in the dining room."

His laugh, echoing all the way to the kitchen, caused Birdie Summerlin to smile. She hadn't heard such a hearty laugh from him since before his only brother, Gerald, had been killed in action.

They settled into a comfortable existence while they waited for the assignment. Dow and Alpharetta were together constantly, keeping their cover as newlyweds. Then early one morning the message from Mittie came.

After breakfast, Dow got up from the table and looked at the woman who wore his rings on her finger. "Let's go for a walk on the beach," he said, for he was suddenly restless, thinking of the assignment.

"Let me get a wrap," she said, and rushed up the stairs to her bedroom.

She took the windbreaker from the closet, put it on over her dungarees, and hurried downstairs to meet Dow and Brewster, the dog, both waiting for her at the door.

"Are you ready?"

"Yes."

They left the house with the dog beside them, and the moment they stepped from the protection of the wall, a car slowly crept into sight down the road. Dow immediately took her hand and said, "Are you ready to act as a newlywed this morning?"

"After you, Dow."

He leaned over and kissed her on the hair. "You really are dotty," he said with a laugh.

"Save your compliments, sir, until they're close enough to overhear," she admonished.

They continued walking, waving to the two men in the car as it passed them, and by the time they reached the beach, Dow shoved his hands into his pockets, against the cold wind. His eyes were pensive as he walked silently down the beach with Alpharetta at his side, her red hair blowing into his face at times.

"I had a message from Mittie this morning."

"Are the plans going well?"

"There's been a slight setback. Our contact in Sweden is being followed."

"Will that delay us?"

Dow leaned down, picked up a small piece of wood, and threw it into the air. Brewster ran up the beach to retrieve it. And Dow pushed his hands back into his pockets.

"Probably no more than a few days. We'll have to use the backup."

When the two reached the point, Dow stopped. "I'm to take you to the airstrip this afternoon, Alpharetta. Mittie wants you to familiarize yourself with the plane you'll be flying."

"What kind is it?"

"An Avro Anson Mk1."

Alpharetta nodded. "Retractable landing gears."

"With two engines—and a range of 790 miles. Probably the most reliable the RAF has, if that's any comfort to you. Tomorrow, you'll fly on reconnaissance, to get the feel of it over the ocean."

"What insignia will it have on it?"

"Swedish, when you make your run. We promised to use a nonmilitary pilot, so you'll carry over a few medical supplies, as if you're on an errand of mercy. But once you reach Sweden and the fragments of the missile are loaded, all identifying marks will have to be stripped from the aircraft. You'll be fair game for both sides."

"A plane without a country?"

"Exactly."

Dow stood looking out over the ocean. "It's not so bad as it sounds from this end, Alpharetta. If you keep to the strict schedule, you should be all right once you get past the coast of Norway. Our fighters will be issued orders that no unidentified aircraft is to be fired upon for one hour in your flight pattern."

"And if I'm late?"

"You *can't* be late. That's all there is to it."

Brewster brought the stick to Dow. The man took it and threw it extra hard along the beach. The dog raced to retrieve it again.

"I just have one more question: Why did you select a woman? Why not a male civilian pilot?"

"*I* didn't choose you, Alpharetta. Sir Nelson did. You'll have to ask him. But I suppose he felt a woman had a better chance of getting through, since the Germans wouldn't suspect a woman. I *do* know there'll be a male pilot, as decoy."

Satisfied with the explanation, Alpharetta suddenly changed the subject. "Race you to the rock," she challenged.

Dow laughed as she started running up the beach. He gave her a few seconds, then took up the challenge. As he ran, he noticed the man on the crag above. How long had he been there, observing them? Dow picked up speed and reached the rock a split second before Alpharetta did.

"What's the matter? Out of practice?" he goaded.

"Brewster got in my way," she replied, out of breath.

"No excuses," he said. "You lose—and you'll have to pay the penalty."

Before she knew it, she was in his arms. His mouth captured hers—a gentle, playful kiss at first. And then, something happened—unplanned, unrehearsed.

They became a man and a woman, caught in the primeval pulse of nature, of wind and waves, roaring and crashing against the landscape. And the kiss, so gentle at first, grew into demand, exploration, as their bodies merged in desire.

The cold wind blew Alpharetta's hair in a feathery trail

behind her, but it had no meaning, for a warmth had invaded her being. Shaken at the awakening of her long-dormant feelings, Alpharetta pushed away from Dow.

"I suppose someone was watching this time, too," she choked.

"Above us, on the cliff." He didn't take his eyes from her. He continued to look, until she broke the locked stare.

"I . . . I think we'd better go back to the house," she suggested.

"Yes. It's much too windy on the beach."

Thoughtfully, silently, they trudged back to the house, with the roar of the wind and Brewster's occasional bark the only sound. No words were spoken until they came within sight of the house.

"Damn," Dow said, barely under his breath, for down the road opposite them came three men, dressed in their best clothes. One carried a large bouquet of flowers, another, a box wrapped with a shabby red ribbon.

"Who are they?" Alpharetta whispered, aware of Dow's reaction to their appearance.

"An official delegation from the village, if I'm not mistaken, coming to present their official good wishes on my taking a bride."

"But I'm not—"

"We both know that," he snapped. Dow waved his hand at the men, and his face changed from displeasure to an encompassing cordiality.

As the two groups reached the gate from different directions, the man who carried nothing ventured, "Good mornin' to ye, Sir Dow."

"Good morning, Miles," Dow replied. "Edgar, Shaun," he added, nodding to the two men with Miles.

"We heard the news in the village," Miles said. "And we're here to express our good wishes to you and your lady."

Shaun, the man carrying the flowers, immediately thrust them into Alpharetta's hands, while Edgar offered the red-ribboned box to Dow.

"Thank you," Alpharetta replied, her embarrassment taken for shyness by the men.

"Lady Pomeroy and I both thank you," Dow replied.

"Please let the village know that we'll be at the tavern tomorrow evening to show our appreciation."

The men, satisfied at his response, put their hands to their heads, as if tipping imaginary hats. Then they backed away and began to walk rapidly down the road.

As Alpharetta stepped into the house beside Dow, she peered at him over the bunch of flowers. "I'm sorry they saw me at close range. That will present a problem for Lady Margaret later, won't it? But maybe they won't broadcast what I look like. Sometimes, men don't notice."

"By tomorrow night, *everyone* in the village will know what you look like. Tradition demands that I buy a drink for all the men in the village. And you, my dear Miss Beaumont, will have to put in an appearance at the tavern with me."

The same hostility he had directed at her that evening at Harrington Hall crept into Dow's voice. And Alpharetta, anxious to escape, fled toward the kitchen to find a vase for the flowers.

Dow took the box upstairs. And if he opened it, he did not confide its contents to Alpharetta.

17

*B*elline Wexford took her time packing. With the buzz bombs ruining everything, she was glad to be leaving London. Her nerves were badly frayed from all the air-raid sirens, night and day.

Never knowing where the rockets were going to hit, she had soon realized that the cutoff of the strange *duv-duv* sound overhead meant that they were coming down immediately. She didn't like to scramble for shelter, any more than she liked having to man the USO canteen.

Almost all the soldiers were gone and BBC radio news reports concerning the fighting in Normandy were somber. Strange, the BBC had ignored what was going on in London, broadcasting only the news of the missiles hitting *south* of the city. But from Bond to Picadilly, the people were complaining, and even blaming the prime minister, as if he were personally responsible for the bombs.

London had been a disaster for her in more than one way. Staying in the hotel with Ben Mark that weekend Alpharetta appeared had not turned out at all as she'd planned. Each time she remembered it, she was furious. He'd called her Alpharetta at the worst possible moment. The entire time he'd been making love to her, he'd been thinking of Alpharetta.

Well, she'd forget about Ben Mark, about London, about Marsh and the entire war, at least for the next few days. She was going to Scotland, to a nice place on the beach, with all expenses paid.

Belline finished packing, closed her suitcase, and left the flat she shared with the other three USO women.

At Lochendall, Alpharetta packed her flight suit for Dow to smuggle into the hangar. She was anxious to try out the Anson and see how it handled close to the water. That gray coastal mist that merged sky and sea was as dangerous as any Lorelei, sending so many pilots to a watery grave.

"Are you ready, Alpharetta?"

She looked up to see Dow standing at the open door between their adjoining bedrooms. Usually the door was kept latched, but she'd forgotten to close it after he had knocked a few minutes before.

She nodded and he walked into her bedroom to get the suitcase. Together they went into the hallway, the door still open between the rooms.

Dow had dressed in uniform for the afternoon, since the small airfield was a military installation, surrounded by a large wire fence and tall metal gates. Identification was needed from even the highest-ranking officer before entry was allowed.

The Rolls-Royce had been brought out for Dow and Alpharetta, and Eckerd now stood beside it. Alpharetta had seen little of the chauffeur since their arrival at Lochendall.

"Good afternoon, Eckerd."

"Good afternoon, Lady Pomeroy."

She stared at him to see if he were teasing her, but his eyes were straight ahead and serious.

The car passed the pub on the corner and went through the fishing village slowly, gathering speed at the end of the street. And all along the way, Dow raised his hand in greeting.

"Are you the laird of the village?" she asked suspiciously.

Dow smiled. "The closest to it, perhaps. My mother was Scottish, and I inherited Lochendall from her, as the second son."

Alpharetta's eyes questioned what her voice could not.

"Yes, I had an older brother, Gerald. You saw his portrait in the gallery. He was to have inherited the title and Harrington Hall. But he was killed in action."

"I'm sorry."

He did not inform her that he had also inherited the woman Gerald would have married, if he had lived, Lady Margaret Cranston. It was the only thing he could do in the circumstances, with his father's heart set on joining the two families that had been friends for so many years. But today he felt fortunate that Meg had never visited Lochendall, even as Gerald's fiancée.

At the gate to the military airstrip, the guards saluted as Dow stopped and showed his credentials. Eckerd drove slowly on to the sheltered side of the hangar, invisible from the road and even from the guards at the gate.

On the tarmac sat two reconnaissance planes—both Avro Anson Mk1s, the kind that normally maintained surveillance along the entire coast of the British Isles.

Twenty minutes later, the two planes took off, one after the other. The first was piloted by Alpharetta Beaumont, the other by Air Vice-Marshal Sir Dow Pomeroy.

They flew over the sheltered arm of the sea beyond the massive gray stone house on the crags—Lochendall. And Claus Mueller, also known as Lewin McGonegal, watched through his binoculars at the window of his house, until they disappeared. Then he went to the wireless to alert the fishing trawler, hidden off the point in the surrounding mist, of this unscheduled flight.

Anxiously he remained by the window, waiting for the planes to return to land. He had been assigned to keep his eye on the air vice-marshal. But he was still angry at Abwehr for not letting him know the man was married or that he was bringing a wife to Lochendall.

He had snapped her picture as she walked from the house, and sent the film on to his contact. Not that she was that important. But intelligence should have all pertinent information on a man who might be planning the heist of the turbine of their downed missile.

Claus's two contacts waited down the road for the reappearance of the Rolls-Royce. In an hour, it headed back to the village, and the two men followed it at a distance. Seeing the black car stop at the pub, they also stopped and casually walked inside to sit at the bar.

With her glowing cheeks the only telltale sign of her recent flight, Alpharetta sat at the small table in the center of the pub. Not long after their arrival, heavy black curtains were drawn at the windows and the owner's wife lit the candles on the tables and the small kerosene lantern at the bar, the main source of light in the room. The pub's old oak timbers might have come from a shipwreck along the coast hundreds of years before.

"Have you had a pleasant afternoon, Alpharetta?" Dow inquired.

"Yes. Oh yes," she responded enthusiastically.

The men at the bar, seeing the glow of her face, the sparkle in her eyes, attributed them to her newlywed state.

Word of Sir Dow's arrival quickly circulated throughout the village. Soon the pub was overcrowded, with old men drinking their free ale at the oak bar while, at each table, entire families, quickly spruced up to come and view the lady of the manor, sat and watched as they drank less alcoholic brew, caring little that their dinners were growing cold in their cottages.

The people smiled; Dow nodded. One old man, fortified by his ale, stopped at the table on his way out and croaked, "A bonny lass, Sir Dow. A bonny lass. The Lord be with ye both."

"Thank you, Hedgins," Dow replied, knowing the old man's weakness for a pretty woman.

After Alpharetta had gone to bed, Freddie Mallory, serving as courier from Sir Nelson Mitford at Air Defense in Middlesex, arrived at Lochendall with messages for Dow.

Mercy, the code name for the Swedish mission, was set. By midafternoon of the next day, when the mist had burned off the coast, Alpharetta would be on her way.

Having seen her handle the plane that afternoon, Dow felt better about the entire caper. And yet a reservation remained. He had tried to discourage her even after she had agreed. But his business was not to interfere with Mittie's plans, only to carry them out to the best of his ability.

He looked at the clock and back to the instructions. He decided not to awaken Alpharetta. She needed a good night's sleep, unencumbered by disturbing dreams. Breakfast time would be soon enough to apprise her of the last details. Dow locked the instruction pouch in his desk, along with the mail packet forwarded to Alpharetta in care of Sir Nelson at Air Defense, and saying good night to Freddie, he went to bed himself.

Birdie Summerlin was a widow in her forties, older than most of the women in the British WAAFs, with three sons in the service. She was a capable woman, with a penchant for laughter, but she'd had little occasion for laughter in the past four years. Like all patriotic British women, she had put her shoulder to the plow, as her father would have said, for she could not see herself sitting at home, knitting, while her sons were fighting.

For the past three years, she had been Dow Pomeroy's staff secretary, with him in Tunis, and moving again to England when he was called back for special assignment. Although only ten years older than he, she had assumed a mothering role with him.

Not that she was against going out with younger men herself. She smiled as she thought of Eckerd and the good times they'd had together. Although the present assignment was a serious one, she and Eckerd were having a lark, pretending to be servants at Lochendall, because of security precautions.

Reggie was the only one who seemed disappointed in the change, for he was the odd man out, with the responsibility of taking care of Brewster, still a baby despite his enormous size.

"The air vice-marshal is taking this sham marriage a little too seriously, don't you think, Birdie?"

"Well, he's a serious fellow, luv," Birdie responded. In bed, with the small reading lamp shining on her book, Birdie remembered the conversation when she had served Reggie his dinner that evening. But with Mallory returning, Reggie would have someone to go to the pub with, on his time off.

Freddie Mallory's arrival at Lochendall was not unexpected by Claus Mueller, for the man was Sir Dow Pomeroy's aide-de-camp. And even with the man on his honeymoon, the air vice-marshal still had responsibilities that could not be shirked. Unfortunately, there was no way Claus could find out what those responsibilities were. He knew that Mallory had brought instructions to him. Yet it was only a matter of time before Abwehr found out what the locked briefcase contained.

The next morning, when Alpharetta came downstairs for

breakfast, she was surprised to see Freddie Mallory already at the table with Dow. She had heard someone come in late the previous night. Despite Dow's wishes for a peaceful night, she had slept little. It was not the arrival of the car that had kept her awake.

"Good morning," she said to one and then the other. Her face denied her restless night.

Freddie, jealous of his commander's welfare, frowned as he recognized the woman who had shared the train compartment with them into London and now waited for Dow to hold her chair for her, as if she had a right to his attention and consideration.

"I think you two have met," Dow said. "Alpharetta, this is Mallory, my ADC." With a twinkle in his hazel eyes, he continued, "Freddie, may I present my wife, Lady Pomeroy."

"You'd better be careful, sir," Freddie cautioned. "Not too many years ago, saying such a thing in front of a witness in this desolate place would have made it legal."

Feeling the disapproval in Mallory's voice, Alpharetta said, "Don't worry, Mallory. This will probably be the shortest marriage on record—or off the record," she corrected. Turning to the woman at her elbow, she asked, "Birdie, do you think I might have an egg this morning?"

"Of course, luv," she said, pouring the tea into Alpharetta's cup. "That nice man, Lewin McGonegal, who clipped the hedge the other day, brought by some gull's eggs this very morning."

She didn't mention that he'd stayed for a hot cup of tea in the kitchen.

Birdie took the other orders and when she had returned to the kitchen, Alpharetta, self-conscious in front of Freddie, asked "Is there any news, Dow?"

"Yes. *Mercy* is to get underway sooner than we thought."

"When?"

"This afternoon."

"Good."

Alpharetta picked up her teacup. She was glad, for if she stayed much longer at Lochendall, she would forget Ben Mark, forget Lady Margaret. She looked out the window at the blue sky, filled with rolling clouds. "It's a fine day for it," she said.

"Yes. We couldn't ask for better," said Dow, feeling strangely depressed. "We have a busy morning ahead of us, Alpharetta. Briefing will be at 0900 in my office."

Gone was the camaraderie of the past week. Freddie, by his presence, had effectively destroyed the intimacy growing between them.

"Oh, by the way, Alpharetta, there's a mail packet for you on the table," Dow informed her.

Alpharetta was pleased that her mail was being forwarded. This time, she hoped to have a letter from Conyer. Duluth never wrote, but left it to his brother to take care of family correspondence. They had drifted apart over the years, with such a long distance between them. Yet Alpharetta remembered that period in her life when the three had been extremely close.

When Alpharetta had finished her breakfast, she picked up her mail packet and walked up the steps while Dow retired to his office.

Dow examined the contents of the briefcase once more—the fake identification papers, Swedish money, the code Alpharetta would use to get in touch with her contact, and, perhaps the most important thing, the maps.

Having read her mail, a quiet, withdrawn Alpharetta tapped on the door promptly at 0900.

"Come in."

Dow sat at his desk, with the map spread over the entire surface before him. He waved Alpharetta to a chair in front of the desk and began his briefing, eyes intent on the map.

"There's been a slight change in the initial plans. A spy is operating somewhere in the village, as I feared. Mittie says the coast guard picked up signals to a boat nearby. The spy is monitoring every takeoff and reporting the time of arrival back to base.

"So Reggie is going to fly reconnaissance from here, taking you, as a passenger, to the Orkney Islands." He pointed to the spot with the wooden baton in his hands. "From there, you'll be put aboard a fishing vessel that will get you to the coast of Sweden—here, through Skagerrak. That's the reason you will have to leave earlier than planned. Then Reggie will fly back to check in at the regular time the reconnaissance usually returns."

He looked up to gauge her reaction, but there was none, only a distant look in her eyes. He frowned. "Are you listening?" he inquired with a sharpness to his voice.

"I'm sorry. I—"

"You're not getting cold feet, are you, Alpharetta?"

"No. Of course not."

"Then follow the briefing."

Again he pointed to the map. Alpharetta leaned over, trying to concentrate on the movement of the baton.

"This means the decoy will fly the plane in after you have arrived by boat. And when the plane is stripped of its Swedish identification, he will take off again. A half hour later, *you*, Alpharetta, will take off in an identical plane—also an Anson. And that plane will contain the missile fragments." He paused. "Are there any questions so far?"

"What if someone talks to me? Or expects me to answer? You know I don't speak the language."

"That's what the contact is for—to make sure no one speaks to you. He will do all the talking for you."

For the best part of the morning, she remained in his office, studying the maps, memorizing the code. By the time she left the room, Dow had a feeling that the mission was doomed.

Damn Mittie for getting him mixed up in such a hopeless situation! Why hadn't the air marshal kept his theatrics to his days at Oxford? Then he felt ashamed. With the missiles threatening to annihilate them all, Mittie had to grasp at straws, at any chance, however small, to gain some measure of defense that all the military forces combined had been unable to provide.

And Alpharetta Beaumont was a necessary part of his plan.

18

*C*oming through the window of the dining room, the light cast patterns upon the linen tablecloth and high-lighted the blue and white Spode soup tureen in the center of the table. The tureen was not filled with soup, but with Scottish heather arranged by Birdie in an attempt to brighten the final luncheon before Alpharetta left.

Sitting at one end of the table, Dow knew that Birdie need not have bothered, for nothing could brighten the luncheon, with Alpharetta seated at the other end and Freddie between them.

The light made an arc around Alpharetta's red hair, giving her an aura of an early Botticelli painting, with her delicate, fair skin, her sad emerald eyes mirroring thoughts that were a million miles away. And Dow, unable to reach her with a touch, or bring her to his side with a command, as he had done earlier when the gardener was watching, realized that something else, beyond Freddie, had subtly put a distance between them.

Alpharetta had little appetite for food and little desire to enter into the sparse conversation between Dow and Freddie.

As soon as the luncheon plates were cleared away, Birdie brought a tray of shortbread. Alpharetta, not wanting to hurt Birdie's feelings by refusing, took the dessert and forced her-self to eat part of it.

Finally Dow cleared his throat. The men had finished eating and were waiting for her. "Don't you think you'd better finish packing?"

"What? Oh, yes, of course. Please excuse me."

Dow watched as Alpharetta walked into the hall, stepped carefully over the sleeping Brewster, and then disappeared.

At the appointed time, Alpharetta came downstairs again. Dressed in a tan skirt and blouse, low-heeled shoes, and a brown sweater draped across her shoulders, she looked as if she were going for a typical afternoon outing instead of heading toward a dangerous assignment, into a stronghold of war, spies, and enemy guns.

Waiting for her at the door, Dow had reverted to his formal, distant manner. Birdie was the one to hug her and whisper, "Good luck, luv," and then to watch as she climbed into the back of the Rolls-Royce.

Reggie and Freddie had already left for the airstrip and so, as Eckerd pulled onto the road, the car contained only Alpharetta and her commanding officer, each silent, with memories to take the place of conversation that neither could manage at the moment.

The schedule was closely coordinated, with arrival time at the airstrip precisely at 1500—twenty minutes after Alpharetta's double was to have arrived from Stanmore in identical clothes so that anyone seeing the woman on her way back to Lochendall in the car with Dow would never suspect that Alpharetta was on her way with Reggie to the Orkney Islands.

"It's unbelievable, Pom, to find such look-alikes," Mittie had confided to Dow that day at Air Defense. "Only the colors of their eyes are different. You see how well this works out. No one will know that the woman pilot is gone, for the other woman will have taken her place."

"Where did you find her?"

"The other woman, you mean?"

"Yes."

"At a USO canteen. That is, after I saw her initially at the Ritz. That's where I bumped into both of them. Lucky for us, what?"

"I don't know, Mittie. I have a feeling you're getting me into quite a bit of trouble. I'm not even married, and you're making a bigamist out of me, supplying me with *two* wives," he had said, chagrined.

"But not at the same time, Pom. And neither one knows the other is involved."

As Dow and Alpharetta rode in silence, Dow remembered the previous conversation with Mittie. Now the scheme had gone too far to be called off. Out of the corner of his eye, he glanced at the woman beside him and it was incomprehensible that anyone else in the world could even remotely resemble Alpharetta Beaumont.

"You have your Baretta?"

"Yes. It's in my shoulder bag."

"Promise me—that you won't hesitate to use it, if necessary."

She looked up into his face, her eyes suddenly luminous with unshed tears. She made no promise, merely shook her head.

In anger he reached out and grasped her arm. "That's an order, do you understand?"

"Dow, you're hurting my arm."

"I'm sorry," he said, relaxing his hold. "But I've got to make you understand. You might be in physical danger—anytime, in any situation. And you're a woman, entirely alone."

"I know."

Belline paced up and down the hangar. She was furious to be kept waiting, hidden away in the cavernous monstrosity, not allowed to show her face outside. She grimaced when she glanced down at the drab, unfashionable outfit she had worn—like a brown bird, camouflaged into the landscape. She had learned long ago that, to be noticed, a woman had to wear the colors that showed off her best features.

The hangar door opened; a black Rolls-Royce drove inside. Belline immediately brightened.

Not waiting for Eckerd to open the door, Dow leaped from the car and, with swift steps, went to meet Belline.

She smiled at the handsome RAF officer coming toward her. The assignment, whatever it was, suddenly promised to be more interesting than she had hoped for.

Inside the car, Alpharetta sat alone. Seeing Belline smiling at Dow Pomeroy in the same manner she flirted with Ben Mark, and realizing that Belline was part of the plan about which no one had thought to tell her, Alpharetta felt betrayed. She stepped out of the car.

Belline, talking with Dow, tensed when she saw Alpharetta. "What are you doing here, Alpharetta?" she gasped.

"I'm just leaving. How are you, Belline?"

"As well as could be expected, under the circumstances. It's been so beastly in London, with all the bombs."

"You'd better not waste time, Alpharetta," Dow interrupted. "You have only minutes to spare."

So there were to be no private good-byes with Dow as there had been with Dow and Lady Margaret Cranston. Alpharetta watched as Dow and Belline climbed into the Rolls-Royce. Then, not looking back, she walked onto the tarmac and boarded the reconnaissance plane, with Reggie in the pilot's seat.

Eckerd drove out of the hangar and, from the car, Dow watched the plane take off. He had deliberately avoided any last words with Alpharetta, for he had wanted to abort the flight. Yet he knew the mission had to go as planned. With a dismal feeling that he might never see Alpharetta again, Dow waited until the plane had completely disappeared. Then he gave Eckerd the order to return to Lochendall. And on the way, it was Eckerd who listened to the talkative Belline. Dow Pomeroy, with a great emptiness in his heart, had thoughts only for the woman who had left him.

Birdie Summerlin, tidying up Alpharetta's room to make way for Belline, changed the sheets on the bed. And although the room didn't need it, Birdie dusted and polished the furniture. The only thing to do was to keep busy so she wouldn't worry over Alpharetta. When she had finished dusting, she straightened the small desk top, removing the blotter to polish beneath it.

It was under the blotter that she found the telegram addressed to Alpharetta. At first, she started to return it to its hiding place. But she had seen too many telegrams like it in the last four years not to be affected by it. She had continually prayed that, as a mother, she would not be the recipient of a message such as the one that she now held in her hands.

By the time Dow returned to Lochendall with Belline, Birdie's eyes were red from crying. Alarmed at her obvious distress, Dow asked, "What's the matter, Birdie?"

"I need to talk with you, Sir Dow, just as soon as I show the miss to her room."

"I'll be in my office, Birdie."

The woman took Belline Wexford upstairs, to the same room used by Alpharetta. "If there's anything you need, Miss Wexford, just let me know."

"Lady Pomeroy."

"What, luv?"

"You're to address me as Lady Pomeroy, I understand."

Her haughty voice caught Birdie off guard.

"And I suggest if you're having some personal crisis, that you forget about it while you're working. I don't care for unhappy people around me."

Birdie's lips tightened. She forced herself to remain civil for her commanding officer's sake.

"If you will excuse me, Lady Pomeroy. Tea will be served at 4:30 in the parlor, if we don't see you before then."

"Oh, I'll more than likely be down after I've unpacked."

In his office, Dow looked out the window toward the sea while he waited for Birdie. What an unsatisfactory, disappointing day all around. And the next three days promised to be even worse, holding nothing but a vast uneasiness for everyone concerned with the project.

As his secretary walked into the office and closed the door, he turned around. "All right, Birdie? What's so disastrous?"

"I thought you should see this, Sir Dow. I found it when I was tidying up Alpharetta's room."

Birdie held out the telegram and waited for Dow to read it.

We regret to inform you that Seaman 1st Class Conyer S. Beaumont and Petty Officer Duluth M. Beaumont, serving aboard the USS Tallahassee in the Pacific, have been listed as missing in action and presumed dead. The USS Tallahassee was torpedoed on June 10, 1944, with no survivors rescued.

Incredulously, Dow looked at the telegram, reread it, and, as if it were burning his hands, released it, letting it fall onto his desk. He sat down in the chair and stared at the brown slip of paper with a sense of horror.

"Alpharetta's two brothers, Sir Dow," Birdie said. "On the same ship."

"The telegram must have been in the mail packet Freddie brought last night. I gave it to her this morning, Birdie, directly after breakfast."

Dow recalled his rebuke as they went over the briefing later. "She didn't say a word about it, Birdie. And all the time, when she was trying to absorb the last-minute instructions, the code, she was living with this." He looked up at Birdie who was blowing her nose. "I should have known something was wrong, just from her reaction." He got up and began to pace back and forth, pounding his fist into the palm of his hand in agitation.

"Poor lamb. You think she'll be all right?"

"I pray to God she will be," Dow responded.

The sound of heels clicking on the landing indicated that Belline Wexford had left her room.

"I'd better go and head off her ladyship before she spoils things," a determined Birdie said, knowing no other way to protect Alpharetta from harm.

"Please close the door after you. I'll keep the telegram, Birdie, if you don't mind."

Dow sat down again in his desk chair. Alpharetta's loss became his own as he was caught up in the memory of those self-destructive days when he had first heard the news of Gerald. Grieving for his own brother, he had challenged death himself, taking suicidal chances in each fighter mission. He prayed that Alpharetta would not do the same.

The telegram could not have come at a worse time. "Alpharetta." He spoke her name aloud, with his entire being struggling in vain to reach her beyond the confines of the walls of Lochendall, to let her know he shared her distress, her sorrow.

Dow suddenly had a great need to leave the house, to stand on the beach and to be absorbed in the primeval calm of sky and sea.

With Brewster at his side, he left the walled compound

behind. Disregarding the man watching the house, he climbed down the bluff where he stood, sheltered by the rock, and gazed out to sea.

"Alpharetta," he said again, but her name was lost upon the wind.

19

*B*eyond the channel, in the Pas de Calais area, Ben Mark St. John, in his fighter bomber, made a sudden dive toward a strange contraption of concrete and metal jutting through the camouflage of tall trees. He had a few bombs left and he always made a habit of emptying his bomb bay before returning to base.

Thinking that the strange object might be a candidate for his last bombs, he reconnoitered and, skirting the trees again, released the remainder of his load.

A sudden explosion produced a ground shock. Quickly soaring aloft to avoid the great vacuum caused by the explosion, a satisfied Ben Mark noted the trail of fire and smoke from below and continued on his way.

Ever since the weekend in London when he'd seen Alpharetta with Marsh, he had been short-tempered and hard to live with. He never should have spent the weekend with Belline. It was a mistake from beginning to end. And worse, it effectively cut him off from Alpharetta, for he knew that, at the first opportunity, Belline would not hesitate to tell Alpharetta about it. Even though she had chosen Marsh over him, there was no guarantee that Marsh would come out of the Normandy invasion alive.

In the distance, a small fishing vessel was reeling in its nets with the catch of the day. Ben Mark made a mock pass at the vessel, and feeling slightly better now that he had given a scare to someone else, he headed for home.

Marsh Wexford, unaware of his cousin's thoughts, had neither the time nor the inclination to sit and contemplate his chances of survival. He was far too busy trying to defend the bridge.

After one day of rest, the experienced troopers had been thrown back into battle, to supplement the green troops that had not fared so well.

"What I wouldn't give for a Tiger tank right now," Giraldo whispered to Marsh as they lay in the muddy marsh beyond the bridgehead. "I'd push the bastards straight off the bridge."

Reloading his rifle, Marsh said, "Why don't you steal one, Giraldo? You seem adept at getting anything else you want."

In a slightly miffed tone, Giraldo replied, "I noticed you drank the wine last night too, Lieutenant."

"It was only fit to gargle with, Giraldo, and you know that. Why couldn't you have been a little more discriminating?"

The men fell flat as the renewed strafing of their position rippled the reeds like a giant wind. The fighting was at an impasse, with American troops cut in two by the bridge. The disabled German tank, sitting in the middle of the bridge, effectively kept the American convoy of trucks and jeeps east of the river from crossing to join the others. And the troops, rather than advancing, had fallen back to defend their rear.

"I know where there're some tanks," Gig piped up once the strafing had passed. "In a grove about five miles away."

"That's panzer division headquarters, idiot," Giraldo replied.

"But when night comes, they only have two guards on duty with the tanks," Laroche said.

"And where did you get that bit of intelligence, Laroche?" an unbelieving Giraldo inquired.

"Maurice Duvalier, the man who rings the bells, told me so. It's important to speak the language, Sergeant," he added to needle Giraldo.

An idea began to take shape in Marsh's mind. If they were successful in stealing one tank, it could be used as a bulldozer to clear the bridge. The small American convoy could then follow behind the moving tank.

"I'm going to see the major," Marsh whispered and left his position near the bridge.

Running a few feet, falling flat, and then zigzagging, Marsh advanced a little at a time until, with a sudden sprint, he completed the run, rolled, and fell into the trench where the major had set up headquarters.

"My God, Wexford," the major said, recognizing the soldier who had landed at his feet. "Haven't you taken enough chances for one day?" He put his pistol back into its holster.

"No, sir."

"Well, what is it this time?"

"Request permission, sir, to use one of the jeeps as soon as it gets dark."

"For what purpose?"

"To steal a Tiger tank, sir."

The major groaned. "And just how do you think you'd manage that?"

"You know the panzer division headquarters?"

The major nodded.

"If you're agreeable, Giraldo, Laroche, Madison, and I plan to drive within a quarter mile of their headquarters, hide the jeep, and go the rest of the way on foot. Laroche says there are only two sentries guarding the tanks at night. We'll pick both sentries off, confiscate one of the tanks, and head back. Giraldo started out in a tank corps—"

"Aren't you oversimplifying, Lieutenant?"

"They're a few things we'll have to play by ear."

"Such as being surrounded by Germans. What if you're challenged by the guard?"

"I speak German, sir. Fluently. Once we're inside the tank, though, we'll have the advantage. And we can clear the bridge for our own convoy to move."

The major stroked his three-day growth of beard. "Certainly the Germans won't be expecting anyone so rash. You'll have the element of surprise in your favor." He stuck his cigar back into his mouth. "Wexford, it sounds just harebrained enough to work."

"Then I have your permission?"

"Heaven help you, yes. And just in case you're lucky enough to get through, I'll have a flag ready."

Marsh quickly zigzagged back to the bridge and his friends. He looked down at his combat boot, nicked by a bullet. He would have to be more careful.

While the four men waited for darkness, the sun painted

the flooded waters of the river gold and purple, while on the bridge lay bodies of soldiers—a surrealistic touch out of place with the pastoral setting.

The sun set and they moved out, one by one, to gather again in the spot where the jeep was camouflaged.

Keeping to the road cleared of mines, Laroche drove the jeep, with Marsh beside him. Giraldo and Madison hung onto the back, their weapons ready as they headed in the direction of the German panzer division headquarters.

After a long day of fighting, there was a silence over the countryside and the least noise, the slightest whisper, carried far beyond its source. Into this quietness the profane noise of the jeep penetrated. But the men were silent, for there was no need for conversation. Each knew exactly what he was to do.

They had been lucky so far, the four of them—training together, fighting together, watching out for each other. They were so attuned to each other, they could move as one force.

The task ahead would not be an easy one. Yet Marsh knew it was a job that had to be done, to settle the score in the land of his natural motherland, occupied for the second time in his lifespan by the Germans.

In his breast pocket he carried the lucky piece sent him by his eight-year-old stepsister, Maya, with a note from Steppie, his adoptive mother. He reached up to assure himself that it was still there.

Marsh had never told Steppie that while he visited the old vicomtesse in Paris, he had driven to St. Mihiel, the town where, as a two-year-old, he had been rescued from the battlefield. And yet he knew Steppie would have understood his desire to see for himself the village and to try to find someone who had known his mother, Ailly.

He would never forget that afternoon spent with the white-haired old woman, Mme. Arnaud, with her gnarled hands clutching the cane that served as a reminder of the ravages of age.

"Her name was Ailly, *mon fils*," she began, repeating the name, as if to summon her memory. "I was her tutor in the château. Her name was stricken from the family Bible and never uttered again by her father, the count, even on the day he died. But what she did saved her entire family from being shot. I think, my son, that little Ailly is in Heaven with the angels, for she sacrificed herself for the good of her family.

"I'm an old woman," she confessed, digressing a moment from the story, "and in these latter years, I have changed my mind on a number of things. Ailly was a victim of war. Afterward, when the peace came, the transgressors, who were men, were forgiven. But the women, their victims, through no fault of their own, were ostracized, to live with the burden of guilt placed upon them by society for the rest of their lives. Or like Ailly, they were allowed to die in disgrace, erased from the book of memory.

"Some people said Ailly should have killed herself rather than live with the German officer. But I knew her; I taught her. For Ailly to take her own life would have meant casting her soul into eternal damnation. It is not up to us to decide whether we live or whether we die. That is left up to *le bon Dieu* in Heaven."

"Do you remember the name of the German officer?" Marsh questioned.

"Not today. My memory is not so good today for names. Perhaps tomorrow. But I do know that you bear a strong resemblance to him. Yet there is something about your smile that reminds me of my little Ailly."

"Do you know where she was buried, Mme. Arnaud? I'd like to visit her grave," Marsh confided "before I leave to go back to Paris."

The old woman smiled. "She is in the ancient section of the family plot, with the unmarked gravestone. Her papa never knew that her maman and I buried her there. Each Tuesday, I go to place flowers on her grave."

Standing in the graveyard where his mother was buried opened the gate to memories long locked away in a small child's mind. People weren't supposed to remember what had happened to them when they were only two years of age. In the cemetery, Marsh wondered whether he'd been told the story so often that he could reconstruct the feelings of terror to go with it—the shell hitting the château; being knocked from his mother's arms, with smoke and fire all around him— and Neal, the downed American flyer, rushing into the house and calling her name, "Ailly! Ailly!"

Yet neither Steppie nor Neal had ever told him of the fallen stone statue or the still, white hand of his mother, barely visible in the debris.

The sound of the shelling in the distance brought Marsh back to the problem at hand. He motioned for Laroche to stop the jeep. Now it was time to proceed the rest of the way on foot.

Heinrich von Freiker, recalled to duty a week before his medical leave was up, sat in the field tent and drank his bottle of wine.

He was in a black mood, summoned as he was from Berlin by von Rundstedt, to take König's place, just when his investigation of Gretchen von Erhard had gotten underway. He knew the young woman was an impostor, masquerading as a mere schoolgirl when, in actuality, she was much older. He had set out to prove it, but his investigation had been cut short with his new orders. The Führer himself knew this Normandy thing was just a diversionary tactic. The real invasion would come when Patton's forces landed at Pas de Calais, and if his leave had to be cancelled, that's where Heinrich wanted to be, in the thick of the fighting.

Heinrich put down the empty bottle, belched, and left his tent for the latrine.

When challenged by the guard, he called out "Freya," and walked on into the darkness.

Marsh and Giraldo, flanking their way from opposite ends of the camp to Laroche and Madison, suddenly froze as a twig snapped under their boots, making a loud noise.

"*Wer ist da?*" a voice called out, challenging the noise.

In the dim light, Marsh could see the outline of the soldier, with his helmet on, his gun with fixed bayonet pointing in their direction. Giraldo looked at Marsh, who silently prayed that they would not be caught in a spray of bullets from a trigger-happy guard. He dared not speak, for they were in the wrong area of camp.

Again the soldier called out, "*Wer ist da?*"

The drunk Heinrich, returning from the latrine, answered, "Freya."

The guard lowered his rifle as his commander came into

sight. And Marsh and Giraldo, happy to be alive, congratulated themselves for learning the password as well.

Farther away, in the compound where the tanks sat like great hulking prehistoric monsters, the two sentries came together, spoke briefly, and resumed a steady pace, with an ever-increasing distance between them.

Watching their pattern, Giraldo and Marsh waited for Gig and Laroche to reach the compound. And in the meantime Giraldo mentally selected the tank he would requisition.

Marsh timed the guards, noting how long it took them to make their rounds and return to the starting point. The third time the guards came together and parted, with backs to each other, Marsh heard the cricket and knew the other two were in position. He responded, waited three minutes, and then gave Giraldo the signal to run for the tank.

As one of the guards reached the remotest part of his walk and was ready to turn, Madison sprang from behind and grabbed him with a choke hold. Laroche thrust his knife into the softness of belly. Laroche, the gentle Cajun, who had gotten sick to his stomach with his first fight in Sicily, was now hardened to the conditions of war, of kill or be killed.

"*Wer ist da?*" The familiar refrain came from the other guard at the slight disturbance. And Marsh, closest to the guard, responded "Freya," as Heinrich had done.

To his surprise, the response brought a swift, unexpected retaliation of gunfire. There was nothing left to do but return the fire and run for the tank. Laroche and Madison did the same, as voices sounded in the distance, and a searchlight went on, illuminating the camp area.

Like groupers threaded through the gills on a fisherman's line, the three fell into the tank, one on top of the other. A machine gun went off somewhere; soldiers finding the dead sentries, called to each other in excited voices, and Giraldo, the only one who could see through the visor of the tank, watched a squad of soldiers running toward them.

The other three held their breath and listened, as metal hatches clanged and reverberated, as the Germans methodically investigated the empty tanks around them.

The four waited for their tank to be next. But after a few minutes, the officer, evidently satisfied that no one had bothered the tanks, called off the search.

Guards were doubled, and the camp returned to normal, while inside the tank the four sweating men moved to a more comfortable position and silently watched while Giraldo familiarized himself with the controls.

A half hour later, Giraldo, not knowing how much diesel fuel the tank had in it, started the behemoth up. With a jerk to its great, wide treads, the tank moved out, while once again, guards shouted and the camp's searchlights went on. But the tank, buttoned up, was secure, the heavy armored plate more than a match for the sentries.

Giraldo crashed into the open road, and with a whoop they were on their way, while the drunk Heinrich von Freiker, putting on his pants again, struggled to comprehend what had happened.

"You sure set off the fireworks, Lieutenant," Madison declared. "Just what did you say to the guard to get him so riled up?"

"Freya," Marsh said. "I would have been all right, if I'd been going to the latrine. But the tank compound evidently had a different password."

"I wonder what the major's going to say when he sees us coming down the road in this thing?" Laroche asked.

"Probably shoot at us with everything he's got," Giraldo answered.

"Hey, Laroche, take off your undershirt," Gig suggested. "We'll run it up on the gun turret, for a surrender flag."

"Hell, we should have taken time to paint a star on it," Giraldo complained.

"That's all right. The major will recognize your driving, Giraldo. He made the lieutenant promise not to let you drive the jeep," Gig quipped.

"The jeep! I forgot all about it," Laroche lamented. "You think the major will be mad at us for not stopping to get it?"

"I expect he'll forgive us, if we clear the bridge for him." Marsh smiled and touched the good-luck piece in his pocket.

In the dark, the armored beast rumbled, wending its wide tracks down the road in the direction of the American soldiers interspersed with members of the French Underground. And the commanding officer, listening to its approach, gave orders to hold fire, on the slight chance that Marsh and his men had been successful in their mission.

Camouflaged behind the trees and dug into the hedgerow country, trucks and jeeps waited, ready to move out.

In what was left of the moonlit night, the tank finally came into sight, with a small white piece of cloth hanging on the gun turret—an undershirt, GI issue.

"Damned if they didn't do it," the major swore, looking through his binoculars. His admiration caused his weathered, stubbled face to break into a grin.

Marsh and his men continued to the base of the bridge, backed up, wheeled slowly to the right, and, using the tank's sixty-ton weight, began the clearing of the bridge, ramming the disabled tank that stood in the way.

The steady drone and rumbling of treads set up a vibration in the distance, and the commanding officer knew the Germans weren't far behind. Now their escape to the other side of the river depended upon the success of one confiscated tank and four men to clear the bridge in time for the convoy to rush across and join the others before the entire panzer division destroyed them.

With his head not as clear as he might have wished, Heinrich von Freiker waited for news after his initial command to pursue. The stealing of the tank smacked of a traitor, and he would take great pleasure in retaliating. If the villagers didn't turn in the members of the Underground, he would round up ten citizens and have them shot. But first he planned on stopping the tank before it could do damage to his own panzer unit—and shooting the bastards who'd stolen it.

Giraldo, gauging each push against the disabled tank, hit it with enough force to jar the teeth and catch the neck in a whiplash. Sparks struck, metal against metal, until a great crash signaled the success of ramming the disabled tank off the bridge.

"Back up, Giraldo," Marsh ordered. "Let's get off the bridge."

But Giraldo, struggling with the frozen left lever, swore. "I can't get it in reverse!" And for a terrifying few minutes, with the rumble behind them vibrating the concrete of the causeway, Marsh and Giraldo both used their strength to try to unlock the behemoth.

Gradually, the lever eased into the correct position.

Gig, suffering from claustrophobia in the enclosed tank, opened the hatch and leaned out to give directions to Giraldo, so that he would not miscalculate and plunge them off the bridge.

"Do we have any ammo?" Marsh inquired.

"No," Giraldo replied. "And not much fuel, either."

As the tank reached the abutment next to the bridge, the American convoy began moving across in a steady flow. A salvo from a bazooka made a direct hit on one of the jeeps. It went up in flames, leaving its occupants on a funeral pyre. The other vehicles rerouted around the burning jeep.

One tank, stolen from the enemy, was the only defense as the men continued across the bridge, while underneath, two swimmers strung the sticks of dynamite along the pilings. It was up to that small group to keep the Germans from sweeping toward the beaches with their reinforcements.

Maurice Duvalier, hidden by the side of the road with three of his compatriots, all over seventy years of age, watched the German tanks pull out, one by one, crashing onto the road where he and his men had hastily planted the mines. Only one portion of the tank was vulnerable—the soft underbelly, like an Achilles heel, undipped in metal armor.

The first explosion brought a tremendous sense of satisfaction to Maurice, who had long waited for his land to be rid of the German conquerors. After the first blast, he expected the panzer division to be more cautious.

True to his surmise, the tanks stopped, turned toward the edge of the road, and, with their flailing chains, sought out the obstacles in their path. Maurice, aware that his maneuver would not stop them completely, but merely buy time for the Americans, was pleased at the havoc he had caused. Silently, he gave the signal to the others. They had done all they could. Now it was time to return to the farm cart and make their way back to Underground headquarters—the farmhouse presided over by his two elderly sisters, Jeannette and Cecile.

Surrounded on all sides by the flooded waters, the narrow causeway was only wide enough for the vehicles to travel single file. With the stolen tank covering their departure, the last truck, the final jeep managed to get onto the bridge just as the first of Heinrich's tanks came into view.

The stolen tank's guns were silent. Only its enormous bulk now protected the rear of the convoy.

"What are we going to do now, Marsh?" Giraldo inquired, seeing the monster headed straight toward them.

The loud report of arms drowned out Marsh's reply, for the salvo, glancing the tank, reverberated into the inside chamber.

"Turn tail and run, Giraldo," Marsh shouted once more. "Get on the bridge."

Again the left track stuck. "Jeez, why did I have to pick a tank with a stubborn lever?" Giraldo wailed.

For the second time that night, Marsh lent his weight and the two men pushed it into reverse.

On the other side of the long bridge, the men from the convoy dug in for the fight, while the two swimmers crouched on the bank with the detonator to destroy the bridge, now that the convoy had finally gotten across.

Marsh had not meant to cut it so close. He had hoped to have enough time to abandon the tank and set it afire to block the Germans. But all four men were trapped inside with no hope of staying alive. If they opened the hatch now, they would be picked off as soon as their helmets became visible.

"Get on the bridge, Giraldo," Marsh ordered.

Giraldo obeyed, while Marsh removed a grenade, weighing it in his hand and feeling for the pin. "When I tell you to scramble, we'll hit the concrete. I'll count to three—Gig, you and Laroche go first, followed by Giraldo."

The two men on the other bank, seeing the German tanks approaching, had only one thought—to push the detonator and destroy the bridge before the tanks reached it.

Almost to the second, the hatch of the stolen tank came open, its occupants crawling along its wide treads, while inside the grenade went off. The double explosion of the bridge and the tank tossed the paratroopers into the air, like the mannequins that had been air-dropped from the gliders earlier, to throw the Germans off the scent of the invasion.

Stunned, they lay where they had landed, atop other bodies on the side of the bridge next to the approaching enemy. The moonlit scene of the peaceful river was once more ravaged by war.

20

*F*or thirty-six hours, Dow Pomeroy had waited for the telephone to ring, for Mittie to call him, to give him some message about Alpharetta. Anything at all, to indicate that she had arrived safely in Sweden, or that the mission had been called off at the last minute.

Instead, there was a blanket of silence, with no communication whatsoever. Dow, used to following each mission's progress from hour to hour, was in a strange situation, cut off from headquarters, unable to do anything more than wait. Finally, he could stand it no longer.

"I'm flying to Middlesex," he told Birdie, and with Reggie accompanying him, he left Lochendall, Belline, and his ADC behind.

Belline, bored with life in such a desolate place, prowled restlessly about the stone house for most of the morning. It was too windy to walk along the beach, so she went back to her room, painted her nails, rearranged her hair, and then rummaged in the closet until time for lunch.

By late afternoon, Belline's fury at being left alone spurred her to action. Going to the closet, she pulled out the green ensemble belonging to Alpharetta, dressed in it, and, in heels much too high for the rugged country, went downstairs to find Freddie Mallory.

Freddie, playing solitaire at the dining-room table, looked up as Belline walked into the room.

"I'm dying of boredom, Freddie," she announced. "How about taking pity on me?"

"You want to play double solitaire?" he asked.

"No. I want to go into the village, but Eckerd won't drive me unless you say it's all right."

"I don't know, Alpharetta. Sir Dow said you were to stay on the grounds until he got back."

"Will you please stop calling me by that ridiculous name?"

"Do you prefer 'Lady Pomeroy'?"

"My name is Belline. Belline Wexford. And I'm tired of pretending to be someone else."

Freddie looked toward the partially open garden window. "You'd better not say that too loudly."

"And who's to care? Or overhear? I think you're all making a mountain out of an anthill, with this secrecy business. And I'm tired of being kept a prisoner in this God-forsaken place."

"It's only for one more day," Freddie said. "Can't you find something to do in the house? Read, or work a crossword puzzle, or—"

"No. I've decided to go into the village, and if you won't take me, then I'll walk."

"In those shoes?" he inquired gently.

"And what's wrong with my shoes?"

"They're really quite attractive. But I daresay you'd find the going a bit rough in them."

"Oh, I expect you and Eckerd will come along with the car after a while." With a satisfied smile, she left the room and went upstairs for her purse. By the time the front door slammed, Freddie had on his officer's coat and was following after her.

"Lady Pomeroy," he called, but Belline didn't turn a-round. She kept walking down the road in the direction of the village.

Claus Mueller, watching the house from his vantage point across the road, noticed with interest Belline's progress. With his telescopic lens, he took several pictures of her.

She was walking differently today. Perhaps it was the shoes. And she didn't look any too happy. No wonder, being left by the bridegroom so soon. As he continued watching, he saw the black Rolls-Royce slowly pull up and stop. The door opened and the woman, smiling, climbed into the car beside Pomeroy's ADC.

Claus left his hiding place and hurried to take the film to his contact in the village.

Behind the pharmacy, in a storeroom set up as a darkroom, Hans Klieber developed the film while Claus waited upstairs. He always enjoyed the brief get-together with Hans, though they dared not speak German, even in the privacy of Hans's apartment. But it was the only time Claus could let down his guard. And while he waited for Hans to come upstairs, he read the decoded message Hans had received from Abwehr about Sir Dow Pomeroy's supposed bride.

Her name is Belline Wexford, an American and a USO hostess in London. There is no record of a marriage to Pomeroy, so it has been assumed that the woman is involved in some secret intelligence work, perhaps with the French Underground. Her brother, Lieutenant Daniel Wexford, is in Normandy with the 82nd Airborne Division. Continue the surveillance until further notice.

A few minutes later, an excited Hans, hanging the CLOSED sign in the front window, climbed the stairs to his apartment over the pharmacy. In his hands, he carried the wet print of Belline.

"Look at this, Lewin," Hans said, careful to call Claus by his alias. "I think the pieces of the puzzle are beginning to come together." He held out the picture for Claus's inspection.

"What is it?" Claus asked, not certain of Hans's meaning.

"Wait. Let me get the other picture." He walked to the desk and from between the covers of a large art book, he pulled the picture Claus had taken of Alpharetta earlier. Putting the two pictures side by side on the table, Hans carefully compared the two and waited for Claus to do the same.

"She's wearing her hair differently today," Claus observed.

"Look again. Do you see any other differences?"

"She seems taller, but that must be due to those idiotic shoes."

Hans remained silent and waited for Claus to continue examining the two pictures. "She isn't wearing her wedding rings," he observed.

Hans, now impatient, picked up a sheet of paper, blocked out the bodies so that only the head and shoulders of both were visible.

"Observe the neck," he said. "You notice the woman in the first picture has a longer neck."

"You mean, there are *two* of them?"

Hans nodded. "Almost identical—perhaps twins. But I'm certain they are two different women."

"But why?"

"When we find out the identity of the first woman, we will know."

Smiling at Claus, Hans said, "You have done an excellent job, photographing them both in the same dress. You are to be congratulated."

Claus beamed at the unexpected tribute as Hans poured two glasses of ale to celebrate the small break in Sir Dow Pomeroy's cover. When he had been assigned to this lonely outpost, to await the invasion of the British Isles by the Führer, Claus had thought the position an important one. But then the invasion had not taken place and he had felt forgotten. All that changed when Hans came three months ago, to take over the pharmacy willed to him by his "cousin" who had died. Claus knew then that the region had become important again.

The sound of the bell ringing at the front of the pharmacy brought a frown to Hans's face. The CLOSED sign meant nothing to the crofters coming into the village at the end of the day. He set down his unfinished glass of ale and peered out the window to see who was ringing the bell so insistently.

"I suppose I'd better go down," he said, seeing the woman. "It might be an emergency."

Hurrying down the steps, he walked through the pharmacy and opened the front door.

"I'm sorry to bother you," the woman said, "but I desperately need some salve for this rash on my arm."

"Come in," Hans replied, looking into the blue-green eyes of Belline Wexford.

By the time Dow and Reggie returned to the military airstrip not far from Lochendall, Dow felt much better. Alpharetta had arrived safely in Sweden via the fishing boat and was a guest on the estate of the countess in whose field the rocket had crashed.

The fragments were hidden in the stables and well guarded. Dow had been assured that the arrangements for their removal were progressing according to plan. Now he had only one more day to wait for Alpharetta's return.

Eckerd, sitting in the Rolls-Royce at the airstrip, was relieved to see his commanding officer walking toward the car. The red-haired woman had put the group captain through his paces for the entire afternoon, refusing to leave the village, even after the few shops were closed. She chose, instead, to go to the pub for dinner. Birdie was expecting them home for dinner, but that didn't seem to matter to the woman.

He climbed out of the car and held the door. "Good evening, Sir Dow."

"Good evening, Eckerd. Where is—er—Lady Pomeroy?" Seeing Reggie immediately behind him, Eckerd hesitated. "Well?"

"She's at the pub, sir, having dinner with Group Captain Mallory."

Dow swore at the news. He quickly climbed in, followed by Reggie. And when Eckerd had closed the door and returned to the driver's seat, Dow said, "To the pub, Eckerd. And be quick."

As they drove out the military gates and onto the main road, great billowing clouds, resembling the fleece of sheep on the nearby lea, rolled in from the sea, and a blustery breeze swept over the road, forming small spirals—dust devils—to dance along the road.

In the pub, the owner's wife, Hilda, frowned as she watched Belline with Freddie Mallory. Somehow it didn't seem right, her being out with another man, especially on her honeymoon.

Grudgingly, she served them a second drink. Lady Pomeroy didn't seem to be in any hurry to order dinner. Keeping her eye on the table, nervertheless, to watch for the signal that they were ready, Hilda waited on the other tables while her husband, McGowan, took care of the bar.

As the door opened, the men at the bar, including Lewin

McGonegal, turned around in one concerted movement to see who had entered. Dow stared for a moment, his eyes adjusting to the dimness of the wooded interior. Seeing Belline and Freddie at the center table, he smiled and walked toward them.

In a voice loud enough to be heard at the bar, he said, "Sorry to be late, darling. Have you been waiting long?"

He leaned over and gave the surprised Belline a perfunctory peck on her cheek as his ADC stood. And Hilda, coming back from the kitchen with a steaming bowl of cabbage and mutton, relaxed at the sight of the air vice-marshal.

"Can I be getting something for ye, Sir Dow?" she asked. "A wee drop of brandy, perhaps?"

Dow laughed. "Now, Hilda, you know no one has any good brandy these days."

"Well, I be saving it, for a special occasion."

"Like the christening of your daughter's new baby?"

Hilda blushed and Dow smiled again. "Save it, Hilda. We really must be going, anyway. Mallory, pay the bill, will you?"

Leaning over and taking Belline's arm, he said, "Darling, there's been a change of plans. We won't be able to stay for dinner after all."

"But—"

He continued smiling while he ordered in a low voice with his teeth clenched. "Get up. Immediately."

Belline had never seen Dow like this before, his hooded hazel eyes those of a peregrine ready to tear its victim to shreds. She rose quickly from her chair and Dow linked his arm with hers, forcing her toward the door, while outwardly he remained cordial.

"Good night, Hilda—McGowan. We'll stop in another time when we can stay for dinner."

"Good night, Sir Dow."

Dow whisked Belline toward the car outside where Reggie and Eckerd waited. As soon as Freddie appeared and climbed into the back, the car sped toward Lochendall with no one saying a word the entire way.

Later, in Dow's bad graces, Belline sat quietly at the dinner table. She preferred to sulk, eating little of Birdie's food, and leaving what conversation there was to the men. She now wore her own clothes, an aqua dress with matching sweater, for the first instruction Dow gave her when they reached the house was to remove the green dress and not ever wear it again.

There had been no mention of Alpharetta then, and no mention of her at the table, yet Belline had a suspicion that the woman was uppermost in the minds of each man around the table that night. She was probably on some secret mission or something. But it couldn't be any more dangerous than dodging the bombs in London.

Piqued at the turn of events and her age-old jealousy of Alpharetta getting the best of her, Belline blurted out, "Did you know that Alpharetta's father was once caught making illegal whiskey?"

Dow, looking at Belline, said, "I believe that was in the thirties, was it not, during your Prohibition?"

"Why, yes, it was," she answered, puzzled at Dow's offhanded acceptance of the information. Had Alpharetta actually confessed her pedigree?

Ignoring Belline, Dow turned to Freddie. "It seems one of the Pomeroys married a Beaumont a century or so ago, according to my father."

Undaunted, Belline tried again. "Her brothers, Conyer and Duluth, were no better. They—"

Dow turned on Belline with such unconcealed fury that she left the sentence dangling in midair.

"You will kindly refrain from speaking ill of the—ill of *anyone*, while at my table. Is that understood?"

Birdie, removing the plate from Belline's place, sloshed some gravy on the tablecloth. "Sorry, luv," she said, dabbing at the stain while giving her commander time to regain control of his temper.

Belline rose from the table. "If you will excuse me, I'm not in the mood for what passes as dessert." She quickly left the dining room and walked to the steps leading upstairs.

"Get out of the way, Brewster," she demanded.

The sheep dog, asleep in his usual place, slowly got up, stretched, and walked several paces farther down the hall to sprawl again.

When Belline reached the bedroom, she pulled out the salve prescription to rub on the rash on her right arm.

By noon of the next day, Hans Klieber had heard from Abwehr. The German secret intelligence had the entire dossier on the woman flyer, Alpharetta Beaumont. Putting the pieces together, they had completed the puzzle, noting her arrival on the fishing vessel and her subsequent visit with the Swedish countess.

Now they knew the seriousness of her mission. Spies had been alerted to monitor her every move, but not to hinder her in that neutral country. Once she took flight and passed the Norwegian coast to the North Sea, the blueprint for her annihilation would be put into action.

For the second time, Hans and Claus celebrated with a glass of ale in the apartment over the pharmacy. And they toasted Belline Wexford for helping them engineer Alpharetta Beaumont's downfall.

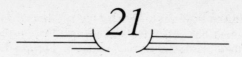

21

*A*long the beach where the wind was driving giant spumed waves against the rocks, Dow looked out over the expanse of gray and listened for the sound of an approaching plane.

But the North Sea played its own dark, deafening symphony—crashing cymbals and tympani.

The mist clouded his binoculars, the salt air whipped his face, but still Dow stood and waited. And listened.

It was on the beach that Dow had begun to awaken, as one long asleep, to experience the feelings that he had long ago pushed away. Strange, that Alpharetta could do what time had been unable to accomplish—to make him feel again, to question his heart and then to discover that love, without his bidding, had invaded it.

The dog Brewster raced up and down the beach, stopping at intervals to look back for attention from Dow. The man picked up a stick and threw it toward the rock. As the dog raced after it, Dow relived that afternoon on the beach with Alpharetta, when he had held her in his arms and kissed her—not because the man was watching them from above, but because he wanted to see if she could summon from his numbed heart what Lady Margaret had been unable to do—a feeling of being alive, of being brought back from the dead, where he had long resided with his brother, Gerald.

His guilt for living was now gone, washed from him by the cleansing powers of the surf against the rocks of Lochendall. It was as if Gerald were in the very wind, whispering to him that it was all right to love—and to live again.

Dow glanced down at his watch. He had hoped to see the plane by now, but still there was no sign. Yet he knew he shouldn't begin to worry until the hour was up, when the cease fire would no longer be in effect for the planes monitored by Mittie at Stanmore.

He walked to the lonely outpost far down the beach, where Gregory Malcolm drank his afternoon tea and viewed the radar screen for enemy ships and planes.

"Any activity, Malcolm?" Dow inquired as the lonely old man opened the locked door to him.

"Not much, Sir Dow," he answered, "beyond the usual fishing boats coming in with their catch."

"What about the plane activity?"

"The day bombers should be passing over soon. Haven't come on the screen yet. Would ye be joining me in a cuppa tea?"

Realizing he was cold and wet, Dow nodded. "Thank you, Malcolm. But I'll get it myself."

With the teacup in his hands, Dow settled down to watch with Malcolm. Every few minutes, he glanced at the time. The hour passed slowly and Dow's anxiety began to mount.

A rumble of thunder slowly moved across the sky and the flash of lightning touched the water on the horizon.

"Looks like we be in for a storm soon."

Brewster, outside, began to bark and run back and forth and whine at the door.

"Be quiet, Brewster," Dow ordered. And the dog, hearing his master's displeasure, sprawled on the ground, his tongue hanging out and his head to one side, listening for the closed door to open.

Finally, dots appeared on the screen and Malcolm became alert, watching the trajectories. "Must be the bombers," he said.

Again Dow glanced down at his watch. For one hour, that northern portion of the United Kingdom had been left defenseless, to allow Alpharetta time to get through. Now she was no longer protected, but a primary target for any plane crossing her air space.

Not able to sit still, Dow got up, left the lonely cabin, and began to hurry up the beach with Brewster at his heels.

Alpharetta, dressed in her heavy flight suit, wiped the cold mist from her goggles. Every few minutes she made corrections to her navigation to compensate for the turbulent downwind that threatened to blow her off course.

She was late, but it couldn't be helped, with the Messerschmitts appearing out of nowhere, strafing her and the decoy plane directly ahead. She had been lucky, moving upward into the cloud bank and losing the Messerschmitt on her tail.

That was the only thing that had saved her. The decoy plane had not been so lucky. She had seen the explosion just seconds before the cloud cover enveloped her. The pilot never had a chance.

Alpharetta took a quick look at her gas gauge. She had gone far off course, so the fuel tanks were half empty even though she still had a long way to fly. But the missile fragments were secure in the hatch.

A squadron of bombers appeared to her right and Alpharetta, taking no chances, immediately sought the cover of clouds until they had passed.

Ben Mark St. John, straggling as usual behind the rest of the fighter squadron, felt particularly pleased at the success of their mission. It wasn't often that they scored such direct hits and got to observe the explosions mushrooming in a chain reaction. The bombers had dropped everything they had on the ammunition train. Ben Mark felt a little sad, though, that they had so little opposition in the sky that day. Just two more to his credit would have made him an ace. And that meant a lot to him.

With his keen eyesight, Ben Mark was the first to notice the plane coming out of the clouds. Suddenly banking to the right, he gained altitude until he could get close enough to read the identifying marks of the plane. He could tell from its shape that it was a British Avro Anson. But the Germans now flew some they had captured, since they had lost so many of their own.

As he came into range, he saw the marks of the plane had been wiped clean, like fingerprints removed from the scene of a crime.

"Unidentified aircraft at port quarter."

Twice Ben Mark gave the plane a chance to identify itself, but there was no response. And he moved in for the kill.

Dangerously close, he made a pass at the plane, his hand on the machine-gun throttle sending deadly bullets toward the cockpit.

There was no retaliation, no defense beyond a sudden maneuver to avoid being hit. Curious now at the refusal of the plane to fight back, Ben Mark made another pass, coming in so close that he could see the holes in the fuselage from the first bullets. He opened up again with all that he had, the tracer fire visible against the dark clouds beyond the wing tip.

This time, there was a response, a voice suddenly breaking radio silence, as if the bullet had caused a short in the cockpit and the transmitter had been turned on accidentally.

It was impossible, but it sounded like a woman. His ears had deceived him, he knew, but in those few seconds, the heart had gone out of his fighting. The plane was crippled, the pilot more than likely wounded. That in itself should be enough to satisfy him.

Ben Mark turned to catch up with the rest of his squadron at the same time the two Messerschmitts, unmistakable in their shape, came out of the clouds and headed toward the unidentified plane, intent on finishing the job that Ben Mark had started.

Ben Mark was under no obligation to defend the plane from its predators, as he would have been if it had given up, using its wings or landing gear to signal surrender after the first shots. He would have followed it to land, and taken the pilot prisoner, if that had happened. It was too bad the crippled plane had not done so.

Defending the weak against superior odds had never been one of Ben Mark's priorities. He remembered being on his Uncle Reed's farm outside Macon, and seeing the sickly yellow chick unable to defend itself from the vicious pecks of the other fowl surrounding it, and Alpharetta crying for him to save the fuzzy creature.

"The biddy's going to die, Alpharetta. It's a fact of life in the barnyard. Only the strong survive. Might as well let the others finish it off now. It'll happen sooner or later."

But the softhearted Alpharetta had implored him to rescue

the chick and put it in a wire coop, safe from the others. And he would never forget that afternoon several weeks later.

"See, Ben Mark? It's well again," his fiancée had said, smiling. "And so fat."

"That's because Eddie has been giving him preferential treatment—and the best mash to eat."

"Shall we see whether he'll be accepted again by the others?"

"I'm not going to rescue him a second time, Alpharetta," he warned. He walked to the coop, lifted the wire, and watched the spindly-legged chick rush toward the others. After an initial vicious peck, the chick was accepted by the rest of the brood.

"Thank you, Ben Mark," Alpharetta said, her green eyes shining with delight as they walked back to the house.

The earlier scene latched itself on to Ben Mark's mind, like a barnacle he was unable to scrape off. He turned to face the Messerschmitts honing in to blast the crippled plane out of the sky.

Dow Pomeroy took off from the airstrip in a new Hawker Tempest and headed out to sea. Directly behind him were Reggie Minton and Freddie Mallory in a second plane, a de Havilland Mosquito Mk1.

Their unofficial reconnaissance mission was to find some trace of the Avro Anson before darkness set in.

Flying along the route that Alpharetta was to have taken, they braced against the strong brisk wind blowing toward land. Down below, the waves rolled in great troughs and one lone trawler listed in the angry sea.

Twenty minutes later, Dow saw an oil slick, and he went into a dive to investigate. Remnants of wood were tossed upon the waves. A downed plane, the debris attesting to its recent demise. But Dow, satisfied that it was not Alpharetta's plane, gained altitude and continued his flight pattern. And as he did so, he ran into the dogfight taking place on the other side of the cloud bank.

He saw the crippled plane immediately, holes in its fuselage, one wing dipping dangerously to the right. And the other, an American fighter bomber, fending off the two Messerschmitts in an uneven battle.

Reggie, to even the odds in the dogfight, joined the American plane in attack of the enemy, while Dow flew alongside the Anson. In a strategic maneuver, Dow eased his own wing tip directly above the Anson's and kept it there, the two planes locked into place, to guide the crippled Anson home.

As the great crags of Lochendall became visible in the last light of day, when the storm made its presence known on land in the howling of the wind across the lea, Dow deliberately gained altitude and speed to uncouple the two planes. He would have to leave the difficult part up to Alpharetta—to land the crippled plane with no help from anyone, not even the control tower. And Dow prayed that the plane would not catch fire as it hit the runway.

Alpharetta, feeling a numbness gradually taking over her body, saw the objects around her assume a hazy, distorted shape. As she let down her landing gear, she shook her head to clear her vision.

Inwardly she heard Gandy Malone's voice shouting, "Lift your right wing, dammit." But this time the plane had a mind of its own, no longer responsible to her as the pilot, for it had been dealt a mortal wound. She heard the sirens wailing, saw the fire trucks racing along the runway, and she knew they were for her.

There would be no second opportunity to approach the runway. The plane was done for. As the last engine sputtered and the gas gauge gave up the ghost, Alpharetta brought the wobbling plane to earth, the fiery rubber wheels protesting the uneven lurch, like some large, awkward seabird, forced off balance, and then skidding on wounded wing, to the sound of its own funeral dirge in siren wails.

At the far end of the field, Dow landed in the Hawker Tempest. And Eckerd, in the Rolls-Royce, rushed to meet him as he started walking on foot toward the scene of the crash.

"Have you seen her? Is she all right, Eckerd?"

"They were just pulling her out of the plane, Sir Dow. I didn't wait to see."

Sargeant Eckerd passed the plane that was now being sprayed with foam, and came to a stop a hundred yards farther down where an ambulance stood with men gathered around it.

"Where is the pilot?" Dow demanded of the young airman closest to him.

"Inside the ambulance, sir."

She lay on the stretcher, her eyes closed, her skin translucent, like a waxen doll.

"Alpharetta!" Dow's cry came from the depths of his heart, the anguish no longer that of a commanding officer.

The bloodstain on her flight suit and helmet revealed that Alpharetta Beaumont had been hit.

22

Hearing her name, Alpharetta opened her eyes. "Dow?"

"Yes, darling. I'm here." He held her hand while the medic examined her right arm, the wound laid bare with the sleeve of her flight suit cut away.

"How bad is it?" Dow inquired of the medic.

"She's lucky. The wound on her forehead is superficial. And the arm looks worse than it really is. No bones broken, that I can tell. She'll be a mite light-headed, because of the blood she's lost," he added, "but she'll be all right."

"Thank God."

The medic took stitches to close the wound and then bandaged her arm. When he had finished, he turned to Dow who had been standing beside her the entire time. "She'll need a tetanus shot and a change of bandages by tomorrow. Other than that, there's not too much else to do except keep her quiet tonight, so the bleeding won't start up again."

"You realize, Massey, that everything that's happened today is top secret? That no one is to mention what has gone on?"

"I understand, sir."

The de Havilland Mosquito came in for landing, and by the time Alpharetta had been taken to the Rolls-Royce, Reggie and Freddie climbed out of their aircraft. Satisfied that they had made it back, Dow ordered Eckerd to drive on, leaving the two to come later in the staff car. As the Rolls drove out of the gate, there was no sign of the plane Alpharetta had ferried. It had been whisked away, its contents to be unloaded in secret.

The rain began in soft, large drops and fog drifted in on the wind. Eckerd, driving slowly to avoid the bumps, leaned forward to see the road through the twilight mist.

Dow, solicitous of the silent Alpharetta, inquired, "How do you feel?"

"Tired. Extremely tired." She turned to him, to look into his hazel eyes. "Thank you, Sir Dow, for coming after me. I never would have made it alone."

Wincing at her new formality, he said, "The play isn't over yet, Alpharetta. You're still to call me Dow."

She looked so vulnerable, half-hidden under the plaid lap robe he had placed around her. He wanted to take her in his arms, to comfort her, to let her know that Birdie had found the telegram. Instead, he announced, "I sent Belline back to London late this afternoon. Her taking your place was nothing but a disaster. Even Brewster was glad to see her go."

"I'm sorry. Belline can be quite charming."

"When it suits her," Dow agreed.

There was so much more that he wanted to tell her. But it was too soon. The honorable thing was to break off with Lady Margaret first, for he knew now that he could not marry her. He had never felt this way about a woman before, except perhaps the one in the portrait gallery. But she was the ghost of Harrington Hall, not flesh and blood like the woman seated beside him.

Birdie Summerlin picked up the oversized black umbrella at the door as soon as she heard the car's engine.

The waiting had been no less painful for her, with Alpharetta out in the storm, and her commanding officer and Reggie and Freddie, too. Eckerd was the only one whose safety was assured—Eckerd and Lloyd, the batman who at that moment was building a fire in the upstairs bedroom belonging to Alpharetta, in anticipation of her arrival.

Anxiously, Birdie watched the Rolls come to a stop. As soon as she recognized Sir Dow, with Alpharetta in his arms, she rushed into the walled yard and, holding the umbrella to shelter the two from the rain, she followed them into the house.

For once, Claus Mueller was not watching. He was certain the Messerschmitts had taken care of the woman flyer.

Dow carried Alpharetta up the stairs, into the bedroom adjacent to his own, with the blackout curtains hiding the warmth and flame of the hearth.

"Birdie, you'll have to help her," he announced, placing her in the chair next to the fireside. "She's weak from a loss of blood."

"What do you want me to do first, luv?" a sympathetic Birdie inquired.

"May I have something to drink?"

"Hot tea?"

"Yes, thank you."

Birdie immediately left the room and went downstairs to the kitchen. A second car pulled into the courtyard, the staff car with Freddie and Reggie, pleased with their role in downing one of the Messerschmitts. They ran for shelter as a thunderous assault brought the storm to Lochendall, full force. And Dow, amid the static on the line to Mittie, relayed the message that the mission called Mercy had been successful.

Several hours later, Alpharetta, helped into her gown by Birdie, lay in bed and listened to the wind and rain lashing the windowpanes. The fire on the hearth was dim and the house began to creak in its unending battle with the sea— slate and stone pitted against the onslaught of salt-encrusted spray.

Dow, unable to sleep, also listened to the wind. A soft sound from within the house, on the other side of his door, alerted him that Alpharetta was awake, too. If he had not been attuned to the least movement, the least sound, perhaps he would have missed it, for the gentle crying was no match for the noise coming in from the sea. Yet it was not unexpected.

He got up, put on his robe, and walked to the door that separated the two bedrooms.

Sitting in the rocking chair before the hearth, Alpharetta held the tear-stained telegram that Birdie had slipped back underneath the blotter.

"Conyer. Duluth." Their names, unbidden, formed upon

her trembling lips. Grief denied required its own retribution, coming like a thief, clawing at tender memories when the heart is weakest and, in dark of night, demanding remembrance.

No memory was exempt. Like a ragpicker, grief plucked at each one, tearing and ripping the memories that were a part of her childhood, before she'd gone to live with the St. Johns—the family cabin, in the shadow of Stone Mountain; the new dress she had been sewing the day the sheriff caught her father and brothers making moonshine; even the stone chimes that Conyer had carved to catch the sounds of the wind as it swept over the porch. She could see Duluth sitting quietly at the oak table in the new cabin, with the light of Ben Mark's housewarming gift—the hurricane lamp—casting shadows on his lean, silent face as he ate his dinner.

Suddenly she became homesick—for her father's arms. But he was dead, too—like Conyer and Duluth. He had lived only a month after being put on parole for making his illicit brew. Conyer, Duluth, and she had buried him in the plot beside the cabin.

Now only the mountain remained—that Georgia granite monolith far older than the Himalayas. And even the comfort of the mountain had been taken from her this night, for she realized that she could never bury Conyer and Duluth at the base of the mountain, with her father. The sea had claimed them, had taken them from her—far too soon.

The wind blew open the window and the sound of the sea roared through the bedroom. Alpharetta cried out and Dow, on the other side of the door, opened it and rushed into the bedroom.

"Alpharetta?"

She stood, caught by the faintly burning embers. "The window. Close the window, Dow," she pleaded. "The sea is coming in."

He attended to the window, closing it and twisting the latch. "It's only the rain," he soothed, walking back to the hearth where Alpharetta stood, shivering and gazing into the embers.

"No, it's the sea. And it's taken Conyer and Duluth. They couldn't even swim, Dow. They couldn't even swim," she repeated. She sank to the hearth, her grief overwhelming her.

"Oh my dear, my dear one," he said, kneeling beside her and taking her in his arms, to comfort her as he would a child, lost from the ones she loved.

Far into the night, as the winds subsided and the sea became calm again, Alpharetta lay asleep in Dow's arms before the hearth, the quilt pulled from the bed to rest on the floor in front of the fire.

Dark dreams disturbed her sleep and Dow soothed her unintelligible sounds with his own, careful of the arm so recently bandaged, the small cut on her forehead where the shattered cockpit had left its mark.

It was in this position that Birdie found them the next morning. Carefully, she closed the door and kept Lloyd downstairs, to give Sir Dow time to wake up and return to his own room before breakfast.

The distant ringing of a telephone awoke Dow. He took one sleepy-eyed view of the time and, alarmed at the late hour, hurried back to his own room. He had no sooner walked into his room than he heard a tap on his door.

"Yes?"

"Sir Nelson is on the telephone, Sir Dow," Freddie's voice informed him.

"I'll come at once." He ran his hand through his hair and opened the door to walk down the hallway to his office.

Picking up the telephone, the air vice-marshal hesitated. All at once he realized that Alpharetta's mission was over and unless he did something about it, she would more than likely be leaving him to go back to her former assignment.

"Pomeroy here," he finally announced.

Mittie wasted no time after Dow identified himself. In sentences that only Dow could understand, he said, "Pom, you've got a bloody raven in your cornfield. And you've got to put up a scarecrow immediately. Do you understand?"

"Last year's, or this year's?" he inquired.

"Last year's, but the scarecrow must wear gray trousers. The old dowager might loan you a pair."

"I understand."

"Good. I'll talk with you in a few days."

Dow stood, looking at the telephone. So there *was* a spy somewhere in the village. And Mittie had ordered him to get

Alpharetta out that night unobserved, and to hide her in the dower house until he contacted him again. Putting his hands into his bathrobe's pockets, Dow returned to his room to shave and get ready for the day. He hoped that Alpharetta would feel like traveling as soon as it got dark again.

Alpharetta remained in her room all morning and rested. She ate little, even with Birdie tempting her with a milk pudding she had made especially for her. "I'm not really an invalid, Birdie," she commented. "You don't have to watch over me every minute of the day."

"And who's to take care of you, if I don't?"

"I'm a grown woman, Birdie. I don't need anyone else."

"Did you tell Sir Dow that last night?"

"What do you mean, Birdie?" Alpharetta asked, for she had been puzzled to discover she had spent the entire night by the hearth. Surely Dow had not remained in her room, once she'd gone to sleep.

Birdie did not reply to her question. Instead, she left the tray by the bed and walked softly out of the room.

Claus Mueller finished his midday meal of sausage and cheese, drank his wine, and started toward the pharmacy where Hans Klieber worked.

His elation was short-lived, for as soon as Hans Klieber closed the pharmacy for his own lunch hour and signaled him to go upstairs, Claus felt something was wrong. He could tell in the way Hans walked.

As soon as they reached the apartment and Hans shut the door, he frowned and asked, "Have you seen the woman today?"

What did he mean? Claus flinched at the question. Finally he recovered enough to ask, "What's the matter? Did the pilots not shoot down her plane?"

"The Messerchmitts vanished. No one knows."

"But the plane was unarmed. The woman *couldn't* have gotten through. It was impossible."

"How many planes returned to base in the late afternoon?"

"I—I didn't notice. The fog closed in and I thought she was already—"

"Idiot! Start looking for the woman."

"Perhaps they shot her down first."

"Or she could have brought back the missile fragments. The Führer is much displeased."

Claus, feeling miserable, tasted the sausage in his throat. Why did Hans always have to ruin his meals? And how did Hans always know the Führer's mind?

Claus, alias Lewin McGonegal, slipped out of the pharmacy when no one was looking. Taking his bicycle from its hiding place, he jumped on it and rode toward the crofter's cottage for his garden tools.

An hour later, Claus propped his bicycle by the seawall at Lochendall and began the garden cleanup. The hedge needed little trimming, but luckily, the storm had strewn behind the debris of leaves and trash. While he worked, Claus listened and watched for some sign of the red-haired woman. But if he saw her, how could he tell which one was the right one— or the wrong one, since there were two of them? And *he* hadn't been able to tell them apart.

At Stanmore, Mittie held the intelligence report in his hands. So the Germans hadn't been able to find out if the missile fragments had been delivered, or whether they had been shot down over the North Sea. Anxious to keep the Germans in suspense, Mittie determined to play the charade out to the end, or for the next several weeks, enough time for the scientists to make their investigation. Let the Germans worry for once, for the V-1 rockets landing in Buzz Bomb Alley had set up a vast chain of anxiety all over the United Kingdom.

He was glad Alpharetta Beaumont hadn't been injured seriously. She was a brave woman. But there were others equally as brave, doing their share. Any nation bombarded by the enemy had to call upon all its resources, male and female. Mittie was careful, though, not to share his philosophy in the joint planning sessions.

At Lochendall, Lewin McGonegal lingered as long as he could in the garden. But he was finally sent on his way by Freddie Mallory. He had not been successful in seeing anyone except Eckerd outside, polishing the Rolls-Royce until its black exterior reflected the sun.

"You are going somewhere—to get the car so nice and shining?" Lewin questioned on his way out.

Quiet for a moment as he continued polishing, the taciturn

Eckerd finally announced, "Today is Thursday. I always polish the car on Thursday."

In the darkness of the night, when the village was asleep, Eckerd brought out the car. Alpharetta's luggage had already been placed in it. With the motor softly purring, two people—Dow and Alpharetta—climbed inside and, without benefit of headlights, the black car slowly wound its way southward to Harrington Hall.

The honeymoon was over, and Alpharetta was to lead a cloistered life in the dower house until her arm had a chance to heal.

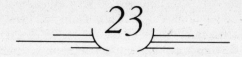

23

*B*en Mark St. John, accumulating enough missions to qualify for a weekend pass, found his way back to London. In his pocket, he carried the letter from Rennie, his mother. The whole sordid mess about Alpharetta's breaking their engagement had finally come to light.

He was mad as hell at Belline for deliberately lying to him, making him think that Marsh was taking his fiancée away from him. Instead, he had been trying to get the two back together in the meeting at the Ritz.

"You're going to be sorry, Belline Wexford," he said aloud as he headed for Rainbow Corner, where Belline worked. She was going to pay for keeping him from Alpharetta that entire weekend.

Then, he remembered. She had a powerful weapon of retaliation that she would use whenever it suited her. Why had he been such an idiot to spend that weekend with Belline?

Walking along the street, Ben Mark couldn't believe the new devastation to the city—whole blocks gone, buildings nothing more than rubble. But luckily, the rockets were coming down in a different place now, south of London, giving the city a breather until the Germans found out that the newspapers were printing the wrong information to throw them off track.

"Sorry, Captain. No officers allowed," the voice said, smiling at him as he entered the door of the canteen.

"I'm not staying," he replied. "I've come to see my cousin who works here. Will you tell Belline Wexford I've arrived?"

"And what name shall I give?"

"St. John."

He felt awkward because of the enlisted men's stares and salutes as they entered the building. He was so much more at ease at Grosvenor House, where the cafeteria served good American food. It was the only place where he could get ice cream on the entire island. But he was well aware of the contention it stirred up among the more conservative element, who censured the Americans for using up fuel for refrigeration. They didn't seem to understand that ice cream was to an American what tea was to the British.

"Ben Mark, what a pleasant surprise," Belline said.

He grunted in acknowledgment. "Can you get off duty?" he asked.

"I'm sure I can. Just let me tell Agnes. How long are you going to be in London?"

"Depends."

Belline smiled. "I'll just be a minute."

In the small café across the street from Picadilly Square, Ben Mark sat opposite Belline and watched her as she ate shortbread with her tea.

"Belline, why did you pretend that Alpharetta and Marsh were interested in each other?"

A surprised Belline set down her cup and frowned. "What is this? An inquisition or something?"

"Just answer the question, Belline."

Playing for time, she inquired, "Who told you any different?"

"My mother. I had a letter from her yesterday."

Belline shrugged her shoulders. "So I was wrong."

Her nonchalant attitude angered Ben Mark. "I'd thought you'd grown up, Belline. Instead, you're still acting the spoiled brat you were back in Atlanta, always causing trouble between people."

A hurt look came into her eyes as they suddenly moistened. "Don't *you* be down on me, too, Ben Mark. I've had enough abuse heaped on me this past week."

"Why? What did you do wrong *this* time?"

"I didn't do *anything* wrong," she denied, "except to agree to go to a God-forsaken place in Scotland and pretend to be someone else. It was a disaster, but I wanted to get away from

London, even for a few days. The buzz bombs had ruined my
nerves.

"I thought it would be fun, but it wasn't. They tried to make
me stay inside the house, but I got so bored that I went into
the village instead. You would have thought I had committed
some terrible crime."

"You're not making much sense, Belline."

"Well, the whole affair didn't make much sense. It was a
hush-hush project and I'm not supposed to talk about it. But
I can tell you one thing, Ben Mark. Your little Alpharetta
isn't as lily-white as you think. She's been posing as the wife
of some air vice-marshal in the RAF. And they went off together on a honeymoon."

"I don't believe you."

"Oh, you don't? Well, who do you think I changed places
with in Scotland, while she flew off for several days?"

At the look on Ben Mark's face, Belline felt better. He
turned white and his hand tightened on the corner of the table.

"When was this?" he demanded.

"Last week."

"What day? What day did you get there? And what day did
you leave? When was the last time you saw her?"

"She was supposed to have gotten back on Thursday. But
I never saw her. They put me on a plane that morning."

Thursday. A week ago. That was the day he had attacked
the unidentified plane over the North Sea and heard the woman's voice that gave him such a twinge in the pit of his stomach.
The same feeling he had now in talking with Belline.

Ben Mark stood up. "Let's get out of here."

"But I haven't finished—"

"Yes, you have." He put money down on the table and,
steering Belline by the elbow, rushed out of the café.

"Just tell me one thing, Belline. Who was your military
contact?"

"I promised not to tell."

"Dammit, Belline. I'm no spy. I've got to get in touch with
the man. There's a terrible possibility that Alpharetta might
be dead. I've got to know."

"Sir Nelson Mitford, the air marshal at Stanmore," she
mumbled.

Ben Mark left Belline at Rainbow Corner. "When am I going to see you again?" she asked.

"I don't know." He dove into a taxi and a disappointed Belline watched as it disappeared.

"Hey, Red, you in the mood for a game of bridge?"

She smiled at the young soldier, a regular at Rainbow Corner. "Sure, Corporal. Let's go bid a grand slam."

Dow Pomeroy, on his way to Harrington Hall for the weekend, stopped in to see Mittie at Air Defense. Ever since he had left Alpharetta in the dower house, with not even his father knowing she was there, he had wrestled with his conscience.

It wasn't fair to Meg to remain engaged to her, when he had no intention now of marrying her. But to go against his father's wishes would take its toll on him emotionally. Regardless, he had made up his mind. He would break with Meg that very weekend. And after a suitable time, he would declare himself to Alpharetta. He could assume his brother's place in many ways. But he drew the line when it came to marriage.

With Eckerd remaining with the staff car, Dow walked into the building and started toward Mittie's office on the second level, where it all began.

Dow remembered the sparks that flew when he first recognized Alpharetta. He had a premonition even then that she would turn his life upside down. And she had.

"Pom, it's jolly good to see you," Sir Nelson said, holding out his hand to Dow in greeting. "How's our patient coming along?"

"I'm on my way to find out, Mittie. And to see my father. He hasn't been well, you know."

"Sorry to hear that. And you'll be wanting to see Lady Margaret too, I expect."

"That goes without saying."

"Yes. Well, remember me to them all—and tell the young red-haired lady how much we appreciate what she did."

"Have you heard from the scientists?"

"They're working on it. A race against time, I can tell you that. Hoped the fighting in France would be further along, but it's a slow process. Lots of casualties, as you well know.

And the troops are nowhere near the missile sites. Poor Monty's got himself bogged down again, despite what the papers say."

"Do you have any further orders for Beaumont?" Dow asked, trying to sound casual.

"She might as well come out of hiding now. Intelligence has picked up the two spies at Lochendall. You were right about one of them, Pom. The gardener, Lewin McGonegal. He was no more Scottish than the Rajah of Kohinoor."

"And the other?"

"The pharmacist. Oh, by the way, Pom. Before you leave, I think you should speak with the young American captain in the next room. He's awfully upset about his fiancée's disappearance."

"What does that have to do with me, Mittie?"

"Just talk with him. His name is Ben Mark St. John."

Ben Mark stood at the window and gazed at the activity below. Sir Nelson had kept him waiting for quite a while. When the door opened, he turned to face him. But the man was not white-mustached, as Belline had said, or nearly as old as he expected.

"Captain St. John?"

"Sir?"

"I was told by the air marshal that you were waiting to talk with me. Something about your fiancée disappearing?"

"Yes, sir. Someone said that Air Defense would be able to tell me where she is."

"I don't see—"

"She was on a special assignment, sir."

"What is her name?"

"Beaumont. Alpharetta Beaumont."

A strange look came into Dow's eyes and then he quickly concealed his chagrin by turning his back and walking to the desk. Alpharetta—engaged. He had not known. As he turned around, his face showed no emotion.

"She's on my staff, Captain," he announced. "And it's true that she's been on special assignment."

The relief was evident in the smile that enveloped Ben Mark's face. "Then she's all right?"

Dow nodded. "Your fiancée is on my father's estate, recovering from her assignment. I'm just leaving for Harrington Hall." Forcing himself to be hospitable, he inquired, "Are you free for the weekend, St. John? If you are, then you might wish to ride with me." It was the least he could do in the light of this development.

"That's good of you, sir. I would appreciate the ride."

"You have luggage?"

"Just my flight bag. It's in the taxi."

"My driver, Sergeant Eckerd, is waiting in the staff car. I suggest you switch your bag from the taxi, and I'll be downstairs in a few minutes."

"Thank you, sir."

"Not at all."

When Ben Mark had gone, Dow remained motionless in the middle of the room, as if he had been turned to stone. Then, with heavy steps, he left the building. It was fortunate that the young American had kept him from making a tragic mistake, but his heart refused to be comforted by the knowledge.

The dower house, located a mile from the main hall, resembled a small cloister, complete in itself with its own gates and its small walled garden where roses bloomed in delicate shades of peach and yellow.

A contented Alpharetta sat on the garden bench and watched the butterflies flutter and then light on the flowers in their unceasing search for nectar.

How lazy she had been the entire week, with her only visitor the doctor who removed her stitches and rebandaged her arm, and her only companion Brewster the sheep dog, who now lay like a great baby on her feet.

"Brewster, do you mind, old chap," she said, affecting a British accent, "moving a bit? My foot has gone to sleep."

Brewster lifted his sleepy head and Alpharetta took that opportunity to withdraw her foot.

The solitary confinement of the past week had not bothered her, for Alpharetta needed the time for her body to heal and for her mind, reliving the memories of childhood with Conyer and Duluth, to accept her grief.

A dower house was an appropriate place for that, designed as it was, for a woman alone—when she was no longer the mistress of a great hall, but a widow. The earl is dead. Long live the earl—a never-ending saga of birth and death, of titles and lands passing from one generation to another.

But Dow's mother had died long ago. There would be no one to occupy the dower house, once old Sir Edward was dead and Lady Margaret had become the chatelaine of Harrington Hall.

Half dozing in the late-afternoon sun, Alpharetta heard a car stop and then the gate squeak as it opened. Warily, she sat up and listened, for she was not expecting anyone.

Dow Pomeroy stood for a moment, framed by the gate, a familiar, strong-boned face with a slight grayness at the temples of his sandy hair; tall, lean, strolling with one arm behind his back and his eyes, deep-set, searching in the shadows of the garden.

Alpharetta stood. "Dow! How nice to see you. I didn't know you were coming."

He stepped into the garden as she began to walk toward him. "Alpharetta, I've brought someone to see you." His voice, cool, distant, was no longer a voice that she recognized.

"Who, Dow?"

"Your fiancé."

She watched, unbelieving, as Ben Mark came into view from behind him. "Ben Mark!"

"I'll leave you two to become reacquainted. And I'll send a car for you later, Captain. You're both expected for dinner at the hall at 7:30."

With mixed feelings, Alpharetta watched Dow disappear as Ben Mark St. John walked toward her, his boyish grin proclaiming his delight in seeing her.

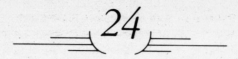

*B*en Mark took Alpharetta in his arms and gave her a resounding kiss. Alpharetta, with an anxious glance toward the gate, whispered, "Stop it, Ben Mark. Sir Dow will see us."

Ben Mark laughed. "The man has a fiancée of his own. I expect he'll be doing the same thing in about ten minutes."

"But . . . I'm not your fiancée, Ben Mark."

"You can't get rid of me that easily, Alpharetta. I know the whole story. You can't run away from me anymore."

"Who—who told you?"

"Don't pester me with questions at a time like this." Again his mouth took possession of hers, stopping any further questions, any further vocal protest. A suddenly cynical Dow, seeing the two embrace, whistled for Brewster and walked back to the car with the dog at his heels.

Alpharetta's sweater, draped over her shoulders, fell to the ground. And Ben Mark's hand, seeking the softness of her skin, came in contact instead with the gauze bandage around her right arm.

His hands dropped to his sides and he stepped back, his expression turning to dismay at the sight of the bandaged arm.

"Alpharetta! You've been hurt."

"A small wound, Ben Mark," she said, dismissing the injury as she stooped to retrieve her sweater. She began to walk back to the bench in the corner of the garden and Ben Mark followed.

"When did it happen?" he demanded, his voice suddenly harsh with urgency.

"Last week. But it really doesn't matter now, Ben Mark. The doctor took the stitches out yesterday, and it's healing nicely."

"But it *does* matter," he refuted.

She sat down on the bench and he stood over her, the scowl so familiar. "I talked with Belline in London yesterday. Alpharetta, were you flying over the North Sea toward the Scottish coast last Thursday—in an unidentified plane?"

Her green eyes widened at the question. "I can't answer that," she replied, taking a sudden interest in the butterfly that had lit on the rosebush near her.

"You cried out, didn't you—when you were hit. When the P-47 attacked you."

"How did you know?" The incredulous expression and her sudden acknowledgment brought a moan that erupted from his throat like a ferocious growl.

He knelt beside her, took her hand, and in utter remorse, whispered, "Forgive me, Alpharetta."

"You? You were the one who . . ."

"Yes. I'm the one who attacked you, who injured you. I'm sure of it. I was going to blast you out of the sky."

"What made you change your mind?"

"The biddy on Uncle Reed's farm."

"What?"

"Well, that's the reason I came back when the Messerschmitts appeared. You were already crippled. I don't think you knew it, but when you were hit, you broke radio silence. I thing the voice was what stopped me at first, even though you refused to signal defeat. Then I kept seeing that poor little chicken you made me rescue in the barnyard—the one getting pecked to death."

His eyes became fierce as he said, "This Sir Dow Pomeroy should be court-martialed, setting you up in such a near-disaster. And I won't mind telling him so."

"No, Ben Mark. Don't blame Dow. It wasn't his fault. I was flying a mission, just as you were. And if it hadn't been for his coming to find me, I never would have made it to land."

"Don't make me feel any worse than I do already, Alpharetta. I've taken the blame for what I did."

"I don't blame you, Ben Mark, any more than I do Sir Dow. It was *my* decision and I knew the danger involved beforehand."

"You've done more than your bit for the war effort, that's for sure. Now it's time for you to stop taking chances."

He smiled a familiar, coaxing smile. "I can get permission for us to be married at once, and then you can go back to the States to wait for me."

He was saying the words she had longed to hear, had dreamed of the entire time she was in training. Why then was she not happier? She looked into his dark brown eyes and shook her head.

"Ben Mark," she said, "Conyer and Duluth are both dead. I have to remain, to take their places, the only way I know how, to do everything in my power to help defeat the Axis. Don't you see? We've waited this long, Ben Mark. We can wait a little longer."

"Conyer and Duluth? Both dead?"

Tears came into her eyes. "They were on the same ship." She looked for her handkerchief, but it had disappeared.

Ben Mark took his, handed it to Alpharetta, and drew her close while the tears flowed.

He had never been comfortable with a woman when she was crying. He sat there awkwardly, patting Alpharetta's shoulder until she drew away, dried her eyes, and made an effort to contain her emotions.

"Are you staying for the weekend?" she inquired, trying hard to engage in ordinary conversation.

"Yes. Sir Dow has been kind enough to put me up at the hall. I'd rather stay here with you, though."

"That's impossible, Ben Mark. You know that."

"But you went away on a honeymoon with the vice-marshal. Belline told me all about it."

She looked at Ben Mark, at his stubborn young face, so different from that of the man who had brought him here. She sighed.

"We were well chaperoned. And you should know it was merely a cover for the mission. Ben Mark, let's not get into a fuss after being apart for so long."

"I can't help being jealous. Having you pose as another man's wife."

"Well, keep it to yourself, Ben Mark. I'd hate for it to become publicized."

"Does his fiancée know—about your Scottish honeymoon?"

"Of course not. Just as no one knows I've been here in the dower house all week, either, while the shrapnel wound was healing."

"I just don't like it, Alpharetta."

"It's in the past, Ben Mark. It doesn't concern us now."

He said no more, for he remembered the night spent with Belline. It was in the past, too, and he hoped it would never concern Alpharetta.

It was growing cool as the sun left the garden, and Alpharetta, with a slight shiver, said, "Let's go into the house."

Two hours later, when they had caught up on all the news from home and shared their own experiences, Ben Mark scowled as the car came to take him back to the hall. Reluctantly he ran his hand over his face and said, "I guess I'd better shave and shower before dinner."

"Yes. Everyone dresses," Alpharetta agreed.

"I'll ride back with the chauffeur to pick you up later. Seven-thirty?"

"Yes. I'll be ready."

He leaned over to kiss her and she watched as he walked out the door and got into the car.

A pensive Alpharetta climbed the stairs, to begin dressing for dinner.

She had not been quite truthful when she told Ben Mark that no one knew she was hiding in the dower house. Sir Edward had known it and had visited with her each day, combining his own loneliness with hers, his own grief at the loss of his son, Gerald, with hers.

In one week's time, she had grown extremely fond of the old man, and because of her friendship with him she had agreed to wear the special white dress that night.

Its lace-trimmed mutton-sleeves hid the bandage on her arm well. Carefully, she buttoned the tiny buttons and when she'd finished, she gazed into the mirror and smiled. Anna Clare would have loved the dress, an heirloom from the past, carefully preserved, exquisite in form. Alpharetta reached for the choker of pearls, fastened them about her throat and, with the matching pearl combs, swept up her red hair. Then she sat at the mirror, and her smile turned into a frown as she viewed the completed image.

After a moment, she rose, took the wrap, and walked downstairs to wait for the car.

With nothing else to do, she stood at the window and watched for the car. Soon it came and Ben Mark was at the door.

Alpharetta rushed to open it. He stood in the doorway, his dark eyes showing amusement at the dress she wore.

"You look as if you've been rummaging in Anna Clare's trunk, Alpharetta. Don't you have something more modern to wear for dinner?"

She immediately became defensive. "It's a beautiful dress, Ben Mark."

"But so old-fashioned. You might have lived a hundred years ago."

"Yes. I could easily be a ghost from the past, couldn't I?"

"Well, come on, my lady. Yon carriage is waiting," he said, sweeping into an exaggerated bow.

"Let me get my purse," she said and soon followed.

So used to seeing Eckerd, Alpharetta was surprised when another man, dressed in the black uniform of a chauffeur, held open the car door. For a moment she felt regret, for she realized things were coming to an end. They would never be together again, like a family, the way they were at Lochendall—Birdie, Freddie, Reggie, Eckerd, and, most of all, Dow.

But hadn't she assured Ben Mark all that was in the past? Just as the woman who'd once worn the heirloom dress was also in the past. Tonight, she was playing a part for the memory of the old man, just as she had played a part in the house at Lochendall—pretending to be the bride of Sir Dow Pomeroy, the man who already had a fiancée.

"We'll be in good company tonight, Alpharetta," Ben Mark informed her on the way past the cornfields that reached to the manor house itself. "Lord Cranston is coming with his daughter, Lady Margaret."

"Did you know he's the one who almost married Anna Clare?"

"I don't believe it."

"But it's true. He told me so himself. You see, when we stopped at Harrington Hall on the way to—on the way to Scotland, he recognized Anna Clare's brooch that I was wearing. The old boy had given it to her himself."

Ben Mark laughed aloud. "I always thought Aunt Anna Clare made up over half the stuff she told us. Maybe she was telling the truth after all.'

"Oh, how I wish she could be with us tonight."

"Uncle Reed probably wouldn't like it."

"No, I suppose not—if Lord Cranston once loved her."

The car stopped in the courtyard and the old butler swung open the heavy door as they approached.

"Good evening, Andrew," Alpharetta said.

"Good evening, Miss, Captain," he said, taking Alpharetta's wrap. "Sir Edward and Master Dow are already in the drawing room."

Feeling slightly self-conscious in the heirloom dress, Alpharetta behaved as she always did when she was a little unsure of herself. She lifted her chin a fraction higher, straightened her spine, and began to walk slowly down the hall.

"I have a feeling you could get lost in a museum this big," Ben Mark said in a low voice, "and not be found for several generations."

"It's big, but there's a warmth to it, too."

"But don't you think it's rather spooky, with that coat of armor greeting you in the hall, first thing?"

"I like the house," she defended.

In the manor house where generation after generation of Pomeroys had lived and died, Sir Edward glanced up at his only remaining son, who at that moment stood by the window and held a glass of brandy in his hands.

It was a special day, celebrated each year in June—Chatelaine Day—to honor all the women over the years brought to Harrington Hall as wives of the Pomeroys. Some said it was a pagan custom, almost like ancestor worship by the Chinese. Yet for the Pomeroy men, it was a time for reflection, for pausing to pay homage to the past chatelaines of the manor and the mothers of the succeeding generations.

Some had brought with them great dowries; others, great

beauty and kindness. Some meek, some outspoken, they carried the keys around their waists, as the symbol of their husband's trust, until other symbols took their place and became more meaningful.

Dow had never known his mother, who died when he was a baby. He had been brought up in a house of men—his father, his brother, Andrew the butler, and even the chef. The only women he had known as a boy were hanging in the portrait gallery—beautiful, cold to the touch, and out of reach, like the titian-haired woman who was supposed to escape her gilt frame at intervals, to haunt the green room where she had once lived and died.

Dow, thinking about it, decided he should also include the assorted maids and his one governess, Miss Wilder. But even her face had faded from his memory, for he had been sent away to school when he was seven.

Sir Edward, watching his son, was tired. That afternoon, he had supervised the gardener as he cut the roses to place in the baskets before each family portrait along the gallery. He'd fought hard to keep the roses amid the vegetables, since the growing of food for the body in wartime was considered more important than food for the soul.

But despite his exhaustion, he felt a sense of anticipation for the dinner ahead. Lady Margaret and Alpharetta had both promised to wear the dresses. He was particularly anxious to see Alpharetta in the special one he had selected for her.

As if in answer to his thoughts, Alpharetta and Ben Mark paused in the doorway and then walked into the room. Sir Edward rose to greet them. At the same time Dow turned from the window.

She stood, framed in the doorway, the military uniform worn by Ben Mark St. John, providing an olive-drab background for the gossamer white, high-necked lace dress with its wide sleeves.

Anchored to his position at the window, Dow shook his head in anguish. The ghost of the titian-haired woman had invaded the drawing room in the form of Alpharetta Beaumont, the woman as unattainable as the one in the gallery. Promised to the man standing beside her, she stirred a primitive passion in Dow that he had never known he possessed.

For one part of him declared war even as he walked toward Ben Mark St. John and extended his right hand in greeting.

A delighted Sir Edward, unaware of the havoc he had played, said, "It's amazing, isn't it, how closely Alpharetta resembles the painting?"

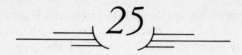

25

Dow took Alpharetta from the drawing room on a pretext of military importance, forcing Ben Mark to remain behind with Sir Edward.

Leading her upstairs toward the portrait gallery, Dow casually said, "I want to show you something, Alpharetta."

The painting had been restored, hung once more in its proper place. The woman in the lace dress, with pearls around her neck, gazed down from her gilt frame.

"Do you recognize yourself?" he inquired.

She looked up at the portrait and down at the dress she was wearing. "It's the same dress," she exclaimed.

"Yes. And your coloring, too, is almost the same."

"Who is she, Dow?"

"She was supposed to have been the most beautiful bride who ever came to Harrington Hall. But also the saddest."

"Why?"

"Even though it was an arranged marriage, it was also a love match. But when she arrived at Harrington Hall from France, she discovered the man she was to marry was dead—killed in a hunting accident. My great-grandfather was the second son who suddenly became the heir."

"And she married him instead?"

"Yes. Because it was already arranged between the families."

"And the green room was hers," Alpharetta stated.

"How did you know?"

"I can't explain it. There was a feeling in the room, as if I weren't alone." She looked at him and suddenly asked, "Why did Sir Edward ask me to wear her dress tonight?"

"We're a pagan lot, Alpharetta. We worship beauty, as well as godliness. And as is the case with many men, some Pomeroys never told their women how much they revered them in life.

"Perhaps it's an assuaging of a collective guilt—to set aside a day in the year to be reminded of them. It's been done every year for the past several hundred years. You'll hear the toasts at dinner tonight. And it's the custom to place baskets of roses before their portraits and at their gravestones. That's why my father was adamant about keeping a portion of his rose garden."

"The roses are beautiful."

Dow nodded in agreement. "Do you grow roses in Atlanta?"

"Yes. But our dogwoods and azaleas are the showstoppers." As she spoke, Alpharetta unconsciously rubbed her arm.

And Dow, seeing it, asked, "Alpharetta, how is your arm?"

"It's healing quite well, thank you."

"I'm glad. I suppose you know that Sir Nelson has given permission for you to come out of hiding?"

"Was that what you wanted to see me about?" Alpharetta was still, her green eyes drawn to Dow's face, and her heart remembering the kiss on the beach. Not like the kiss that she had shared with Ben Mark several hours earlier.

"Alpharetta." Dow took one step closer to her, his eyes tracing the shape of her mouth as he, too, remembered Lochendall.

Voices in the hall caused him to drop his arms to his sides and halt where he was.

"That must be Meg and her father," he said.

"Then we'd better go back downstairs," Alpharetta suggested, vaguely disturbed at their conversation.

"Yes, of course."

Lady Margaret was also in white. Alpharetta recognized the dress she was wearing, for it too was captured in the portrait gallery.

"Oh, there you are, Dow." Meg smiled and self-consciously ran her hand along the seam of her dress where the dressmaker had attempted to hide the fact the seams had been let out. But the dress, long stored, showed a difference in color where the seams had been disturbed.

"I see you have on Agatha's dress," Dow said.

"Yes. And I don't dare breathe," she admitted with a laugh.

As the six sat at the table that night with the scent of wax candles combining with the perfume of roses, there was a solemn formality broken only occasionally by conversation. A feeling of anticipation pervaded the dining hall where priceless goblets of the finest Venetian glass and porcelain plates with gold matched by the gold vermeil of tableware had been brought from storage for their annual use. The five-branched silver candelabra had been replaced with gold ones, in the shape of blackamoors holding torches high.

Alpharetta sat at the table like a small jewel, her dress of mellowed lace renewed in the glow of tapering flame, bringing to the heart of Dow Pomeroy a knowledge of the past, a renascence of his family history that had nothing to do with Lady Margaret Cranston, seated to his right.

Sir Edward cleared his throat and stood, holding a goblet of wine—deep red—and began the ages-old ritual, naming each chatelaine, from Madelaine, the first, to his own wife, Katerine.

As he lifted his glass, the others did the same. And when he had finished, Sir Edward set down his goblet. "In the old days," he explained with a twinkle in his eye, "the Pomeroys broke their glasses against the fireplace, after the toasts. But in modern days, we became more frugal."

He looked at Dow and said, "Are you ready, son?"

"Yes, Father."

Dow stood, while Andrew, nearby, brought the vermeil tray. On it were the heavy keys—to the wine cellar, to the food pantries and cupboards—all attached to a white satin waistcord.

"Alpharetta, would you please come and stand by me?"

Surprised, she stood and walked toward Dow, her eyes questioning his action.

"It is fitting for Alpharetta to be wearing the dress of Desirée Pomeroy. One hundred years ago, she came to this house as a bride. Chosen by the one she loved, she married another, yet her sorrow was kept to herself. Honor and duty clothed her well. As the heir, I offer you the symbol of our trust and devotion, Desirée Pomeroy, née Beaumont. Wear it in peace."

Dow took the satin rope with the keys and handed it to Alpharetta. And as Ben Mark frowned, his fiancée, her eyes unable to break their strong bond with Dow's eyes, slowly tied the rope around her waist.

Sir Edward then stood at the other end of the table and waited for Andrew to bring the second tray.

"Agatha Pomeroy, née Edmundton, will you please stand?"

Lady Margaret, on cue, with a self-conscious brushing back of her brown hair from her forehead, stood and walked toward him.

On the tray lay a jewelry case—ancient dubonnet velvet. Sir Edward opened it, removed a necklace of rubies and diamonds from it, and turned to Margaret. With hands tremulous with age, he placed the family jewels around Meg's neck and closed the clasp.

"Agatha, to you belongs the betrothal necklace, binding you forever to the house of Pomeroy. Wear it with grace, until that day when the ring upon your finger replaces it, as a matron replaces a maid."

Meg glanced quickly toward Dow. Unlike the chatelaine's keys that Alpharetta wore about her waist and would give up at the end of the evening, the necklace was Meg's, to seal her betrothal to Dow. Meg's face concealed her displeasure at Dow's lack of attention to the actions of his father. He was far too absorbed in the other woman at the end of the table.

Alpharetta was also unaware of Meg, for the impact of Dow's revelation had hit her hard—her own family name upon his lips—Beaumont, Desirée Beaumont.

Could it be that the same coloring, the same facial structure, like the Hapsburg chin, had been passed on by some common ancestor from generation to generation, branch to branch, until the blood could no longer acknowledge kin, except in the Beaumont name and the titian hair, evident in the portrait gallery and in her own mirror as well?

And was her close resemblance to this Desirée, of whom

she had no prior knowledge, the cause of Dow's first, hostile scrutiny on the train from Prestwick?

Whatever it was, Alpharetta felt a kinship to the woman whose dress she was wearing. But much more devastating, she felt the strong magnetic pull toward Dow Pomeroy.

After a final toast, Sir Edward suggested, "Shall we adjourn to the drawing room?"

Ben Mark, relieved that the ceremony was over, rose and claimed Alpharetta. If he'd had a choice, he knew exactly what he would do—remove the satin cord from Alpharetta's waist immediately. He had let his jealousy get the better of him as he watched Dow and Alpharetta together, even though Lady Margaret had been given the betrothal necklace. For Dow had acted as if he were binding Alpharetta to his side, instead of Lady Margaret. But that was ridiculous. Still there was something between them he couldn't quite put a finger on. He knew, for his own sake, that he should remove Alpharetta from Dow Pomeroy's influence, and the sooner the better.

Cornering Dow in the drawing room, Ben Mark scarcely disguised his impatience. "Sir Dow," he said, "I want to marry Alpharetta immediately and send her back to the States. She—"

"No, Ben Mark," Alpharetta interrupted, her voice strangely distant, as if his words had drawn her from another world. "We've already discussed it."

With Lady Margaret at his side, Dow glanced impersonally from Ben Mark to Alpharetta. In a low, cold voice, he replied, "I'm afraid your request is impossible, Captain. Miss Beaumont is still on my personal staff. I cannot give permission at the present time."

Ben Mark, forced to accede to a superior officer, clamped his jaw shut, but his dark eyes revealed his anger at the air vice-marshal's decision.

"Dow, aren't you being a little hard on them?" Meg inquired. "Couldn't you get someone else?"

"Meg, this is a military matter. I would appreciate your not becoming involved."

A strangeness pervaded the drawing room, as if the occupants were caught between two worlds. It destroyed all camaraderie, all attempts at casual conversation, despite Lord

Cranston, despite Sir Edward. And Alpharetta, under stress, began to feel the throbbing in her head.

"Dow, do you think I might leave now?" she inquired, being careful not to be overheard.

"That won't be necessary," he replied. "The green room is yours for the night."

"But I don't have—"

"I've sent Betty to the dower house to pack your overnight bag. She should be back in a few minutes."

"You didn't have to do that—"

"And we'll move the rest of your things into the hall tomorrow. It's no longer imperative for you to hide out. The spies have been shot."

The lateness of the hour had taken its toll on everyone in the drawing room. Lord Cranston rose from his chair in a lumbering manner, then steadied himself and called to his daughter in a bellowing voice.

"Margaret, my dear, it's time for us to be on our way."

Sir Edward also rose from his chair, the stiffness of his joints apparent in his slow, measured movements. Like two magnificent old stags far beyond their prime, they stood surveying the room with no fight left in them, merely a longing for peace and a comfortable bed.

Yet in the room, an unspoken challenge remained between the two younger men. On their arms were two women, one sensuously beautiful, the other pleasing to the eye until compared to the first. And the primitive display of warring antlers was but thinly disguised by the veneer of civilized society, as the two men in military uniform, with medals on their chests attesting to their prowess, silently braced for the primeval struggle for male supremacy, with one woman as the prize.

Once the good-byes had been said and Dow had walked to the door with Meg, Ben Mark, leaning toward Alpharetta, said, "If you're ready, too, I'll ride back to the dower house with you."

"That won't be necessary, Captain," Dow commented, returning to stand beside them. "Alpharetta is being moved into the hall."

Once again, Ben Mark felt thwarted. He looked at Alpharetta and again toward Dow. Alpharetta, seeing the transformation on his face, tensed.

"Let's go for a walk, Ben Mark. I feel the need of a little fresh air. Just let me say goodnight to Sir Edward."

"While you're at it, you can give him his keys, too," Ben Mark suggested.

In the garden, with its formal parterres bathed by the silver of the moon, Ben Mark made no pretense at hiding his anger. He dragged Alpharetta to a bench sheltered by vines, sat down, and fumed.

"You're not his property, Alpharetta. If you told him you were going, there's nothing he could do about it."

Stubbornly she replied, "I still have a job to do, Ben Mark."

"Horse manure! You're dazzled by the man, his title, and this manor house. If you stay around, you're going to be hurt. He's going to marry Lady Margaret, and you're going to wind up like Anna Clare. If you think someone like him is going to hitch himself for life to a moonshiner's daughter . . ."

"Is that how you see me, Ben Mark?" Alpharetta inquired, her voice a warning that Ben Mark had gone too far.

He quickly backed down. "I don't hold that against you, Alpharetta. After all, it was *my* father who loaned your father the money for the still."

"And became his partner," Alpharetta added.

Ignoring her comment, Ben Mark continued, "It's just that we understand each other. And I don't think you would fare well with all this British snobbishness around you."

Alpharetta smiled as she remembered the snobbishness of Atlanta, and the unhappiness of so many people when an anxiously awaited invitation was never received; when people left town to avoid having to admit that they had not been considered important enough to attend the annual azalea party given by one of society's leading matrons. Because of her guardian's prominence, she had been included. But she would gladly have given her place to another. Alpharetta had learned long ago that human worth was measured in inner qualities, not in whose garden one sat for a brief moment in history.

"I think we should go in now, Ben Mark." Alpharetta stood

and the dark-haired man beside her suddenly took her in his arms and began a slow, lingering kiss.

From the window above, Dow Pomeroy looked down into the garden at the merging figures and felt an unquenchable sadness.

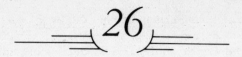

26

A troubled Alpharetta removed the lace dress, hung it in the armoire of the green room, and sat down before the ancient mirror. Her thoughts went far beyond her own reflection to a longing for something that had no visible face or form. It was a dream, binding her, like the satin cord around her waist earlier, to some unfathomed element in the English soil. And sensing this, she knew that her engagement to Ben Mark was a mistake. Yet she was powerless to do anything about it.

The day had turned out far differently than she had expected, and the headache that had threatened all evening blossomed as she knew it would. With no hope of resting peacefully, she climbed into the tester bed and stared at the ceiling, while praying for sleep to ease the stress of the day.

Marsh Wexford also stared at the ceiling, his massive headache undiminished by the cold, wet cloth upon his brow.

He was surprised to be alive, to be in a bed with a roof over his head, and to be wearing a white nightshirt instead of his uniform. The last thing he remembered was the explosion of the tank, the disintegration of the bridge.

At the sound of footsteps, Marsh cautiously listened. The old man, coming to replace the cloth on his forehead, was relieved to find Marsh awake. "You are feeling better, *non?*"

"I have a grandfather of a headache," he admitted.

"That is to be expected, landing as you did on the ground beyond the tanks. Lucky for you that the Germans thought you were dead."

"Where am I?" Marsh asked, feeling foolish at the mundane question.

"On the farm belonging to my sisters," he replied. "Le Bois Rouge."

"And your name?"

The old Frenchman was the one who hesitated this time. "I am called Maurice Duvalier, bellringer. That is sufficient."

"The others. What about the others with me?" Marsh asked, trying to prop himself up on one elbow.

"Two are safe elsewhere. The sergeant was taken prisoner. He awoke at an inopportune moment. There was nothing we could do."

Marsh groaned as he thought of Giraldo and lay his head on the pillow again.

The sound of a motorized vehicle pulling into the yard invoked a quick response from Maurice.

"Not a word, monsieur," he whispered. "It might be the German SS officer looking for you. Unfortunately we were seen spiriting you away."

Marsh lay still, his breathing noticeably loud in the silence of the small attic room, with its sharp-angled half-ceiling. If he were discovered, Marsh knew the old man and all his family would be shot for harboring him from the enemy.

A woman's voice from below carried upward through the small shaft, her indignant tones matching the harsh voice of the interrogator.

"Watch your words, old woman, or I'll set fire to you on top of the nearest haystack."

"I am too old to be another Joan of Arc," she protested, looking him straight in the eye. And in a sudden, coaxing voice, she added, "All I want you to do is stop scaring my poor little chou-chou." She picked up her dog and murmured comfortingly to him while the soldier laughed.

Then, catching himself, he scowled and warned in a stern voice, "If you see him, you are to report him to me at once. You know the penalty for not reporting."

"Of course, monsieur. We shall both be on the lookout for the American, won't we, chou-chou?"

The little dog yelped as if in answer. And the SS officer, without bothering to investigate further in the house of the two elderly sisters, climbed into the staff car and drove out of the farmyard. While Cecile held on to her dog and watched him disappear, her older sister, Jeannette, just inside the door, lowered the loaded gun and put it back in its proper place behind the flour cupboard.

Hearing the car leave, Marsh struggled to get up, but Maurice held out his hand to stop him. In a low whisper the old Frenchman said, "You must remain quiet for a little longer. The Germans always come back a second time, hoping to catch us unawares."

Freitag, true to Maurice's words, hid the staff car behind a haystack and stealthily approached the yard again on foot.

Maurice's grandson, Ibert, aged six years, was playing with his ball as the SS officer came into view. The German motioned for the child and Ibert, leaving his ball on the ground, walked toward him.

"Little boy, what is your name?" he inquired.

"Ibert," the dark-eyed child replied, looking curiously at the officer and waiting.

"I have a son about your age," the officer confessed. "And he loves chocolates. Do you like chocolates, too, Ibert?"

"*Oui, monsieur.*"

"Would you like one now?"

The child glanced cautiously toward the house where his great-aunt, Cecile, stood in the doorway, and then back to the officer, who now knelt by the boy and reached into his pocket.

He pulled out a chocolate wrapped in gold foil, similar to the Swiss ones Monsieur Simon had once sold in his store. Ibert's eyes grew wide as the German slowly unwrapped it, revealing the luscious milk chocolate in the shape of a wreath.

"This is yours if you promise to tell me the truth, Ibert. Will you?"

The little boy solemnly nodded.

"Have you seen a wounded American paratrooper?"

"*Oui.*"

Ibert reached out for the chocolate and the SS officer laughed at the greediness of the child. He broke off half the chocolate and gave to the boy, while he kept the other half.

Ibert, popping the small piece of candy into his mouth,

rolled his eyes like a connoisseur and announced, "*C'est merv-eilleux!*" Then he reached for the other half.

"Not so fast, Ibert. First, you must tell me *where* you saw the paratrooper."

"Why, hanging from the church steeple, monsieur. Everyone saw him, the night of the invasion . . ."

Freitag growled and snatched back the other half of the chocolate. He stood up and, looking down into the solemn face, he had a feeling that he had just been outmaneuvered by one small French boy.

Ibert shrugged as the man stalked to his car. The boy nonchalantly turned his back, retrieved his ball, and, childlike, began bouncing it as he counted, "*Un, deux, trois, quatre, cinq . . .*"

Upstairs, his grandfather, Maurice, listened for the sound of the engine the second time as the German drove out of the hay field, onto the road.

Finally, Marsh sat up on the side of the bed. His head swam and the room leaned out of perspective as if it had been designed by Van Gogh.

"You have the head-swimming?" Maurice inquired, watching him.

"Yes."

"It will go away in the next few days," the Frenchman assured him.

"I can't wait that long. I have go get back to my division immediately. Would you please bring me my uniform?"

"That would be suicide, Lieutenant. Remember, there is no bridge. You must wait for the armies to cross the river and reach you."

"But you're in danger. Your entire family. You could be shot for hiding me."

"You are not the first. I could have been shot anytime these past four years for my activities. A few more days won't make the difference."

Unable to sit up any longer, Marsh put his head on the pillow and closed his eyes.

"I will have Cecile bring you some soup and a little wine to settle your stomach."

Maurice left the hidden room, walked carefully down the steps, and stopped to listen every few treads. Then he proceeded cautiously to the opening adjacent to the cupboard in the kitchen. He tapped once; his signal was returned, and he stepped into the kitchen. Faded blue gingham lined the shuttered window, and ancient blue crockery hung from hooks in the ceiling beams.

"A little soup for our guest, Jeannette," he announced. "He is awake now."

Ibert, seated on the small stool next to the window, had just begun peeling potatoes. He looked up and inquired, "May I take it to him, Grandpapa? I wish to see the big American for myself."

Maurice smiled. "If you promise not to talk him to death, little one."

Jeannette also smiled and nodded in the boy's direction. "Ibert deserves a special treat. He didn't tell the German officer anything at all."

Unusually philosophical for one so small, Ibert shrugged his shoulders. "The chocolate was not worth being shot, Grandpapa. Perhaps if he had offered me a bicycle . . ."

Maurice's eyes twinkled as he reached out to tousle the child's hair. "You shall have your bicycle, Ibert. After the war. I promise you."

"A red one, Grandpapa?"

"*Oui*, Ibert. A red one."

Maurice's eyes misted as he looked at the little boy, so frail and yet so spirited. Ibert was the only one of his son's family to escape the massacre by the Germans. François, his wife Danielle, and their two older children, Siméon and Vachel, were lined up against the wall and shot with the rest of the village after the German soldier was killed. Only Ibert survived, because he had been asleep in the trundle bed beneath the larger bed.

Freitag drove back to the panzer division headquarters to report to Heinrich von Freiker. The road was clear of all fighting, for the Americans had disappeared three days earlier and the tanks were on hold. The fierce fighting along the beaches would spread inland soon, and once the American armies returned, Heinrich and his men would be ready for them.

Losing the Tiger tank was a blemish on Heinrich's record,

and he was determined to erase this blot at the earliest possible moment, before the news got back to Berlin. He had even given up his nightly allotment of spirits, which put Heinrich in a terrible mood. But his head was clear. He needed that to plan his retribution.

"In my opinion, the wounded Americans are clearly in the vicinity," Freitag announced. "And I have no doubt that the Duvalier sisters are involved, although I do not think they are hiding anyone in their house."

"I am not interested in your opinions, Freitag. I want proof. And I want the Americans caught."

Freitag's face turned a beet hue. He was a professional soldier, not used to the verbal abuse he had been forced to take ever since joining Heinrich's staff. "The American jeep is hidden under a haystack in their field."

At this information, Heinrich's bad temper abated. He smiled, not widely enough to show his teeth but enough for Freitag to feel some small measure of vindication.

"Do you wish me to confiscate it?"

"*Nein.* We will wait and see who comes for it. Put a guard detail around the farm, Freitag. At once."

"*Ja, mein Sturmbannführer.*"

The small boy sat quietly in the attic room as Marsh ate the soup. Ibert had promised not to bother the man with questions, although the American spoke French.

Finally, unable to stand the silence any longer, Ibert said, "I polished your boots, monsieur, while you were asleep. Grandpapa let me."

"Thank you, Ibert," Marsh replied, taking a bite of the freshly baked bread.

"Do all Americans have such big feet?"

Marsh put down the soup bowl for a moment. "Not all."

Coming into the room to check on the man, Maurice admonished his grandson, "Ibert, you must not bother our guest with your questions."

"That's all right. Back home I have a little sister, Maya, who's only a year or so older than Ibert. I'm used to questions."

He reached toward the bedside table to retrieve his good-luck charm—the Stone Mountain commemorative coin—to show Ibert. "See? This is the coin she gave me for good luck."

He allowed the curious Ibert to examine it. "Is it like my St. Christopher's medal?" the boy inquired. "Are these the American saints?"

"Not exactly. They were the brave men of the South."

"On their horses," Ibert added.

"Yes. And my little sister, like the other schoolchildren, bought a coin to help raise money to finish the carving on the mountain of rock. She gave hers to me to carry on each parachute jump."

"I should like to see this mountain of stone," Ibert said solemnly, returning the coin to Marsh.

"Perhaps someday you will."

"Come, Ibert. It's time to go downstairs again."

"Do I have to, Grandpapa?"

"Yes, little one. The lieutenant must rest to get his strength back."

Maurice turned to Marsh. "If you need anything during the night, tap twice on the floor. My room is directly below."

For two days, Marsh remained in the attic room. The combination of rest and food provided a healing balm for his bruised body. But his mind was troubled over the three men who had been with him—Giraldo, now a prisoner of war, if they hadn't shot him, and Gig and Laroche, hidden in another farmhouse somewhere.

The guard detail stationed to watch the farm had little to do, for there were no comings and goings, except for the two elderly women, one old man walking to the barn each evening to attend to chores, and the small boy who played in the yard and fed the few remaining chickens.

On the third day, Marsh, impatient to leave, counted the hours until nightfall, for he had decided to take the jeep and ride toward the sound of guns as soon as it got dark. His pistol was his only weapon, and he had little ammunition for it.

"I wish you would wait another day," Maurice said, bringing him the fresh uniform that Jeannette had washed and ironed.

"I can't, Maurice. I'm a soldier."

"But one with a big headache," Maurice replied.

"The headache and dizziness are almost gone," he assured him. "No, I must go. Each day I stay puts you in graver danger."

At panzer headquarters, Heinrich received the word. The Americans had broken through and von Runstedt had ordered him to pull out immediately to avoid being caught in the pocket. An ill-tempered Heinrich called Freitag into his presence.

"We're pulling out, Freitag. In one hour. The Americans are sweeping around our flank. We cannot wait for the French at Le Bois Rouge to show their hand. They must be dealt with at once. You understand, Freitag?"

The German hesitated.

"Kill them, Freitag. I don't want a single one left living. That's an order."

"The boy, too, *mein Sturmbahnführer?*"

"Everyone—the old man, the women, the child, the animals. Set fire to the haystacks, the house itself. Take a squad with you and leave immediately."

As the haystacks caught the warm glow of the setting sun, the smell of potato soup permeated the kitchen, the aroma causing Ibert to drop his ball and begin to walk toward the farmhouse.

Suddenly, one of the haystacks in the field became a torch, lighting up the countryside. Maurice, coming out of the barn, looked toward the setting sun and saw the fire.

"Run, Ibert, into the house," he shouted.

Cecile, standing in the doorway with her small dog in her arms, was powerless to stop the nightmare. She saw the explosion as the jeep, hidden in the haystack, disintegrated. German soldiers appeared with their machine guns spraying the farmyard as they ran, bringing down Maurice. And Jeannette, pulling the rifle from its hiding place behind the flour cupboard in the kitchen, gave a cry as she saw Cecile slump to the ground beyond the open doorway.

Marsh, pulling on his combat boots upstairs, heard the sudden fire of machine guns, and he knew that what he had feared might happen had come true.

He rushed down the stairs with his pistol in his hand. Too

late. Jeannette, the indomitable old white-haired French-woman, lay just inside the door, red blood rushing to meet her pale brown hands, still powdered with the flour of freshly kneaded dough.

Marsh kicked the kitchen door closed and barricaded it. Then, taking the rifle, he broke the windowpane and crouched below the wooden sash. The barn began to burn and the russet-colored chickens squawked in terror, as if a fox had suddenly invaded the farmyard. Marsh's rifle shot brought down one German soldier as he hurled a lighted torch toward the house.

One weapon, one man defended the farmhouse from the enemy, until the sound of vehicles arriving and the noise of other guns drove the Germans from the conflagration they had started on the farm called Le Bois Rouge. But they were quickly apprehended and taken prisoner—the six who still remained alive.

"'Allo!" a voice called out from the yard. And Marsh, inside, responded in English, for the uniforms of the soldiers were American issue.

As some of the soldiers struggled to put out the fire in the barn, Marsh removed the barricade from the kitchen door. In the glow of burning haystacks, he walked slowly, cautiously, into the yard toward the Americans.

Maurice, the bellringer, a member of the French Underground for four years, lay where he had been hit. Marsh, realizing the old man was dead, could no longer see clearly for the tears in his eyes.

"The bastards! The damned bastards!" he said. For a moment he knelt beside the Frenchman. Then he rose and walked slowly toward Cecile and her toy poodle, both caught in the machine-gun crossfire of the enemy.

He felt a hand on his shoulder and a voice in his ear as one of the officers said, "Come, Lieutenant, and climb into the truck. There's nothing more you can do for them."

But Marsh, realizing Ibert was nowhere in sight, began calling, "Ibert! Where are you, Ibert?"

There was no sign of him in the yard. Shouting the little boy's name, Marsh rushed back into the house.

A slight whimper behind the flour cupboard was the only

sound. Marsh followed the droplets of blood upon the floor until he came to the small boy crouching behind the cupboard, while the aroma of potato soup floated through the kitchen with its faded gingham curtains and its crockery moving slightly from the vibration of the guns.

"Ibert!"

Marsh leaned over and picked up the child with the slightly injured leg, and held him close.

"Grandpapa!" Ibert cried. "Grandpapa is dead."

"Yes, Ibert. Grandpapa is dead. They're all dead."

"But he promised me a red bicycle. After the war," he sobbed.

Marsh cradled the child in his arms as he had cradled his little sister, Maya, when she had hurt her knee. "You shall have your bicycle, Ibert. I'll buy you one. That I swear."

The little boy looked up into Marsh's face. "You won't come back," he said.

"I promise, Ibert. I'll find you and bring the bicycle to you."

"You swear—by your American saints?"

Marsh reached into his pocket for his good-luck piece. "By my American saints. And I want you to keep this as a pledge."

Marsh took the commemorative coin showing the images of Lee, Jackson, and Davis carved on the mountain, and placed it in the little boy's hand.

"I'll find you, Ibert. Wherever you are. Now, let's go and locate a medic to bandage your leg."

A sober Marsh Wexford walked slowly out of the farm kitchen with Ibert Duvalier, small victim of war, in his arms.

27

*B*y July, as Marsh returned to Leicester to begin training for another invasion, George S. Patton, Jr., the general most feared by the Germans, was allowed to cross the channel.

As he set foot in Normandy with his Third Army, the first command given to him since the Mediterranean invasion, he stood upon the heights and sensed the destiny that friend and foe alike were determined to wrest from him.

While Heinrich von Freiker threw his tanks into battle with a vengeance, Patton was not allowed the same privilege, for Bradley, in charge of the 12th U.S. Army Group, still took orders from Montgomery, in command of land armies.

And so, for Patton, waiting for battle on the whim of his greatest rival, the man he had beaten to Messina on the island of Sicily, the month of July went slowly. It took him only a few steps closer to his destiny, while Montgomery remained bogged down at Falaise.

July was not the best month for Adolph Hitler either, for a group of his own military men had conspired to murder him in his bunker fortress.

In Berlin, Heinrich's father, General Emil von Freiker, walked along the *Strasse* with his old friend, Wilhelm von Sydow. A bloodbath had begun, marking Hitler's retribution against anyone who might have been remotely connected to the conspiracy, including thousands of innocent relatives.

"The fools! They should never have tried to kill the Führer," Emil said, his voice betraying his emotions.

"But the man is mad, Emil. You know that."

"The *world* is mad, Wilhelm. Why should he be any different?"

"Von Kluge has chosen to take poison. The Führer gave him a choice of that—or being shot. One of the most decorated German generals—forced to end his life in such an ignoble way. That is the tragedy. And I hear that he suspects Rommel, as well."

Emil nodded. The two men, approaching the symphony hall, became silent. For one more evening, music, the gentle soother of savage thoughts, would again erase the horrors of war.

Emil walked to his regular seat, followed by von Sydow. The general frowned as he read the program. The work of von Hammer, not his favorite, was to be performed that night. The *Kindertotenlieder*, sung by Frau Emma. For Emil, there was only one song cycle by that name—the one composed by Mahler. But Mahler was a Jew, his works banned by the Third Reich.

Von Sydow, also taking note of the program, pointed to Emma's name and whispered to his friend, "She is on the list of five thousand, Emil. Her daughter, too. Her husband was a distant cousin of General Max Bucher."

Emil stared at Wilhelm in disbelief. "She had nothing to do with—"

"I know. A pity. But if there's any consolation, it will be several months before she is picked up. Her name is toward the end, and few people have access to the entire list."

Seeing the expression on Emil's face, von Sydow apologized. "I'm sorry, Emil. I fear I have spoiled your evening with such news."

Emil sat, frozen to his seat, listening to von Hammer's *Songs on the Deaths of Children*, sung by the great voice of Frau Emma von Erhard, unknowingly lamenting the death of her own daughter, Gretchen.

And the old general grieved for his lost son—the one he had abandoned at St. Mihiel in another war—the child that, feature for feature, was his own image. The regret washed over him in the tragic tones sung by Frau Emma and, as he sat, caught up in the sadness of the words, Emil began to question such fatalism. What if the woman were warned? Did she have anyplace to hide from the Gestapo? Was it possible that he might find some way to tell her, without becoming involved himself?

That thought was his only consolation as he listened to the music. At the same time, Hitler, recuperating from the slight injuries sustained in his bunker fortress, was consoled by the knowledge that his Vengeance rockets, the A-4s, were nearly ready to begin their deadly journey from their launching sites in Holland to wipe out every inch of English soil, and were even aimed toward New York, the premier city of the Americas. Soon, all of his enemies would be annihilated.

Belline Wexford, struggling with her old enemy, the jealousy that encompassed her whenever she thought of Alpharetta Beaumont, listened to music of a different type.

Her USO unit had finally moved out of London, into country to the north, where Ben Mark's bomber squadron was stationed. The USO was taking over an old storefront, furnishing it with chairs, tables, a fountain; and Belline, in her coveralls, with a kerchief to protect her head from the dust, finished cleaning the countertop, to the rhythm of the jitterbug tune coming from the record player in the corner.

She had not minded coming ahead of the others to get the place in shape before its opening, for it would give her some time with Ben Mark.

The news that Ben Mark had reconciled his differences with Alpharetta and was again engaged to her, had not sat well with Belline, just as the idea of Alpharetta's visit that weekend was not something she looked forward to, even though Marsh was bringing her.

Her stepbrother Marsh was lucky to be alive after Normandy. And for that Belline was grateful. She gave an extra hard swish of the cloth on the counter top as she thought of how near Alpharetta had come to disaster—and survived.

But after tonight, she would once again have Ben Mark to herself, for Alpharetta wouldn't want him after hearing the news.

Alpharetta sat beside Marsh in the borrowed jeep and engaged in quiet conversation as Marsh drove on the left side of the road. As the navigator, she held the map that Dow had marked for her. Even then, she was unsure that they had made the correct turn, for the highway signs, taken down at the beginning of the war, were still nonexistent.

The fighting in Normandy had left its mark on Marsh. Not just in his medal for bravery and his promotion to captain, but in a subtler way. He was reticent about that invasion and the upcoming one, and Alpharetta did not press him.

"I'm surprised you two got back together so quickly, Alpharetta," Marsh said.

"So am I, Marsh. But Ben Mark had a letter from Rennie. I guess Anna Clare talked with her. It's a little disconcerting, isn't it, when the whole world knows your secrets?"

Marsh laughed. "It's difficult to keep things from one's own family, Alpharetta." He then reached out and touched her hand. "I'm sorry about Conyer and Duluth. I didn't know until Steppie wrote me last week."

"It's easier for me now, Marsh. At first, I was so angry with the sea, but somehow, I feel closer to them when I look at the water."

Marsh slowed the jeep at the crossroads and Alpharetta, looking at the map, announced, "I think we'd better stop to ask for directions. And maybe we can find someone serving tea. I've sort of gotten used to it since being assigned to Sir Dow's staff."

"Another Anglophile," Marsh teased, shaking his head. "Just like General Eisenhower." Then his face grew serious. "I guess you've heard what a lot of American units have called him."

"What?"

"The best general the *British* ever had."

"He's still giving priority to Montgomery?"

"Yes. The 82nd has already been assigned to him, as well as the bulk of supplies. And the 101st has been given to him too, for the next invasion."

"Dow said the British don't have any more troops, Marsh. Even in reserve. They lost so many before we got into the war."

"That's true. Most of the Allied Army is made up of Americans."

Marsh stopped the jeep, parking it in the town square sit-

232 · *Frances Patton Statham*

uated at the top of the hill. The two got out, stretched, and began walking down the narrow cobbled street in the direction of the wooden sign advertising the Wayside Pub and Tearoom.

"It's too bad that Ben Mark couldn't have the entire weekend free," Marsh said.

"I'm grateful he could even have a day off, on such short notice."

"Belline and I will make ourselves scarce tomorrow. . . ."

"There's no need for that. It will be like old times—the four of us together."

"But Belline spoiled it for you the last time the four of us were together."

"That was in London, when I hadn't seen Ben Mark for all those months. No, Marsh. We understand each other now. Everything will be all right."

They entered the wood and wattle shop where summer flowers bloomed in window boxes, where a plump young woman in white apron and cap showed them to a corner nook with an old love seat. The table was covered by a faded red cloth, and on top of that was a smaller cloth—a white square embroidered with lace on the corners, with matching napkins.

"Tea? For both of you?" the young woman inquired, watching Marsh fold his tall frame into the space behind the table.

"Yes, please," Alpharetta answered, "and a little something to eat. Sandwiches? Scones?"

"My mum is just taking some shortbread out of the oven. And I can fix you some cucumber sandwiches."

Alpharetta smiled and nodded. As soon as the girl left, Marsh said with a teasing voice, "It's a good thing I brought some additional food with me. I'd starve otherwise."

"But you wouldn't dare open a can of Spam in front of the waitress, would you, Marsh?"

"Who said anything about Spam? I brought some sockeye salmon, some cheese, crackers. . . ."

Marsh stopped suddenly, for D-Day loomed in his memory—with Gig, Laroche, and Giraldo. Giraldo, now a prisoner, perhaps hungry that very moment. And little Ibert, losing everyone he loved . . .

Alpharetta, seeing the pain cloud Marsh's brow, said quietly, "It hurts—to remember too much, Marsh."

He looked in surprise at the perceptive Alpharetta. "Yes, it hurts," he admitted, realizing that only another with the same pain could understand so well.

The others in the tearoom were politely distant to the American paratrooper and the woman in uniform. All over England, the same scene was being re-enacted. Almost no village was exempt from the sight of American soldiers with their wives and sweethearts. For the Americans, if resentful of the favoritism Eisenhower showed the British, also showed their favoritism for skin as fair as the rose and the special patriotism that mobilized them all, even to the princesses in the palace, who could fix the motor in a car as easily as any mechanic in a garage. Yet to the close observer, there was a telltale sign indicating that the woman with Marsh, despite her uniform, was not British. For she held her silverware in the American way.

Soon the two were back on the road again, the man at the petrol station reaffirming that they were headed in the right direction. And Alpharetta was grateful for the information, which was the only thing that the man could offer, having no fuel to sell. But it didn't matter. Marsh had brought extra cans of gasoline as well as extra tins of food.

Within the next hour, the movement of planes overhead indicated that they had almost reached their destination.

"Belline said to look for a storefront with a small sign on the door," Marsh announced as they crossed a small bridge on the outskirts of town. "The canteen is so new they haven't put up the large sign on the building."

White, rolling clouds filled the sky and a distant rumble of thunder answered the roar of the planes, the sounds almost indistinguishable from one another.

"I hope that's not an omen of what the weather's going to be like this weekend," Alpharetta murmured, glancing toward the sky. "It seems it's rained almost every day for the past week."

"You brought your mackintosh with you, didn't you, just in case?"

Alpharetta laughed. "I brought my *raincoat*, Marsh, if that's what you mean. Sir Dow is the one with the mackintosh."

Marsh grinned. "Thought you might have become British through and through," he teased. "I watched you back there,

Alpharetta, in the tearoom. You could have been pouring tea all your life, it looked so natural."

"Stop teasing me, Marsh, and help me look for the USO sign. Did Belline say which side of the street it was on?"

"The left."

"There it is," Alpharetta said. "Or rather, there it was," she added, for they were passing the building just as she spied the sign.

Marsh swung the jeep around, making a U-turn in the middle of the street, causing a woman on a bicycle to glare at him.

"Sorry," he yelled. The woman smiled and started off again, as Marsh came to a stop at the curbing before the storefront.

Alpharetta removed her hands from in front of her eyes. Breathing a sigh of relief, she laughed, "You've started driving exactly like Ben Mark," she accused.

"Just be glad you're not riding in a Tiger tank."

"I heard about that caper, Marsh. Is that why you and your men got the medals—for stealing the tank?"

Her question went unanswered, for at that moment, the door to the canteen swung open and Belline, still dressed in the dirty coveralls, with the kerchief about her hair, came out to greet them.

"Welcome to Paradise Lost," she exclaimed.

"Belline!" The smile on Alpharetta's lips vanished, for in front of her stood a vastly changed Belline—thin, with large, dark smudges under her eyes.

Marsh, also noticing the drastic change in his stepsister, asked, "Have you been ill, Belline?"

"Why, no, I'm fine," she assured him, her voice sounding brave and slightly tremulous. "Come on in, you two. I've been expecting you for the past hour."

28

In Belline's small walk-up apartment over the canteen, Alpharetta sat on the bed as she threaded the needle to repair the hem of her uniform. All evening she had tried not to say anything about the change in Belline's appearance. But after Marsh, who also noticed Belline's lethargy and lack of appetite, had brought them back from dinner at the local pub and driven on to the base where he was to bunk for the night, Alpharetta could no longer keep silent.

"All right, Belline. Now that we're alone, will you please tell me what's wrong?"

For a moment Belline glared at Alpharetta without saying anything. Then she replied, "If you really want to know, Alpharetta, I'm pregnant."

"Oh, Belline, no."

"Well, it's not as if I wanted it to happen."

"I know, Belline. It's just that . . ." Alpharetta stopped and started again. "Is the—the father willing to marry you?"

"I haven't told him yet."

"You'll have to tell him, Belline. Immediately. That is, if . . . I presume he's a soldier?"

"He's an airman, stationed here in England."

"Do you love him?"

Belline nodded.

"And he must love you, too. Otherwise . . ." Alpharetta's voice trailed into a mere whisper.

"He's engaged—to someone else."

Alpharetta turned abruptly, a wariness possessing her. The

two red-haired women stared at each other, and Alpharetta sensed the answer before she asked the question.

"Is it . . . Ben Mark?"

Again Belline nodded. "I didn't mean for it to happen, Alpharetta. You had broken your engagement to him, and seeing you for the first time after that in London—with Marsh—he misunderstood, Alpharetta. And *I* misunderstood. I thought he had finally gotten over you—and that he loved me, the way he used to when we were children. I didn't know the two of you would ever get back together."

"I don't suppose he ever loved me as much as he loved you, Belline," Alpharetta soberly responded. "Maybe that was the real reason for my breaking our engagement in the first place. But Belline, you know I won't stand in your way—especially now."

"Well, whatever you do, don't tell Marsh. I don't want him to know yet."

"Of course. I'll keep your secret." Alpharetta busied herself hanging her uniform on the door and smoothing its creases. Without looking at Belline, she said, "When I see Ben Mark tomorrow, I'll talk with him. That will make it easier for you." Then, walking slowly back to the bed, she continued, "And I'll inform Marsh on the way back that Ben Mark and I decided we weren't suited for each other, after all. So when you two get married, it won't be such a surprise."

"Thank you, Alpharetta. I won't ever forget this. You can't imagine the burden I've been carrying, ever since I found out—about the baby. But what if Ben Mark refuses to marry me?"

"He won't, Belline. I'll see to that."

When the light had been cut out, a satisfied Belline lay quietly in the dark, thinking. It had been much more effective to announce the baby than to merely confess that she and Ben Mark had spent the night together in London. Alpharetta probably would not have believed that of him. But with the baby—even Ben Mark would have to accept it as the truth.

Alpharetta, also lying in the darkness, gave up trying to sleep. Multiple images bombarded her—her life in fragments in no particular order—the times with Ben Mark at the airfield, the dinner at Rennie's when she had just gone to live with Reed and Anna Clare, the day at the stadium when she'd gone with Ben Mark to see the President of the United States. She waited for sadness to overwhelm her, but surprisingly, her eyes were dry, her only sadness was for Belline—and for Ben Mark.

She didn't look forward to the next day and the embarrassing confrontation with her fiancé, or to being questioned by Dow upon her return. Turning over on her side, Alpharetta decided that, except for informing Marsh, she would keep the breaking of her engagement to herself. There was no need for Sir Dow Pomeroy to know.

All night, Alpharetta was conscious of the bombers. And by early morning, long before it was time to get up, she heard the steady downpour of rain.

Unable to stay in bed any longer, she finally got up and tiptoed to the window, where she peered out at the deserted street.

From the twin bed next to hers, Belline said, "Do you mind heating your own tea, Alpharetta? I've stopped eating breakfast."

"I don't mind, Belline." Then, remembering their conversation the evening before, a solicitous Alpharetta said, "Let me fix you a cup, too."

"No. I think I'll just stay in bed this morning, and go back to sleep."

Alpharetta didn't argue. Wrapping her robe around her, she found the small cupboard and the teakettle, and within a few minutes, sat down in the makeshift kitchenette—a small cubicle beyond the bathroom—to eat her breakfast of tea, toast and jam. Outside, the rain continued, riverlets streaming along the small windowpane where light struggled to come inside. Wasting no time, she finished eating, washed her cup and plate and hurried to the bathroom to draw her bath.

The plumbing was ancient and rattled as she turned on the water in the claw-footed tub, with its porcelain slightly chipped along the edges. Her white towel hung on the coiled pipe that once warmed the bath towels for the storekeeper's comfort, but had long since been disconnected. And above the lavatory a utilitarian mirror hung, too high up for Alpharetta to see herself as she brushed her teeth.

Regardless of her accommodations, Alpharetta felt lucky to have a place to sleep for the weekend. By Tuesday of the next week, when the canteen opened formally, the other USO women would arrive, filling all the bunks in the two small bedrooms upstairs.

Alpharetta finished her bath, dressed in her uniform, and as she stood on tiptoe trying to see into the mirror to brush her hair, she heard the insistent knocking on the door downstairs. That could mean only one thing—Ben Mark and Marsh had arrived.

Walking into the bedroom, she looked toward Belline, who sat up and yawned. "What time shall we come back for you, Belline?"

"By lunchtime," she answered.

Alpharetta rushed down the steps and opened the door to Ben Mark, standing with a large black umbrella sheltering him from the driving rain.

"Well, it's about time," he said and dashed into the building, shedding the rain from his trench coat. Ben Mark grinned as Alpharetta stepped back to avoid getting her own uniform wet. But in a teasing mood, he reached out, lifted her in the air, and gave her a resounding kiss.

For an instant, Alpharetta forgot everything that had plagued her through the long night—the conversation with Belline, the responsibility that rested so heavily upon her. Ben Mark had always been able to do that to her—to make her forget everything but the pleasure of seeing him, of being with him again.

"Put me down, Ben Mark," she scolded as she laughed. "My uniform is wet, and it's all your fault."

"What do you expect, when you open the door to a drenched airman?"

The door, still ajar, blew wide open with a gust of wind. Alpharetta looked outside, and, not seeing Marsh, inquired, "Didn't Marsh come with you?"

"He dropped me off first. He'll come back in a half hour." Ben Mark, making himself at home, took off his trench coat, hung it over a chair, and said, "You think the canteen can afford a cup of coffee for an officer?"

"I'll see. I'm not sure the supplies have come yet.

Belline . . . " Alpharetta suddenly stopped, remembering the woman upstairs in bed.

"Where *is* Belline, by the way?"

"Upstairs. She'll be down a little later."

"She never was one for getting up early."

Unusually quiet, Alpharetta walked behind the counter and began to search for a coffee can and the urn that was a standard item in all canteens. But once she had located the box in which the urn rested, she said, "I don't think you'll be able to drink thirty cups, Ben Mark. Maybe I'd better go upstairs for the small tea kettle instead. You don't mind instant coffee this one time do you?"

"All of it tastes about the same—pretty awful. Just so it's hot."

While Ben Mark sat at one of the tables and looked out the window at the rain, Alpharetta went upstairs to the small apartment. And as she passed through the bedroom, Belline lifted her head, and asked, "Have you talked with him yet?"

"No. I haven't had a chance. He wants a cup of coffee, Belline. Is it all right if I take the kettle downstairs to heat some water?"

"Sure, I told you I won't be using it."

A few minutes later, Alpharetta sat opposite Ben Mark and watched as he sipped the hot liquid. "Aren't you going to have a cup with me?"

"No. I've already had breakfast." She continued to watch him. After hesitating, she finally said, "Ben Mark, there's something I need to discuss with you."

"And it must be serious, judging from your frown. What have I done wrong, Alpharetta?" he teased. "Not told you how beautiful you are this morning?"

"I wish it were as simple as that. I—I'm afraid it's much more serious. It's about—Belline."

Warily, he set down his cup. His eyes became guarded as he waited for Alpharetta to continue.

"Belline is going to have your baby, Ben Mark."

Underscored by the rain against the storefront, the silence grew as an incredulous Ben Mark stared at the woman he was engaged to marry.

"That's impossible," he said, his voice barely audible over the downpour outside.

"Is it, Ben Mark?"

A dark scowl, so familiar, marred his features. "What has Belline been telling you, Alpharetta?"

"That . . . that the two of you spent the weekend together in London. Do you deny it, Ben Mark? There's no need to do so. And I don't hold it against you. It happened, I know, before you and I got back together. Oh, Ben Mark, don't you see—this is so hard for all of us. Belline is upstairs, suffering from morning sickness. And she's too embarrassed to tell you."

"I don't believe it. She's doing this to tear us apart, just as she did in London—to try to keep us from getting married. I should have married you immediately when I found you, instead of deferring to that Sir Dow Pomeroy."

"It wouldn't have worked, Ben Mark—with this between us."

"Well, I'm certainly not going to marry Belline. And you can tell her that."

"You'll have to, for the sake of the child. I'm releasing you, Ben Mark, from our agreement. But one thing you must promise me. Let me tell Marsh that we've broken our engagement, without revealing the real reason. We'll pretend to have had a fuss."

Ben Mark stood up and slowly put on his trench coat. "We won't have to pretend, Alpharetta. I'm leaving right now. You can tell Marsh anything you want to. I don't care."

"Aren't you going to wait and see Belline?"

"No. I'm hitching a ride back to base." He picked up the black umbrella in the corner and stalked out into the driving rain.

"Will we see you later?" Alpharetta asked from the doorway.

There was no answer. Ben Mark continued walking down the street, his back rigid, his steps angry as he sloshed through the puddles and crossed the street to the corner, until he was out of sight.

An unhappy Alpharetta walked back to the table and sat fingering the empty cup that Ben Mark had held. She had made a mess of the entire situation, even though she'd spent half the night rehearsing what she was going to say. But no amount of rehearsal had prepared her for the actuality.

Putting off telling Belline, Alpharetta remained downstairs. As Marsh swept into the canteen, he waited for his eyes to become adjusted to the dim light. Seeing Alpharetta alone, he asked, "Where's Ben Mark?"

"Good morning, Marsh. Did you get soaked, too?"

Without answering, Marsh repeated his question, "Alpharetta, where's Ben Mark?"

The red-haired woman stood. "He's already gone back to the base."

"But I dropped him off here less than a half hour ago. What happened, Alpharetta?"

"I'm afraid we've had an awful fuss."

"You haven't even had time to greet each other properly, much less engage in a spat."

"Oh, yes we have. I'm afraid it's over, Marsh. I can't possibly marry Ben Mark. I should have known it before now."

Walking to the table, Marsh pulled out a chair and sat, leaning his elbows on the rungs. "Do you want to talk about it, Alpharetta? Or do you want me to go find him and bring him back?"

She shook her head. "No, to both questions, Marsh. It would never work."

Peering closely at her, Marsh demanded, "Did Belline have anything to do with the breakup this time?"

"No. This was just between Ben Mark and me. No one else was involved." She looked up from the floor and said, "Marsh, do you think we might leave by this afternoon, instead of waiting until tomorrow?"

"You won't mind riding in the rain? You'll get awfully wet."

"Even that's preferable to remaining here another day."

"You don't think Ben Mark will change his mind and come back to make up with you?"

"It's too late for that, Marsh. Entirely too late."

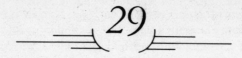

29

*I*t was also too late for Heinrich von Freiker to do anything about the Americans overrunning his position. Wheeling the great tanks of his panzer division, he barely escaped to a negligible safety.

The quick dispersal of tanks was always a dead giveaway, indicating the Germans were abandoning an area. Now, with the tanks gone, the German infantry was in a last-ditch defense prior to retreating, for the U.S. Third Army had broken through.

By August 1, the thong holding him to earth was finally released from Patton, the war hawk. He was now free to begin the great flight of his armored tanks, sweeping in winglike motion across the difficult terrain of Normandy. He knew intimately the corduroy roads that William the Conqueror had taken—the only roads on which his tanks could travel without getting bogged down. And in his pocket, he carried his plans for crossing the Rhine, pinpointing the same spot Napoleon had chosen—Oppenheim.

Farther north, the more cautious Montgomery hammered away at the stiff resistance that his Canadian and British armies encountered around Caen and Falaise. But by the end of August, as the U.S. Third Army reached the Seine, one hundred miles ahead of any other army, the Canadian First Army finally sealed off the gap at Falaise. But the Germans had slipped an entire army through the gap, 35,000 who lived to fight another day.

Now, making up for the time lost, the British Second Army swept through Brussels, and by September 4 entered Antwerp, the prize that the Germans had struggled to keep, knowing that the Allies desperately needed a supply port closer to the front. The seven-hundred-mile round trip over the terrain of Normandy from the initial beaches wasted valuable time in supplying the vast armies, north and south, on two fronts at once.

But Montgomery became cautious once more, refusing to move his army until his supplies had been replenished. And in stopping, he allowed German control of the fifty-four-mile Antwerp estuary to continue, making the inland port and its facilities useless to the Allies. And once again, the fight for supplies between the two Allied armies accelerated.

No one in London at SHAEF headquarters had expected the U.S Third Army to make such a spectacular breakout, and so the army had outrun its lines of supply. The tanks and the trucks desperately needed gasoline. Ammunition, food, medicine—all were in short supply. Even then, two of the Third Army's divisions had established a bridgehead over the Meuse at Verdun. And the Germans, who considered Patton their most formidable enemy, were alarmed by the exploits of his army.

Montgomery was not only aware of Patton's advances, but of the first V-2 rockets devastating London from a base in Holland. And on September 10, he flew to Brussels to meet Eisenhower, the Supreme Commander—to present a daring plan to hasten the end of the war.

Montgomery brought with him his own administrative and supply officer, but demanded that the Supreme Allied Commander not be given the same consideration. And Eisenhower, who had so admired the British, if not Monty himself, concurred with Monty's request and came alone, without his own staff advisor. In that meeting, Eisenhower gave him what he wanted—priority over Patton in men and supplies.

On that day, with the freeing of the Antwerp estuary forgotten, with van Zangen's army allowed to escape through the estuary, as the panzer divisions had done across the strait in Sicily, Operation Market-Garden was born—the invasion of Holland and the securing of five bridgeheads around Arnhem. Montgomery was given the First Allied Airborne Army, with two American parachute divisions, first priority on all supplies, and the trucks from the First and Third Armies to carry those supplies.

In that action, Eisenhower effectively stopped Patton in his armored-division tracks—a feat that the Germans had been unable to bring off.

Captain Marsh Wexford, back in his old barracks in England with Gig and Laroche, began training for the first daylight drop in the 82nd Airborne's history, this time under a British commander. And the objective assigned to their group was the area between Nijmegen and Grave, south of Arnhem.

Unlike the invasions of Sicily and Normandy, which had taken months of planning, Operation Market-Garden was due to take off in days, the largest air drop that had ever been assembled, with planes and gliders from twenty-four different airfields.

The commander of the British Second Army, General Dempsey, was not enthusiastic about Market-Garden. His intelligence staff had received disturbing reports from the Dutch Resistance of a massive buildup of German troops around Arnhem. But this intelligence information was completely disregarded at the headquarters of the 21st Army Group.

A week previously, the fleeing German troops had swept through Holland on every available vehicle—confiscated bicycles, carts, and anything else with wheels.

The news was out. The Allied armies were coming. And the Nazis, civilian collaborators as well as the German soldiers, began a frenzied trek for the German border.

Remnants of divisions, armies without their equipment, tanks, men dazed from battle and uncertain of the route to the border—all clogged the roadways and passed through the towns, fear written on their faces, and dust scattered over their uniforms to hide the skull and crossbones of the SS troops, the black suits of the tank brigades. No one appeared to lead them. They went, without direction, like lemmings rushing toward disaster.

The Dutch, thinking the war would be over in a few days, celebrated their liberation by bringing out their orange armbands. They climbed to the roofs of their houses to watch and jeer the rabble passing by. And they waited with flowers to greet the Allied troops they were certain were directly behind.

One day passed, then two. Soon they realized the war was not over: their freedom was not yet secured. For the seventy-year-old Field Marshal von Runstedt, wily and battle-scarred, stopped the rout, took the rabble of soldiers from van Zangen's army and began to regroup them into fighting units. And Bittrich, in charge of the battered, tankless II SS Panzer Corps, did the same, bringing the elite corps to an area near Arnhem for reorganizing. And in that triangle of Arnhem, Nijmegen, and Oosterbeek, they shaped them into proud-once-more units of the Third Reich.

On September 15, two days before Operation Market-Garden, SS officer Heinrich von Freiker drove to the De Groot Hotel in Berg-en-Dal, not far from Nijmegen. Horst, his aide, was at his side.

Seeing his commander glance impatiently at his watch, Horst said, "The hotel is only a few more kilometers, my Colonel."

"Good. I'm getting hungry. And I have no wish to eat these dried-up sandwiches packed this morning."

"If the hotel is anything like it used to be before the war, you will have much fine food and wine."

"You've been—to the hotel?"

"*Nein*, my Colonel. But my employer spent his honeymoon there and he said it was very beautiful and well appointed. That was before the war, of course."

Heinrich nodded and watched the road. He was glad the bombs had not destroyed the vacation spot. Situated in the backwaters, it was still intact, the high ground of woods overlooking the flat terrain of pear orchards and small waterways beyond. It extended for five miles toward the Waal River, where the 1800-foot-long Nijmegen bridge rose in a brilliant example of mathematical ingenuity.

The town itself was well defended with antiaircraft guns and a regiment of SS troops in the city, and slightly beyond, in the forests and wooded areas, several panzer divisions.

But Heinrich wanted to forget about war for a few days. He wanted to rest and recuperate, to drink without fear of a raid. A stirring of desire made him think of Gretchen von Erhard. He should have a woman with him to assuage his desire. But not just any woman—only Gretchen, to punish her in a fitting manner for her crime of illusion, for despite her schoolgirl demeanor she was as much a woman as any other.

Heinrich smiled as the hotel came into view. It was even more beautiful than he had been led to believe.

"This will be a good time for us, Horst, *hein?*" Heinrich said in a jovial manner.

"*Ja*, my Colonel," Horst replied, relieved that the officer seemed pleased.

At the same time that Montgomery and Eisenhower were meeting in Brussels, a pleased Sir Dow Pomeroy had just found new quarters for his personal staff on the southern coast of England.

The entire Fighter Command had been moved from Stanmore because of the rockets. Big artillery guns, both Brithsh and American, were positioned along the downs to fire channelward at the missiles. For the rockets, many times more deadly than the buzz bombs, traveled at a speed faster than sound, making it impossible to track them by radar.

Birdie Summerlin, with Alpharetta accompanying her, examined the space in the four-bedroom house not far from the batteries, and mentally allotted the space into living quarters and offices.

"This room all right for you, luv?" Birdie inquired, looking toward the red-haired woman at the door.

Alpharetta, walking into the upstairs bedroom, nodded.

"We'll have to share it, I'm afraid."

"I don't mind, Birdie. When I was in training," Alpharetta replied, smiling, "I would have been happy to share bed and bath with only one other."

"Freddie and Reggie will have the two small bedrooms downstairs, and Sir Dow, the master bedroom at the end of this hall. I can't think of any other way to arrange it."

"I would have thought you and I would be assigned to women's quarters somewhere, Birdie," Alpharetta commented. "I'm surprised that we'll all be together again, as at Lochendall."

"Oh, Sir Dow was specific about that. Only Eckerd and Lloyd will be over the garage at the gate. Well, come, luv, and give me a hand before Sir Dow gets here."

It had been almost a month since Alpharetta had seen Marsh, Ben Mark, and Belline. That weekend had been such a fiasco. But Alpharetta had said nothing about it to her commander. As far as Dow was concerned, she was still engaged to Ben Mark. And she had vowed to say nothing to dispel that belief. It would be too difficult, too embarrassing, to explain the breaking of her engagement—for the second time.

How could she, after what Dow had said on the day she returned?

"I have decided I've been too selfish, Alpharetta. I'm withdrawing my objections to your marriage. If you and your captain wish to get married, I won't stand in your way."

But the wedding that was being planned was not her own. A doctor had confirmed Belline's pregnancy. Ben Mark was now resigned to marrying Belline for the sake of the baby. It had been a hurried thing, for the wedding had to take place as soon as Ben Mark obtained a pass.

That first evening, as the incessant barrage of guns finally showed signs of lessening, a subdued Dow sat and watched Alpharetta reading Ben Mark's letter by candlelight. And he waited for the request he had dreaded and expected ever since he had withdrawn his objections to their marriage.

Alpharetta folded the letter and, seeing Dow watching her, she inquired, "Sir Dow, if it's all right with you, I should like to take off this coming Saturday and Sunday."

She was long overdue for a pass. He knew that. Not trusting his voice, he merely nodded and returned to reading his newspaper. Not long after that, he left the room to retire for the night.

For Dow, the new house held no pleasure. His own life was as drab as the blackout curtains at the windows. He was tired, too. Tired of the war that eroded his life and now threatened to write the finishing chapter on the love he had kept hidden. Alpharetta.

Her name formed on his lips, even as he went to sleep, the night punctuated by the barrage of heavy guns seeking to defend the land from the dreaded rockets.

Late Saturday morning, September 16, Ben Mark's wedding day, Alpharetta dressed out of uniform and watched from the upstairs window for her taxi to arrive.

She had a strange feeling that she was reliving her life, each event shuffled in a time warp, to be used again, like drawing a card from the same deck, in a different sequence.

It had been over a year since she had waited for another taxi—yellow—to pull up into the allée of trees bordering the house in Atlanta. The weather had been miserably hot that day in July, not like the cool English weather of this September Saturday. Strange that her remembrance was keyed to the contrast in the elements—one day so hot and dry, the other cool, with the ever-present hint of mist and rain.

She saw the London black taxi slow and creep past the gates and she hurried downstairs.

As the taxi left with its passenger, Sir Dow Pomeroy, watching from his office window, closed the heavy draperies, relegating the room to darkness and gloom, to match his somber mood.

30

*I*n the age-old abbey that had seen its share of conflict and peace, sorrow and serenity through the years, Belline Wexford, strangely peaceful, stood at the chapel entrance and waited her turn to walk down the aisle.

She was dressed in white, in a knee-length dress and a smart little bridal hat, a veiled wisp purchased prematurely, soon after her arrival in England with the USO. But that no longer mattered, for the day she had planned all her life—her wedding day with Ben Mark St. John—was now here. True, it was not quite the way she had initially planned it, but the fact remained that Ben Mark would be *her* husband in a few minutes, and *not* Alpharetta's.

Ted, a fellow air corps officer, stood at the altar with Ben Mark. As the peal of the organ heralded the beginning of the procession, Belline watched her one attendant, Elsa, the girl from the USO, walk in slow, measured steps down the aisle.

The fanfare of the organ alerted Belline that it was now her turn. She began the walk toward Ben Mark. Her head lifted a little higher, the slight flush on her cheeks a giveaway of the triumph she felt at that moment. Her eyes wavered from Ben Mark's to search for Alpharetta in the pew. But she had evidently chosen not to come. Slightly disappointed, Belline continued down the aisle, where the minister in his robes began the traditional ceremony. "Dearly beloved . . ."

The exchange of rings, the repeated vows, took little time. With the flourish of the organ, the ceremony was over and the recessional began.

Among the sheltered archways facing the green, the reception table had been set up, presided over by other members of Belline's USO troop. Even a small wedding cake had miraculously appeared, but in less than a half hour, with the threat of rain, the crowd, having demolished the wedding delicacies, began to disperse.

Showing no emotion, a subdued Ben Mark watched the guests leave. The two people he cared most about had not come—Alpharetta and Marsh. One by choice, and the other because his leave was suddenly canceled.

In the early afternoon, Alpharetta returned by taxi to the house on the battery where Dow Pomeroy, his head on the desk in his downstairs office, had drifted into an uneasy sleep. He was alone, for he had not only given Alpharetta the weekend off, but the rest of his staff, too.

The purr of the car's engine, the closing of the door, were not sufficient to waken him fully. Thinking he was alone, Dow had not bothered to close his office door from the hallway. As he heard the tap of steps inside, he quickly lifted his head and listened. And through sleepy, unfocused eyes, he saw a blur of blue move past the open door.

"Who is it?" he demanded, his hand tightening on the holster atop his desk.

Hearing his voice, the woman stopped. "It's Alpharetta."

Startled, he glanced down at his watch. Only two hours had gone by since the taxi had come for her.

"Is something wrong?"

"No nothing. I changed my mind. I decided not to go to Ben Mark's wedding, after all."

At the expression on Dow's face, Alpharetta explained in a distant voice, "He married Belline today. Now, if you will excuse me . . ."

Dow stood dumbfounded as Alpharetta made her way up the stairs. So Captain Ben Mark St. John had not married Alpharetta, but had married Belline instead. His mind alternately accepted this information, then refuted it, and finally accepted it again.

His shoulders straightened; a heavy burden fell from his heart. Suddenly Dow grinned boyishly, stuck his hands in his pockets, and, with a spring to his step, walked back into his office to contemplate this magnificent, unexpected good fortune.

Birdie Summerlin had gone home—to be with one of her sons on leave. And so Alpharetta, with the room to herself, crawled into the twin bed for a long-awaited nap. Within minutes, exhausted from a lack of sleep the evening before, she fell into a deep slumber.

The house remained quiet and an hour later, when Alpharetta awoke, she felt refreshed, strangely exuberant, her dreams, always the first clue of changed relationships, demanding exploration, translation. By all rights, she should have been despondent. But no tears stained her pillow, no disquieting memories from her sleep plagued her.

She sat up and, like one removing her bandages to view the mortal wound, she traced the edges of her mental scars. Like the light scar on her right arm from the shrapnel wound that had healed itself in the weeks after the trip to Sweden, they were barely perceptible.

"He isn't worth it, Alpharetta—even if he *is* my own cousin." Marsh's words echoed in her thoughts, part of her mind refuting Marsh's words, the other part acknowledging what she had tried to conceal from herself ever since that day in the dower house.

The emotion she felt for Ben Mark was no longer love, but a genuine liking, for she had seen glimpses of him that no one else had seen—the true worth under the bravado, the spoiled exterior. And she realized, for the first time, that she would never have been able to give him what Belline offered—total devotion. There was a part of her that would remain forever aloof, that small, independent spirit that bound self with self, a portion of her complete from the rest, unaligned and free as the gulls passing over the house in the blue-gray of the sky and sea beyond.

Feeling good about herself, Alpharetta got up and dressed in dungarees and a ribbed sweater. She had a great desire to walk along the downs with her new independence of heart.

Braced against the wind, Alpharetta drank in the smell of the sea, the nervous call of birds, flying in and out of the mist that now began to swirl in variations of images recalled from Lochendall.

Great waves crashed into the seawall and spilled white-flecked foam, which was carried inland by the wind as the conspiracy of air and water continued its unending vendetta against the land.

Separated by the sea channel, the land under Alpharetta's feet and the land containing the rocket-launching sites were measured not in miles, but in rocket speed—a mere five minutes apart. Yet a sense of remoteness encompassed the downs and all of England, for the majority of the people had not equated the tremendous explosions with the new weapon of the Germans.

Alpharetta, straining to see through the worsening mist, saw a figure moving toward her. She recognized Dow.

"Race you to the seawall," she shouted, conjuring another image of Lochendall.

"I'll race you back to the house instead," he shouted. "We're in for another blow."

"That's too far to run," she complained.

The wind at her back gave her a push, propelling her against her will toward Dow. He reached out, placed her arm in his, to Alpharetta's protest.

"But I'm not ready to go back," she said.

But the weather, no respecter of her wishes, became her adversary. The heavens opened and the rain came down, making the prospect of shelter far more desirable.

"I'll build a fire, while you change into dry clothes," Dow said as they reached the house.

"What about you?"

"I'll get the fire going first. Don't worry about me."

Chilled by the sudden drenching, Alpharetta needed no further prompting. She should have put a scarf over her hair, but her regrets came too late.

The soft glow of logs in the fireplace drew Alpharetta into the downstairs sitting room. His sandy hair still showing traces of dampness, Dow poured two glasses of wine at Alpharetta's appearance.

"Here, this will help to warm you," he said, handing her one.

She took the wineglass and sank to the pillow before the hearth, while Dow watched her.

"I had hoped to go into London tonight," she said ruefully.

"That's off limits for you, from now on, until the rocket sites are overrun."

"Oh? You didn't say anything about that earlier, when you gave me the pass."

"No. But now you're my responsibility, more or less."

"Less."

"What?"

"You didn't keep Birdie from making the trip. I don't mean to be impertinent, but I should think you would give me the consideration you gave Birdie—especially on my time off."

"You don't understand. Birdie is a widow, with grown children—not an impetuous redhead who takes unnecessary chances."

Instead of becoming angry, Alpharetta laughed.

"What do you find so amusing?"

"Oh, several things. But speaking of chances, what do you think the odds are then for finding something for dinner? Did Birdie leave any food for you in the refrigerator?"

"If you find anything, you may have half of it."

"If I prepare it?"

He nodded. "Lloyd's gone, too."

"Now, *you're* the one taking chances. Has it occurred to you that I might not be able to cook?"

"Surely if you're able to read an aerial map, you can read a cookbook, too, Miss Beaumont."

Alpharetta smiled, sipped her glass of wine, and dried her hair before the fire. Dow was relaxed—in a good mood. She wasn't sure what Birdie would say when she found out the two had spent the evening together with no one else in the house. But at the moment, it didn't seem to matter.

Later, as the two sat at the small table beyond the hearth, candleglow answered the hearth in rhythmic fire, a silent language that needed no interpreter, for its power was older than speech itself—bypassing human lips for the primitive yearnings of the heart.

Dow lifted his wineglass and acknowledged the fire's power. He knew he had to be careful not to alarm Alpharetta, like all males in the presence of a firebird, who could vanish at will, leaving only the promise of its return five hundred years hence.

31

By noon of the next day, Sunday, September 17, the great air armada left England, the noise lasting for hours, a sound that cancelled speech and even the church bells' tolling.

Rushing out of the house on the downs, Alpharetta was joined by Dow. Together, they watched the sky carpeted overhead by planes, tip to tip, blotting out the sun's rays and casting an almost solid shadow on the land. Now Alpharetta knew why Marsh Wexford's pass had been cancelled.

In broad open daylight, and on a Sunday, too, Captain Marsh Wexford had boarded the transport for the air portion of the Holland invasion, while other groups all over England waited their turn in the most massive movement of airborne troops ever undertaken.

Seated next to Gig and Laroche, Marsh unconsciously reached toward his pocket to finger the good-luck piece as he had done each time before jumping toward the enemy. But the commemorative coin was gone—given to little Ibert Duvalier as a pledge for his return to France.

A strange sense of loss pervaded Marsh and then he chided himself for such superstition.

Seeing Marsh's action, Gig inquired, "What's the matter, Captain? Forget something?"

"No. Not really." Marsh shrugged, reluctant to discuss it. He turned his attention to the continuous drone of the great armada that promised to fill the skies, not only for this day but for the next three.

"It's going to be different this time," Marsh said aloud, to no one in particular.

"Yeah. This time Laroche is going to watch out where he lands," Gig teased.

Laroche, ignoring the barb, said, "It's going to be different, too, without Giraldo. Wonder where he is now?"

"Probably trying to escape," Marsh answered.

The three became silent, forged in friendship despite the difference in rank, for survival was the greatest bond of all, tying them with the comradeship of fighting together in Sicily, Italy, and Normandy.

Marsh looked around him, noticing the new faces—those who had been added to the combat team in place of the paratroopers left behind with each battle. And he knew that his cousin, Ben Mark, with only two days' leave, would be playing a part in the Allied invasion later in the week.

The 82nd Division, Gavin's airborne troops, hardened from battle, scars on their bodies—medals of valor that could never be taken away—now braced for another jump in a roulette of time, for by all odds, few should have survived this long—especially Marsh, Gig, and Laroche after the tank episode.

Jumping with them this time was the 101st Airborne, the Screaming Eagles of Matthew Ridgway—two American divisions hammered far too thin, with one British division and a Polish brigade. They all shared the impossible tasks ahead—to secure the towns and the bridges for Montgomery's troops and tanks to get to Arnhem, a front far too long, too narrow, a corridor one tank wide, with treacherous canals, ditches, and the unceasing flow of the Waal River, the greatest barrier of all. Nijmegen was the key. Without the capture of the Nijmegen bridge, the entire operation would be a failure. And it was up to the 82nd Airborne to capture it.

The contour of the land became visible. Low hanging clouds parted into expanses of blue. The sun highlighted the terrain, the rays sweeping over the waterways, picking up the reflection of trees and villages, windmills, and even the deer that roamed freely in and out of the forests. The long shadow of the afternoon now extended over quiet Dutch farmhouses, gardens, and woods as the silk canopy filled the skies.

Scattered for miles by the pilots in their drops from Sicily to Normandy, the commanders of the combat teams of the 82nd Airborne had learned their lessons well—to take their losses at the beginning in a concentrated drop, rather than risk losing half their troopers in an ineffective sprinkling all over the countryside.

". . . Put us down in Holland or put us down in Hell," Colonel Mendez charged the pilots, "but put us all down together in one place."

Near the town of Groesbeek on the eastern side of the wooded heights, the pathfinders Marsh, Gig, and Laroche descended. The bright sunlight presented an added danger. But seeing the landscape clearly, they maneuvered their parachutes like sails to avoid the areas of water that had been so disastrous in their landings in Normandy.

Marsh Wexford, landing in a farmyard on the other side of the woods from the De Groot Hotel, quickly unharnessed himself from his parachute and ran for cover, just as an unsuspecting Heinrich von Freiker picked up his napkin and began his lunch in the hotel dining room.

Coming down within a few hundred yards from where Marsh had landed, Laroche divested himself of his parachute and ran in the same direction.

Gig, holding a basket carrying a small brown puppy of undetermined pedigree named Lester, let go of the basket at the last possible moment, as he hit the soft, marshy polder land between the dikes. Rescuing the puppy, he zipped the mascot in the top of his combat suit and joined the rest of the team.

"Let's get on with it," Marsh said, looking back at the sky for the planes that were to follow.

In a matter of minutes, he and his men marked the area with small stoves and brightly colored strips to signal the special zone for the artillery units, gliders, and General Browning's Corps headquarters directly behind them.

"Help me, Laroche," Gig whispered to his friend, as he retrieved the large cargo parachute containing a machine gun.

Hidden in a ditch, Marsh and his team set up their defense weapons against the enemy and waited for the paratroopers and the Waco gliders to land. Large, lumbersome birds of wood, the military gliders plummeted from the skies, some landing intact, others splitting open at the moment of impact to reveal weapons and jeeps, the majority of which rolled out, unscathed.

In the midst of the first wave of troopers, a Dutch intelligence officer, familiar with the land and the language, came down. He helped to guide them down a dirt road—half the men on one side, half on the other, reverting to the irrigation ditches at the sound of armored vehicles in the vicinity.

Finishing his meal at the De Groot Hotel, Heinrich frowned in displeasure at being disturbed.

"What is it, Horst?" Heinrich inquired.

"We are being attacked, my Colonel, by paratroopers."

Cautious at the news, Heinrich laid down his napkin and, listening, heard the unmistakable drone of planes. With an epithet, he arose from his chair and walked to the large window giving a view of the low ground beyond the higher elevation of the hotel. As far as he could see, planes, gliders, and paratroopers filled the sky.

"Why do they always have to come at mealtimes?" he fumed, feeling his digestion react uneasily to the sight. Without waiting for an answer, he ordered, "Get the car, Horst. We'll try to reach Student's headquarters at Vught. He'll need me."

"It's already outside the door, my Colonel." He held out his commander's pistol belt.

The serving girl Anje, watching Heinrich secure the belt around his waist, felt a sense of elation, which she hid carefully in a bland expression as she approached the table.

"Are you not having dessert, Herr Colonel?" she inquired.

He glanced longingly toward the pastries, shook his head, and left the nearly empty dining room while Anje cleared the table and hurriedly carried her tray of dishes back to the kitchen.

The few remaining civilians in the dining room stood by the large window and watched the troopers descend from the sky in every direction.

As she walked into the kitchen, Anje said, "Quick, Huls, the gravy is boiling over." Her voice contained an urgency that was not lost on the chef. He wiped his hands on the large white apron surrounding his pot-bellied form.

"Watch it for me, Anje," he said, leaving the kitchen for the chef's pantry, forbidden territory to any other worker.

Inside the pantry, hidden under a wooden barrel, a telephone rested—a direct line to the Dutch Resistance headquarters five miles away.

"The flour that I ordered has come," he said to the voice at the other end of the line. "I can now begin baking the birthday cake."

"Very good. When did the flour arrive?"

"A few minutes ago. It will be a large birthday cake."

"Then I shall tell Clodjie. She will be pleased."

He quickly hung up the telephone and started toward the door.

"Where is Huls?" the maître d' demanded as he walked into the kitchen.

Anje gazed at Gerd, the Dutch Nazi collaborator standing before her. In a voice loud enough for Huls to overhear, she replied, "He's gone to the pantry for more supplies."

Alerted, Huls picked up the chocolate he had been hoarding and a tin of special flour. As he almost bumped into Gerd, Huls smiled and, in a confidential voice announced, "I have decided to make special cakes for tonight's dessert, with chocolate. Anje says the guests are extremely nervous."

"A good idea, Huls, even if we have nothing to worry about. Anje, you can stay this afternoon to help him."

"But I—"

"Anje will only get in the way, Gerd. I want my kitchen to myself."

"As you wish, Huls," the man replied, giving in to him, for Gerd knew that he could not do without Huls, despite his prima-donna temperament.

Trying to appear unhurried, an excited Anje left the hotel grounds for the small house she shared with her aged grandfather.

As communication wires were cut by the Dutch Resistance, the German general Model, thinking the main attack was to be on Army Group B's headquarters, hastily evacuated the Tafelberg and the Hartenstein, taking with him his military maps and little else. He had no way of knowing the real targets—the five bridges and surrounding waterways designating the northern route to Germany. The only thing he knew for certain was the invader's descent from the skies.

Marsh, with his first objective completed, requisitioned one of the jeeps from a freight glider. Soon his team was on its way from the drop zone.

The jeep, containing Gig and Laroche, also held two new members of the pathfinders team—Megan and Howard.

When the enemy fire became too intense, they would abandon the jeep for a ditch. Then they would resume their advance. In a narrow street where enemy fire suddenly strafed the path in front of them, the five jumped and rolled into the protection of a doorway not a moment too soon. Within seconds, the jeep was afire, with the explosion of the gas tank drowning out the other street noises.

"Jeez, that was close."

"Too close," Marsh replied, his hand unconsciously reaching for the good-luck piece that he no longer carried.

ott im Himmel! Look, Horst," Heinrich said, spreading the papers from the captured briefcase onto the nose of the crashed Waco glider.

Horst looked uneasily, but not at the Allied military papers, for he was acutely aware of the scene of death—the crashed glider, dead paratroopers, his own dead countrymen, the area fought over only an hour or so earlier and now deserted, a cyclorama of battle, posed for a wide-angle photograph, with the slight breeze murmuring through the band of trees bordering the marshy field, like a brief, lonely whisper.

Horst held the pistol in his hands and waited warily for his commander to walk back to the car, for despite the quietness, snipers could be lurking in the nearby woods.

While Horst remained concerned for his commander's safety, Heinrich examined the papers from the briefcase. He couldn't believe his luck. Battle plans, with maps, the names of the units involved—their goal of five bridges—a detailed invasion plan of Holland. And he was the sole German possessor.

Handing over such valuable information to Army Group B's headquarters would be quite a coup for him. He could see the recommendations, the promotion long overdue—if the plans were genuine and not something planted by the Allies, as they were in the habit of doing to throw the Wehrmacht off track.

He shifted the papers, recognizing the same units he had fought against in Sicily, Normandy, Italy. His eyes narrowed at the sight of the 82nd Airborne unit—the one that had given him such a black eye in Normandy, the one that had driven him from his comfortable villa in Sicily in the middle of the night. Paulina di Resa, in the green silk caftan, her long flowing black hair against the pillow, became a fleeting image in his mind, and a slight regret permeated his consciousness. He had not meant to shoot her, only scare her into confessing where she had hidden the priceless icon. If it had not been for the paratroopers— Yes, it was all their fault. *They* were to blame for his losing such a treasure.

The face of the blond paratrooper had haunted him ever since that one encounter in Sicily. For a brief moment he had thought he was going mad, seeing his own father before him.

Carefully, he read that portion of the plan that involved the American airborne unit. If Heinrich were lucky, the American was still alive and heading for the ultimate goal— the bridge at Nijmegen.

He smiled. He would have ample time to turn the battle plans over to General Student and get to Nijmegen, to wait for the unit and hopefully for the blond American paratrooper who so resembled his father. And this time he would destroy them all.

"Horst, start the car."

"Yes, my Colonel," Horst replied, glad to leave the scene.

Like Marsh in the jeep, Heinrich in the German car detoured to avoid heavy artillery fire. For that reason, it took him much longer than usual to reach Student's headquarters at Vught. The guards at the gate demanded to see Heinrich's identification before he was allowed to enter the compound.

As Horst slowed the car in front of the steps, Heinrich leaped from the car with the briefcase, returned the guard's salute, and walked into the cool, black and white tile hallway.

In an imperious voice, Heinrich informed the general's aide, "I must see the general immediately. I have captured the entire battle plans for the Allied invasion."

"He's on the telephone. Please have a seat, Herr Colonel."

"This is of the utmost importance," Heinrich informed him. "Tell him that Colonel von Freiker is here," he demanded.

Hearing the name—General von Freiker was a special friend of General Student—the aide rose from his desk, tapped on the closed door of Student's private office, and opened the door slightly.

Through the narrow slit, Heinrich saw the general's back as he sat on top of the desk, his black boot impatiently tapping the fine old mahogany as he talked into the mouthpiece of the black telephone.

"Well, then, try the field telephone again, if you can't reach him by this one."

With his hand over the speaker, Student turned toward the door. "Yes?"

"Colonel von Freiker is here to see you—on urgent business."

"Show him in."

Again, Student turned his back and resumed speaking into the telephone as Heinrich entered the room, stood, and waited for the general to finish. Gazing about the room, Heinrich saw that it was no different from any other headquarters, with the wooden paneling, the picture of Hitler staring from the wall, and the large Nazi flag with black swastika that overpowered the room. He took the briefcase and unobtrusively laid the papers out on top of the massive desk, its corners marked by gold escutcheons, the grain of the wood polished to a mirrorlike sheen.

"Well, keep trying every few minutes," Student spoke again, "and let me know as soon as you reach him."

With a sigh, Student hung up the telephone and turned to greet his visitor with a somber face. "Heinrich, my boy. What disastrous news do *you* bring with you?" he inquired.

"Not disastrous, my General—I think I have found the entire invasion plans of Field Marshal Montgomery."

A cautious Student looked at the papers and asked, "Where did you get them?"

"In a crashed glider, not far from your headquarters."

As Student sank into his chair and began to examine more closely the papers on the desk before him, Heinrich watched for the general's reaction. Waving a hand in Heinrich's direction, an absorbed Student said, "Sit down, Heinrich," as if he were still the small child Student had once dandled on his knee.

"It could be a hoax . . ."

The disappointing words were immediately tempered with, "But I don't think so. Heinrich, I believe these are genuine. And if they are, it is a retribution from the gods."

Inwardly glowing, Heinrich said nothing as Student continued examining each map. "So this is why I haven't been able to reach Model. British paratroopers have landed right in his midst. But Bittrich should make short shrift of them with his tanks, if we can keep Horrock's army from reaching them. I'll have to call von Rundstedt and see if he can get in touch with either Model or Bittrich."

Under Student's orders, Heinrich hurried to meet up with a panzer division alerted from the Reichswald, just over the German border near Wyler. The rendezvous point was to be a small castle on the Holland side used by Abwehr to monitor the Dutch Resistance forces.

Colonel von Freiker was not the only one headed for the Raalte castle. Anje, still dressed in her serving uniform of black and white, had not gone home from the De Groot Hotel. She had met the groundskeeper at the end of the drive and his news had changed her mind.

Never before had the Dutch Resistance been able to infiltrate the castle, but if luck were with her, she would find the files unattended.

Somewhere within the military complex was the list of collaborators. But even more vital was a list of the Resistance fighters, complete with code names. They had been betrayed by a double agent, and one by one they had been arrested and shot.

Now, if the groundskeeper's information were true, Anje had the opportunity to destroy the evidence against them and to find out the name of the double agent so that the Resistance might deal with him. People like Gerd, the maître d' at the hotel, while annoying, had stated their allegiance to the Nazis and the members of the Resistance had carefully avoided letting men like him learn what was going on in the underground. She and Huls were always careful around Gerd.

For three years, Huls had been protective of her, taking the brunt of Gerd's ire, seeing that she in no way became suspect for her activities. Now Anje wanted to do something for Huls, for she sensed he was in danger.

He had sent her home that afternoon. But it was vastly more important to seize this opportunity to destroy the evidence against her friends in the underground.

The Raalte castle, hidden in an out-of-the-way grove of trees, looked peacefully quiet as Anje approached it on foot, after hiding her bicycle. The heavy, slightly ajar gates, indicated the speed with which the occupants had fled the castle. Still, Anje was cautious.

Looking to her right and then her left, Anje hurried inside, leaving the front door open as she had found it. She wasted no time in locating the tremendous file room, with its metal cabinets reaching almost to the ceiling.

She began pulling out file after file of correspondence from Berlin, from the Reichstag—mountains of papers that had no meaning for her. As time passed and she still found nothing of value, she suspected that correspondence so sensitive to security would not be kept in the regular file room, but more than likely in the commandant's office—perhaps his personal safe.

Leaving the file room, Anje walked down the hall and pushed open doors until she stopped on the threshold of a paneled office, decorated in much the same manner as the one Heinrich had just left, with the required picture of the head of the Third Reich in prominent position, balanced by the flags on each side. Two tall metal cabinets towered against the far wall.

For a member of the underground, the opening of a locked cabinet presented little challenge. Anje removed a hairpin from her neatly coiffeured head. But there was no need to use it. The files were unlocked, indicating once again the haste with which the commandant had fled.

Pulling open a drawer of the first cabinet, Anje began rifling through the large brown envelopes, different from the material in the file room.

As she pulled a particularly fat envelope from its resting place, two pictures fell from the envelope and dropped to the floor at her feet. When she stooped to retrieve the pictures, she drew in her breath, for she recognized a familiar face—Huls, in his chef's uniform.

Her hands began to tremble as she quickly returned the pictures to the envelope. Her one thought was to take the damning information and hurry back to the De Groot Hotel to warn Huls.

The sound of boots in the hallway suddenly alerted Anje

that she was no longer alone. She looked at the windows behind her. They were covered with bars. One door, and only one, provided an exit from the room. She had made a fatal error in her haste, for she was trapped in the room. Hugging the envelope to her breast, Anje darted under the massive desk just as the door to the office opened.

For an instant, Heinrich stood in the doorway, his eyes adjusting to the inside light after the harsh glare of the afternoon sun. Gradually, the room took shape, the telephone on the desk drawing him into the room. He decided to try to reach Model again.

As Heinrich's steps brought him closer to the desk, Anje withdrew the stiletto from her garter, and waited to be discovered in her compromising position. She crouched like a cornered wild animal, ready to strike at the first moment of attack by the enemy.

Heinrich, standing on the other side of the desk, reached for the telephone and removed the receiver from its hook.

"Hello," he said into the mouthpiece and then jiggled the hook up and down. "Hello." The line was dead.

"It's no use, Horst," he said to the man standing guard at the threshold. "The lines were probably cut by the Resistance the moment the first paratroopers came down. Why don't you go and see if you can find something to drink? It might be a long wait for the tanks."

"As you wish, my Colonel."

The retreating steps of the second man told Anje that she was now alone in the room with one German colonel, waiting for armor to arrive. And she knew she had to do something to bluff her way out before he came around to sit at the desk.

"Herr Colonel?" she inquired in a frightened, girlish voice.

"*Ja*? Who's in here?" Heinrich demanded. "Where are you? Identify yourself."

"It's me—Magda. I'm hiding—under the desk."

"Come out where I can see you."

"You won't shoot me, will you, Herr Colonel?"

He made no promises.

Anje, cautiously placing the stiletto back into her garter, crawled out from under the desk and came face to face with the same man she had served lunch at the De Groot Hotel several hours earlier.

Forcing herself to remain calm, she gave no evidence that she recognized him. But it was obvious that Heinrich recognized the young woman standing before him.

"How did you get here?" he demanded.

"By bicycle—as I do every day." Her baffled expression made him impatient.

"No. You're lying. You work at the De Groot Hotel. You have no business being here."

A smile caused the dimple to show in the young woman's cheek. "You must have me mixed up with my cousin, Anje. *She's* the one who works at the De Groot."

Still suspicious, Heinrich inquired. "Why were you hiding? Under the desk?"

"I—I hadn't finished my cleaning. I was afraid Herr Blockhead—" Anje covered her mouth in chagrin as Heinrich suddenly smiled. "I mean, Herr Commandant would be angry. And so I stayed. But when I heard footsteps, I thought it was the paratroopers, and that's why I hid."

In a stern manner that disguised his mirth at her use of the commandant's nickname, he accused, "No. You're lying. You're Anje. And you came to cut the communications lines."

"Please, Herr Colonel. The lines were cut long before everyone left, including the commandant."

"Where did he go?"

"Back across the border."

Satisfied, Heinrich relaxed. Yes, that would be just like him, for he had no stomach for fighting. "Finish your cleaning, Magda. I expect the commandant will be back in several days."

"Yes, Herr Colonel."

He moved toward the door as he heard Horst coming back down the hallway. "You're certain you're not Anje?" he inquired again.

"Oh, no, Herr Colonel. I'm too clumsy to be a waitress." The small glass paperweight fell off the desk and broke.

Staring in dismay at the broken shards of glass on the floor, Anje said, "The commandant will be angry at me for this."

"Yes, I expect he will, Magda," Heinrich replied, as he faced Horst coming into the room. "You found something to drink, Horst?"

"Yes, my Colonel," he replied, frowning as he saw the woman in the room with his commander.

In a dry voice, Heinrich explained her presence. "Anje's cousin, Magda. She's the cleaning girl here. Well, what have you found, Horst? And where is it?"

"In the sitting room. I thought you would be more comfortable there." He continued to glare at the woman picking up the pieces of glass from the floor.

Heinrich nodded, closed the door, and motioned for Horst to lock it behind him, leaving Anje trapped again, with bars at the windows and the only exit lost to her.

Anje heard the sudden closing of the door and the click of the key, and she knew that Heinrich had not believed her flimsy story.

Silently, she waited with her head pressed against the door and listened to the double set of steps as the two Germans made their way down the hall. At least Heinrich had not assigned his aide to guard duty before the locked door.

Anje walked back to the desk and reached under it for the envelope containing the pictures, the information on the Dutch Resistance. And her eyes, unbelieving, examined again the picture of Huls and the information in his dossier.

Huls, her friend, was the double agent! No, it couldn't be true. *Gerd* was the Nazi collaborator, not Huls. But the chef's own handwriting condemned him, as his information condemned the network of Resistance workers in that district, his contacts in other cities, and even the telephone operators working in the exchange.

She looked at the real names and labeled code names opposite them, one by one. One code name remained alone with no identification beside it. *The Griffon*—operating independently in the district, no clue as to his cover.

Anje, remembering Gerd's actions, his close monitoring of Huls, and his avowed loyalty to the Nazis, began to suspect that Gerd might well be *The Griffon*. What better cover than working in the hotel where Nazi officers came and went and, slightly drunk, talked with loosened tongues to a known collaborator or sympathizer?

She must get out—to warn the underground of Huls, the

betrayer in their midst. A sadness overwhelmed her. Then Anje began to pick the lock. Hidden in her chemise was Huls's dossier. The others she had destroyed, setting fire to the bits of paper in the metal wastebasket.

A steady rumble of tanks in the distance caused the ground to tremble, the windows to rattle. Anje, opening the door to the hallway, peered down the long corridor and glanced toward the curved marble stairs that led to the second floor. With her shoes in her hands, she fled toward the front door and put on her shoes and began to run through the compound, past Heinrich's staff car and toward the wooded grove where she had left her bicycle.

As she reached the bicycle, she stopped. Leaning against a nearby tree was Heinrich, and directly beyond him was his aide, Horst.

Anje stared at Heinrich and then at Horst, her hands tightening their grip on the handlebars of the bicycle. A satisfied expression passed over Heinrich's face at the dismay he had caused.

Pitching the empty wine bottle into the brush, Heinrich lazily gave Horst the order.

"Shoot her, Horst."

"My Colonel?"

"I said shoot her, Horst. Immediately."

Horst gazed apologetically at Anje, removed his gun from its holster, and aimed. The muffled shot rang over the countryside, answered in kind by the din of the moving tanks.

Anje's hands loosened on the handlebars. The bicycle fell, and the seventeen-year-old member of the Dutch underground crumpled to the soft earth, her fall dislodging the picture of Huls, the double agent, from its hiding place, to lie beside her outstretched hand.

Satisfied, Heinrich said, "Come, Horst. I hear the tanks. It's past time to start for Nijmegen."

For over ten hours, Model, the commander of Army Group B, who had fled his overrun headquarters at Oosterbeek for Bittrich's quarters in Doetinchem, had no idea of the extent of the invasion or the importance of the Arnhem bridge. He only knew that his army had been cut in two by British paratroopers and he had mistakenly thought that his headquarters had been their prime goal.

But farther south, General Student and Heinrich von Freiker were well aware of the plans, and they now put into action a massive assault to stop the Allies from meeting their goal.

As darkness descended in the town of Mook, Marsh, Gig, and Laroche, plus the two new members of the team—Howard and Megan—were exhausted from the continuous fighting from village to village. They were holed up in the cellar of a deserted house to eat their K rations, cold, without benefit of anything to wash it down, while around them, the sporadic sound of guns signaled a lull in the fighting.

For the first time that day, Marsh surveyed the two rookies—the tall, calm, aristocratic Megan, and the smaller, nervous Howard, who ate in a crouched position, as if he were ready to flee at a moment's notice.

The seasoned Laroche, tired and hungry, looked around the temporary shelter and complained, "Never heard of a wine cellar without wine."

"Why don't you try the water faucet in the kitchen?" Gig suggested, busy feeding bits of K rations to Lester, the small brown puppy he'd carried all day. He dumped the few remaining drops of water from his canteen on his fingers for the puppy to lick. "If you're that thirsty."

"And get my head blown off? You think I came all this way for a drink of water? If I'd wanted that, I would have dunked my head in the canal."

"Or landed in another well."

"That's getting old, Madison, reminding me of that."

"Stop your bickering," Marsh ordered, his patience worn thin.

The sound of heavy boots on the floor overhead caused the five to freeze and listen. Their thirst was forgotten as they swapped messkits for their rifles, took positions against the barricade of barrels and waited. Rapid fire outside the house was answered in turn by enemy rifles above Marsh and the other paratroopers.

"I think the Germans are directly above us," whispered Megan, one of the new men.

A grenade thrown from the street into an upstairs window caused the cellar to rain down plaster upon their heads and a wooden beam to sag dangerously.

"Let's get out of here," Marsh said, moving toward the back entrance, for he had no wish to be buried alive.

"You think the shed next to us is unoccupied?" inquired Mel Howard, the other new paratrooper.

"We'll know soon enough," Marsh answered, glancing toward the outbuilding of stucco, with its sloped roof of faded tile.

Heading toward the door, he was stopped by Gig. "I'll go first," Gig volunteered. "I can run the fastest. Just let me get Lester zipped up here."

"Why not send the dog first?" Megan suggested, to be answered by a furious glare from Gig.

"We'll give you cover," Laroche commented, also ignoring the suggestion.

With the animal safely zipped into his combat suit, Gig edged toward the door, glanced out into the small garden area between the buildings, and suddenly streaked through the rows of bright yellow sunflowers to the safety of the next building.

No fire strafed the garden. But Laroche, going next, was not so fortunate. From the upper windows came the sound of rifles. Laroche fell flat in the dirt, concealed by the few sunflowers with their heads intact. Marsh, shooting from the small opening in the door, aimed his rifle toward the windows and, out of the corner of his eye, watched to see if Laroche had moved. The almost imperceptible stirring of sunflowers gave Marsh hope that the little Cajun was still alive.

Mel Howard, without waiting for a signal, rushed from the doorway, causing Marsh to swear. But it was already too late. He went down in a burst of fire before he had reached the halfway mark in the garden.

"Have you got a grenade left, Megan?" Marsh demanded of the one remaining paratrooper. His voice was harsh.

"Yes, sir."

"Well, give it to me. And after I throw it, run like hell. Are you ready?"

"But what about *you*, sir?"

"I'll be all right if the grenade hits its mark."

Marsh removed the pin from the plastic in his hand, hurled it toward the windows where the enemy guns had pinned them down, and, in an urgent voice after the explosion, commanded, "Run, Megan!"

The young paratrooper, hunching low, swept past the door and a split second later Marsh followed, his large frame a target for any guns still in action.

Megan reached the shed with the others, but Marsh, searching for Laroche, paused long enough to lift the wounded Cajun into his arms and carry him toward the shed.

"Medic!" Marsh yelled, his voice loud enough to be heard throughout the town. There would be no more fighting for Laroche in Operation Market-Garden.

As the smoke from the grenade cleared and silence reigned in the small Dutch garden with its miniature windmill barely turning in the breeze, Marsh cautiously went back into the garden for Howard. The man was dead. He already knew that but he brought him into shelter anyway.

"You hurt bad, Laroche?" Gig asked, leaning over his buddy.

Before answering, Laroche inquired, "Is my arm still there, Madison?"

"Yeah."

"Then I don't hurt so bad."

Gig tore a strip of cloth from Laroche's shirt and used it as a tourniquet to stop the flow of blood while they waited for the medic to reach them with his stretcher and claim Laroche for the hospital and Mel Howard, on his first jump, for the list of those killed in action.

Now the odds were catching up with the four veterans who had survived the Sicily campaign. First Giraldo, and then Laroche. But neither was dead. There was still hope for both.

Without saying a word, Marsh and Gig looked at each other and tightened the muscles in their stomachs. They knew that, at any moment, they too might be separated from each other.

Once the three able-bodied paratroopers left the shed, Marsh decided it was safer to go from rooftop to rooftop, for then they could see below the approach of enemy vehicles from all directions.

For the townspeople, caught in the fighting without prior warning and, hiding in their attics and other sheltered places carved out in their houses, the sound of combat boots overhead was a strange noise. Some, unable to resist looking out their gabled windows, saw men, used to the air, hopping, surefooted, minus their parachutes, as if the wings on their uniforms had given them some special ability over their land-grounded brothers.

The pathfinders, fighting with one unit and then another of Gavin's troops, finally reached the Maas-Waal canal at the same time the British paratroopers, farther north, were taking the upper end of the bridge at Arnhem. As Marsh, Gig, and Megan approached the banks of the canal, the crossing of the wide expanse of water was already underway, soldiers in flimsy canvas boats hidden by a cover of smoke.

Gig, watching the loading of boats, turned green. "Thirteen! I'm not about to get in a boat with twelve others. That's positively unlucky."

"You didn't add the three engineers already in each boat," Marsh countered.

"Well, that's more like it. Guess Lester and I will chance it after all."

After he climbed into one of the boats with Marsh and Megan and they had pushed off, Gig became silent, listening for the sound of guns on the other side of the canal.

Caught in a swirl of current, the flimsy boats began to spin in all directions, and the soldiers resorted to using the butts of their rifles to help paddle. But then enemy machine guns on the opposite bank found the boats as the smokescreen vanished.

"Hell, we're just damn sitting ducks," Gig said, sorry that he had been persuaded to set foot in the canvas boat. He took off his helmet and began to bail water, as Marsh and Megan and all the others plugged the holes with every bit of canvas at their disposal to keep the small craft afloat until they reached the other side.

They were at the mercy of the Germans and their guns. But against all odds, the flotilla landed with only a small percentage of casualties, and rushing the positions of the Germans, the men secured the crossing.

Two combat teams now raced for the town of Nijmegen, that city reconstructed by Caesar after its destruction by Claudius Civilis; the legendary residence of Barbarossa, Charlemagne, with its breathtakingly beautiful view of the Lower Rhine again under fire.

Approaching the outskirts of the town, the men under Reuben Tucker engaged in hand-to-hand combat with the enemy for every inch of the city. From house to house they fought, as they had in Mook, Grave, Groesbeek, their destination, the five-storied bridge, to reach it before the Germans blew it up in their faces.

By the time Marsh arrived, the magnificent bridge still stood. A steel monster with a life and soul of its own, the bridge spanned the river like Bifröst, the legendary, mythical bridge connecting Earth to Heaven. In the darkness, Marsh drew in his breath at its design—even more forbidding than he had imagined.

"You think we still have a chance to take it?" Megan inquired beside him.

"If they don't blow it up in the next few minutes," Marsh answered, awed at the steel structure looming before them.

34

As Marsh and the others fought for the bridge at Nijmegen, they were painfully aware of the race against time, for the British airborne unit fighting at Arnhem was isolated.

The landing fields had been overrun by Bittrich's panzer divisions, their presence dismissed by Montgomery's headquarters in spite of the Dutch Resistance reports.

Farther back in line, south of Eindhoven, men in the British 8 Corps sat down and cried as they heard the paratroopers at Arnhem begging for covering artillery fire that did not come. By all rights, 8 Corps should have been up front with them, for they had perfected the communications system with the troopers, retuning the frequencies of the large radio sets that went out as the troopers dropped with the radios on their practice jumps.

For months, the radio men of 8 Corps had lived with the troopers, eaten with them, and called them by name. But by a quirk of fate, 30 Corps, judged nearer to the battle scene than 8 Corps, was selected by the high command at the last minute to take over their duties. And the switch to an unrehearsed team spelled disaster for the paratroopers, with no radio contact, their supplies of ammunition and food landing amid the German-held fields, and the weather in England grounding the planes carrying reinforcements.

The division, with enough food and supplies to last two days, struggled through the hell that now encompassed them—men wounded, without water; their commanding general, Urquhart, trapped in the attic of a house completely surrounded by Germans, with the two ranking officers at log-gerheads over the course of action they should take.

The paratroopers, regardless of nationality—American, British, Polish—felt a special kinship with each other. Knowing that the British could not hold out much longer, the men of the 82nd fought fiercely for the Nijmegen bridge, while listening for the sound of Horrock's tanks behind them.

"Where are the damned tanks?" Gig called out to Marsh. "They should have been here before now."

"They got held up at Son," Marsh replied.

"But that was yesterday."

Marsh was grimly silent, his mind on the sniper in the next house.

The brief silhouette in the window, the steady fire of one rifle and then a lull for reloading registered in Marsh's brain. The German sniper was the major obstacle directly between the three paratroopers and the others fighting on the bridge.

Marsh, tired and irritable at the delay, left his position to reconnoiter at the back of the red-tiled house with the parapets overlooking the street, while Gig and Megan continued to fend off the fire from another direction.

Into the semidarkness Marsh went, using the barrel of his rifle to open the rear door of the house. Stealthily, he began to climb the narrow stairs. Holding his breath, he stopped as the stairwell creaked. But the arms fire outside camouflaged the sound.

Looking below him to make sure the enemy had not infiltrated the house behind him, he saw instead a dining-room table set for dinner, its contents bathed in the last vestiges of sunlight. Crisp, clean white linen, a loaf of bread, pale yellow flowers were juxtaposed against shattered glass, as if the owner of the house had suddenly left the table when peace turned into war.

The resumption of fire above caused Marsh to rush the remaining steps. Flinging open the attic door, he saw the sniper whirl from the window to fire at the unexpected intruder.

Marsh, quicker in his aim, won the brief exchange of shots. Not taking time to record in his memory the physical characteristics of his adversary, Marsh crept toward the parapet. From that vantage point, he could see up and down the length of the narrow street. For the moment, nothing now stood in their way to the bridge.

To Gig and Megan concealed below, he called out, "I've got the sniper. Run, and I'll cover you."

First one and then the other drew out of the alleyway, running and ducking, while Marsh crouched on the widow walk and guarded the street until he saw that the two men had passed onto the bridge structure itself.

On the other side of the bridge, the German commander, seeing his own position worsen and, fearing for the loss of the bridge, gave orders for its demolition.

As Marsh, racing to catch up with the others, reached the bridge, the German officer commanded, "Now, Corporal!"

He waited for the detonator to set off the dynamite fitted into boxes painted the same shade of green as the bridge, while paratroopers worked frantically to cut the wires before the feat could be accomplished.

When nothing happened, the German officer frantically shouted to his corporal, "Now—again. Push the detonator!"

The corporal tried again, pushing downward on the handle of the detonator box with both hands. But once again nothing happened, and in desperation he looked at the officer.

They had waited too late to destroy the bridge. The wires had been cut.

The Germans at the north end of the bridge opened fire with all they had. The Wehrmacht had been unable to keep the paratroopers from seizing the lower end. Now it was up to them to hold the northern end until the panzer divisions, with Heinrich von Freiker in their midst, could negotiate the few kilometers to Nijmegen.

Pinned down by fire from the opposite end, Gig took the whining, squirming Lester from the top of his combat suit and set him down beside him on the abutment of the steel bridge while he reloaded his rifle.

"Stay, Lester," he ordered. But the puppy, tired of his incarceration for the greater part of the day, disobeyed Gig. Like a child suddenly freed of restraint, he took off toward the middle of the bridge, his small belly swollen with the last of Gig's K rations, his short tail wagging at the two troopers farther ahead.

"Hey, Madison," Megan called. "Your dog's getting away."

Turning his attention from his rifle, Gig began to whistle for the dog. "Come here, Lester. Come back, puppy. You're going to get your head blown off."

The whistling, the shouts were of no concern to the puppy. Lester continued forward as fast as his short, stubby legs would carry him.

Swinging his body over the railing, Gig began to run after the puppy, to rescue him before a stray German bullet put an end to his short life.

"Madison, come back. That's an order!" Marsh's voice shouted the command, his words echoing in triplicate in a staccato sound back and forth across the river.

But Gig, like the puppy, had a mind of his own. He was too close to Lester not to try a rescue. As Gig's hands reached out for his pet, a burst of machine-gun fire leveled all three paratroopers brash enough to leave the shelter of the abutment for the middle of the bridge.

Gig fell in a riddle of bullets, the puppy barely beyond his grasp.

"Madison!" Marsh shouted again—too late. Anguish filled his heart, spilling over to cloud his vision, while the lump in his throat railed against the sudden death in twilight.

Marsh leaped from his defensive position, throwing everything he had into battle, as if he were the only one fighting the Germans. He rushed down the bridge, his combat boots making a thundering noise on the metallic surface, while Lester, the small brown puppy, thinking it a game, leaned over and licked Gig's still face and waited for the dead paratrooper to tuck him once again into the top of his combat suit.

There was no time for last rites, no time for rescuing the dead from the bridge. The living were too busy demanding retribution from the enemy, seeking vengeance for life lost in the battle.

Events of Gig's life whirled in Marsh's mind, even as he fought. The episode of the donkey in Sicily, the Great Dane in Normandy. Because of his love for yet another animal, Gig had lost his life.

Now Marsh Wexford was the only original member of his combat team left to fight. At that moment, his own safety was not high on his list of priorities.

Denying everything but the need to get even, Marsh was

in the vanguard to reach the other side. His grenade, thrown into the concrete bunker, effectively put it out of commission. And the remaining troopers rushed down the bridge, to take and hold the northern end.

As Horrock's tanks rumbled through Nijmegen and reached the bridge, a great shout went up from the survivors of the 82nd Division. At great cost, they had secured the bridge—the last formidable obstacle between Nijmegen and Arnhem.

"Go, tanks!" someone shouted, waving them on to cross the newly taken bridge. But the great rumble of tanks began to diminish as each motor cut out, and the tanks settled down for the night on the approach to the bridge.

"What's the matter? You afraid to cross?" one disgruntled paratrooper called out at the delay.

"You want us to come over and lead you by the hand? What's the matter with you guys? You can't stop now!"

"We have to wait for the infantry to catch up with us," was the reply.

An unbelieving 82nd Airborne Division—tired, bleeding, hungry and thirsty, aware that their airborne cousins were being decimated at Arnhem only eleven miles away—became livid.

"Georgie Patton wouldn't have stopped for the night," one declared.

"Yeah. You can bet on that. He would have gone straight through tonight—infantry or no infantry—to rescue every last one of the troopers."

"Instead of stopping off for tea."

Officers and enlisted men of the 82nd Airborne were extremely bitter. And none more so than Captain Daniel "Marsh" Wexford.

Heinrich von Freiker heard the disappointing news. The bridge at Nijmegen had been captured intact by the Americans.

He would have preferred meeting them before the bridge but, armed with the knowledge of their route, he was not unduly alarmed. Still, he did not quite believe the road chosen for the tanks to get to Arnhem—the dike road, on high ground, indefensible from enemy guns on each side. The most gifted student in either Dutch or German war college would have failed his examination if he had chosen that route to Arnhem, in preference to the lower road.

But it was to his advantage that the British planners of the invasion had evidently not consulted the Dutch. They had good reason, because of the double agents. But the Americans, more trusting, had utilized members of the Resistance, making it possible, despite their plans being known, to take every objective assigned to them.

Things would be different from now on, Heinrich pledged silently while he stood on the high ground and looked in the direction of the bridge. At first light, he promised a devastating blow in two directions—on the dike road, and later, nearer the bridge itself.

"Back to camp, Horst," he suddenly ordered his driver in clipped, guttural tones.

They drove to the bivouac where the tanks had been camouflaged. The offensive of Market-Garden had ground to a halt for the night, and an impatient Heinrich longed for sunrise when he would personally annihilate Horrock's tanks and break the back of the Allies' offensive in their attempt to rescue the paratroopers still struggling to hold on at Arnhem.

"Heil, Hitler!" he said, returning the salute of the special guard as he reached his tent directly beyond the tanks sent from the Reichswald.

Marsh deliberately chose a resting place for the night where he could be alone with his grief. Megan had gone down on the bridge.

He was tired of the war, of the price paid for each plot of earth, red from the blood of men dying to keep a madman from taking over the world. And he was tired of the generals in their immaculate uniforms, in their comfortable beds that night, far from the cries of the wounded and the silent recriminations of the men they had sent to their deaths.

Marsh, the shy and gentle giant, had experienced more than his share of suffering. He longed to wake up from the nightmare and to hear Gig whistling his favorite tune; to see Laroche whittling his alligator from a stick; and to watch Giraldo losing at poker, as he had on the night before their jump into Normandy.

Finally, a troubled and exhausted Marsh, the stubble of beard on his chin a reminder of the fighting without cessation, relaxed into sleep as his mind continued the nightmare, dreams distorted by what he had lost in these frantic days of fighting in Holland.

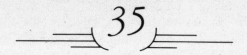

35

Along the suicidal dike road, the tanks from Horrock's 30 Corps began their advance. The German guns opened up, with the panzerfaust weapons completing what the guns missed.

In less than one hour, hopeless chaos reigned—tanks destroyed and burning, blocking the narrow corridor that was unprotected on both sides.

Heinrich looked through his binoculars and felt a sense of elation at the destruction. But the elation was tempered with the realization that it was not only the British tanks he had sworn to annihilate, but the infantry—specifically the American 82nd Airborne Infantry that had taken the Nijmegen bridge intact the previous evening.

Like a gladiator assessing the strength of his opponent, Heinrich sensed this was the moment to strike in another direction—in the pocket of woods where the infantry was grouped in hand-to-hand combat.

This time, *he* had the advantage. This time, *he* would make sure that the All-American Division did not escape him as it had in Sicily and Normandy.

Heinrich, in a reckless mood, decided he would get into the fight personally, the same as the young American general Gavin, who had jumped with his troops and, by all reports, had slept on the ground with them.

"You may follow if you wish," Heinrich announced to the sad-eyed Horst, as he climbed into the lead tank. "At a distance, of course." For Horst had protested being left behind.

With the goggles over his eyes, Heinrich raised his hand to signal the tanks to move out for their positions.

Captain Marsh Wexford, with a new company of men to lead, left the safety of the slit trench he had dug the evening before, ate a chocolate bar for breakfast, and climbed into a jeep with a driver named Smitty, assigned to take him to headquarters for briefing.

"You read German, don't you, Wexford?"

"Yes, sir."

The commanding officer seemed relieved. "Well, we just captured a bunch of panzerfausts last night, with their instructions. The first thing I want you to do is translate them, so our men can assemble the weapons. Pretty good, huh? Using the German's own weapons to knock out their tanks."

"It's about the only thing that will penetrate the armor—especially the Tigers," Marsh agreed.

"Wonder why the U.S. never developed one this good?"

"I guess no one ever had the guts to tell the Pentagon that their antitank weapons didn't work."

"Yes. Well, get to it, Wexford. We'll probably need them in the next few hours."

With Marsh translating the instructions into English, the men assembled the weapons in a short time. Now they were ready to move out on foot, taking the panzerfausts with them.

The sound of big guns in the distance pinpointed the main battle along the dike road. Black smoke and the acrid smell of burning rubber filled the sky. Suddenly, as machine guns ripped through the trees within the pocket of woods beyond the dike, Marsh and his men jumped for cover. They had deliberately fanned out in a wider sweep, infiltrating behind the German line of defense.

"Let's go," Marsh whispered, crawling on his stomach through the brush toward the machine-gun nest that defended that portion of road.

The platoons of soldiers followed and, circling the dug-in position of the Germans, they rushed it with rifles blazing. As smoke filtered through the woods and drifted upward to meet the mist, a bird, oblivious to the battle, lit on the tree next to the machine-gun nest—more intent on the insect crawling along the bark than on the three dead German soldiers being removed from their positions behind the guns.

While two of the troopers took possession of the placement, the others slowly worked their way forward, their goal to infiltrate each position along the line behind the bigger guns trained on the dike road.

Turning to his right where Gig usually fought, Marsh felt a sense of loss as he looked at the freckle-faced youth beside him. Then like lightning that gave no warning, a thunderous, dark scowl replaced the sad visage, for zipped into the youth's combat suit was Lester, the small brown puppy.

"What are you doing with that dog, Corporal?"

"I found him on the bridge, sir. He's no trouble. I—"

"Get rid of him, immediately!"

"But sir . . ."

"That's an order!"

A miserable young soldier began to unzip the top of his combat suit, while the friend next to him attempted to intervene.

"He's just a harmless little puppy, Captain."

"You heard me, Corporal."

"Yes, sir." The two young soldiers exchanged glances, and the corporal, wondering what had caused the captain to be so angry, gently placed the small brown puppy on the ground.

"Fall back in line, Corporal. To the rear. Innes, take Harris with you and scout ahead for the next several hundred yards."

The reluctant corporal left Lester by the roadside, while an inconsolable Marsh Wexford began the next phase of infiltration without looking back at the abandoned puppy.

A chill in the morning air and the dampness of the ground where Marsh had slept made his bones ache, as if he were an old man divining the change of seasons. Even his throat felt sore and Marsh was conscious of the uncomfortable cold mist that invaded his lungs and caused his breathing to become labored as he led his men onward through the woods.

He hated the fall rains and winter weather in Europe, coming without warning to numb his fingers, rendering them clumsy in the reloading of his weapons. They should be supple, quick to deal with Germans hidden behind the trees throughout the forest.

At the exchange of fire ahead, Marsh dropped to the ground and, from his place behind a log, listened and watched for the two soldiers to return from their scouting.

He blew on his hands to warm them, but the expiration of breath changed into a cough—raw, barking. It penetrated the woods and gave away his hiding place. Forcing himself to stop in the middle of the cough, he covered his mouth and wheezed, feeling his lungs protest at the same time.

When the wheezing had subsided, there was no sound except the gentle patter of morning rain on the leaves and the telltale rattle of tanks where they had no business being.

Five minutes passed, then five more. The two soldiers sent ahead did not return. Marsh, uneasy, said to the man beside him, "Bring the panzerfaust with you. We'll go ahead and see what's holding them up."

The two moved out in the direction of the road, careful not to break cover or give a clear view of themselves to the enemy around them. Their progress went unchallenged, unprotested, which aroused Marsh's suspicions. Something was wrong ahead. He wasn't certain what it was, but the feeling remained, that primitive instinct that caused the adrenalin to begin flowing, an autonomous thing that had nothing to do with logic or reason.

"Wait for me here," he ordered, "and cover me. I'm going ahead."

Marsh slowly wound his way forward, until he came to a bend in the road where his view was obscured. His senses tingled with alertness as his breathing grew more labored.

Hidden at the bend in the road was a single German tank, camouflaged, its menacing gun waiting to blast the entire company the moment it swept around the curve.

Realizing the soldiers were slowly making their way through the woods to this central point, Marsh knew what he had to do. He hurried back to the soldier waiting with the panzerfaust and he exchanged his rifle for the more powerful weapon.

"There's a German tank ahead," he said. "Go back and warn the others about the ambush. I'll try to knock it out."

"I'd feel better, Captain, if I went forward with you."

"Do as I say, soldier. Enough troopers have already died, without more falling into a trap at this late date."

All his anger, his hurt was directed at that one tank and its occupant, as if the war were now being fought between two men, like David and Goliath. Forgotten was the promise he had made to Paulina di Resa in the villa in Sicily. He had a vendetta of his own to settle—for Gig, Giraldo, and Laroche. But the German in command of the tank was the same man Paulina had sworn him to avenge when she had drawn the cross of blood in Marsh's hand.

Marsh slung the panzerfaust over his shoulder and slowly began to reweave his way through the woods to the position on the other side of the road from the hidden tank.

The panzerfaust instructions he had translated from the German ran through his mind—the range of effectiveness a mere thirty-three yards, much shorter than the bazookas the infantry had been trained to use against enemy tanks. In Sicily, Marsh had learned not to rely on the bazooka against the Tiger tanks. But he had seen the panzerfausts in action against the U.S. Army tanks, and he was well acquainted with their destructive power.

As Marsh advanced, the two soldiers he had sent ahead watched and listened in desperation, while the trench knives of their German captors were held at their throats to keep them from warning him.

While Heinrich von Freiker also listened for the sound of advancing troops, Marsh continued forward. He was committed to knocking out the tank with the panzerfaust with its finned projectile. And he would make sure he was much closer to it than thirty-three yards. He was determined to make no mistake, no error in judgment, for he had only one projectile between the tank and his company.

With the panzerfaust hoisted to his shoulder, he came within range of the tank, the rain-soaked forest disguising his steps, but not the cough that forced its way past his lips. He stopped and listened, and then moved on.

Ten more yards to go, and he would be almost face to face with the enemy.

It was now or not at all, for the gunner had started whirling the large turret gun into position toward the wooded area where he was hiding.

In a sudden rush, Marsh left the dubious safety of his hiding place, crouched at the edge of the road and positioned the panzerfaust on the ground.

"Fire!" The order, loud and penetrating, came from Heinrich for the tank gunner to fire.

As the sound exploded all around him in the forest, a relieved Marsh realized the gun was positioned too high to reach him. He took the panzerfaust and fired it, its projectile spewing toward the tank. It hit and the tank erupted in flames.

For one second's purgatory before hell began, the two opponents stared at each other—Heinrich in his immaculate black SS uniform covered by a raincoat, and Marsh in the dirty, wet combat suit he had worn for six days straight.

As a piece of metal struck his foot, tearing the leather of his boot into shreds, Heinrich screamed. In disbelief he saw the blood trailing—his own blood—as he fell over the side of the burning tank and rolled in the wet leaves to put out the fire that scorched his hair and filled his nose, nearly suffocating him.

The powerful gun of the tank, fired a few seconds before the panzerfaust, dug up the forest, splitting a nearby linden tree in half, to fall on the unsuspecting Marsh only moments after he had fired the projectile.

Now Marsh lay pinned to the forest floor at the bend in the road, the trunk of the tree too heavy to lift from his body, his rifle left in the woods beyond, and a frenzied Heinrich von Freiker, dragging his foot behind, heading toward him with his side arms drawn.

36

*I*n a paroxysm of coughing, with the heavy weight of the tree across his chest and legs, Marsh felt the dripping of the rain on his face.

His luck had run out. A sadness overwhelmed him. The commemorative coin, the promise he had given to little Ibert Duvalier—all were gone.

Once more he struggled against the weight that pinned him down, but it was hopeless.

With the wounded German officer staring down at him, examining every inch of his face as he aimed carefully, Marsh waited patiently for death. He would have preferred his blood spilled, not in Holland, amid the canals and soft polder land reclaimed from the sea, but in the land of his birth—France—to be near the mother he had never known in life. Reunited in death—two wars apart.

He heard the click of the gun and he closed his eyes.

"*Nein*," a guttural voice cautioned. "We need him for questioning."

At the sound of the voice, Marsh opened his eyes to see another German officer staring down at him.

But Heinrich ignored the voice. He aimed and fired at Marsh's head. Marsh felt nothing, heard nothing except the explosion in his ears.

A dazed and weakened Heinrich looked at the pistol in his hands and back to the soldier still alive on the ground. He had missed him at close range.

Heinrich raised his pistol and, attempting to focus his eyes, he aimed again at Marsh.

The other officer deflected the gun with his hand. "*Nein*," Heinrich. You are not to shoot him."

"You already have two prisoners, Karl," Heinrich argued. "That should be enough."

"But this is an officer. He is much more valuable to us. Come, Heinrich," he ordered, confiscating the side arms. "Horst is bringing up the car to take you to the hospital."

"Karl . . ."

"Leave him to me, Heinrich. You're bleeding to death."

Looking toward the trail of blood through the leaves, Heinrich became sick. His vision blurred again and his mind, once more playing tricks on him, saw his father staring up at him from the forest floor.

Horst arrived, jumped from the car, and lifted his Obersturmbahnführer in his arms.

"Promise me, Horst. You will kill him."

"Who, my Colonel?"

"My father. I tried to shoot him but the bullet missed."

Horst, worried that his commander had received a concussion from the tank explosion and was out of his head, said nothing, but continued to the car. He left the scene as the two captured paratroopers were led from the woods to help remove the tree trunk pinning their captain to the ground.

In the house along the downs, Alpharetta and Dow sat in the parlor with Birdie, Freddie, and Reggie.

Eight days had elapsed since the two had watched the great air armada pass over them. Eight days of waiting for news of the fighting.

No mention had been made of Marsh's division, the 82nd, or the other American one, the 101st. It was as if a conspiracy had silenced any information about four of the bridges, with only the British soldiers fighting near the Arnhem bridge mentioned, and that news increasingly somber.

Waiting for the night's newscast by the BBC, Alpharetta sat patiently, quietly, her ears attuned to the latest development of the invasion that was rapidly turning into disaster. But still, she hoped to hear something about the Americans fighting in Operation Market-Garden.

As a chilled Alpharetta got up for her sweater, Birdie said,

"I think this is it, luv." Quickly she sat down again and, folding her arms for warmth, shivered and listened.

Arnhem was declared a disaster. The few remaining British paratroopers had been evacuated in the night—two thousand of the original ten thousand, a massacre by the Germans. Birdie's eyes filled with tears.

As Alpharetta waited to hear what had happened to the Americans, how many had been killed, the telephone rang in Dow's office next to the parlor.

Freddie, answering the phone, motioned to Alpharetta through the open door. "It's for you," he said.

A surprised Alpharetta rose and walked into Dow's office. She stared at the telephone, hesitating to pick it up. She didn't know why her heart should react, even before she knew who was on the other end of the line. Finally, with Freddie staring at her from the door, she lifted the receiver.

"Hello?"

"Alpharetta?"

"Yes?"

"It's me—Belline."

The words were muffled, and sounded far away.

"Is anything wrong, Belline?"

Unintelligible sobbing sounds took the place of words, and Alpharetta, listening to the incoherence, grew alarmed. "What's the matter, Belline? What's happened? Belline?"

Struggling to make herself understood, Belline finally managed to speak. "Ben Mark's been killed."

A stunned Alpharetta, hearing the words, refused them. All week, she had been thinking of Marsh and the danger he was in. It never occurred to her that Ben Mark was the vulnerable one. Now it was her turn to remain silent, as if she had lost all ability to speak.

"Alpharetta? Did you hear me? Ben Mark is dead."

"No. There must be some mistake, Belline."

"There's no mistake. I have the telegram in front of me."

"If he were shot down, he could still be alive."

"His plane exploded in the air. Ted, the best man at our wedding, called me a few minutes ago."

Alpharetta swallowed. A great hurt lodged in her throat—for Belline, for herself, for Rennie, and the unborn baby. She clutched the telephone and listened to Belline's sobbing, as she tried hard not to do the same.

"Belline? Belline?"

There was no more conversation for the moment. The telephone only served to carry inchoate sounds of grief, with Alpharetta powerless to comfort Belline in her sorrow. The ache in her throat remained as a new fear overtook her. In tones that sounded alien to her own ears, she managed to say, "And Marsh? Have you heard anything from Marsh?"

"Not a word," Belline sobbed. "For all I know, he's dead, too."

"Don't say that, Belline. Pray to God nothing's happened to him, as well."

"Right now, I'm not even sure there *is* a God."

"Where are you? I'll get permission from Dow to let me come and be with you."

"There's nothing you can do, Alpharetta. I just wanted you to know, since you loved Ben Mark, too."

The line went dead and Alpharetta, staring at the black telephone, the harbinger of tragedy, slowly hung it up. She did not return to the parlor where the others were sitting. Her grief was too new to be shared. She raced through the hallway, opened the front door, and fled into the night.

Dow, with one ear to the radio and the other alert to the telephone call, heard the front door close. Something was wrong. He had been with Alpharetta too long not to sense it. Excusing himself from the room, Dow grabbed a flashlight from the hall table next to the door and dashed into the night, the beam of light searching for the red-haired woman who had fled in the fog.

"Alpharetta! Where are you? Come back."

His voice was taken up by the wind and carried into the night. Alpharetta continued to flee until a rabbit hole caused her to pitch forward onto the grassy downs. The breath was knocked from her as she hit the ground.

Like a miniature searchlight seeking out the planes in the sky, the small flashlight beam in Dow's hands struggled through the fog, revealing Alpharetta on the ground.

Hands suddenly lifted her to her feet, but no voice inquired as to her state of health or mind, for the worst had been assumed.

"I'm all right," she protested. "You don't have to help me." Alpharetta backed from him and brushed the dirt from her skirt.

"What's the matter, Alpharetta? Why did you leave the house so suddenly?"

Turning on him as if he were the enemy, Alpharetta retaliated, "The *war's* the matter—Americans getting killed in every battle. And their deaths, their victories, too unimportant for the British to mention."

He ignored the lashing out at him. This was not like Alpharetta, venting her hurt upon another.

"If you're speaking of Arnhem, Alpharetta, naturally it's uppermost in our minds. Our airborne troops have been slaughtered. You heard the news. We've lost eight thousand of our best troops. Britain has no more men to take their places. For us, Arnhem is another Dunkirk." His sad voice went unnoticed.

"And you think we can afford to throw away the lives of our own soldiers? The 82nd and 101st are in the same invasion. You think somehow they've all miraculously escaped death?"

"No, Alpharetta. I don't think that."

"Then why can't we hear what's happened to them? Why does the news have to come from a telephone call?"

"Who rang you up a few minutes ago?" he demanded.

"Belline." Alpharetta wiped the tears from her eyes.

"And?" he prompted.

"Ben Mark is dead."

"Oh, Alpharetta, I'm so sorry."

Before she knew it, she was in his arms, his voice caressing as his hands caressed. The wind gusted over the downs and lashed the two in an embrace. Their lips touched—seeking, comforting—in the mistaken knowledge that love had been denied them both.

Not understanding his emotions, a suddenly angry Dow pushed her from him. Maintaining his grip on her arms, he stared at her and tried to fathom her inmost thoughts.

"Don't grieve for him, Alpharetta. It's not your place. Belline is his wife, not you."

"How can I help it? Poor Ben Mark. He'll never see Atlanta again. Never see his own child."

Tears began streaming down her cheeks as the revelation hit Dow with unexpected impact.

"There's to be a child?" he asked in an incredulous tone.

Alpharetta nodded.

"How soon?"

"In less than seven months." Alpharetta, realizing that she had just breached Belline's confidence, said, "I shouldn't have told you, Dow. Promise me, you won't tell anyone about it."

A grim Dow replied, "Don't worry, Alpharetta. Your secret is safe with me."

"Thank you," a miserable Alpharetta replied. "You see, for Belline's sake . . ."

"There's no need to say any more about it."

It never occurred to Alpharetta, absorbed in her grief, that Dow had completely misunderstood her when she had confessed about the baby.

"Are you ready to come back to the house now, or would you rather stay out awhile?"

His voice was gentle, different from his anger of a few moments earlier.

"I can't go in now, looking like this."

"Are you up to walking?"

"Yes."

He tucked her arm into his and occasionally shone the flashlight on the path, while Alpharetta sought to draw her emotions under control before facing Birdie and the others.

37

The next morning, Air Vice-Marshal Sir Dow Pomeroy abruptly left his headquarters on the downs. Only Eckerd went with him, Reggie and Freddie having taken off on a special reconnaissance flight. The two women remained behind with only the batman, Lloyd, to call upon if they needed help.

A saddened Alpharetta, feeling obsolete, made up her mind. She was tired of looking at aerial photographs and trying to identify the rocket-launching sites amid the camouflage of trees. Because of Ben Mark, she wanted to start flying again—to ferry planes across the channel to the fighting zones.

Finishing her morning tea at the breakfast table, Birdie set down her cup and with a pensive sigh looked at Alpharetta seated across the table.

"I suppose I *should* use today to straighten the files," Birdie commented. "And then start answering the intelligence questionnaire that Ultra is so fond of. What are you planning to do this morning, luv?"

"Make a request for transfer."

"What are you talking about?"

"Birdie, I want to start flying again—this time ferrying planes across the channel."

"Sir Dow won't like that. Won't like that at all," Birdie cautioned.

"There's not much he can do about it, Birdie. I'm only on temporary assignment to him. And my special mission was completed a long time ago."

"But he relies on you, Alpharetta. You're the best aerial spotter around."

"I still haven't been successful in finding the rocket-launching sites, though. Sometimes, when I look at all the still photographs, I get a feeling that it's a floating crap game—the same kind our gardener, Eddie, and his brother were involved in, moving the game to a different place each Saturday night to keep from being caught by the police."

"That's impossible. We all know that. It's just that the Germans have camouflaged the sites so well. Why don't you give it another try this morning, Alpharetta—with those photographs Reggie took several days ago?"

"I still won't find anything unusual, Birdie. I've looked them over time and again."

But with nothing else to do, Alpharetta sat at a corner table with the photographs, as the sound of the typewriter clicking away at the other end of the office indicated that Birdie had become absorbed in her own work.

Alpharetta had gotten little sleep the night before. She was numb with grief over Ben Mark's death—just as she had been when she received the telegram about Conyer and Duluth. Only later would the actual horrible truth hit her. And until then, she knew she must keep her mind busy.

Inch by inch Alpharetta moved the magnifying glass over the photographs and searched for some small deviation from the ones taken the week before.

She kept going back to the same picture time after time, re-examining it, moving the glass up and down to try to make some sense of the strange, cylindrical device half hidden by the trees surrounding it.

The position of the cylinder was horizontal, not vertical, and on it was the barest suggestion of a wheel she hadn't noticed before. Alpharetta became excited at the idea of a wheel. And the remark about the floating crap game, spoken facetiously, suddenly made sense.

If it were true. No, it was too heavy, too cumbersome. But what if the rocket launchers were actually mobile? Couldn't that be the reason no one had been able to destroy them? The planes had bombarded the same sites again and again, but still the V-2 rockets kept coming over London. An im-

patient, excited Alpharetta stood up, carried the reconnaissance photograph to the window, and, holding it up to the
light, examined it again under the magnifying glass.

"Birdie," she called out, interrupting the woman at her typing—something she had never done before.

Birdie finished typing the sentence and then looked up
from her desk. "Yes? What is it, Alpharetta?"

"I think I've found it."

"What? The launching ramp?"

"It's not actually a concrete ramp, Birdie. It's a huge mobile
unit on wheels. Can't you see? We've been looking for the
wrong thing. That's why we haven't been able to make any
progress. The Germans move it from place to place—hiding
it in the woods. Come and take a look. You can see a portion
of wheel, if you look closely."

Birdie left the desk and walked to the window where Alpharetta stood.

"You see? The barest suggestion of a wheel? It must be
movable, Birdie. It *has* to be."

Not nearly so excited as Alpharetta, Birdie inquired, "But
how could they fire such huge rockets from the ground like
that? Wouldn't they stay close to the ground instead of going
into a trajectory high enough to reach England?"

Deflated as she considered Birdie's point, Alpharetta suddenly smiled. "No, Birdie. The wheel in the picture could be
hydraulic, used to position the rocket vertically—*after* it's
loaded."

Though still not convinced, Birdie was pleased to see Alpharetta so excited. Perhaps with this new development, she
might forget the idea of leaving Sir Dow's staff.

Birdie went back to her desk, while Alpharetta walked to
the file cabinet. Now, with a new direction to pursue, Alpharetta pulled out other reconnaisance photographs, spread
them on the floor, and began to look for the launching unit
in a vertical position. If she found it in two different positions
that fact would be convincing evidence to present to Dow
upon his return.

A quarter of an hour later, Alpharetta found it—the same
type cylinder, as vertical as the trees around it.

Her unconscious sound of pleasure completely disrupted

Birdie's train of thought. "You found what you were looking for?"

"Oh, did I disturb you again, Birdie?" she inquired, unable to disguise her pleased expression.

"That's all right, luv. It's time to take a break anyway." She rose from the desk and walked toward the table where Alpharetta had sorted out the three telling photographs from the rest. "You found something, did you?"

"Yes. More than enough evidence to convince Sir Dow."

"I'm so glad, Alpharetta."

Gathering up the other photographs, the younger woman asked, "Do you want to see, Birdie?"

The woman shook her head. "I won't be able to tell anything about them. I haven't the knack for it."

"Then I'll lock them in the files again," Alpharetta said, "and I think I'll go for a walk. My eyes are tired."

"You do that, luv. And I'll just get on with my typing."

While Alpharetta contemplated what Dow might say about her discovery, the air vice-marshal had his mind on other things.

Sitting up front in the staff car with Eckerd, Dow had been silent for the last hour. His father would be surprised to see him, unless Meg had alerted him of his sudden trip.

All along the way to Harrington Hall, Dow silently rehearsed what he would say to Meg. With his eyes on the road, Eckerd knew his commander was wrestling with a vexing problem.

Eckerd always enjoyed driving into Yorkshire, the place where he was born. There was something about the moors that he loved. And when his father had moved to Leeds, Eckerd remembered how desolate and lonely he felt, bound by dirty streets and sooty buildings, when he had known the freedom and fresh, clean air of the moors.

Still wrestling with words that stubbornly eluded him, Dow was only vaguely aware of his surroundings as they passed through the cathedral city of York and began the approach to the little town of Pocklington.

"We're almost there, Sir Dow," Eckerd said, smiling. It was a habit of the past four years, to awaken Sir Dow at the place where the sign had once stood.

But Dow was not asleep this time. In fact, he had slept little for the past twenty-four hours—ever since he had followed Alpharetta onto the downs, after her devastating telephone call.

Ben Mark St. John was dead. If Alpharetta had ever thought to get him back, that dream was now dead with the man.

The familiar landscape appeared and Dow, looking along the stretch of vista which the threshing machine had deprived of its corn crop, grimaced. Like some poor sheep shorn of its wool, the vista was now bare stubble.

At that moment, the land army girls, dressed in fatigues, passed by and waved. They had just come from the fields and the lorry was loaded with fodder for the animals for winter.

The long summer days had given way to fall, with a chill in the air, a sudden rush of wind whipping over the fields and moors. And the trees, buffeted by the wind, were losing their leaves in the prelude to winter, revealing the nests built in their forks.

Animals had the right idea, an instinct for survival, building nests and scurrying to bury their acorns. They were much smarter than the men who sat and planned for the next battles, which were even more destructive than the wintry blasts.

Dow shook his head, as if to clear it for other thoughts. He himself was far better at planning complicated air maneuvers and intelligence missions than a single confrontation that, however dignified in the execution, still remained an unpleasant task.

He was not looking forward to the meeting with Meg, or the repercussions to follow in his own house. But his feeling of protection for Alpharetta overrode everything else.

As the car drove into the courtyard of Harrington Hall, Dow said, "Eckerd, I'll not be long. Stretch your legs, and then be ready to leave again in twenty minutes."

Lady Margaret, with a dark shawl over her shoulders to keep warm, left the school housed in a massive old hall a mile away from her own residence, and climbed into the governess cart pulled by Nicky, the piebald pony.

It was quite a comedown, the lady of the manor relegated to the governess cart to go back and forth to the school where refugee children from the London streets had been relocated.

For some of the children, the school was now a way of life, their activities in the crowded streets of a crowded city long forgotten, just as making do was a way of life for Margaret, whose Rolls-Royce, lacking petrol, now stood in the carriage house and was brought out only on rare occasions.

There was no need for her to guess why Dow was making a special trip to see her. Ever since he had brought the red-haired woman on his staff to Harrington Hall and placed her in the green room, Meg had suspected that their engagement might be in trouble.

If the war had not come when it did . . . But what was the use of living in the past? The war *had* come, taking Gerald from her. Solid, steadfast Gerald, not nearly so exciting as his younger brother, Dow. Meg had been comfortable with Gerald, as she was even now with Dow's ADC, Freddie Mallory. But she never felt completely at ease when she was with Dow, despite his attempts to make her so.

For a fleeting moment, Meg allowed herself to think Dow's visit might be for another reason, but then she remembered Chatelaine Day when Sir Edward had given her the betrothal necklace. Dow had not even noticed, for his eyes had been for the other woman. He must love her very much. And because of that, she knew what she must do.

Meg had just enough time to wash her face and comb through her hair before Dow arrived. Farnsworth, the butler, opened the door, as Meg walked down the stairs.

"Dow," she called from the foot of the stairs. "How good to see you again."

She came forward to meet him, offering her cheek for him to kiss. Far more calmly than she thought possible, she said, "I was just going for a walk. Would you like to join me, instead of sitting in the drawing room? We haven't made a fire yet."

Slightly startled, Dow replied, "Why, yes. A walk would be very pleasant." He took his hat from Farnsworth and placed it under one arm, while he offered the other to Meg.

Within a few minutes, they were in the garden, far from the inquisitive ears of Lara, the maid. Meg wanted no one to overhear their conversation.

"I read the tragic news in the paper this morning," Meg prompted the silent Dow.

"Yes. It looks as if the war will last another winter."

"It must be awfully disappointing to Monty, even though he said the invasion was ninety percent successful."

Dow stared at Meg. "It was a failure, Meg. A blasted failure." His voice was harsher than he intended. "I'm sorry, Meg, for sounding off like that."

"You have every right to do so, Dow. I know what a strain you've been under, with the rockets—everyone blaming everyone else, the Prime Minister, on down, for not stopping them."

Spotting the bench in the far corner of the garden, Dow said, "Let's sit down for a while, Meg. I came to discuss something other than the war, but I'm finding it extremely difficult to come up with the words."

For an instant, Meg's emotions gave her away. Then she steeled her trembling lips, and her soft brown eyes revealed nothing as she turned to Dow and smiled.

"Dow, don't look so distressed," she assured him. "I already know what you're going to say. And it's all right. Really it is."

He gazed at her with a questioning look.

"You want me to release you from our engagement."

Dow's eyes held no joy, merely pain. When he did not deny it, she continued, "From the first time you brought her to Harrington Hall, I somehow knew you were falling in love with Alpharetta Beaumont."

"But I . . ." He ceased abruptly and stared at the astute Meg, with her ability to see into his heart. "I didn't want it to be this way, Meg."

"I know. But war does strange things to relationships." Seeing how miserable he looked, Meg insisted, "It's better this way, you know, for I could never marry a man who loved someone else. That happened to my mother and she never got over it." Meg's voice became less audible. "I suppose you'll be marrying her soon?"

"I haven't spoken to her yet."

A bittersweet smile formed on Meg's lips. Of course he would not have said anything to Alpharetta. His code of honor would preclude that, while he was engaged to someone else.

Staring into the distance toward Harrington Hall, Dow said, "The hardest part will be to tell my father—and Lord Cranston. They'll both be extremely disappointed."

"It won't be the end of the world for them, Dow. Just so

long as they can continue playing cribbage together. But if you don't mind, I'd rather be the one to break off the engagement—just for appearances."

"Of course, Meg. I'll say nothing about it. And you may paint me into a black knave and throw arrows at me, if you like."

"I don't think that's necessary, Dow." Meg stood up. As if the embarrassing conversation had never taken place, Meg reminded him, "You and Sir Edward are expected for dinner tonight."

"Won't that be awkward—in the circumstances?"

"I should think we would always be friends, Dow, even after you marry Alpharetta. And Father and I would expect you for dinner, as we have in the past. That won't change."

A new respect for Lady Margaret Cranston went with Dow as he returned to Harrington Hall. Also traveling with him was the uneasy burden he had deliberately chosen—to protect Alpharetta from scandal, as she bore another man's child.

Watching him climb into the waiting car, Meg realized she had not told Dow that her friend, Macris, had written her about the wedding in the ancient abbey on the downs with Ben Mark St. John as the groom and someone other than Alpharetta as the bride. From that information, she had known that Dow's request for freedom would soon follow.

38

*I*n the small hours of Sunday evening, long after everyone else had gone to bed, Alpharetta sat by the fire in the parlor and gazed at the dying embers as she contemplated the last few months on Sir Dow's staff.

Already the request for transfer was on his desk. As soon as the paper work went through, she would be on her way. The only question was: where? She no longer wanted to stay in England. But she couldn't return to the WASPs, since the U.S. Air Corps had phased out that program. Perhaps she would apply to the WAACs as Mary Lou Brandon had done.

All evening she had waited for the sound of Dow's car. It was imperative to show him the aerial photographs at the earliest possible moment, to have him confirm her suspicions about the rocket-launching devices. If they proved to be true, then her time had not been wasted. And it would be an appropriate memorial to Ben Mark, if her discovery should keep other people from dying.

Lulled by the peace and silence of the room bathed in a pale candescence, Alpharetta closed her eyes and laid her head on the cushion by the hearth. Not intending to go to sleep, she nevertheless drifted into a light slumber before Dow's car turned into the drive.

At the gate, Dow said, "Just let me out here, Eckerd, and you can put the car up. I'll walk the rest of the way to the house."

"What about your luggage, Sir Dow?"

"Bring it to the house at breakfast time. That will be soon enough."

And so it was that Alpharetta, sleeping by the hearth, did not hear the car and was not aware of Dow's footsteps as he deliberately tiptoed into the silent house.

Halfway up the stairs to his bedroom, Dow changed his mind and retraced his steps down the hallway to his office. Carefully checking that the blackout draperies were drawn despite the relaxation of the defense regulation, he turned on the light.

Dow sat down at his desk to go over his mail and any messages that Birdie had left for him.

He was immediately depressed as he recognized Meg's handwriting on the first letter. Turning to the metal file tray at his right, he took out the papers to examine instead, glancing quickly through the sheaf for any that needed his immediate attention. Alpharetta's request for transfer was sandwiched between the completed questionnaire and the staff report Birdie had left for him to sign.

He sat with the transfer papers in his hands. They were no longer relevant, for Alpharetta would be going nowhere else except Harrington Hall. Setting them aside, he signed the other papers and reports, and then began a report of his own, using the typewriter, while he waited for sleepiness to send him looking for his bed. He should never have allowed himself the luxury of a nap in the staff car on the way back. Now there was no telling when he would get to sleep.

The clacking of the typewriter permeated Alpharetta's slumber. Like one waking up from a bad dream, she lifted her head and looked around her. The fire was out; she was cold and uncomfortable.

Alpharetta listened, but the noise in the office stopped. Perhaps it had been Reggie or Freddie, unable to sleep. When she glanced at her watch, she saw that it was one A.M., far too late to stay up any longer waiting for Dow. She stood and yawned just as the office door opened and Dow Pomeroy came into view.

Seeing her, Dow said "Alpharetta, what are you doing up so late?"

"I was waiting to see you. But I must have gone to sleep by the fire," she confessed.

His eyes softened at her admission. "If it's the transfer . . ."

"No, I wanted to show you the aerial maps. I think I've found something really important. Could you take a quick look? Now?"

"If you're not too exhausted to show me. You really should take better care of yourself."

A puzzled look passed over her face. *He* was the one who had just returned from a long, tiring trip.

They went back into his office. At first Dow was not impressed with Alpharetta's theory or her pinpointing the merest suggestion of a wheel. And yet her argument held logic. The more he thought about it, the more logical it became. Certainly, it could be the reason for the stalemate even if it *did* make the resolution of the problem more complex.

Looking from the map to Alpharetta, Dow said, "If it's true, you realize the headache it brings."

"Yes. The launching sites can't be overrun as Montgomery had hoped."

Tightening his jaw, Dow vowed, "We'll have to step up the bombing of all supply trains. It's the only way to make certain the rockets don't reach Holland from Germany. If they have no rockets to fire . . ."

"Then their launchers will remain idle," she finished for him.

"You've done a valuable service, Alpharetta. Now go on upstairs to bed. You and I are going to have a long day tomorrow with Mittie at Fighter Command."

Alpharetta, pleased to be included, said, "Do you want me to put the maps back?"

"No, I'll do that."

"Then, good night, sir."

His frown turned into a smile at her formality. "Good night, Alpharetta. Sleep well."

For a long time, he remained in his office. At 1:45 in the morning, Dow locked the maps into his cabinet, cut out the lights, and walked up the stairs to his own bedroom at the opposite end of the hall from where Birdie and Alpharetta were sleeping.

By ten o'clock the next morning, Dow and Alpharetta sat in conference with Sir Nelson Mitford, his aide, and two other aerial target spotters. They pored over the three maps and discussed Alpharetta's theory, substantiated by a recent intelligence report sent from a young Dutch boy through a friend in Switzerland.

Despite the doubt of one of the experts, Sir Nelson was convinced. "The prime minister will be pleased," he announced. And the man, nicknamed the Pelican because of his awkwardness, took special pride in the fact that it was Alpharetta who had evidently come up with the answer.

As they were leaving, Mittie took the air vice-marshal aside and chided, "I remember the day, Pom, when you weren't at all pleased that I assigned that young woman to your personal staff. How do you feel about her now?"

Keeping his face sober, Dow said, "She still hasn't learned how to salute, Mittie."

Alpharetta lifted her chin in defiance as they stared at her from across the room. Mittie chuckled at Dow's reply and teased, "But she has other attributes far more important. By the way, how is Lady Margaret?"

"Very well, thank you. I presume you know that we're no longer engaged to be married."

"No, I was not aware." Mittie cleared his throat. At a loss for appropriate words, Mittie said aloud what he was thinking at the moment.

"I suppose no one can forget she was Gerald's girl, first. Well, bear up, old boy," he said, patting him on the shoulder. "And be careful. First love is full of innocence. But second love is fraught with danger. And it comes jolly soon."

Mittie's platitude did not make Dow feel any better, for Alpharetta's first love had evidently not been so innocent. But Dow had no right to judge. The war had done strange things to them all, making them live for the moment, since the tomorrows were so few. That was why he mustn't waste any more time before speaking to Alpharetta.

They left Fighter Command and rode in silence until they had almost reached the house. Alpharetta, unable to keep silent any longer, said, "You'll sign my transfer now?"

Before answering, Dow looked toward Eckerd in the front seat, then back to Alpharetta at his side. "I need to talk with you about that. Are you up to walking the rest of the way?"

Alpharetta laughed. "You sound as if I've suddenly developed an infirmity. I confess I had a birthday last week, but

I'm not quite over the hill. Of course I'm up to walking, if that's what you want to do."

Dow tapped on the window that divided the front seat from the rear. He motioned for Eckerd to stop, and the two climbed out of the back seat to walk the remainder of the way.

They had not gone more than a few steps when Dow said, "There's no need for the transfer, Alpharetta. For you the war is over."

She bristled at his words. "I can still fly, Dow. And I plan to do so, as long as I can."

"I know how you feel," he said with sympathy in his eyes. "But you've done your share, Alpharetta. *More* than your share. You need someone to take care of you, now. And I plan to be that someone."

"I don't think I understand you."

Impatiently, Dow looked around, at the lack of privacy. "Let's walk on the downs toward the channel—and I'll explain."

Still puzzled, Alpharetta accompanied him until they were out of sight of the house. With the wind whipping in from the channel and the crash of waves in the background, Dow stopped in a sheltered band of small shrubs where an outcropping of rock provided a seat.

"Do you remember the time, Alpharetta, when we were on the beach at Lochendall and I kissed you?"

"The spy was watching us from above."

Dow shook his head. "That wasn't the reason. I merely used him as an excuse. I fell in love with you that day, Alpharetta. And that love has grown stronger every day."

"Dow, you mustn't tell me these things. Lady Margaret . . ."

"Meg and I are no longer engaged, so I have every right. I was planning to ask you to marry me when you had recovered from your shrapnel wound, but then your fiancé suddenly appeared."

"Ben Mark. Yes, I remember that afternoon in the garden at the dower house."

"But he's dead, Alpharetta. And the living have to go on living—to salvage what's left. I made arrangements this morning with the authorities for our marriage. The red tape will take another week."

"But I—"

"No excuses, Alpharetta. I love you and that's all that matters. And one day, I hope you will grow to love me, too."

It was happening too fast. But she had no time to come to terms with his words. His arms, his lips claimed her, dredging up memories of the time when she had posed as his wife at Lochendall. And the same love that had been a newly wrought thing, lying dormant beneath the surface of their lives, now blossomed into fullness.

She ached with love lost—her father, Conyer, Duluth, Ben Mark—her strength gradually eroding with each new loss. Dow was offering her a haven of love from which she would never have to venture alone, and Alpharetta, not understanding her vulnerability until that moment, had yet to fathom the full proportion of his gift.

She was in his arms, her head against his shoulder, and her heart was at peace.

In a secrecy that Alpharetta did not feel necessary, Dow arranged the wedding ceremony for the following Saturday.

"Birdie will be hurt," Alpharetta commented, "when she discovers we didn't even let her know."

"It's much better this way. Safer for you."

"If you're thinking of that weekend when we were alone in the house . . ."

"Among other things. No, it's much better to announce the *fait accompli* than go through the fanfare preceding it."

"If that's what you want. But how are you going to explain this suddenness to your own father?"

"You may leave that up to me," he said, ending the conversation.

When Saturday arrived, Alpharetta, at Dow's request, dressed in her uniform and casually left the premises in a taxi, as if she were to be gone for the day. She would have preferred wearing something more bridal, as Belline had done. But there had been no time for shopping, not even for a new nightgown. The one concession she had made was replacing her usual pink wool thermal underwear with the white silk camisole she had brought with her from Atlanta. Because of the cold and dampness of the English weather, it had received little wear.

Carrying her shoulder bag, Alpharetta left the house on the downs and rode into London, to wait for Dow in the lobby of the Ritz Hotel, a place filled with bittersweet memories of Ben Mark, Belline, and Marsh, of girlish dreams of innocence shattered by war like the windows that faced the Thames. Overshadowing the journey was the ever-present threat of the Vengeance rockets.

Approximately fifteen minutes after Alpharetta had arrived at the hotel, Dow came, not in the staff car with Eckerd but in a black taxi, just as Alpharetta had done.

She rose to greet him as his eyes sought her out. "The taxi is waiting. Are you ready?"

"Yes."

He helped her into the back seat, gave directions to the cabbie, and then reached over to hold her hand, as if she needed to be comforted, which indeed she did. The entire affair had been too hurried, clandestine, and Alpharetta, withdrawing her hand, said, "Dow, I'm not sure we should be doing this. . . ."

"It's too late for second thoughts, Alpharetta."

His tone was that of her commanding officer, brooking no disobedience on her part. She sighed and folded her hands in her lap to keep them still. The actuality of her wedding day was so foreign to her romantic dreams, and yet she was certain of her love for the man seated beside her. And that was all that mattered.

The wedding took place in a consulate room, with strangers witnessing the signing of papers, the legal documents declaring that she and Dow were man and wife. With wedding congratulations ringing in her ears, they hurried down the steps, one brief kiss, one brief ceremony binding them together for a lifetime, neither one certain of its allotment.

Alpharetta stared down at the plain gold band, the large emerald on her finger—the same rings she had worn when she had posed as his wife. At that moment, she felt no more married to the man beside her than she had previously.

"We'll have a quiet lunch at the Ritz," he said, glancing down at his watch. "It's already arranged."

She had no thought for what she ate. The mirrors, the palms, the garlands of gold, and the pink tablecloths dipping to the floor recalled an earlier day when she had sought out Ben Mark, and danced with Marsh instead. The scene was the same but her emotions were vastly different, happiness replacing the tragedy of love long vanished. Dow was right. The sorrow was Belline's. Gazing at her husband, so serious, Alpharetta smiled at him and reached her hand toward him, taking him by surprise. And in that gesture, she sealed her allegiance to Dow Pomeroy.

At the end of the meal, Alpharetta went to the powder room. She stared in the mirror, as she had done earlier, but a special radiance now replaced the tears of yesterday.

"Thank you, Sir Nelson," she whispered, "for stepping on my foot that day." She added color to her lips, dropped a coin into the plate for the maid, and then returned to the table.

As soon as she was seated again, Dow put into words what he had been avoiding for the entire meal. His headquarters had been transferred to the Continent.

"Alpharetta, my plane is leaving for France—in one hour."

Stunned at his words, she stared at the man she had married.

"Did you hear me, darling?"

"I—I don't believe you."

"It's true. I should have told you earlier, I suppose."

"Yes, you should have."

"But I didn't want to spoil the short time we had together."

Alpharetta stood abruptly, her hurt undisguised. A feeling of betrayal swept over her.

"Sit down, darling. People are staring."

She wanted to disobey, to run from the room, but her anger made her weak and she sat down again.

Calmly, soothingly, Dow continued, "Eckerd has orders to take you to Harrington Hall on Monday."

"It seems you've thought of everything, Dow, except my own wishes."

"Where else would you go, Alpharetta? Birdie will be closing up the house on the downs, and it's far too dangerous for you to get a flat here in London."

"I could go with you."

"No, Alpharetta. You're my wife now. Your place is at Harrington Hall."

Dow glanced down at his watch. "Eckerd should be waiting to take me to the airport. I'll put you in a taxi first, for you to return to the downs."

"And I'm to say good-bye here—in public—as if nothing has happened today but a casual luncheon?"

"It's far better this way, Alpharetta. Believe me."

"I've made a mistake, Dow. I should never have let you talk me into marrying you."

Dow stood and, ignoring her comment, ushered her out of the Ritz. Eckerd, parked down the street, saw them as they walked onto the pavement. He pulled out, directly behind the taxi Dow signaled.

"I'll write you, darling."

"Don't bother." Without looking back, Alpharetta climbed into the taxi, removed the gold band and emerald from her finger, dropped them into her shoulder bag, and stared straight ahead, seeing nothing for the tears that clouded her eyes.

39

In the crowded boxcar filled with other prisoners of war, Captain Daniel "Marsh" Wexford breathed the stale and putrid air and listened in the darkness to the sound of the train slowing in its rush through the German countryside.

He had been shuttled back and forth, changing trains, hiding in the tunnels when Allied planes had strafed and plowed up the tracks of steel.

At times, he had been forced out of the car, to work on the rail bed, but the labor had been a welcome relief from the cattle car filled with men reduced to animal status, without food or water for long periods of time.

Marsh's chest still hurt when he coughed. In fact, he was almost certain he had a fractured rib from the tree trunk. But he was lucky to survive at all. It was not often that a gun fired point blank missed its target.

The train stopped. The cattle car was uncoupled and pushed onto a side track. Marsh waited for the sound of the outside bars being released and the guttural order to disembark. Instead, even the small opening for air was locked shut.

"You might as well settle down for the night, Captain," a voice at his knee cautioned. "They won't let us out until daylight. Scared, I guess, that some of us might escape in the dark."

An uneasy group of men shifted and shuffled, trying to ease themselves to the floor, but it was impossible because of their number.

Suddenly, an hysterical voice erupted from the opposite end of the car. "I've got to get out of here. I can't stay cooped up any longer." He began to rattle the side of the car. And his voice, gaining volume, shouted, "Let me out of here, you bastards. I'm a man. Not an animal."

"Quiet, fella. You'll only bring trouble."

He paid no attention. "You hear me, you damn bastards? I'm dying of thirst," the man shouted at the top of his lungs, before his neighbor clapped his hand over his mouth to shut him up.

Too late, Marsh heard the irate voices of the guards. The kicking against the boxcar was answered by a round of machine-gun fire that penetrated the wood, bringing disaster to the men crowded together inside.

"Oh, Jesus—I'm hit. I'm hit," a voice cried.

"Oh Lord, have mercy. Save us."

The moaning began, quiet, with no hope of relief. The outburst had been dealt with effectively—no one else was going to bang against the sides of the car for attention.

A soft voice began singing "Abide With Me." It was taken up by Marsh and the others who could still sing, their voices forming a *quodlibet* to the moans of the wounded—two separate melodies entwined as one, raised to the God who seemed to have deserted them.

When daylight came and the prisoners who had survived the machine guns were let out of the boxcar, none was in any condition to attempt escape. The irony was that without the air holes made by the machine guns, most would have suffocated during the night.

As a weak and thirsty Marsh jumped to the ground, he was singled out by the guards, with three others, for a special detail.

"You will have to earn your bread and water this morning," the head guard advised. "You will start digging graves for the dead."

Ten men had been killed by machine-gun fire. Now, with shovels thrust into their hands, the work detail prepared a deep trench for burial. The others, seated by the tracks, watched and waited for the job to be completed. Only then would they receive water and a small allotment of black bread.

Far too soon, without time to eat, they were brought to their feet. "We walk now," the head guard announced.

Marsh looked at the men, the majority unable to walk a long distance. "The men are weak," he said to the guard. "How far are we to walk?"

"No more than four kilometers," the guard replied.

They began, some able to go by themselves, others needing assistance. The stragglers were prompted with a rifle butt in their backs when they fell too far behind.

One mile, and then two, they continued. As they came to a wooded area, the men were forced into a single file, with hands over their heads.

Just beyond them, in a clearing, stood the prisoner-of-war camp, surrounded by barbed wire, a tall metal fence, and a tower overseeing the small huts sprinkled throughout the compound. They had reached Stalag 13, the unluckiest camp of all, judging from the faces of the SS troops who watched them file into the compound.

For two weeks they had been herded together in the most unsanitary conditions, without benefit of soap or water. Coming out to inspect this new wave of prisoners, the commandant turned up his nose and backed away.

"Bring out the hoses," he ordered his subordinate and disappeared into his quarters to wait by the warm stove.

As animals penned together are sluiced on their way to the slaughterhouse, so the prisoners were doused by the hoses under massive pressure, while the howling wind swept in from the mountains, signaling the beginning of winter.

Heinrich von Freiker stared down at his foot as the doctor changed the dressing. Two of his toes were missing. He could never hope to walk again without a limp.

He was going home to recuperate, for his hospital bed was needed for those being brought in daily.

"I should have killed him, Horst," Heinrich said to his aide waiting to take him to Berlin. "You see what he has done? He has maimed me—for life."

"You are lucky, my Colonel—to be alive," Horst reminded him.

A week later, as Emil von Freiker drove past the rubble along the Wilhelmstrasse and headed toward the hall where the Berlin Philharmonic was tuning up for its evening performance, he was thinking not only of the fate of Heinrich, but also of the entire *Vaterland*. They had both been lucky, for von Runstedt, with Bittrich, had turned the Holland invasion into a rout, buying a little more time for the Third Reich.

The invasion had also bought a little more time for the final list of people waiting to be arrested because of the attempt on Hitler's life, for the Führer had reinstated von Rundstedt as commander of OB West, thus taking him away from the purge, something the field marshal should never have been involved in to begin with.

But now, with the invasion successfully defeated, the purge had begun again, and through von Sydow, Emil had received word that Frau Emma was to be arrested soon. Her only sin was in being related, by marriage, to a general suspected of having a part in the assassination attempt. But if Emil had his way, the voice of the great Frau Emma would be spared.

The success of his elaborate preparations, which included a car waiting for Frau Emma the moment the concert was over that evening, depended upon the mercy of the Allied bombers that had been pounding the city incessantly.

It was a miracle that the Brandenburg Gates and the Reichstag were still standing, while all around them, other buildings, other artistic works had joined the rubble. Like Hamburg, like Köln, Berlin was now a ghostly skeleton of its former days of glory.

But the music remained—the soul of Germany, recalling the days before the madman had taken over—and it was for this that Emil lived. He knew that, despite the victory in Holland, despite the propaganda put out by Goebbels of new weapons, new advances, the days of a warring Germany were limited. The Luftwaffe was gone; the Russian front a disaster. They had lost too many men. They could not survive much longer.

Emil was getting old. Tired of war, not suited for peace, he asked only that the end might be an honorable one and that his son, so changed, could once more become the man he was before the war. And yet even as he wished it, Emil knew it was impossible. Heinrich had tasted power; he had destroyed entire villages with their people, and had boasted openly about it.

There was a vast difference in being a soldier and in being

a slaughterer of women and children. Emil longed for the old days when things were different, but it was too late, too late. The history of Germany was being written in the blood of its innocent victims. And Heinrich, with his sword, was part of it, relegated by Himmler to do a henchman's work.

The street became narrow through the rubble and Emil's driver had difficulty getting past the other vehicles. If the bombers came back that night, Emil feared that the way of escape could easily be blocked for the woman.

Recuperating from his wound, Heinrich had needed no persuasion from his father to attend the performance that night. Already he was in his seat, with his eyes carefully searching each section—orchestra, loge, balcony. He saw that the guards were already in position in strategic places near each exit.

Because of his foot, Heinrich would never go back to the panzer division. But his vast anger could be forged into another instrument of death, for Himmler had allowed him, as an SS officer, to transfer to the Gestapo.

Yes, he would enjoy the concert. Knowing that his father would be hearing Frau Emma for the last time heightened his anticipation of the evening.

He had never liked the woman, and a firing squad was good enough for her. But Heinrich had planned something else for her daughter, Gretchen—arranging for her death certificate so Himmler would never know what he had done with her.

"Good evening, *Vater*."

"Heinrich."

Emil took his seat beside his son. The lights lowered and the music began. For father and son, each unaware of the other's plans, the music went unheard. Emil listened for bombers in the sky, for air-raid sirens, while Heinrich watched the blond Gretchen, seated in the shadows of the opera box on the far wall opposite him. Occasionally, when his father glanced in his direction, Heinrich put down his binoculars, faced the orchestra, and pretended to listen.

In the opera box, Gretchen sat and gripped her handkerchief to keep her hands from trembling.

She and her mother had gone over the plans time and again.

After the intermission, Gretchen was to slip away as soon as her mother started singing, when all eyes would be on the stage, and the opera box enclosed in darkness.

The design of the box, with a staircase to the dressing rooms below, was a well-guarded secret, known to few people beyond the manager of the hall and certain members of the orchestra who slipped back and forth to listen, when their exotic instruments were not required for a portion of the program.

The orchestra finished the first half of the program and the crowd began to file out for intermission. The audience gathered in small groups, drinking their schnapps and wine. Men in uniform were casually situated at each exit, no different from any other night, with the usual sprinkling of officers throughout the crowd.

The bell sounded the end of intermission and Heinrich, watching the young woman as she walked toward the heavy draperies that enclosed the box, nodded to the SS officer to take his place directly beside the box. He would make certain that she did not escape after the program.

The lights lowered; the manager, joining Gretchen in the box, applauded as the great Frau Emma von Erhard walked onto the stage with the conductor. During the noise of the applause, Gretchen, with a fleeting glance toward her mother, opened the small trap door, climbed through, and closed it after her.

The manager, still applauding, pushed the rug over the telltale spot with his foot and slid his chair a few inches back.

Down the stairs Gretchen went, her soft slippers making no noise. When she had reached the dressing room, she quickly gathered the small bundle from its hiding place in the wardrobe closet, stuffed it into the empty violin case, and hurried through the alley to the waiting Horch.

A voice, low, disguised, inquired, "Is your violin a Stradivarius, Fräulein?"

"*Nein.* It is an Amati."

With her correct answer, he said, "Get in."

Clutching the violin case holding her fake ID, her ration card, and a change of clothes, she did as she was told. The car started up, the purr of the engine making little noise in the night. As the car began to edge through the alley, Gretchen became alarmed.

"Wait. We have to wait for my mother."

But the man, pressing his foot on the accelerator, answered, "Your mother is not coming, Fräulein."

"Yes, she is. Stop. Oh, please stop. We must go back."

The driver paid no attention to Gretchen. When she attempted to open the door, the driver said, "Don't be a fool, Fräulein. You will kill yourself if you try to jump." And he locked all the car doors to prevent such an occurrence.

Inside the hall, the sound that Emil feared was heard. The lights went out; the music stopped. Shrill sirens took over, bombarding the nerves with their incessant noise, while the audience scurried to the bomb shelter directly beneath the hall.

Outside, large artillery guns rumbled. Searchlights penetrated the heavens to pinpoint the offending bombers. But their underbellies, painted black, were camouflaged against the black of the sky, making it difficult, except by gambler's chance, for the guns to shoot the marauders out of the sky.

A sadness overtook Emil as a different emotion touched Heinrich—anger at the interruption of his triumph, cutting short the evening as he sat deliberately savoring the plans he had made for Gretchen von Erhard.

In the darkness, Heinrich shouted to the guards. "Stop her! You must not let her escape." But his voice was lost in the noise of the audience rushing to safety. "Give me the flashlight!" Heinrich ordered, grabbing one from a guard. And with its beam showing the way, he walked up the steps to the loge and the box where Gretchen had been sitting.

He thrust the draperies back and searched every corner, but the box was empty. "Fool! You let her get away," he ranted at the young SS officer still stationed at his post outside the box.

"It happened so suddenly, *mein Obersturmbahnführer*," he apologized. "The people came out in such a rush. But surely, she is in the shelter with the others."

"For your sake, I hope she is."

Heinrich left a miserable young officer and hurried toward

the shelter where the entire audience hovered in groups of twos and threes. Like the klieg light in the heavens, the beam of light from Heinrich's confiscated flashlight swept impatiently back and forth, up and down, searching out the blond girl, Gretchen. Despite the havoc outside, the guards stood at each exit, following orders not to take shelter as the others had done.

Aggravated by the pain in his foot, Heinrich became a madman, close kin with his supreme commander. As rage took over, he became his own victim, searching for the one who had disappeared in the darkness, as if she had been whisked away by gods determined to keep her from Heinrich's grasp. But if the daughter had been lost, Heinrich was gratified that the mother had not flown, as well. At least something could be salvaged from the disaster of the evening.

"Stop! No cars are allowed!"

The gruff voice at the barricade at the end of the street brought the black Horch to a halt. But the driver, oblivious to the action around him, had only one mission—to get Gretchen out of the city.

Showing the order signed with Hitler's own High Command seal, he said, "I must get through immediately."

The man saw the small, anonymous figure in the back seat and curled his lips in disgust. He had enough to do without being bothered with the mistresses of high-ranking officers.

"I take no responsibility for her safety," he said, returning the papers to the chauffeur.

"She is my responsibility," the cold voice replied. "Yours is to let us through."

Resenting the arrogant voice of the driver, the man in the Home Guard grudgingly removed the barricade for the black car to edge through.

As the car left the bombarded city, fires had already started and the sound of wailing ambulances joined the cacophony of terror.

Finally the artillery guns stopped. And Berlin was left to cope with the same devastation that Hitler had meted out so unflinchingly to the cities of Europe and the British Isles. Once again, the victims were people unfortunate enough to be in the corridors of war, their nationalities of little consequence.

Three days later, in a small castle hidden in the Bavarian Alps, Gretchen von Erhard awoke.

A maid, several years younger than she, knocked on the bedroom door and, with a slight curtsey, carried a breakfast tray to the fine old poster bed, carved with the story of Rumpelstiltskin upon its four posts—a German woodcutter's whim designed to please the blond daughter of the house, long dead.

"Good morning, Fräulein. You are awake?" she asked the shadowy figure lifting her head from the soft down pillow.

"Yes. I fear I have slept for a very long time."

"That is to be expected—coming as you did, so late in the night."

The maid walked to the draperies and opened them wide. Smiling, she turned back to the bed, where the sunlight now revealed the Fräulein's face.

The buxom young country maid, with the same pink round cheeks of her six sisters, gave a start as the shadowed figure became visible in the late-morning sunlight.

Hair, long and blond and slightly tousled from a restless night, blue eyes the color of robin's eggs, and a flawless, creamy complexion as perfect as the white lace of her gown greeted the maid in the figure of Gretchen. Her supple, slender body was now free from its bondage of formless schoolgirl's uniform and ugly black stockings.

Gretchen rose and, with the tray in her hands, walked toward the small table by the window.

"I think I'll have my breakfast here, in the sun," she said, smiling at the dark-haired maid.

"I brought you a newspaper also, Fräulein," the maid informed Gretchen, finding her voice again.

Quickly, she curtseyed as if in the presence of royalty. Suddenly remembering to introduce herself, she said, "My name is Heidi. When you're ready for your bath, please pull the cord." She pointed to the needlepoint bellpull near the door and then was gone.

The newspaper lay forgotten on the tray where Heidi had

placed it, for Gretchen was reveling in the taste of coffee, which she had not sampled in three years. Available only on the black market where it was beyond the budget of Gretchen and her mother, coffee was a forgotten luxury. Only when she had finished the cup did she remember the newspaper.

She unfolded it carefully, and as she turned to the inside, the small headlines leaped out at her. With incredulous eyes, she read: THE GREAT FRAU EMMA VON ERHARD IS DEAD!

"No," Gretchen cried out, pushing the newpaper from her. It wasn't true. It couldn't be true. But the newspaper drew her as it repelled, and she began to read the article, detailing the circumstances of her mother's death.

"*Mutter,*" Gretchen said aloud, the anguish in her voice transforming itself into tears that trailed down flawless cheeks. The dampness marred her vision and made it impossible for her to read further. She should have stayed in Berlin. She should have waited for her mother before going to the car. And yet even as she thought this, she knew her mother had not planned it that way.

She had found the letter hidden in the bundle of clothes, with her ID card.

By the time you read this, my *Liebchen,* you will know that we have been separated for the first time in our lives. I am too well known to hide. Whatever happens, do not be sad for me. Death means little to me, if I know that *you* have survived. For as long as you are alive, I live too. Good-bye, my darling, and do not grieve for me.

Frau Emma's admonition went unheeded. Gretchen, brushing back the tears, struggled to read the newspaper account of what had happened.

The great dramatic soprano, star of the Vienna Opera House, and, more recently, soloist with the Berlin Philharmonic Orchestra, succumbed to injuries suffered in the air raid that took place in Berlin this past Wednesday evening. She died as she had lived—with a song in her heart.

Frau Emma will be laid to rest in a state funeral, beside

her late husband, General Gustav von Erhard, in the family plot at Götterung on Monday at three in the afternoon. There are no immediate survivors.

The article ended:

The singer was distantly related to General Max Bucher.

With one sentence, the newspaper had refuted the Nazi propaganda. For in publishing the name of one of the generals in the conspiracy, the link was clear. Frau Emma von Erhard had been murdered by the Gestapo.

For a long time, Gretchen sat by the window. Then she drew the draperies and, with the room as dark as her heart, she threw herself across the bed and wept.

Much later in the afternoon, with her grief fully spent, Gretchen rose and dressed in the change of clothes she had brought with her in the violin case.

As she dressed, she began to make plans to attend her mother's funeral at Götterung, while Marsh Wexford, in Stalag 13, began to make plans for his escape.

40

M y son. My own son! How could Heinrich have done such a thing?"

A haunted General Emil von Freiker, with his military briefcase at his side, rode toward the Reichstag, his route unvaried for the past three years.

The despondency over Frau Emma's unwarranted death gripped him, bringing an ache that refused any comfort. He would never be able to go to the symphony without remembering Heinrich's deed—destroying what had been, for Emil, an oasis of joy amid the madness.

He walked up the steps of the Reichstag like an old man, with stooped shoulders and a heavy heart.

"Emil," a voice called out.

He turned around to see his longtime friend von Sydow motioning to him.

"I must talk with you, Emil. Privately."

Emil gave his briefcase to the guard inside the door and retraced his steps to the curb where von Sydow waited. If it were of a confidential nature, the street was safer than the military offices inside, where all conversations could be monitored.

"Let's walk together," von Sydow suggested, taking Emil by the arm as he signaled his driver to follow in the car. "I've made an important discovery that I think you should know about."

"Not another attempt on the Führer's life, I hope."

"No, nothing like that."

"Good. We cannot afford another purge."

"I've just returned from a visit to one of the prisoner-of-war camps, Emil. It was quite a shock to see a young paratrooper who could have passed for your double twenty-five years ago. Blond, blue-eyed, your same height . . ."

"And what's so surprising about that, Wilhelm? There must be many men in this world who resemble other men."

"But let me finish. I asked the commandant to let me see his dossier. Emil, he was born in St. Mihiel, during our occupation there in the last war. He's the same age your little Hans would have been."

Emil stopped in the middle of the street and stared at Wilhelm. "The child died—in the fire, with his mother. No, Wilhelm. There's no possibility this American could be my son. It's a coincidence—nothing more."

"The reports could have been wrong. After all, we had moved out before the fire. He could have been found alive by one of the American soldiers."

Emil shook his head. "The past is dead and buried, the same as the child."

"The paratrooper was badly beaten—by the guards, for trying to escape."

"Wilhelm, it's no use. I have only one son, Heinrich," Emil insisted bitterly. "The one who arrested Frau Emma and arranged her death."

"Perhaps you're right, Emil. You have only one son. For the other won't last long in Stalag 13."

"Dräger has him?"

"Yes."

"Even if he proved to be my other son, there's nothing I could do for him."

"He goes by the name of Wexford, in case you change your mind."

Wilhelm left him hurriedly, saluting with a "Heil Hitler!" for the sake of the driver bringing his car to the curbing. Emil watched the car depart, then slowly walked back to the Reichstag.

All day, Emil was haunted by the possibility that the son he had abandoned in France, with his mother, Ailly, was still alive.

Many times he had regretted that day when he was ordered

to leave St. Mihiel, with the Americans at his heels. It had come as a surprise, being overrun by a fledgling army whose effectiveness had been more or less dismissed in the first war. Now, twenty-five years later, that American army was a force to be reckoned with. Without it, the Führer would have defeated the British long ago.

A measure of excitement began to fill Emil's body. His military bearing returned, his shoulders straightened. There would be no harm in just going to see the boy, he decided.

Emil picked up the telephone and his aide in the outer office answered immediately.

"Put me through to Colonel Dräger at Stalag 13."

An unhappy Dräger sat at his desk and drummed a devil's tattoo with his fingers. He never liked it when the generals at the Reichstag came to snoop around. It always spelled trouble. But Freiker had at least been courteous enough to announce his arrival, giving Dräger an opportunity to clean up; for, like many of the old-timers from the Wehrmacht, Freiker still believed in the Geneva Convention. They, however, didn't have to deal with recalcitrant prisoners day after day.

He had forty-eight hours to turn the camp into a model prison. He would order special food in the mess for the prisoners and get them cleaned and shaven. Dräger frowned. A few of the prisoners would have to be hidden from sight. But that presented no problem.

"Kurt," he called to the guard standing on the other side of the door. "Come in here."

The guard moved quickly, stood at attention before Dräger, and waited for him to speak.

"We're having an inspection in forty-eight hours. I want you to take the three paratroopers who tried to escape and throw them into the Hole, until the inspection is over."

"Are they to be punished again?"

"No. I want no dead men on my hands. But withhold any food or water for the next forty-eight hours."

Two days later, when Emil arrived at the camp, a smiling Dräger was ready for him.

"Herr General, how good to see you," he exclaimed as von

Freiker climbed out of the vehicle and stood to his full height of well over six feet. "I have a hot meal waiting for you—the same hot meal, incidentally, that the prisoners are eating at the moment. I hope you don't mind having the same fare as the prisoners."

Emil's hooded eyes stared down into Dräger's as he spoke. "It is always gratifying to know the prisoners are well fed."

"Yes. Well . . . come inside," Dräger offered, suddenly defensive under von Freiker's gaze.

Emil showed no impatience with Dräger. He ate the meal and drank the wine. And when he had finished, Emil, cautious not to mention the Wexford name, said, "I should like to inspect all barracks, Dräger."

The colonel, thinking the general would soon tire, began with the best and newest of the huts and left the worst ones for last. Despite the advance warning, many of the huts would not stand a rigid inspection.

"I don't know who he is," one British prisoner whispered, when Emil had gone. "But I'm grateful to him for the hot meal."

"How did it taste without all that treacle over it?" a Canadian teased. For the guards made a practice of sinking their bayonets into each can of food sent from home, and by the time the British prisoners received their boxes, sweet syrup had spilled over everything.

"So that's what was missing," the Englishman said, grinning. "I knew the cook forgot to put something in the stew."

Far from tiring, Emil went to all barracks and quietly looked over the men as he searched for a young paratrooper as tall as he.

Dräger became more nervous as the afternoon wore on, and he began to suspect that von Freiker had been sent on a special mission.

"This is the last hut, Herr General," Dräger said, relieved that von Freiker had not seemed to notice there were no mattresses on the cots in the last two huts.

"And there are no more prisoners in your care?" Emil asked at the end of the tour.

"There may be one or two on duty digging a new latrine behind the compound."

"Well, let's go back to your office, Dräger. I'd like to look over their files. The majority are American, I presume?"

Infuriatingly for Dräger, Emil took his time. Pulling out one file and then another, he seemed no more interested in one man than another. But all that time, Emil had steeled himself to read the file of the paratrooper, Wexford. Coming almost to the end of the names in the file, he saw there was no one by that name. He had seen no man in the barracks or on the grounds who could even halfway have passed as his son. Von Sydow was mistaken. Either that, or Dräger had killed him.

Finally Emil looked up. "I understand an American paratrooper by the name of Wexford was put under your care recently. Why is his file not with the rest?"

Dräger's grip tightened on his holster. Something was afoot. The general knew something that he didn't. Dräger decided to tell the truth.

"He may be one of the three who attempted to escape. If so, he is being punished."

"How?" Emil demanded.

"He has been put in the Hole."

"In this weather? He will freeze to death, Dräger."

"Herr General, may I remind you that he is the enemy—that he attempted to escape, and was caught."

"I want to see him. Have one of your guards bring him to me."

"He's not a model prisoner, Herr General. I cannot guarantee—"

"Have him brought to me regardless, Dräger."

The Hole, dug into the side of the earth, was like a mine shaft, pitch black, cold and damp, the ceiling too low for Marsh to stand up straight. But it didn't matter, for he was weak, as were the other two, from a lack of food.

The heavy gate began to swing open and Marsh shielded his eyes from the sudden glare of sunlight.

"Wexford," the guard shouted. "You are to come with me."

"What about the others?"

"They stay."

"Then I stay, too."

"*Nein*, you come with me. It has been ordered."

"Go on, Wexford. And when you come back, bring me a steak and a beer," one man requested, his sense of humor still intact.

With the prisoner in front of him, the guard walked across the compound to the commandant's headquarters. And Emil, standing at the window, watched.

The prisoner towered above the guard. Emil was too far away to see any other characteristics besides the prisoner's height. Suddenly impatient, he picked up the binoculars from Dräger's desk and walked back to the window. A few moments later, he returned the binoculars to the desk.

"He is to be fed, Dräger," Emil ordered, "and made presentable before I question him."

"Yes, Herr General."

Forty-five minutes later, a curious Marsh sat in a detention cell. His tongue, swollen earlier from a lack of water, was now almost back to normal. He felt much better.

"You will stand for General von Freiker," a voice ordered.

Marsh obeyed, his stance proud, his blue eyes wary at the approach of the German general.

"You are Captain Daniel Wexford?"

"Yes. My serial number is—"

"That is not necessary, Captain. I have not come to question you on military matters."

Both were aware that the only information Marsh would be required to give was name, rank, serial number. Still, Marsh remained wary.

"Bring me a chair, Private," Emil ordered, "and then you may wait in the outer room."

Kurt, the guard, obeyed. When Emil and Marsh were alone, with iron bars separating them, the general sat and motioned for Marsh to do the same.

"I have seen your dossier," Emil began. "And I see from it that you were born at St. Mihiel."

Marsh neither confirmed nor denied it.

"When did you go to America?"

"My name is Captain Daniel Wexford. My serial number is 264—"

"Was your mother's name—Ailly?"

The name caused Marsh to falter. Staring at the German general, he examined his strong, angular face in a new light. His features had been ravaged by age, but they were similar to his own. As Marsh stared at the older man and saw what he might become in time, so Emil stared at the young paratrooper and remembered what he had been.

Neither betrayed his thoughts to the other. But the name Ailly had drawn a response against Marsh's will. The name hung in the silent air, binding father and son together.

"Is there anything you wish?" Emil finally inquired.

"Yes."

"Name it, and if it's within my power . . ."

"Two of my men are still in the Hole. I want them released and given food and water."

"I will see to it."

Emil stood, reluctant to go, yet afraid to stay. "Good luck, Captain Wexford."

"Thank you, Herr General."

Marsh was returned to his barracks soon after the general left camp. And the two men were released from the Hole, as he requested.

Three days passed. The bruises suffered from the beating began to heal, but there was little food to eat.

On the morning of the fourth day, a guard came into the officers' barracks for Marsh. "We go into the forest to gather firewood for the commandant," he said. "You come."

"Now see here, you can't take him," a fellow officer protested. "It's against regulations for an officer to do manual labor."

Marsh quieted him. "Maybe I'll find a rabbit for our supper. We could do with a little meat in our gruel."

"You know the regulation about fire—"

"We'll worry about that when we have something to put in the pot," Marsh cautioned.

He climbed into the truck with the other men. The gates opened and the well-guarded prisoners left the compound for the nearby forest.

In twos the prisoners worked, gathering twigs and small branches that had fallen to the forest floor. The commandant would be warm during the winter, even if the prisoners were not allowed to build fires for themselves.

As Marsh bent over for a limb, he felt a rifle prod him in the back. "You are to come with me," the guard announced in his gruff voice.

When Marsh was slow to respond, the guard used his rifle butt in a ferocious blow. "At once."

Holding his side, Marsh straightened and began to follow the guard. The other men kept their eyes downward while they continued to gather firewood and bundle the sticks together.

"I've had just about enough of your—"

"Silence." The guard now prodded Marsh until the two were out of sight of the others. And when they had reached the band of trees on the lower edge of the forest, the guard motioned for Marsh to stop. He pointed to a tall tree in the distance.

"You will find a rucksack on the far side of the conifer. I will look the other way for five minutes. And in another fifteen, I will return to the truck to sound the alarm and release the dogs."

Marsh's eyes narrowed at the guard. Either someone wanted him shot—or someone had arranged his escape. But which?

There was only one way to find out.

Long before the twenty minutes were up, Marsh heard the dogs. And he realized what the guard had done—taken the bribe money and then given the alarm earlier than he had promised. Unless he could outwit the dogs in the next few minutes, he was assured of being captured—a second time.

Stopping beside a large oak tree in the forest, Marsh retrieved the prison shirt from his rucksack. If only he had a can of pepper. He would sprinkle the shirt liberally, plant it in the bushes, and when the dogs found it and sniffed it, their sense of smell would be hampered temporarily.

The dogs' barking was closer, louder, and Marsh knew he had to think of something else in a hurry, or the German shepherds would run him to ground.

He did the only thing left for him. He swung onto a low branch of the ancient oak and climbed almost to the top. He took the prison shirt and tied it to a high limb, then carefully swung toward the limb of the next tree. If he could keep in the air for awhile, he might be able to escape.

From his vantage point in the tree, Marsh looked back. He saw the guards with their dogs fast approaching. He gazed frantically in the other direction, at the mountainous stream that curved its way through the wooded terrain. And he knew his only salvation lay in that direction.

Like the obstacle course at Fort Benning at the beginning of his paratrooper training, Marsh went, hand over hand, edging from one tree limb to another, without putting his feet on the ground until he reached the last large oak in the woods.

Around the water's edge the vegetation changed to smaller trees—trees far too small to accommodate Marsh's weight. Behind him, the barking of dogs grew into an uproar. They must have discovered his shirt tied high up in the first tree he had climbed.

With a feeling of impending doom, Marsh jumped toward the green willow next to the water, dangled precipitously as he heard the wood crack, and braced his body for the inevitable fall. Barely missing the bank, he landed with a splash. It was only then that Marsh felt he stood a sporting chance to escape.

41

At Götterung, high in the hills where the ancestral *Schloss* of the von Erhard family lay in disrepair, Heinrich von Freiker set up his headquarters for the capture of Gretchen.

His rage had finally abated, and now he looked forward to the calculating cat-and-mouse game with the young woman. He congratulated himself on the news releases concerning Frau Emma's mock state burial. He had seen that she received far more news coverage than she deserved, but he knew that wherever Gretchen was hiding, the news would reach her. And that was the important thing. Otherwise, his entrapment would take much longer.

A shell of its splendid ancient self, the *Schloss* had been stripped of its valuables. No family portraits gazed from the walls; no silver steins sat on the sideboard in the dining hall waiting to be filled for the lord of the manor.

With the cunning that had helped him survive time after time, Heinrich had taken one wing for himself, trusting to his subordinate to make him comfortable. His military vehicle was hidden in the barn, so there would be no outward sign that the *Schloss* was inhabited.

The cold and dampness had made his foot ache more than usual. Heinrich longed for Horst to build a fire, but smoke rising from a chimney would alert Gretchen that the manor house was occupied and drive her away. So Heinrich withstood the discomfort.

As Heinrich, draped in an army blanket, sat in the faded wing chair of the master bedroom and shivered despite all attempts at keeping warm, a cold Gretchen, dressed as a young boy, carefully made her way through the woods on horseback.

She knew every trail, every meandering stream in the vicinity of the *Schloss*, for, as a child, she had ridden over the land many times with her father, his proud demeanor, his iron-rod posture at odds with the gentleness he exhibited with animals and with his daughter.

She had been off at school when it happened—the nightmare that never seemed real, her father dragged away and shot when he refused the post offered by Adolph Hitler. She knew that her mother had never forgiven herself for being away in Vienna at the height of the opera season. Frau Emma felt she could have persuaded him to take a less severe stand.

The childhood memories rose to envelop Gretchen as she came to the apple orchard where trees, ancient and gnarled, spread their limbs in all directions.

"*Vater! Vater!*" she said, the hurt returning to her throat.

The apples were nearly gone. Gretchen, performing the ritual that had bound her spiritually to her father in childhood, got down from the horse and, selecting one apple for the animal and one for herself, stood very still at the edge of the orchard. As she ate the fruit, she relived those earlier days when they had been a family—together. And as she had so many times before, Gretchen, standing in that spot, knew that just over the rise beyond the orchard, she would be able to see the family *Schloss*—if it were still standing.

Caution now slowed her, for the open field beyond the orchard gave no hiding place from curious eyes.

Not far from the *Schloss*, Marsh Wexford, escaped prisoner of war, sat in a sheltered copse and finished the last of the black bread.

He was hopelessly lost. The map in his rucksack was of minimal use without a compass. In the distance, snow already covered the mountain peaks. And the late-afternoon wind carried the promise of frost. Marsh stood up. He would have to seek better shelter soon.

Hoisting the rucksack to his shoulders, he began to walk. Like a mountain climber, Marsh trudged, helped by the long stick he had fashioned the day before to seek out the dangers beneath the layer of leaves. He prodded the ground in the same way he had when searching for land mines at the drop zones. The stick had already found an animal trap. And Marsh felt extremely lucky that the steel had snapped on the stick instead of his foot.

Avoiding the barn, Gretchen galloped quickly across the stone bridge and disappeared from view. She urged the horse into the stream directly beneath the bridge, for the ground beyond was soft and she wanted no hoofprints broadcasting the direction in which she traveled.

Buildings, long deserted by the herdsman and his family, lay east of the *Schloss* and overlooked the cemetery where her ancestors were buried—where her mother, too, was to be laid to rest.

Gretchen followed the stream bed until it began to deepen. With a slight tug to the reins, she coaxed the horse up the bank and traversed the field until she came to the herdsman's simple rock cottage with its attached animal shed.

For a minute or so, she observed the cottage to make certain it was still unoccupied. Then she climbed down and led the horse into the yard.

Like Gretchen, Marsh avoided the massive stone barn. But he had no hesitancy in seeking shelter for the night in the *Schloss* itself. Approaching from a different direction, he slipped into the turret wing where two exits provided a measure of safety if he were forced to retreat in a hurry.

While Marsh foraged for food in the root cellar, Horst prepared a suitable meal for his commander. Unaware of each other in separate wings of the same house, Heinrich and Marsh—archenemies—settled down for the night.

The slow, steady sound of rain pelting the roof of the herdsman's cottage awakened Gretchen long before daylight. A slight whinny from the shed indicated that König, the horse, was uneasy too. Gretchen arose and groped her way toward the shed to reassure the horse.

"It's all right, König," she whispered, patting him on the flank. Crooning to him in the half-light of early dawn, she calmed him and then went back to bed. Gretchen knew that by daylight she would have to allow him to graze in the meadow, for the stored hay was moldy. If she were careful, she might even chance going to the *Schloss* to look for some salt for the horse.

The rain stopped. The sun edged through the cracks of the wooden shutters. Gretchen arose, brushed her hair upward and then hid it under the cap. That was the extent of her toilette, for she had slept in her clothes for added warmth. Without taking time to eat the meager food left from the previous day, she walked to the shed, put the bridle on König, and led him to the field where she hobbled him to keep him from straying.

Then she set off on foot in the direction of the *Schloss*. She had not gone far when she heard a vehicle. The sound of the motor grew louder and, in alarm, Gretchen raced back toward the field to unhobble the horse and lead him into the shed. It was imperative that neither she nor König be seen. She ducked into the cover of bushes and watched an old motor truck pass by on the road in front of her. She kept her fingers crossed that the three men inside the open truck would continue on their journey without becoming suspicious.

The vehicle passed dangerously close to the herdsman's cottage. But it kept going, only braking for the curve as the road wound down the hill toward the cemetery.

The truck stopped; the men got out and took their shovels with them. Gravediggers. They had come to dig her mother's grave. Now it was too late to put König back into the shed. Gretchen would have to leave him in the meadow until the gravediggers had finished.

She came out of her hiding place and began to trace her route once more to the *Schloss*.

Marsh woke to the sound of footsteps. Quickly, he grabbed his knife, left the corner where he had bedded down for the night, and hid behind the drapery. At that moment he was sorry that the rucksack had not contained any weapon more lethal than the trench knife. But it would have to suffice if he were cornered.

His hand tightened on the hilt of the knife as he watched

two men enter the room. Standing only ten feet from his hiding place was the German officer who had fired at him in the forest beyond Nijmegen. He held his breath and sweated despite the chill of the air.

"Horst, I like this room better than the one in the other wing. Please move my things in here this morning."

"I will do that, my Colonel, as soon as I have prepared your breakfast."

"The gravediggers have already come?"

"*Ja.* I sent them on to the cemetery."

"Good. We will have to make the funeral appear genuine, even if there is no body."

"You think she will come—by this afternoon?"

"If she doesn't, then I have planned the trap for nothing."

"And what are you going to do to her, Herr Colonel, once she is caught? Shoot her?"

A harsh laugh filled Heinrich's throat. "Not at first, Horst. After several days, she may beg to die. But I shall decide later what I will do with her."

"You'll have to be careful, my Colonel," Horst cautioned. "It will not be like the young Dutch girl. Someone may recognize her at the funeral."

"That doesn't bother me, Horst. Her death certificate is signed. How can a woman already dead cause trouble? No, Gretchen von Erhard is of no consequence. There is no one left to give her aid. Her life is entirely in my hands now."

Heinrich turned his back and began to limp from the room. As the door closed, Marsh's hand began to relax on the hilt of the knife. His mind spun with unanswered questions. Who was being buried—or *not* buried? And who was Gretchen von Erhard?

He had little time to ponder these questions. He needed to rescue his rucksack, which had been in view all the while, and get out of the room before the two reappeared.

From the edge of the trees, Gretchen stood for a while and observed the *Schloss*. A tile had fallen from the turret to the ground. And grass had sprung up in the cracks of the stone courtyard. Her father had taken such pride in the *Schloss*, and it hurt Gretchen to see it in such poor condition.

Cautiously, she began to reconnoiter, running a few steps, then stopping to listen. Breaching the last few feet beyond the servants' entrance, Gretchen reached the slanted door to the root cellar. She removed the rusted metal bar, opened the door, and slid her way through the chute as she had done when she was eight years old.

Feet first, she tumbled onto the dirt floor inside. Colored bottles lined the shelf at the window, and the cobwebs obscured the small amount of sunlight that tried to peek between the bottles. As Gretchen began to grope beyond the barrels that once contained dried apples, she bumped into one and sent it rolling.

Up above the cellar, Heinrich lifted his head at the noise. "Do you think it might be . . ."

"Hush, Horst, and listen."

Heinrich got up from the table, removed his pistol from its holster, and walked toward the service entrance.

Gretchen picked her way through the dried, shriveled apples that now lay in every direction. More accustomed by now to the dim light, she made certain she did not make any more noise. And she began to look for a block of salt, to take back to the horse.

Unsuccessful in finding the salt, Gretchen knew she could not return to the courtyard in the same way she had come. She stopped and listened. The house was silent, beyond the slight scraping of a tree limb and the whistle of the wind through a broken windowpane.

When she didn't hear anything else to alarm her, she began to climb the stairs toward the honeycomb of pantries surrounding the mammoth kitchen, with its stone fireplace large enough to roast a whole pig or lamb on the spit; its ovens suitable for baking twelve fresh loaves of bread at the same time. But that was long ago. She would be lucky to find even a little salt hidden in one of the cupboards.

As Gretchen opened the door, Marsh watched from his hiding place but did nothing to call attention to himself.

She went from one cupboard to another, until she found a small amount of salt in a wooden cannister. Then, like a ghost, she disappeared through another door.

Two other men stood at a window in another part of the

Schloss and watched her progress as she darted from the service yard and into the trellised arbor. And although she was dressed as a boy, both Horst and Heinrich recognized her.

"Why don't you arrest her now, my Colonel?"

"And spoil the fun of this afternoon? Horst, I'm disappointed in you. The drama must be played out to the end."

"She escaped previously. You are not afraid that she might get away again?"

Heinrich's lips tightened at the suggestion. But he relaxed when he glanced down at his watch.

"The soldiers have already surrounded the estate. No, Horst. Not even a dog can slip through the net I have prepared."

Although Marsh did not overhear Heinrich's boast, he soon discovered the truth of his words. From the moment Marsh had hidden behind the drapery in the bedroom that morning, he knew he had selected the wrong place for shelter. If a funeral were to take place, then the *Schloss* would be running over with people. It would be better for him to get out before all the activity began.

With the rucksack over his shoulder, Marsh left the *Schloss* being careful to avoid the wing that Heinrich had requisitioned.

But too late. Guards were already stationed at the bridge to cut off his escape. Two others stood before the massive barn. And down below, at the road winding to the right of the *Schloss*, two more sentinels had taken their places. Marsh was hemmed in. The only thing left to do was to go back into hiding, until Heinrich had arrested the woman who was coming to the funeral.

Only he could not return to the *Schloss* itself. He would have to find a new place to hide until the danger was over.

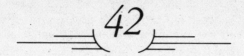

At three o'clock in the afternoon, Gretchen watched the slow procession of black move over the road to the family burial plot.

A priest led a small group of mourners behind the funeral wagon that held her mother's coffin. Draped in black bunting, the wagon lumbered laboriously, a groan of the wheels protesting each turn.

The iron gates to the cemetery opened; the wagon continued until it reached the freshly dug rectangular cut in the earth, then stopped.

In the cracked mirror, Gretchen took a last look at her reflection. She wanted to make sure the rolled legs of her trousers were not visible beneath the dark cape that covered the boyish clothes. Satisfied, she swapped her tweed cap for the black hat with mourning veil that she had brought with her from the house in the Bavarian Alps. With a small bouquet of the last wild flowers, she hurried down the hill to join the end of the procession.

From his hiding place overlooking the cemetery, Marsh Wexford also watched the procession. A rotund town official walked directly behind the priest. Marsh had seen many like him throughout Europe. He was dressed in black, with a ribbon across his stomach and a medal signifying his importance to the Nazi regime. Behind him came a handful of stragglers—official mourners, no doubt, little more than spies—interspersed with a few shabby villagers whose prayers for the wife of Gustav von Erhard might be genuine. Farther back into the cemetery, the gravediggers waited, with the old truck holding their shovels and a large tarpaulin to cover supplies from the rain.

As Marsh observed the solemn gathering, his eye caught a movement of black to his left. He lowered his head and watched a figure carefully descend through the brush.

The black cape, the hat with mourning veil concealing the facial features, seemed much too large and somber for the small figure beneath. What was the person doing, approaching the burial ground so stealthily?

The realization of who it might be struck Marsh with a sudden force. Gretchen von Erhard. Could she be the woman for whom Heinrich had set his trap? This small figure—more like an unprotected child than a woman?

"Gretchen? Gretchen von Erhard?"

She froze at the calling of her name.

Marsh's voice was little more than a whisper. "You're walking into a trap."

"Who's there?" Gretchen questioned, for Marsh was invisible to her. But his words had immediately brought fear to her heart.

"A friend."

"If you're a friend, then show yourself."

Ignoring her entreaty, Marsh continued, "Heinrich is waiting to arrest you. He has the place surrounded."

"What . . . what can I do?" Gretchen asked, wary of the man she couldn't see, yet even more fearful of Heinrich von Freiker.

Marsh, having seen the hobbled horse in the meadow, said, "You came by horseback?"

"Yes."

"Where is it now?" he inquired, for the horse had disappeared.

"There's no need for you to know."

"Gretchen, don't be stubborn. If you want me to help you, then you must not make me waste time looking for the animal."

"In the shed attached to the herdsman's cottage. It's in the vale just over the hill."

The priest, standing at the foot of the grave and lifting his eyes to Heaven, saw Gretchen on the hill. It was too late for her to hide, for the priest motioned to her and indicated he would wait to begin the service until she had taken her place with the rest of the mourners.

"I'll have to go on. The priest has seen me."

"Then meet me at the truck as soon as you drop your flowers on the coffin. Be careful. And Gretchen? Roll up your trouser leg. It's showing."

Gretchen glanced down quickly. A twig had caught on the right cuff and forced it down below the cape's hem. She stooped down to fix it and then finished walking toward the cemetery, to stand at the back of the group of mourners. When she was in place, the priest began the service for the dead.

While Heinrich and Horst stood on the road leading from the *Schloss* and watched from that vantage, Marsh left his hiding place in the brush and went to search for the horse. He banked on the priest's taking his time with the funeral.

While he searched, his mind was busy, planning the escape of both Gretchen and himself. A few minutes later, when he had found the cottage and located the horse in the shed, he took a sack of moldy grain and created a dummy, the same as he had done with rags the first time he attempted to escape from the prisoner-of-war camp. Only this time he strapped the dummy onto the saddle. And when he had covered it with the old threadbare blanket he'd carried in his rucksack, he was ready. His only regret was in losing the blanket, for the nights in the mountains were extremely cold.

Leading the horse by the reins, Marsh skirted the cemetery and brought him to the edge of woods beyond the truck where the gravediggers waited. And there he hid König.

When the priest had finished with the service, Gretchen shed no tears as she dropped the few flowers onto the coffin and walked away. She edged toward the empty truck, as she had been instructed, and glanced briefly at the three men seated a small distance away. While others filed by the deep cut in the earth where the coffin had been lowered, she vanished into the woods.

Seeing the woman in black disappear, Heinrich sounded an alarm. He motioned for the guards to pursue her and cut off her escape. But at that moment, Marsh, with an apology to König, placed a sharp burr under the saddle of the horse, gave him a slap, and watched him bolt. Gretchen's cape, tied hurriedly over the sack wrapped in the black blanket, flapped behind the horse.

"Stop the horse!" Heinrich shouted. But König kept going at a rapid pace. He cleared the barricade, raced over the bridge, and galloped toward the apple orchard while the guards watched, helpless to stop him.

"Follow the horse," Heinrich ordered Horst.

"We will get bogged down, my Colonel."

"Do as I say!" he repeated, enraged at the turn of events.

The car set off cross-country, but the terrain was too wet. The vehicle bogged down, axle-deep, into the soft earth as König disappeared through the trees.

A disconcerted town official looked at the priest for a cue. The funeral was over. There was no need for the mourners to remain. The caisson left; the priest began to walk from the cemetery. The mourners followed, as the three gravediggers started shoveling dirt into the hole.

Once the people had gone, Marsh, with his cap pulled low over his eyes, casually walked toward the gravediggers. In German, he ordered them to stop.

"Colonel von Freiker wants the empty coffin removed."

"But the body . . ."

"There is no body," he growled. "The coffin is empty." And Marsh crossed his fingers that he had heard Heinrich correctly.

"Dig it up and I'll put it on the truck."

They did as Marsh instructed. Clearing the coffin from the dirt, the men hauled it up with the same rope that had been used to lower it.

"He is right," one of the men said, grinning at the others.

"I will take it and clean it up, while you fill the hole."

"If we had known there was to be no body, we would not have dug so deep a hole."

"And then it would have been questioned by the priest," Marsh answered.

"That is so," another man agreed, and began to spade the

dirt. He glanced once or twice at Marsh, dressed little better than he. But he didn't question Marsh's presence or his orders. He was used to being told what to do.

While the gravediggers continued with their work, Marsh took the empty pine coffin on the other side of the truck, where the gravediggers could not see it. With their backs turned, he motioned to Gretchen behind the large monument beyond the truck.

He removed the lid and Gretchen climbed inside the box. A slight whimper escaped her as Marsh closed the lid.

"It's all right," he whispered. "I'll leave enough air for you."

He lifted the coffin to slide onto the back of the truck and then covered it with the tarpaulin, being careful to loosen the lid as he had promised.

When the men had finished, they brought their shovels and placed them in the truck. Now began the most dangerous part of the plan. The guards, stationed at the bridge, knew that three men had entered. Only three could get out again without arousing suspicion.

"Which one of you is staying to guard the grave?" Marsh inquired, for he had no way of knowing which was the driver.

"Herr Mueller said nothing about staying. Our work is finished."

"Colonel von Freiker has changed that order. One of you will remain until the guard comes to relieve you. Which will it be?"

Two of the men looked at each other. "Hermann, you live closest," the older man volunteered.

"Then Hermann, you stay," Marsh ordered.

An unhappy Hermann watched the truck leave the cemetery and start up the winding road around the *Schloss*. Sitting in the back of the truck, Marsh pulled the cap farther down on his face as the vehicle stopped at the barricade.

The guards, thinking that Gretchen had already escaped, paid little attention to the men in the truck. After a cursory glance, they removed the barricade and the driver left the *Schloss* behind.

The village lay below the *Schloss*, and the truck headed east in that direction. Shortly before they reached the town with its tall spire in the center and its houses lying in squares around it, Marsh tapped on the coffin. "Climb out," he whispered, "but stay under the tarpaulin."

Hidden under Marsh's jacket was the tweed cap Gretchen had left in the herdsman's cottage, for he knew she would need it once she had disposed of the veiled black hat. He pulled it out and pushed it under the tarpaulin that flapped in the sturdy breeze.

With only the canvas separating them, Gretchen could feel Marsh's heavy jacket against her as he kept the tarpaulin from flying off the truck and exposing the coffin.

"Who are you?" Gretchen suddenly asked.

He looked toward the closed windows of the cab of the truck. "An American."

So he was in just as much danger as she, or perhaps even more.

"Where are you going?"

"Switzerland," he replied in a low voice.

"You're headed in the wrong direction."

He pressed his hand against the tarpaulin to warn her. The truck began slowing down and then came to a stop to allow a farmer with his cow to cross the road.

When it started up again, Gretchen whispered, "I can help you, if you like."

"How?"

"I know this country well. I could be your guide."

Marsh was not certain that he wanted a guide who was being hunted by the Gestapo. Yet he had gotten hopelessly lost by himself.

Taking his silence for acquiescence, she said, "Where are we now?"

"Just coming to a long bridge. I'll have to get you out of the truck soon."

"I'll meet you in the alley behind the *Biergarten* at eight o'clock."

The next time the truck slowed, Marsh pressed the tarpaulin. "There's no one in sight. Just slide to the end of the truck, and I'll keep you covered."

Gretchen edged her way to the end of the truck as Marsh held down the canvas. He looked toward the two men inside the truck, but they were more interested in a woman sitting in the window of a house. With their attention riveted on the window, Gretchen jumped down, remaining in a crouched position at the curbing until the truck picked up speed and disappeared.

Another block and Marsh tapped on the window to stop the truck. "You can let me off here," he mimed, since they were unable to hear him with the glass rolled up.

The driver nodded and stopped. He rolled down his window and inquired, "What shall I do with the pine box?"

"You may sell it," Marsh stated. "The colonel does not mind."

The two men grinned. Coffins brought a good price. The money would buy many a stein of beer during the winter. "*Danke*," the driver said.

"*Bitte*." Marsh waited for the men to drive off. Then he retrieved his black armband, signaling a recent bereavement, making it easier for him, as a stranger, to use his food card.

The rucksack. He had forgotten and left the ruck sack in the coffin. Nervously, Marsh felt for his ID and ration card. They were still in the pocket of his jacket. But his combat boots were in the rucksack, with the map and trench knife.

How could he have been so careless? What could he do about it? Absolutely nothing. By now, the guards would have discovered the gravedigger at the cemetery. And the search for the fourth man would be on. The only thing he could do was to stay out of sight until dark and meet Gretchen in the alley behind the *Biergarten*. He didn't dare use his ration card in the meantime, for any stranger would be remembered when the Gestapo began to question the storekeepers.

43

*B*y the next day, Heinrich's anger had spawned a murderous obsession. He sat at a desk in the *Schloss*, with the contents of Marsh's rucksack laid out on a table, while the tower clock in the nearby town clanged its chimes over the countryside—three times, like the cock's crow, announcing betrayal.

He stared at the guard standing before him. But the only sound in the room, besides the steady crackle of a fire, was the nervous tapping of Heinrich's baton against the side of the desk.

"And the three gravediggers have also vanished?" Heinrich inquired in a deceptively benign voice.

"*Ja*, Herr Colonel."

Gretchen von Erhard was already listed as dead. He could not issue a warrant for her arrest, or else he would be called upon to explain to Himmler. But the escaped prisoner who had, in turn, helped Gretchen to escape, was another matter. He knew they were together. And if he captured one, he would capture the other.

"Horst, bring me the dossier on the escaped prisoner from Stalag 13."

Heinrich stared down at the information before him. His eyes narrowed at the man's picture. Captain Daniel "Marsh" Wexford. Atlanta, Georgia. 82nd Airborne Division. Was he destined to be plagued by the same American over and over, like a bad dream that kept recurring night after night? And the worst nightmare of all was that his own father might have had a hand in the escape.

There was one way to find out. "Horst, get Dräger on the field telephone," Heinrich ordered, closing the folder with a snap.

Horst, obeying, went outside to the caravan, the mobile unit containing the communications equipment.

An hour later, an exhausted Gretchen lay asleep in a barn while Marsh heated water over a hastily made fire.

He almost hated to waken her, for it had been an extremely long, hazardous day. But they would have to press on after they had eaten. It was too dangerous to remain in the same province with Heinrich, for Marsh felt certain that he would be after them both.

Sitting by the small fire pit he had dug in the earthen floor of the deserted barn, Marsh turned his hand palm up and stared at it, as if the cross Paulina di Resa had drawn in it were still visible.

Emil von Freiker. Heinrich von Freiker. Marsh had no doubt now that the general had arranged his escape. All this time, he had wondered about his father. Now he knew. But seeing him was not as he'd imagined it would be. There was no instant emotion, only curiosity and a tacit acknowledgment between two men who could never be more than enemies, for Marsh could not forget his mother, Ailly, and what the war had done to her.

He gazed at the sleeping Gretchen, so vulnerable. A pawn of war, too. And perhaps it was because of his mother, Ailly, that he had not remained in hiding until Gretchen had been caught, but instead helped her to escape from Heinrich.

"Gretchen," he called softly. "Wake up."

When there was no response, he walked over to the pile of straw where she lay and placed his hand on her arm to give her a gentle shake.

Her blue eyes opened instantly—large, alarmed, but with the softness that comes from sleep.

"What is it?" she asked, sitting up. Her long blond hair had come loose as she slept. It framed her small face until she quickly twisted it into a knot on the top of her head and hid it under the tweed cap.

"The food is ready. That's all."

She walked to the fire, stiffly at first, like a young colt not yet certain of its legs.

"What time is it?"

Marsh looked down at his watch. "Four-thirty."

Gretchen took a cup of tea. After holding it for a moment to warm her hands, she lifted it to her lips. "We still have over an hour of daylight," she commented.

From her remark, Marsh knew that Gretchen was also thinking of Heinrich and the Gestapo.

Dividing the brown bread, Marsh said, "I still cannot fathom a country destroying its own people. What did you do wrong, Gretchen—or your mother, for that matter?"

Gretchen took a bite before answering. "Germany was never my country. I am Austrian, as my father was. He refused a commission offered by Hitler. And he was executed for it."

"But your mother had no part in that."

"All my mother ever wanted to do was to sing—and to protect me from the Nazis." Gretchen looked up at Marsh. "She was an American, you know."

"No, I didn't know."

"But she became an Austrian when she married my father. It was after the Great War. She went to Vienna to study with Professor Hartzig. And a year later, on the night of her debut at the Vienna Opera House, she met my father." Gretchen suddenly smiled.

"My father always enjoyed telling the story of how she turned him down the first time he proposed. She was afraid he would make her give up her singing to become a *Hausfrau*."

"Evidently, he convinced her otherwise," Marsh replied.

Gretchen nodded and continued with her eating. "He was so proud of her. I remember sitting as a child in the opera box with him, and watching my mother on stage. But then— things changed. . . ."

A forlorn look replaced the brief happiness that her memories had dredged up. "Finally, even her voice couldn't save her from the Nazis."

"Where will you go, Gretchen?"

"I don't know. But that isn't important for the moment. Where will *you* go, once you have escaped?" she asked in return.

"Rejoin my division."

Marsh began to put out the fire and erase the telltale signs of their use of the barn. He wanted no farmer shot for harboring them. "Have you finished?"

She hurriedly drank the last of the liquid. "Yes," she responded and handed the cup to Marsh to put back into the tattered bag that had replaced the sturdy rucksack.

The two walked to the barn door and as Marsh left, and Gretchen waited until he had given her the all-clear sign. Then she too exited the barn.

Small snowflakes drifted down and landed on Gretchen's face. The mountains in the distance were completely covered with snow, and a filmy haze stretched over the valleys where smoke drifted upward to meet the clouds. The fall had been cold and rainy. Now winter had come early, making it difficult for people without homes and a warm fireside.

Gretchen was cold, but she did not complain. She was sorry, though, that she had been unable to keep the black cape. She could have put it to good use.

At the same time, Marsh lamented the loss of his trench knife and the blanket. But he had been lucky to acquire a pocketknife in the town before he'd met Gretchen in the alley behind the *Biergarten*.

A drone of planes overhead prompted Marsh to dive for cover. He forced Gretchen down into the narrow ditch with him. The earth shook while the sky behind them lit up with smoke and flames, as the incendiaries found their mark. Marsh, seeing the fire so close, was sorry they had left the barn.

A sudden strafing along the ditch plowed up the ground near them and made Marsh seek other shelter.

"Let's get out of here," he said, crawling down the open ditch toward the group of trees ahead. Directly after him came Gretchen, determined to keep up.

Once Marsh deemed it safe to move, the two began walking again. Flakes of snow multiplied, hiding the ground before them.

As he looked at Gretchen, Marsh saw that her lips were almost blue. "Here, take my jacket," he said, removing it.

"No. I'm all right. You keep it," she said, refusing his offer.

He began to walk faster, urging her on to shelter. What a

pity they had not been able to keep the horse. It would have made the journey much easier for the girl.

In the twilight, a tall tower rose from the next village, and Gretchen stopped for a moment to listen to the bells. They were a replica of the bells of the previous village, but they echoed over the mountains and the valley far more urgently.

Covered by the first snow of the season, the town took on a special quality, as if it might have been designed by an artist for a picture postcard. If there were any signs of war and rubble, they were hidden under the blanket of white.

Mesmerized by the sight, Gretchen said, "It's beautiful, isn't it, Marsh?"

He smiled at the shy manner in which she said his name. "Yes—beautiful, but treacherous. We can't go down. We'll have to find shelter somewhere else."

Gretchen knew the wisdom of his decision, and yet she was disappointed, for she remembered the village from her childhood when she had gone there as a child with her father to buy a present for her mother's birthday.

It was precisely this familiarity with the village that made her remember the shepherd's hut on its other side. The shepherd had carved exquisite animals from wood, and she had begged her father to take her to his hut after they had bought a crystal piece in a shop in town.

If the old shepherd were still alive, she knew they would be safe that night.

"I know a shelter—if you don't mind walking a little farther."

Gretchen said it almost casually. She had not complained of the fast pace or the cold that had penetrated her bones and was making her feel slightly numb and sleepy. "It's on the hillside beyond. We'll have to walk around the village to get there."

"Can you make it that far?"

"I have no other choice."

Gretchen took the stick that Marsh had fashioned for her, dug it into the steep hillside, and began the climb downward, to skirt the village in the valley and to gain the higher elevation on the other side.

All at once, the world became silent. The bells in the village ceased ringing. Even Gretchen's footsteps were silent, car-

peted by the snow. It was as if the village had been put to
sleep for a hundred years. At that moment, Gretchen felt that
she, too, could sleep for a hundred years.

The meager sun that had lain on the crest of the mountain
suddenly fell behind it, plunging the earth into layers of purple—magenta, violet, and aubergine. Like glasses of wine
staining a cloth of linen, the colors gradually spread over the
snow, changing its appearance to a darker hue.

An animal howled in its lair and a night bird flapped its
wings as Marsh and Gretchen passed by. No one else disturbed the winter scene.

About the time that Gretchen despaired of ever finding the
shepherd's hut, its dim outline appeared out of the darkness.

"There it is," Gretchen said, pointing to the rude structure
that offered no welcoming light. "I'll go ahead and see if Rei-
ner still lives there."

Her timid knock, her soft calling of his name brought no
response from within. Gretchen tried the door, but it was
locked. Seeing her lack of progress, Marsh stepped forward,
put his shoulder against the wood, and forced the door open.

Once Marsh had lit a match and looked around the room,
he saw that it had been unoccupied for a long time. He set
down the tattered bag, closed the door, and lit the old wax
candle that still sat in the middle of the rustic table. He ignored Gretchen as he settled into the hut and investigated
the corners for any unwanted guests.

By the time he turned back to Gretchen, she was slumped
against the empty hearth with her eyes closed.

"Gretchen!" Marsh said, walking to her and bending over.
"You mustn't go to sleep yet."

He reached out to touch her. Her skin was icy cold.
"Gretchen, wake up," he urged, for she was chilled far beyond
what was safe. He began to rub her hands vigorously. He
removed her wet shoes and stockings and placed her small
feet into his hands to warm them, too.

Removing the bedcover, he shook it out and wrapped it
around her and held her close to him, to absorb his own body
warmth.

Her teeth began to chatter and she protested the intimate
touch of his body against hers.

"Don't be afraid, Gretchen," he said. But he didn't mind

her struggle against him, for it served to awaken her. He was afraid that if she went to sleep in her state, she might never waken again.

As she opened her eyes, she pushed against him to free herself and Marsh let her go.

Standing up, he left her. He had not planned to build a fire, but Gretchen had made him change his mind. And he would take the opportunity to dry their shoes and socks before the fire, as they warmed themselves.

After a few false starts with the damp wood, the fire finally caught. Gretchen, realizing what Marsh had done, looked at him in the glow of the fire.

"Thank you, Marsh, for making me stay awake."

He smiled. "I didn't want to lose my guide."

They sat, toasting their feet on the hearth, with socks and stockings hung to dry and shoes propped to one side of the hearth. They drank the hot tea he made from melted snow, but saved the rest of the bread for morning.

As the flame began to die, Marsh said, "You realize we cannot keep the fire going all night? We don't have enough wood. And it's too dangerous."

Her sober mood matched his. "I was afraid of that. But it felt wonderful to be warm again. Even for a little while."

Marsh looked at Gretchen, so ill-clad for the winter weather. And he decided he would go into the village the next day to purchase warmer clothes for her. If that left little money for food, so be it.

When the fire went out, Marsh wrapped Gretchen in the bedclothes and cradled her in his arms. She did not protest this time. It was necessary for survival.

For one brief night, Gretchen von Erhard felt safe in the midst of the nightmare.

44

The next morning, as Gretchen slept, Marsh put on dry socks and his brogans and tramped back to the village. He had debated waking her, but decided at the last minute to let her rest.

Taking a branch to erase his footprints outside the hut, he had also erected a barrier inside the door to awaken Gretchen in case someone else should attempt to seek shelter under the same roof.

By the time he reached the village, Marsh knew what he wanted. And he found it in the window of a small shop off the main street. He stood outside and gazed at the boots and coat. But their price was exorbitant, far too expensive for his pocketbook, although the items were not new.

As he started to walk on, the proprietor opened his door. "*Guten morgen*," the man greeted the dejected Marsh. "You like the coat—the boots?"

Marsh nodded. He was surprised that the man was friendly, for strangers were usually looked upon with suspicion. Perhaps the possibility of a sale had made the man react in an uncharacteristic manner. "But I don't have enough money," Marsh informed him.

"The coat is very fine—and warm," the proprietor remarked, as if he had not heard Marsh. "Come in to examine the coat, and see that I have told you the truth."

Marsh politely declined. There was no need to waste time. But a German soldier coming down the street made him change his mind.

"I will do so," Marsh said, for he did not want to show his identification card, if he were challenged.

He followed the man inside. After he had examined the coat and agreed that it was a fine one, he took an interest in the boots. He measured them with his hands while he recalled the size of Gretchen's feet as he had rubbed them warm the previous evening.

As soon as the soldier had passed by, Marsh turned to the proprietor. "*Danke*. I will think about them."

"You have something of value you would like to swap, perhaps?"

Only by hiding it had Marsh been able to keep his watch. For the guards at the stalag regularly relieved new prisoners of their possessions. But Marsh had put it on his wrist again when he and Gretchen had set out. Now, he saw what the proprietor was proposing—the watch in return for the coat and red boots.

"I have no shoe stamp," Marsh countered.

"The boots are not new."

"You would take the watch in exchange for the coat and boots?" Marsh knew the answer before it was spoken.

"It could be arranged."

Not wanting to appear too anxious, the tall blond man slowly removed the watch from his wrist for the proprietor to examine. After a moment or two of checking it, the owner of the shop, pleased at its excellence, said, "The coat and boots are yours, *mein Herr*."

"Could you wrap them? I wish them to be a surprise."

The proprietor nodded. He went behind the counter, and took out some ancient newspaper and string. Within a few more minutes, Marsh left the village with the parcels under his arm, while the German soldier continued his rounds on his black bicycle.

At the sight of the bicycle, Marsh's memory stirred. "Grandpapa promised me a red bicycle—but he is dead." Marsh still remembered little Ibert Duvalier's words on that tragic day in Normandy.

Later, when Marsh returned to the shepherd's hut high in the hills, an incredulous Gretchen stared at the warm coat, at the boots, and then back toward Marsh.

"Are they for me?"

"Well, they're hardly my size," he teased.

A disconcerted Marsh watched as Gretchen burst into tears. "You don't like them?" he asked.

"I haven't had a new coat in four years."

"It isn't new."

A look of fear came over Gretchen's features. "How did you get them? I thought you didn't have much money."

"I had enough," he answered, not anxious to let her know he had exchanged his watch for the boots and coat. "Do they fit?"

Gretchen tried on the black coat with its fur-lined hood and stood back for Marsh to judge.

"A little large," he announced.

"That doesn't matter. It's warm. It's beautiful. Thank you, Marsh." Her eyes sparkled as he had never seen them. Happiness, however brief, had made a dramatic change in her, even in the way she held her head.

"Now for the boots," Marsh prompted.

Gretchen sat on the old wooden stool and Marsh helped her with each boot. She stood up, walked proudly back and forth.

"We will get over the frontier much faster now. I promise not to lag behind."

Gretchen reached out her hands to Marsh. Their eyes met as she moved toward him. Standing on tiptoe, she kissed him on the chin. "Thank you," she whispered. "I will never forget your generosity. Perhaps someday I can repay you."

As the wind whistled down the old fireplace, Marsh's eyes remained on the young girl's face, angelic in the light filtering from the cracks around the door.

"Gretchen, each day becomes more dangerous now, as we approach the frontier."

She stared at the man whose teasing manner had so rapidly vanished.

"You must promise me that regardless of what happens, if we become separated before we reach Switzerland, you will write to me in care of the American Embassy in London, to let me know where you are."

"The war may last a long time, Marsh. So many things could happen in the meantime."

"Promise me, Gretchen." His hands tightened on hers.

"I promise."

They left the shepherd's hut in silence and began the dangerous trek toward the frontier guarded by SS troops whose duty was to shoot anyone who attempted to escape over the mountains.

For eight days, Marsh and Gretchen dodged border patrols, hid in deserted monasteries, found sanctuary in the isolated way stations that dotted the mountains. With little to eat, with nearly all their money gone, they traipsed over the mountains to the frontier and finally stood within view of the Bodensee, the two-hundred-square-mile lake that lay on the border between Germany and Switzerland and became Lake Constance once the waters were within Swiss jurisdiction.

This was the destination they had striven for, driving themselves almost beyond human endurance as they traveled entirely by foot, for any other way would have subjected them to suspicion and possible arrest.

After dark, they approached the lake town with caution. As usual, a cathedral spire provided a landmark for them.

"Wait inside the cathedral, until I come for you, Gretchen."

"Where are you going, Marsh?"

"To the alehouse, to try to find someone to take us across the lake."

Inside the cathedral, Gretchen remained on her knees for a long time. The candles flickered, burned low. Worshipers came and went out, but Marsh did not return.

Dwindling one by one, the worshipers stood, gave the sign of the cross and left, until Gretchen alone remained.

Finally a robed priest walked down the aisle toward Gretchen. "The Lord be with you, my child."

She looked up at the tall, thin priest standing beside her. "Thank you, Father." But she made no move to go. She *couldn't* leave until Marsh came back for her.

As she returned to her prayers, the priest walked on, making the rounds of the cathedral, checking each entrance. At last he walked back to where Gretchen knelt.

"My child, you will have to save some of your prayers for tomorrow. It is past time for you to go home," he reminded her gently with a smile.

"Father?"

"Yes?"

"I . . ." Gretchen stopped. She was so tired, so afraid. But she couldn't trust the priest with her fear. For he was German. And she was wanted by the Gestapo, as was Marsh. And he had not come back.

"You are in trouble, my child?"

"No. That is—" She stood up. "Good night, Father."

Her clothes showed that she had traveled a great distance. And her face revealed a haunting desperation. Gretchen began to walk rapidly down the aisle, but she didn't get far before the priest caught up with her.

"Would you like to have supper with me—and tell me what is troubling you?"

Gretchen hesitated. "No, thank you, Father. I . . . I have to meet someone."

"Here, in the cathedral? Is that why you have remained for such a long time?"

She finally nodded.

"I might be able to help you," he whispered, his eyes suddenly seeking out the dark places to make certain no one overheard.

A cautious Marsh left the alehouse to get Gretchen. He had left her far too long. And he was disappointed that he was not bringing good news with him. He had been unsuccessful in finding someone to take them across the lake, for the German soldiers had been everywhere. And each hour they stayed in the town increased the danger of their being caught.

Marsh walked toward the cathedral and backed into a doorway whenever he heard someone on the street. Peering to the right and to the left, he hurried onto the south porch and attempted to enter the transept. But the cathedral was locked.

"Marsh?" a voice called out from the other side of the door.

"Gretchen?"

He waited as he heard a key turn in the lock. A priest in black stood before him. "Come in quickly," the priest urged. And Marsh obeyed.

As Marsh and Gretchen ate a simple hot meal and waited for a member of the Resistance to come and smuggle them aboard a boat to freedom, Heinrich von Freiker waited in more comfortable quarters in a resort hotel overlooking the Bodensee.

"Enter," Heinrich called out when he heard the tap on the door.

A pleased Horst walked into the room. "They are both under surveillance, my Colonel."

"Where are they now?"

"In the care of Father Kristophe at the cathedral. He has arranged their escape in the early hours."

"The tunnel is being guarded? As well as the cathedral?"

"*Ja*, my Colonel."

Heinrich smiled. "Good. This time, they won't escape. And as for Father Kristophe, his evening prayers tonight will be his last this side of Hell."

Heinrich clasped his hands before the fire. He relished the hour when he would tell his father what had happened to Captain Daniel "Marsh" Wexford, after he had taken such pains to arrange his escape. But it hadn't worked. Heinrich had been able to track him to the lake. And with Marsh, he would destroy the underground escape route for the enemies of the Third Reich. As for Gretchen, he had other plans for her.

"Wake up, my child. It's time to leave."

Fully clothed, Gretchen sat up. The lantern flickered against the stone wall. The sound of footsteps was muffled, while low-speaking voices exchanged last-minute briefings in the tunnel. Gretchen followed the priest with his lantern. In the tunnel she searched for Marsh. But all three men were priests. Marsh was nowhere to be seen.

"Come, Gretchen," a priest whispered.

"No. I can't go without Marsh." She looked up into the priest's face. His grin spread wide as she recognized him.

"Just don't ask me to say a *Te Deum*," Marsh confessed.

"Come," Father Kristophe urged, holding the lantern high.

They followed through the passageway, a torturous labyrinth winding toward the lake.

"We stop here," Father Kristophe said.

The tunnel now divided into two forks, like a two-headed Medusa.

"We will go separate ways," Father Kristophe advised. "It's safer."

He indicated for Gretchen to follow him, while Marsh walked with Ernst, the other man also dressed in priestly robes.

For a moment, Gretchen felt separated from a part of herself when she was separated from Marsh. For ten days she had shared her life with him. She had become so accustomed to being with him that she had not slept well without his presence in the room under the cathedral. But of course, the priest would not have condoned their sharing the same room while they were under his care. She stared in the direction that Marsh had gone, and then hurried to catch up with Father Kristophe. Soon she and Marsh would be together again.

Because of his housekeeper, Father Kristophe had become increasingly uneasy about using the old tunnel. And that's why he had decided to send the American soldier down the newly completed section that would bring him out fifty yards beyond the lake dock.

At that point, shortly before sunrise, when the waters of the lake lapped softly against the docks, and the wind had not yet gathered force to sweep down the streets, Father Kristophe blew out the light in his lantern. Silently, he turned a handle, and the opening in the tunnel became visible.

He waited for the signal from Ernst. And when it came, Father Kristophe waited a minute longer, while the two dark shadows moved toward the dock and disappeared into the small boat. Then he and Gretchen left the safety of the older tunnel opening. They too had almost reached the dock when the klieg lights came on, catching Gretchen in their harsh glare.

The sirens began pulsating their raucous screams into the air. SS troops began to converge from every direction, while Heinrich von Freiker limped to the parapet above and watched the drama taking place below.

"Gretchen!"

"Gretchen!"

Two voices shouted to her at the same time, two voices from different directions.

"You cannot get away. You are surrounded, Gretchen," Heinrich called out.

She stood in the glare of the lights. She and the priest, Father Kristophe. The lights had not found Marsh, already in the boat.

For one brief moment she turned her head toward Marsh, and then slowly began to walk in the opposite direction, toward Heinrich.

Marsh, realizing what she was doing, threw off Ernst's restraining hand as he resolved to rescue her.

"It is too late, Captain. They have already caught her."

But Marsh would not be restrained. He stood up to climb back on the dock.

With lightning speed, Ernst hit Marsh over the head, and the paratrooper, dressed as a priest, crumpled into the stern of the boat.

Amid the noise farther down the dock, the small boat left the banks of the Bodensee. Later, Marsh Wexford woke up on the excursion boat that plied the waters of Lake Constance.

"I'm glad to see that the damage was not permanent, Captain," Ernst said, wringing the wet towel to place on his head. "I was afraid I had hit you too hard."

A heartsick Marsh climbed unsteadily from the cot, and despite Ernst's objections, even though they were in safe waters, he went on deck. With his priestly robes scarcely hiding the German-made brogans, Marsh Wexford braced himself against the wind and stared back at the snow-covered mountains in the distance.

"Oh, Marsh. How beautiful. Perhaps someday I can repay you."

Gretchen's voice haunted him as he remembered the morning he had given her the warm coat to wear. She had repaid him far beyond anything he deserved. For she had sacrificed herself in order to save him.

"Gretchen," he whispered, willing his very soul to reach her at that moment. And the paratrooper who had fought in Sicily, Italy, Normandy, and Holland, who had faced death time and again without flinching, now wept at the unhappy prospect of living.

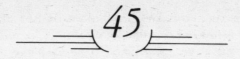

The hopes of the Allies—to win the war against Germany with a single thrust through Holland—had not materialized. Now they braced for a cold, bitter winter war on a broad front—with Montgomery in the north and Patton and Bradley in the south.

Alpharetta also braced for a cold winter—in the dower house on the Pomeroy estate. She had vowed not to spend a night in Harrington Hall again until Dow returned.

Sharing the dower house with her was Belline, who had come at Alpharetta's invitation. It was the least she could do in Ben Mark's memory, for it was too dangerous for Belline to stay in London while she waited for the birth of his child.

Unaware of Dow's mistaken idea about the baby, Alpharetta sat in the parlor with her coat on and read the letter that the post had brought from him that morning.

"I'm glad that Belline is with you until the birth of the baby, for the Germans are on the march again, and I'm not certain when I will be able to come back for a visit. I shall try to get home at Christmas, but if that is not possible, rest assured that I will be there in time for the birth of the child."

Alpharetta reread the paragraph. And it puzzled her just as much the second time. Finally, she shrugged her shoulders, folded the letter, and went to put the kettle on for tea.

Even though she was not staying at the hall, Alpharetta saw Sir Edward every day. He had taken to calling at the dower house each afternoon, especially since Belline spent a large part of the day in bed on doctor's orders, and Alpharetta did not like leaving her.

Now she saw him walking briskly down the lane. She smiled and went to the door to open it as soon as he reached the steps.

"Good afternoon, Sir Edward. Do come in."

"Good afternoon, 'Retta," he replied, removing his cap as he walked inside. "How is Belline today?"

"She's feeling better, thank you." She looked toward the table where Dow's letter lay. "I heard from Dow today."

"So did I," Sir Edward acknowledged. In a teasing manner he added, "He asked me to keep an eye on you."

"You haven't told him, have you, that I'm staying in the dower house with Belline?"

"No. Not at all. Even though I don't understand why you're not at the hall."

"This house is easier to heat," she defended, rising from the chair to place another log on the fire.

"You're right about that. Harrington Hall has always been impossible in winter."

"Then perhaps you should move in with *us*, Sir Edward."

He cleared his throat and reached for the pipe in his pocket. "Now that's what I would like to discuss with you."

"You mean, you might consider it?"

For a moment, the look on Sir Edward's face was blank. Then understanding brought back his usual demeanor.

"No, not that. What I want to discuss is your continuing to call me Sir Edward. That won't do, 'Retta. Won't do at all. You're Dow's wife now." He looked at her rather sheepishly. "Would it be too difficult for you to start calling me—Father?"

Alpharetta stared at the old man sitting before the fire and tapping his pipe. She had liked him from the first moment he had taken her to see his still, when Dow had stopped for the night on the way to Scotland.

Her green eyes sparkled. So he had accepted her as a daughter. She smiled and, looking across the room at him, she inquired, "Would you like your tea now, Father?"

"Whenever it's ready, 'Retta," he replied, relaxing his body to fit the curves of the upholstered rocking chair before the hearth. As Alpharetta walked to the kitchen, he filled his pipe with tobacco, then leaned over to get a light from the flames on the hearth.

When the sun began to wane, Sir Edward left the dower house to return to the hall. For a while, Alpharetta stood and watched him go. His departure was slower, less brisk than his arrival. If it were not for Belline, she probably would have swallowed her pride and moved into the hall to keep the old man company. Alpharetta shivered and went back to the fire. Now she understood the old saying that English winter ended in July and began again in August.

Later that evening, as Belline remained upstairs, Alpharetta sat by the hearth in the same rocking chair that Sir Edward had occupied. She worried over the strange letter from Dow, much like the dog, Brewster, going back to sniff the fox's den, even though the fox had long fled.

It was almost as if Dow thought *she* was having Ben Mark's baby, instead of Belline. That was it. But surely . . .

Abruptly she stood up, found the letter, and held it to the light. She began to reconstruct that evening on the downs after Belline had called her about Ben Mark's death. That was when it started. Surely Dow didn't think Ben Mark had made her pregnant and then married Belline? Had she not made it clear to him that *Belline* was the pregnant one?

But Dow had arranged their marriage hurriedly, and then left without consummating it. There could be only one logical explanation for that. He had thought Alpharetta was already pregnant with Ben Mark's child. And Ben Mark was dead.

Now it all fell into place, and a furious Alpharetta left the house for a long walk. If she stayed inside any longer—in the house where Dow had put the rings on her finger before their mock honeymoon—she knew she would explode. For the marriage was still a mockery, no more real than the honeymoon at Lochendall.

She would write him immediately. No, she wouldn't. Let him discover the truth for himself upon his return, whenever that might be—Christmas or later. It didn't matter to her.

Christmas of 1944 came and went, hardly observed at all, for the Germans, mounting a massive offensive in the Ardennes, had broken through a weak link in the defensive line. All leaves were cancelled.

Back with his division, Marsh Wexford was thrown into yet

another battle, in snow that was waist-deep, while Germans, dressed in American uniforms, infiltrated the line and added to the frustration of the battle.

Patton, fighting in the south, received the urgent telephone call from Bradley. "Georgie, how soon can you get to Bastogne with your tanks?"

"I'll be there in forty-eight hours, Brad."

Bradley, the commander of 12th Army Group, knew that was an impossibility. No one could turn tanks around and get that far in heavy winter snow in that short a period. The men would have to wait for relief at least ninety-eight hours, for Patton was a soldier, not a magician.

But true to his word, Patton wheeled an entire army around and drove his tanks unmercifully, and within forty-eight hours the U.S. Third Army had arrived at Bastogne to give relief to the trapped Americans.

Toward the end of February, Marsh Wexford and his division were pulled out of the line. They returned to their billets in Sissone, France. For them, the winter war had ended.

Two days later, the travail of Belline, Marsh's stepsister, began in the dower house at Harrington Hall.

"Alpharetta, I want you to know . . ." Belline, holding on to Alpharetta's hand, stopped speaking as another pain took her breath. When she had relaxed, she suddenly said, "If anything happens to me, I want you to take the baby."

"Nothing's going to happen to you, Belline. Think of something else. Think how beautiful your baby's going to be."

"Yes. He'll look just like Ben Mark."

"Or *she* might look like you or me."

"Alpharetta, I'm sorry . . ."

She cut Belline off. This was no time for regrets or recriminations. "The past is over and done with, Belline."

The doctor seated at the bedside looked at Alpharetta. "I think you'd better go downstairs. Nurse Mortain will take over now."

"Don't leave me, Alpharetta. I need you." Belline reached out toward her and Alpharetta, caught between the two, looked at the doctor again.

He sighed. "All right. But please don't get in the way."

And so it was that Alpharetta was present in the room when Ben Mark's son was born—hair as black as midnight, an angry voice protesting his entrance into a war-torn world.

Later, Alpharetta held him and stared down into his contented face. The baby was a miracle—just as Marsh's escape was a miracle. Vaguely, Alpharetta remembered Dow's letter about his plans to be present for the birth of the baby. But he had not gotten home after all. The war had kept him on the Continent.

Five days later, as Alpharetta sat by the downstairs fire and soothed the hungry baby while Miss Mortain heated the bottle in the kitchen, a car drove up the lane and stopped at the gate.

When the knock came, she hurriedly wrapped the blanket around the baby and went to unlock the door.

Standing in front of her was Dow, his face dark with anger. "Dow!"

"What are you doing in the dower house?" he began, paying no attention to the child in her arms. "Your place is at Harrington Hall, as my wife."

"But I—"

He cut her off. "I presume there's a nurse for the baby?"

"Yes. Miss Mortain. She—she's in the kitchen."

"Then will you hand the child over to her? I'm taking you to the hall immediately. I'll come back later for them."

"But you don't understand, Dow—"

The nurse came from the kitchen with the bottle in her hands. "I'll take the wee bairn now, my lady," she said, seeing the man in the room.

"Miss Mortain, this is my husband, Sir Dow. He's just come home on leave. I . . . I'm going to the hall with him—but I'll be back later."

"Take your time, Lady Pomeroy. And don't worry about the bairn. He's in good hands with Nurse Mortain."

"Where's your coat, Alpharetta? It's freezing outside."

"In the closet. The navy-blue one."

He got the coat out and helped her on with it. Then before she could object, he had lifted her into his arms to carry her to the car.

She hadn't intended for their first meeting to be like this. And now, too late, she realized she should have written him the truth instead of allowing him to go on thinking that *she* was the one expecting the baby.

He draped the plaid lap robe around her, cranked the car, and started it in the direction of the hall.

Alpharetta stared at the man at her side. And her anger matched his because of his behavior, disrupting the calm atmosphere of the dower house and practically kidnaping her from it.

With his jaw set, Dow drove slowly, carefully, as if she were made of breakable china.

"Dow, before this goes any further, I need to talk with you."

"Not now, Alpharetta. I'm too angry to listen."

The fog was beginning to close in, spreading itself over the land, bare of the grain that had been harvested in the fall.

Dow drove up to the door, got out, and once again lifted Alpharetta into his arms.

Andrew, the butler, appeared at the door. "Good evening, my lady," he said, not blinking at the strange sight of Dow carrying his wife into the hall.

"Good evening, Andrew," she managed to say as Dow swept down the hallway to the curved stairs that wound up to the second floor.

As they reached the landing, Betty, the maid, was coming out of the green room.

"Everything's ready, Sir Dow. There's a good roaring fire going."

"Thank you, Betty. I'll turn my wife over to you for the moment."

"Certainly, sir."

The maid walked directly behind them and into the green room, where the flickering flames from the hearth spread a soft glow over the green silk moiré walls, the draperies drawn against the cold. A brief reflection of the two appeared in the old patinaed mirror as Dow passed it by and set Alpharetta gently into the chair.

"I'll wait outside," he said and left the room.

Alpharetta continued to sit in the chair with her coat wrapped around her as she stared into the flames.

"I'll help you to undress, whenever you're ready, my lady."

She looked around at Betty. The maid was standing by the bed and touching the exquisite negligee ensemble draped across it.

"It has to be from Paris, ma'am."

Alpharetta rose from the chair and walked to the bed. The negligee and robe were ivory-colored, with russet fur lining the wide cuffs of the long dolman sleeves and the hem.

The red-haired woman realized she would have no privacy with Dow until Betty had done her duty and left.

Dow waited impatiently in the hall, and when he saw Betty come out of the room, he walked in again.

Alpharetta stood by the fire in the ivory robe, her green eyes accented by the silk moiré of the walls while the ivory satin of the robe bathed her porcelain skin in its softness.

Dow gazed at her without saying anything. And then he began in a pained voice, "You're quite beautiful, Alpharetta. It seems that motherhood agrees with you."

"You didn't have to marry me, Dow," she said, the anger beginning again.

"I know that, Alpharetta." His voice was curiously mild. "But I chose to do so, even under the circumstances."

"No, Dow. What I have been trying to tell you is that it wasn't necessary for you to . . . to save my honor. The baby isn't mine. *Belline* is the mother. That's the reason she and Ben Mark were married—because of the baby.

"Don't you see? *Our* marriage is a fraud. The same as it was at Lochendall."

She began to remove the rings from her finger. "As soon as Belline is able to travel, we'll both leave—with the baby. I'm sure you'll be able to get an annulment with no problem, since our marriage was never consummated."

With no move to take the rings, he stood looking at her, as if he didn't quite believe what she was saying.

"You mean, the baby you were holding a few minutes ago isn't yours?"

"No. I've told you. He belongs to Belline. Now, if you'll kindly leave the room, I'll put on my own clothes and go back to the dower house."

Relief at the news was evident in Dow's face. However hard

he'd tried to mask it, the knowledge that the baby was not a girl, but a boy, had disappointed him. For that meant another man's son would become his heir. Yet for Alpharetta, he had been prepared to accept the boy as his firstborn.

Fleetingly, Dow thought of the wedding gift Miles and the other two men had brought to Lochendall from the village. He had never told Alpharetta what the box contained—the handmade lace christening gown and bonnet, sewn for the next master of Lochendall—the secondborn son. Now he had just discovered there was no firstborn son for him to claim, either.

"You can't leave, Alpharetta."

"I not only *can*, but *will*. I don't need your pity, Dow. No marriage can be built on pity."

"What about *love*, Alpharetta?"

Startled, she looked into his face. His eyes, his jaw had softened from the earlier granite hardness.

"What about—love?" she repeated warily.

"I want you as my wife, Alpharetta—as I did at Lochendall. I know you don't love me, but in time . . ."

He reached out and took the rings from her. And then he took her hand and placed the rings on her finger again. "You remember the first time I did this? 'I suppose a husband would give you jewels to match your eyes, Miss Beaumont.'"

"I remember," she whispered.

He took her gently in his arms. "I won't let you go, you know. And after tonight, there'll be no grounds for annulment."

He began to tease her with his kisses, slowly, tantalizingly. "Dow?"

"Hush, darling."

The old mirror reflected the two wrapped in each other's arms.

Once again Dow lifted her and carried her to the bed of his ancestors. A glow encompassed the room as love blossomed with an eternal flame that spread on wings of fire to ignite one man and one woman in its ecstasy.

*B*y the first week of March, the U.S. First Army entered Köln and the troops of the U.S. 9th Division secured a bridgehead at Remagen. During that time, Montgomery was poised for his offensive in the north.

Once again the field marshal was allotted all the supplies and men he had demanded, to the detriment of the American armies in the south.

The lack of gasoline in the Third Army became so grave that each time Patton was summoned to a meeting at Allied headquarters, he drifted in on an empty tank and had his driver tap the headquarter's tank for enough fuel to return the general back to his own army.

On the other side of the Rhine, the Germans watched Montgomery's preparations, the giant stockpiles being amassed. They built up their defenses, preparing for the set piece, Montgomery's trademark in battle.

On March 22, one day before the British Second Army began crossing at Rees, troops of the U.S. Third Army, with little gasoline or ammunition, slipped across the Rhine at Oppenheim, the same spot chosen by Napoleon more than a century earlier.

Sicily was being relived. Again Patton had stolen Montgomery's thunder, as he had done at Messina.

Now, the four Allied armies—British, Canadian, American, Soviet—began to converge toward the heart of Germany from three directions. And by the end of March, the last V-2 rocket hit England.

In Berlin, Emil von Freiker sat in the back of his Horch and looked around him as his driver took him toward the Reichstag.

He knew the end was near. The Third Reich was now an empty shell waiting to be crushed under the invader's boot. For the sake of the people left—the civilians, the women— he prayed it would not be the Red Army that reached Berlin first.

On this April morning, Emil had a sudden desire to see his boyhood home one last time. He tapped on the glass to get his driver's attention. No one would miss him at the Reichstag. The day would be far better spent in living out old memories.

They drove into the countryside, where the land still appeared whole despite the leveling of cities throughout the Reich. In the shelter of trees swelling with the promise of spring, Emil got out of the car to stare at the house in the distance.

"Wait here, Schmidt. I won't be long."

He had no wish for witnesses, even his driver, for it was a journey into the past, where only he could go—alone. But as he pushed open the door, voices greeted him. A woman began to cry, as a man laughed harshly. Heinrich? Was it his son Heinrich?

For a moment, he stood and listened. "Please, Heinrich. I beg you. Kill me, as you did my mother."

"In good time, Gretchen. I have not finished with you yet. You have burrowed yourself into my soul, and I cannot get enough of you. I knew you would be like this, the moment I laid eyes on you."

"I want to die, Heinrich. I can't stand the sight of you. I can't bear for you to touch me again."

"Beg all you want. Your repulsion only increases my desire."

"Heinrich!"

The man whirled at the sound of his name. "What are you doing here, *Vater*?"

"Release the girl at once."

Heinrich, off balance at the intrusion of his father, grew

composed again. "*Nein, Vater.* She is my mistress. You recognize her? The great Frau Emma's daughter? Gretchen von Erhard?"

"What has happened to you, Heinrich—to turn on your own people?"

"They are enemies of the state and the Führer."

"I cannot allow you to mistreat her."

"There is little you can do, old man," Heinrich said in a disparaging tone. "And if you do not leave me alone, I shall arrest even you. Oh, I know what you have been up to. You arranged the escape of the paratrooper from Dräger's stalag. Your—"

"I'm warning you, Heinrich. Release her."

At first he didn't see the pistol in his father's hands. And when he did, he became afraid, for he had taken off his own gun belt.

"Gretchen, you are free to go," Emil said, still looking into his son's face.

"Horst, come here," Heinrich shouted.

Gretchen pulled away from Heinrich and ran from the room.

Emil called after her, "Don't go back to Berlin. Head south—toward Patton's army."

Emil and Heinrich stood facing each other, taking the measure of each other. Father and son.

"So the paratrooper got away?" Emil inquired.

"Yes. He was lucky."

Emil suddenly smiled. He had no hesitation now in pulling the trigger.

As Gretchen ran from the house, she heard the sound of a gunshot.

For a moment, Heinrich looked at his father. And then he collapsed on the floor.

Schmidt, hearing the shot, drew his pistol and raced into the house as Horst ran up the stairs from the wine cellar. Both heard a second shot, and by the time they reached the room, Emil too lay on the floor.

"He killed his own son." Horst shook his head in disbelief as he leaned over Heinrich's body.

Schmidt, staring down at the dead body of his general, replied, "It was necessary. Herr General was an honorable man."

On April 30, Hitler killed himself in his bunker and on May 7, 1945, Germany made a formal surrender at Rheims.

The war in Europe was finally over. The greatest war machine that had ever been devised by one nation had finally been defeated. Despite the petty jealousies, the rivalries, the egos of the commanding generals, the deed had been done through a joint effort of free nations, under one supreme commander.

One basic fact can never be denied or distorted by history— the bravery of the soldiers who, like Marsh Wexford and his men, left their legacy of freedom in places like Ste.-Mère-Église, Nijmegen, Gela, and Trois Ponts, in the Ardennes.

But for Marsh, the war was still unfinished. He remembered his promise to the boy, Ibert Duvalier. He remembered his entreaty of Gretchen von Erhard. And he lived for the day when the vigil and the search could begin.

But the United States was still at war with Japan. And talk began that the majority of the soldiers in Europe might be shipped to the Pacific. For Marsh and the others, the sudden reprieve came on August 14, 1945, when Japan surrendered. On September 2, the articles of surrender were signed, making it official. The world was finally at peace.

Now began the search of each orphanage in Normandy, the requests through official channels for help.

"Captain, you must realize there are thousands of war orphans—some too young to remember their names, their families."

"But he's six years old. Ibert wouldn't forget his own name."

"Many have chosen to forget *everything*. Their memories are too painful for them to live with."

While Marsh looked for the child, he also haunted the American Embassy in London on a regular basis. No hope was given for Gretchen von Erhard, either.

"There is no guarantee that she came out of Berlin alive. And if she did, she might be in Russia."

In late November, as the gusts in the channel made the crossing hazardous, Marsh went back to France and renewed the search for Ibert.

In an obscure little town forty miles from Le Bois Rouge, Marsh stopped the car at what was to be the final spot of the day. It was a rural area, and down an old dirt road was an unpromising building, with the roof needing repair, the fence leaning at an angle.

Marsh got out of the car with little hope. He stood watching the children at play. They were dressed poorly, their skinny arms and legs covered in navy blue, with caps of the same color on their heads. Most seemed happy, hopping up and down to keep warm, running in circles, bouncing a ball.

All except one small boy. Making no attempt to join in the play, he sat apart from the others, his small hands clutching a coin.

Marsh stood at the fence and watched. There was something familiar about the child, and yet he couldn't be sure. It had been more than a year since he had seen him.

"Ibert?" Marsh's voice called out, but the child paid no attention. He must have been mistaken.

The other children stopped their playing. They stared at the man and back to the little boy who had not looked up.

"Ibert," a child said. "The man is calling you."

The child seated by himself finally looked up. For one brief moment, a glimmer of hope passed over his face and then was gone.

"Ibert?" Marsh called, louder this time. "Ibert Duvalier?"

The child stood, as if awakening from a dream. He began to walk toward the fence, slowly at first. And then he began to run, as Marsh found the gate and rushed to meet him.

"Monsieur, monsieur," Ibert said, his face filled with emotion. "You have come."

Marsh swung him from the ground, up into his arms.

"You kept your promise. You kept your promise." And in his hands, he clutched the coin all the tighter.

While Marsh waited in Paris for the official papers on Ibert to be processed, he again contacted the American Embassy in London. There was still no message from Gretchen. Reluctantly, he realized he could not remain in Paris forever. He and Ibert would have to leave soon for the United States.

The week before Christmas, Europe was again covered by snow, as it had been the previous year when Marsh had fought in the Ardennes. And once again, tragedy struck.

The hero of the Ardennes, General George S. Patton, Jr., died from injuries sustained in an accident.

A saddened Marsh knew he could not leave Europe until he paid his last respects to the Liberator, the man who had turned an entire army around to help defeat the last major offensive of the Germans.

And so it was that on Christmas Eve 1945, Marsh, with Ibert at his side, stood in the cemetery at Hamm, Luxembourg, with a multitude of people, both soldier and civilian, and waited for the funeral cortege to arrive.

Staring over row upon row of white crosses, Marsh sensed that Europe was gathering a hero to its bosom. The old warrior was coming to rest among his own troops.

The man had been a paradox—religious and profane, rash and deliberate, proud and humble, aristocratic and earthy, but always a man of honor; rich in his own material possessions, yet a pauper, begging for supplies for his troops, who, on the day of their greatest victory, received not a drop of gasoline from supply.

Marsh watched as the high-level brass passed by in the official honorary escort, the stars and braid signifying some of the most important military men in the world—with the exception of one man, General Walter Bedell Smith, Eisenhower's aide. For Patton's wife, Beatrice, had struck the name of his greatest detractor from the list and substituted the name of Patton's orderly, Sergeant Meeks, the black man who had watched over the general in life and now, with tears in his eyes, accompanied him to his final resting place.

When the flowers had been laid upon his grave, when the bugles had blown and the crowds begun to disperse, Marsh waited while the small French orphan, Ibert Duvalier, left his side and walked to the mound. Ibert slipped the commemorative coin out of his pocket and, kneeling down, buried it in the soft earth next to the white cross.

"He needs it more than I do," Ibert explained. "For I shall see the mountain for myself."

In complete trust, he put his small hand in the paratrooper's larger one and, together, they joined the crowd leaving the cemetery.

The people filed out, wave after wave, passing through the gates with the golden eagles on each side declaring that portion of hallowed land as American.

All at once, Marsh stopped where he was, for in the crowd ahead he saw a woman dressed in a black coat with fur-lined hood, and small red boots on her feet to protect them from the snow.

"Gretchen!" Marsh yelled, and began the frantic effort to reach her before she disappeared. When he realized Ibert could not keep up with him, he swung the boy into his arms.

Towering over the crowd, Marsh yelled again, "Gretchen! Wait!"

At the sound of her name, the woman turned. Her eyes widened at the sight of the tall blond man rushing toward her. Her hand went up to her cheek in a nervous gesture and she began to move rapidly away, seeking refuge in the crowd, as if deliberately avoiding him.

But Marsh was determined not to lose her. "Gretchen!" he called again, racing through the crowd until, at last, he reached out to take her arm and stop her forcibly.

With the crowd milling around them, they stared at each other, Gretchen attempting to back away even as he held her arm.

"Why didn't you write me?" he demanded. "I've stalked the American Embassy for months—waiting for word that you were still alive, that you were all right. Did you forget your promise to me, so soon?"

Her eyes were sad. "No, Marsh, I didn't forget."

"Then, why didn't you write?"

"Let me go, Marsh. Please. There can never be anything between us. Too much has happened. Heinrich—"

She choked on the man's name. Her lips began to tremble as her voice deserted her.

There was no need to confirm what he had known all along. "Where is he?" Marsh demanded.

In a whisper Gretchen replied, "He's . . . dead."

Marsh's eyes showed his satisfaction at the news. Now he would not have to track him down. He was already dead.

The memory of Gretchen deliberately walking toward Heinrich at Boden See so that Marsh might escape, had haunted the American for months, as the words spoken earlier by Madame Arnaud at St. Mihiel had haunted him.

"She was a victim of war, my little Ailly. She lost her life but she gave it willingly to save her family."

Madame Arnaud's words had come full circle, to encompass another war. But Gretchen was still alive. Marsh smiled. He was certain.

"This is Christmas Eve, Gretchen," he replied in a gentle voice. "A day of miracles. I've found you again. And that's all that matters."

"He found me, too, mam'selle," Ibert stated. "Just as he said he would."

"And the three of us are going home soon—to Atlanta. Come, Gretchen. It's time to celebrate our good fortune."

He smiled and drew her to him.

"Marsh, you're . . . sure?" she whispered.

"Never more sure of anything in my life."

Tragedy turned into joy as the three rejoined the crowd and left the hallowed ground.

On that same evening at Harrington Hall in England, a quiet, subdued Lady Alpharetta Beaumont-Pomeroy, aware of the ritual taking place in the Luxembourg cemetery, sat at dinner with her husband and his father.

Belline had left England with the baby. But they shared their Christmas Eve with Lord Cranston, Meg, and Freddie Mallory, who had begun to call on Lady Margaret Cranston once Dow had married Alpharetta.

The hall was hung with greenery, the work of Alpharetta, and the aroma of roast goose and plum pudding rose from the silver trays presided over by Andrew.

Later, when the dinner was over and their guests had gone, Sir Edward, Dow, and Alpharetta sat before the fire in the family drawing room, their memories, their thoughts on other times, other Christmases, when the Allied cause seemed lost and the people grasped for heroes like straws in the wind.

As Sir Edward dozed before the fire, Dow stood up and turned toward Alpharetta. "Are you ready to call it a night, darling?"

"Yes, Dow. If you are. But what about Father?"

"I'll get Andrew to help him to bed."

Arm in arm, Dow and Alpharetta climbed the stairs, walked slowly past the portrait gallery where Desirée Pomeroy posed regally in her gilt frame.

As the two walked into the green bedroom, Dow, realizing the cause of Alpharetta's quietness, said, "Don't be sad, darling. The ground of Luxembourg won't keep him forever. I wouldn't be a bit surprised if, fifty to a hundred years from now, your General Patton is found stomping over another battlefield, leading his men. You heard him say we'll have to fight the Russians, someday. And I fully expect him to come back from Valhalla to do it."

Alpharetta, looking at her husband in the mirror decorated with golden garlands of flowers and birds, smiled. "I think *one* ghost is enough to worry about, Dow, without conjuring another."

"I doubt that you'll see Desirée haunting these halls ever again. True love has finally won. And I think she would be pleased at the outcome. Remind me to place an extra rose by her side next year."

His hazel eyes took on a golden glow as his hand touched Alpharetta's cheek. "Merry Christmas, darling," Dow said.

"Merry . . ." The final word was muffled by kisses, sweet to the taste, for Dow had taken her in his arms.

Outside, the parterres, the long vistas to Harrington Hall waited for spring, when the earth would once again bloom with beauty to feed the soul. But an impatient Dow, in the green room of damask silk, could wait no longer. In the arms of the woman he had kept in his heart since time began, he found joy, love, and a long-awaited peace on that Christmas Eve of 1945.

About the Author

Frances Patton Statham lives in Atlanta, Georgia. She has received four national and three regional awards for her novels, including the prestigious Author of the Year Award in fiction from the Dixie Council of Authors and Journalists in 1978—the first time this award went to the author of an original paperback—and again in 1984. A lyric coloratura soprano with a master's degree in voice, Ms. Statham recently won the Frank Stieglitz Memorial Award for an original music composition, "Song Cycle for Soprano, Flute, and Piano." She is the recipient of numerous prizes for her oil paintings and watercolors. Her previous novels are *Flame of New Orleans*, *Jasmine Moon*, *Daughters of the Summer Storm*, *Phoenix Rising*, and *From Love's Ashes*. She is presently at work on a new novel.